"How do you survive the unen[...] about war, grief, guilt, and grapp[...] and finally taking the risk and acknowledging the ones that you do. Moving and full of heart."

—Caroline Leavitt, *New York Times* bestselling author

of *Is This Tomorrow* and *Pictures of You*

"With its gripping plot and seasoned prose, it is hard to imagine that *Casualties* is Elizabeth Marro's debut novel. She writes of a mother's worst nightmare, and offers no easy answers. B[...] end of her novel we care for her characters, an[...] find the elusive redemption they so [...]

of *Burning Man*

"Conflicting human [...], missed opportunities, and the random luck [...] raw challenge the true-to-life, complicated characters in Elizabeth Marro's page-turning novel. This is an important story set against the drama of today's volatile world that asks moral questions yet, ultimately, resides in the heart."

—Judy Reeves, author of *Wild Women, Wild Voices*

"There's an emotional jolt early in the pages of Elizabeth Marro's debut novel, *Casualties*, that reminds us not all battle scars start on the battlefield. The bell-like tolls of this tragic event will reverberate throughout the rest of this heartbreaking novel as Ruth and Casey, two strangers broken by grief and regret, reluctantly join together on a cross-country road trip. Elizabeth Marro made me care about these two people so much that by the end of the novel I'd forgotten they were fictional characters, and I was ready to call them up to see how they were doing and if they'd finally found their way toward peace and forgiveness." —David Abrams, author of *Fobbit*

"Marro's debut novel is a gritty tragedy that unrelentingly addresses painful issues of war, suicide, and the shady dealings of defense contractors . . . Through her characters' soul-searching and self-discovery, Marro provides a clear sense that, while the past can't be undone, the future always offers a chance to make amends, and the human spirit can triumph over pain and find hope in family and forgiveness. This is a tortured novel and yet a redemptive one. It isn't a happily-ever-after story, but Marro casts a ray of hope that a good life can be lived after terrible tragedy."          —*Kirkus Reviews*

# Casualties

## ELIZABETH MARRO

BERKLEY BOOKS
*New York*

BERKLEY

**An imprint of Penguin Random House LLC**
**375 Hudson Street, New York, New York 10014**

PUBLISHING HISTORY
Berkley trade paperback edition / February 2016

Library of Congress Cataloging-in-Publication Data

Marro, Elizabeth.
Casualties / Elizabeth Marro.
p. cm.
ISBN 978-0-425-28346-2
I. Title.
PS3613.A76933C38 2016
813'.6—dc23
2015031689

PRINTED IN THE UNITED STATES OF AMERICA

10  9  8  7  6  5  4  3  2  1

Cover photo: Rainy Road Through a Window copyright © Anthony Scibelli / Getty Images.
Cover design by Lesley Worrell.
Text design by Kelly Lipovich.

Penguin
Random
House

*For Edward Marro, with love*

# ACKNOWLEDGMENTS

The path to finishing this book was long, with many switchbacks and false turns. I would not have made it to the end without the practical, technical, physical, spiritual, and loving support of many people and one dog. Here they are:

For their patience, enthusiasm, and frank critiques, I thank my large and talented San Diego writing community beginning with Judy Hamilton who has read more versions of this book than anyone else and still remains my friend. Special thanks goes to Mary Jean Newcomer, Elizabeth Fitzsimons, and Jean Brandl who were there at the beginning. Jeanne Peterson, Melanie Traci, Melanie Hooks, Cuauhtémoc Q. Kish, Cheryl Carroll, Neal, Jill Hall, and Pamela Hunt Cloyd helped me through subsequent iterations. The following writers helped me to the finish line: Judy Reeves, Greg Johnson, Anita Knowles, Scott Barbour, Leslie Nack, and Jeffery Pinkston.

To Rae Francoeur: Thank you for forty years of unfailing friendship and for never letting that friendship cloud your keen editor's eye. Your fearlessness in your own writing has been an inspiration. Your advice and willingness to share your own experience, from writing that first sentence to publishing your own book, helped to light the way for me.

Thank you to Sheila Ragan, Bruce Bauer, Frank Barrancotto, Kay Chilcote, Laurie Scott, and Mary Anne Small Capistrano for encouraging me, helping me keep my balance, and for that fabulous cake.

The talented Megan Mulry connected me with my fabulous agent, Allison Hunter, who in turn matched me up with my equally fabulous editor at Berkley, Jackie Cantor. Amy Schneider and Pam Barricklow made sure my work shone in the best possible light. These women ushered me from the land of unpublished novelists to the land of published novelists. I will always be grateful.

My parents, Mary Power Donovan and Peter Guest, taught me to love the written word and never made me stop reading or writing unless it was absolutely necessary. Thank you to my siblings, Peter, Mary, John, Kit, Sam, Laura, Peter, Nancy, Ted, and Lib for cheering me on, and to Paul Donovan and Jen Ellis for adding their voices to the chorus. My Marro family, Miki, John, and Patrick, have been hugely supportive every step of the way.

Rory Donovan, my son and navigator, thank you for your special brand of insight and humor and for teaching me about mothers and sons.

And Ed Marro, my husband, my partner, my love, thank you for believing in me and for making it all possible.

A few more words . . .

As I wrote this book, I crossed paths with three Marines who made their mark on me, and reminded me why it was important to try to write it. Remembering Will, his friend Roger, and the young Marine who sat next to me at the Peace Resource Center of San Diego and shared so openly his confusion about coming home when his brothers remained behind.

I'm grateful to Sergeant Major Kenneth W. Strickland USMC, Retired, for his guidance when I had questions about procedures, deployment, and other aspects of Marine Corps life. Pamela Hunt Cloyd provided me with photographs and details about Camp Lejeune and answered questions that only a writer and military wife could. Donna Swisher of Pacific Water Therapy provided assistance with insights and resources for understanding the challenges and options faced by those with amputated limbs. Any errors here are my own.

The convergence of the wars in Iraq and Afghanistan and the explosion of the Internet made it possible for those of us who are not in the military to learn very nearly in real-time about the day-to-day lives of those fighting and those who wait at home. Even after some of the blogs, videos, interviews, and social media pages of active-duty military were taken down, the voices of those at war or adjusting to their lives upon returning home found ways to get through. These stories grabbed me early and wouldn't let me go. They guided me along the way. I am grateful.

There are many excellent books on the subject of Iraq and the Marines. Here are a few I consulted during the writing of this novel:

*The Blog of War: Front-Line Dispatches from Soldiers in Iraq and Afghanistan*, edited by Mathew Currier Burden

*Operation Homecoming: Iraq, Afghanistan, and the Home Front, in the Words of U.S. Troops and Their Families*, edited by Andrew Carroll

*Winter Soldier: Iraq and Afghanistan: Eyewitness Accounts of the Occupation*, by IVAW and Aaron Glantz

*Shade It Black: Death and After in Iraq*, by Jess Goodell with John Hearn

*War*, by Sebastian Junger

*Making the Corps*, by Thomas E. Ricks

*Keeping Faith: A Father-Son Story About Love and the United States Marine Corps*, by John Schaeffer and Frank Schaeffer

*Jarhead*, by Anthony Swofford

# New Beginnings

# CHAPTER 1

July 2004

At some point it may no longer be possible to start over. Ruth has worried about this before, but on the morning after her son's nineteenth birthday, she feels cold with the certainty of it. There will be a time when Robbie is too old to recover lost ground, when all his mistakes have calcified into a mass so large and impenetrable that neither one of them can break through.

Not for the first time, her assistant reminds her that she may be making too much of things.

"He's only nineteen. He's going to be fine," says the voice coming through the Bluetooth wedged in Ruth's ear. "Whatever you do, don't lose your temper."

"Temper? What temper? I'm a San Diegan now. We don't have tempers. We have one great day after another. It's the law or something, isn't it?"

Ruth cranks opens her kitchen window with one hand and pours her third espresso with the other. She stares at the spot of driveway where Robbie's truck is supposed to be. It's nearly ten o'clock. He's fourteen hours late.

"Don't say I didn't try," Terri says with a sigh. "I'll move the rest of your morning appointments. Let me know about the afternoon."

Ruth barely hears the click in her ear when Terri hangs up. A truck is approaching. She stretches forward to get a better look, but it's just the maintenance crew for the golf course she has never used a day in her life. And never will. This house is just one more failed start; they moved here because it was closer to the third and last high school she'd found for Robbie. He hadn't bothered to show up. They'd kicked him out before she'd finished unpacking the last box. Now she's stuck too far away to see the Pacific but close enough to catch its scent on a morning like this when the breeze is right.

Enough. Her turn will come—and when it does, she'll be living so close to the ocean that the sound of waves will lull her to sleep every night and wake her every morning. Right now she has to focus. Ruth turns from the window and scans the community college brochures fanned out on the table in front of her. *Discover Your Potential*, invites the cover of the booklet on top. Every guidance counselor and teacher Robbie had had used to go on and on about his potential. He must still have it in there somewhere.

She'll have to broach the subject strategically. She can't, for example, remind Robbie that he said he'd be home last night so they could cap off his birthday weekend in the desert with a good dinner. Last night is history even though the tray of lasagna she'd bought remains, untouched, in the refrigerator next to a thirty-dollar Death by Chocolate cake, also untouched. She can't let him know about the splinter of pain that burrowed deeper with every hour she sat alone waiting for him, hoping that he'd do what he said he'd do. She thought she'd seen his eyes soften for a millisecond when she suggested the kind of dinner he liked, no pressure, nothing he had to dress up for.

But that's how things have been going for years now. One minute there's that softening, a glimpse of the boy who used to lift his arms and smile when she walked into a room. The next minute the boy disappears into a six-foot-two-inch hulk of muscle and fat shrouded in black T-shirts and baggy jeans. The light that made his eyes look like amber honey vanishes. He can freeze her out with a single look.

The roar of an engine pulls Ruth back to the window. A gray pickup loaded with a dirt bike and an ATV screeches into the driveway where it sits, shimmying to the bass that pounds into the pavement and rattles the windowpane. Ruth's resolve cracks a little with every pulsing beat. She gulps the rest of her espresso and lets the cup clatter into the sink.

When the truck shudders to a stop, Robbie tumbles out, eyes squinting and his mouth open in a laugh. He's on the phone. Ruth wishes now she'd gone to work. This whole conversation would go better tonight, after he'd slept a little and she'd had a chance to regroup.

Then Robbie's in the kitchen bringing three days of sweat, beer breath, and cigarette smoke with him.

"Hey, what're you doin' here?" He shoves his phone into the pocket of his sagging camouflage shorts, pushing them further down his hips.

"Happy birthday."

Even she can hear how bitter she sounds. She sees his grin of surprise fall away before it gets started. Had he been happy to see her? He's already shrugging; there's the hunch of his thick shoulders and the smirk she has come to hate.

"Thanks." He heads for the refrigerator but stops at the table. "What's all this?" He snatches up one of the brochures and looks at the picture of young men and women on the cover, grouped on the grass as if they and their laptops were part of the landscaping. "This supposed to be my birthday present?"

Ruth thinks of the computer that Terri researched, bought, and wrapped, waiting for him on his bed. She wishes now she'd put it somewhere else. She needs more time. He's staring down at her now, chin jutting out a little, like he's challenging her to explain herself.

Ruth takes a deep breath and tries for a smile. "I just thought you might find something you like in there, something that might help you decide what you want to do with your life."

"Got all that dialed in."

Ruth thinks of the garage where he works part time, fixing dirt bikes, motorcycles, and those tricycles his friends race in the desert. Then she sees her brother back in New Hampshire, head always stuck under the hood of a truck or car, or half-buried in the engine of someone's farm machine. He'd given up on himself without even trying. She wasn't going to let that happen to Robbie. "I'm talking about a career. It's not too late. You can find something that—"

"I'm starved. What's in the fridge?" Robbie grabs the door of the refrigerator.

"Don't turn your back on me. We're going to get this settled. Now."

He swings around to face her. "I was going to save my news for later, but I might as well tell you now."

Ruth doesn't want to hear; she's heard it all before. "You need a real job. With a real future." They've both heard this before too. She pauses, searching for words that are new, that will penetrate.

"That's what my news is all about."

Ruth feels her jaw cramp with the effort of biting back a sarcastic *What now?* Maybe he's gotten that girl, his boss's daughter, pregnant. He's going to spend the rest of his life getting tattoos and living for weekends in the blazing sun with beer, engines, and a couple of kids. He's going to let his mind, that alive, curious mind she'd once been so proud of, go to waste. Is he trying to spite her by hurting himself? Ruth's train of thought is rumbling so loud and fast she doesn't realize at first that Robbie is still speaking. "What did you say?"

Robbie's chin still juts out as though he's expecting trouble, but he is searching her face the way he used to when he was a boy and wanted to see if he'd pleased her. He starts over, speaking slowly, deliberately, as if each word is loaded with explosives and must be uttered with care.

"I said I decided to work for Uncle Sam. Kinda like you only I joined the Marines. Signed on the dotted line last Friday. A couple months and I'm outta here."

Ruth feels a sudden slipping inside, even though she can't move. "That's impossible."

Robbie's eyes harden and he smirks again. "They want me. A few good men. Guess I'm good enough for once. Besides, there's a war on—but you know all that, right?" He rubs the tips of his thumb and forefinger together and imitates the sound of a cash register. "Cha-ching."

Ruth grips the edge of the chair in front of her. She wants him to take it all back, the announcement he made so proudly and now his insulting tone that somehow makes her job sound dirty. The military couldn't run their wars without the civilians she found for them. She helped men and women make money they needed, more than they could ever make doing the same jobs at home. But they were adults, not nineteen-year-old kids.

"No!"

Robbie shrugs, but his eyes stay focused on hers. "Not your call. For once, I'm doing what I want to do."

"I'll tell them the truth and they'll kick you out." Ruth has no idea if this is true, but she'll try anything.

"What're you talking about?"

Ruth ticks off a list on her fingers. "You flunked out of school after school. Rehab was the only thing that kept you out of juvie. What about the psychiatrist, your depression. Do the Marines know?"

"Got my GED, and that other shit's been over for years."

"Two years, barely two years."

"Long enough."

"You could go to college. It's not too late. All you have to do is—"

"When're you going to give up on that? Your kid's not college material, Ruthie. I'm just a motorhead who wants to beat up a few bad buys and spread freedom."

Each word out of his mouth seems to put more distance between them. She has to stop him; she has to find some way to fix this.

"You think what I'm doing is stupid, don't you?"

Ruth hears him but she's running through her mental Rolodex for the name of anyone who is connected, who can help her get him out. Then she realizes that if she tries that, she'll be marked as the carpetbagger she's always felt she is. The company she works for is filled with ex-military. Proud is what she is supposed to feel. Proud is what they will expect of her. Too late, she registers his question and, helpless, she sees his hurt before he tries to look tough again. *No, not stupid*, she wants to say. *You're all I have.*

"Think about it, Ruthie," Robbie is saying now, leaning against the refrigerator. "You'll be the mother of a Marine. For the first time ever you can brag about me a little, if you want."

Words she has been meaning to say for years crowd into her throat.

"Stop calling me that."

"What?"

"Ruthie. I'm your mother. Don't forget it."

She is crying. She expects him to look away; it's what he's done the few times she has ever cried in front of him. But he doesn't. He straightens and takes a step toward her. When he speaks again, all the mockery is gone.

"I'm doing this because I have to, Mom. Be proud of me. Just give it a try, okay?" She understands that he means to sound tough, final, but Ruth hears the uncertainty he is trying to hide. She hears it and, in a flash of instinct, understands that he is asking her not to hear it.

He's put himself out of reach. The balance between them has shifted. Then, through the tears, through the loss threatening to engulf her, Ruth feels something that frightens but also exhilarates her.

She is relieved.

It is the memory of this relief that will haunt her in the months to come. It will start to unsettle her tonight when they eat the lasagna and carve up the chocolate cake. It will continue to disturb her when Robbie leaves for boot camp, and later, when he is assigned to duty nearly three thousand miles away at Camp Lejeune. It will scald her when she learns he has been deployed to Iraq. Each day she will think back to this day and remember how she nodded and wiped her eyes. She will remember how Robbie's body seemed to loosen, open up, how he squared his shoulders and embraced her as if he'd been practicing all his life for this moment. Sometimes she thinks she will be haunted every day by the memory of the relief she felt when Robbie asked her to let him go. And she did.

# Homecoming

# CHAPTER 2

July 2008

The banners seemed to come out of nowhere. They rippled along the chain-link fence right up to the main gate that separated Camp Lejeune from the tattoo parlors, strip clubs, motels, used-car lots, and bars along Route 24, each scrawled, painted, or stitched with words that had been saved up for this moment. *You are our hero! We love you Daddy! Welcome Home Son.* Some of the Marines pressed against the windows of the bus, whooping and clicking cameras. Others reached for cell phones and dialed the wives, mothers, fathers, sisters, and brothers waiting to meet them inside the gates. "Soon, baby, soon." "Almost there."

Robbie waited for the tide of euphoria to take him. Instead he picked up the anxiety behind the shouts and grins stretched too wide and too tight. He smelled it beneath the stink of diesel fuel, swampy feet, and sweat.

Korder's elbow jabbed Robbie in the ribs. Robbie slammed him back, but Korder kept looking at his phone.

"She's got us a motel room. Says she's loaded it with food and booze; we don't have to come out for three days. Christ, now that

I'm here, I can't fuckin' believe it." Korder let out a bark that was supposed to be a laugh.

The darkness inside Robbie shifted and stretched like an animal waking. He looked out the window, wanting to fill up on the light that spilled down on the caravan of buses bearing his unit through the main entrance. Most of his unit. In seconds he no longer saw the banners or the sweeps of moss hanging from the pines. He saw the outpost, a concrete school building surrounded by concertina wire and a wall of sandbags covered with as much grit and dirt as they contained. Inside, his cot sat jammed tight against others in a space reinforced by wood framing and more sandbags. He saw the coffeemaker, Korder's Xbox, the daisy chain of power cords they'd rigged to keep things going. He saw Garcia in full gear, Kevlar on his head, stretching his neck like a turtle toward a small mirror nailed to a two-by-four so he could pop a zit.

"There's the armory," Korder said. Garcia disappeared. The bus rolled to a stop. Just a few more hours to go. They would check their rifles in at the armory, get their barracks assignments, and then climb back on the buses that would take them across the base to the waiting families and friends, and those whose Marines were dead, but wanted to be there anyway, to see and hug the ones who lived.

"Your mom'll be glad to see you." Korder stood, but he couldn't go anywhere until the bus started to unload.

Robbie shook his head. "I told her not to come."

There was no point. He'd be through with active duty in another couple of months and then he'd be in the reserves unless he re-upped. His mother had already started thinking again about schools, sending him e-mail after e-mail with links to colleges he could attend once he got back to San Diego. She'd sent pictures of a new house she'd built near the beach with another picture of his truck in the new garage. Her e-mails were like brochures for travel in a country called Home. Before his laptop died, he'd looked at the messages to see if his mother wrote anything besides *This place looks great* or *You'll love this,* and then deleted them. He saved only the ones she sent—about her business trips, the weather, her workouts, the construction of the new house—that ended with *Be safe. I love you, Mom.*

He would reread them just to arrive again at the last two sentences. Sometimes he felt a tug, like the nibble of a trout on a line he'd been casting for hours. For a few seconds he felt the promise of something he couldn't see but knew was there. If he looked too long, though, the words read like one of the commands Ruthie used to squeeze out when he was a kid and she was racing to make a flight. "Finish your math. Be good for the babysitter. I'll call you tonight. I love you." Even if she was furious with him, she said "I love you," like she was reminding herself, or just making sure she covered all her bases in case the plane went down. When she said "I love you," nine out of ten times it meant she was leaving him.

That was the problem with letters and phone calls from home, he'd once said to Garcia; they could make you want everything back the way it was, even stuff you hated. Garcia hadn't answered him. He was staring at his girlfriend's new Facebook page. She'd posted a picture of herself in the lap of a guy Garcia knew from home.

"I hate her, man, I hate the bitch," Garcia kept saying. Peterson jumped on him to make him stop. Hanny, Korder, and Robbie had to pull them apart. None of them wanted to see Garcia's pain or be reminded that their own lives could be going to shit and there wasn't a damn thing they could do about it.

"Fuck your girlfriend, fuck the Internet, fuck letters from home," he'd told Garcia that night. "It's all different now. No one back there knows anything about you anymore. You got us."

Two nights later, they helped to zip his arm, his leg, and what they could find of his powerful body into a black bag.

That was what was still out there waiting for him and every other Marine on these buses. After the hugs, when the signs were propped up in the corners and the balloons collapsed on the floor, it would be you and the things the desert had done to you or the people you cared about. . . . Meanwhile, all the people who'd been left back home, worrying, wanted their due. Ruthie wanted him to get it right this time. That was what her e-mails were really all about. A do-over.

Panic struck Robbie like a cobra. His breath seemed trapped in his lungs. He tried to focus on the Marines lining up outside the bus to turn in their weapons, but he felt his mother's presence, even here in North Carolina. He saw her standing with her arms open, eyes eager and expectant, not knowing that he couldn't breathe, couldn't even do this simple thing. He felt a hand grip his left shoulder.

"Get it together, O'Connell," said Korder. "Get it together."

He stood. He wasn't sure if he'd done it on his own or if Korder had yanked him up. All he knew was he was standing and his lungs were working. He sucked in air and heaved it out: in, out, in, out. A little better now.

"Ready?"

Robbie nodded. He shook himself free of Korder's hand and stepped into the line of Marines moving off the bus.

# CHAPTER 3

Ruth guided the Jaguar to her parking spot in the company garage with the kind of blind instinct produced by years of routine. She'd told herself she'd make her decision when she arrived, but here she was, still torn between Robbie's wishes and her own impulses.

She decided to leave the car running until she made up her mind. She could wait for Robbie to come home "his own way," as her friend Neal put it when he warned her to be patient. Or she could hop a plane tonight for North Carolina. All Ruth wanted was to see him, even if it was just for a few hours. That would be enough time to let it sink in that he was really home, really safe. After that, she could wait a little longer for the Marines to finish with him.

Screw patience. Ruth reached for her purse and extracted her phone. It wouldn't hurt to check for flights.

A text from Robbie greeted her from the display of her Black-Berry: *all gd call u sn*. When had he sent it? Damn it. She'd been listening and watching for word from him, and now all she had was another text with the same message he'd been sending since he'd called her after landing. Eighteen days ago and counting.

A knock on the driver's-side window made Ruth jump. The phone fell into her lap. Danny. She switched off the ignition and waited for Danny, security man, garage attendant, and self-appointed valet to RyCom's senior executives, to step back so she could open the door.

"Jag need a wash today, Ms. Nolan?"

"Yes, please, Danny." Ruth wasn't sure if she was sorry or grateful for the interruption. Either way, his smile pulled her into the start of another workday, the kind of day that had gotten her through both of Robbie's deployments. No doubt this one would offer more than enough to keep her occupied while she waited a little longer to hear from her son. She grabbed her purse and briefcase. "There's some dry cleaning in the back, too."

"I'll take care of it." A glint of silver flashed beneath Danny's mustache when he smiled again. His warmth and his eagerness spread like a balm over Ruth's agitation.

*I'll take care of it.* Magic lived in those words. Ruth felt her lips relax into a smile as she strode toward the elevator that would take her up to RyCom's main entrance. In fourth grade she'd figured out that the way to escape her tormentors at recess was to raise her hand every time Mrs. Pelletier needed someone to clean erasers, stack books, or help Rainey McKinnon with her math. At sixteen, she'd told the manager of the North Woods Lodge & Restaurant he didn't have to train another waitress for evenings. "I'll take care of it," she'd told him. He'd made her an assistant manager in her junior year.

The strong magic came, though, when Ruth learned to see a problem—and come up with a solution—before others even knew it was there. Initiative. Like Danny's and maybe a few of the people hunching over their computers right now to make sure she had what she needed for her business development meeting, which would start—Ruth looked at her watch—in exactly eighteen minutes. She punched the button for the elevator that would take her up to the ground level and the main entrance of RyCom.

As the door opened, she came face-to-face with Gordon Olson, or as much of his face as she could see through the cigarette smoke that rose between them.

"You look pleased with yourself, Ruth."

"Good morning to you, too, Gordon."

She stepped aside to let him out, but he just shook his head. "Just riding up and down until I finish this." His eyes slitted as he inhaled again.

Ruth forced herself to step inside the elevator. The man brought out the mule in her, as her grandmother used to say. She wouldn't give him the satisfaction of an elevator to himself.

"Think you can hold your breath to the next floor?" Gordon said. He smiled a lipless smile as he exhaled. His face was the color of wet sand, and every wrinkle looked like a fissure formed when the tide goes out. He was only sixty-five. He looked eighty.

"How are you not dead yet?" Ruth said, waving the smoke away.

"God doesn't want me. The devil doesn't seem to want me. Guess you're stuck with me."

The elevator bell dinged as it hit ground level and Ruth burst through the doors before they'd opened all the way, but his voice caught up to her.

"Not so fast. Got a couple of questions for you."

Ruth glanced at her watch. "Let's walk and talk."

Gordon inhaled one last time. He dropped the cigarette and ground it into the granite walkway, then fell into step beside Ruth as she walked toward their building. "How're things looking in the body business? We hitting our marks?"

*We.* That was rich. Ruth remembered how he'd rolled his eyes when she'd proposed the whole idea five years ago. "We're a tech company, not some temp agency," he'd said. Don Ryland was the one who counted, though, and he'd liked the idea. He'd been willing to try anything that would keep his company out of Chapter 11. But she knew that it was the Transglobal deal that was driving Gordon's interest. The whale of all defense contractors wanted to buy RyCom, thanks to the success of her "body business." He'd get millions out of the deal, so would Don, and more importantly, so would she. That was what initiative could do.

"We've renewed all existing contracts or are about to," she said. "A few new RFPs are coming this week. KBR is close to signing another eight-hundred-million-dollar contract."

"Close? Close doesn't count."

"What's the matter, Gordon? Afraid the lungs'll petrify before you get your payout?"

"I don't count my winnings until I can hold them in my hand." He stopped at the next elevator but didn't press the button, only looked at her through his heavy-lidded eyes.

Ruth felt heat start to rise again from her neck toward her face. "I'll take the stairs," she said as Gordon pressed the button for the elevator that would ferry him up to the executive floor.

"I'm not finished, Ruth."

"Catch me later, I've got a meeting," Ruth said over her shoulder. She felt him watching her as her heels clicked across the atrium floor.

He and Don knew about the house, of course. They knew she had gone for it, overspent on the waterfront lot, on the construction itself, and even the Jaguar. Ruth had bought the car used from one of Neal's friends who'd gotten overextended. She'd imagined driving it to the airport, picking up Robbie, letting him have the keys to drive it home. This was the reason she'd drained the account holding the last of the loan she'd taken out. She already owed nearly two million dollars. What was another sixty thousand? For the first time in her life, Ruth had bet on the come, as Don used to call it. Spending money she didn't have, was how her grandparents would have put it. The size of her mortgage was more than a hundred times what they'd earned from the farm or the woods around it.

Damn Gordon Olson. She had the KBR contract to deal with, a whole day of meetings and phone calls about the Transglobal deal, and—

"Morning, Ms. Nolan," sang Marcia, the receptionist. She sat like a wren on her eggs, peering over her half glasses from the center of her control station. The circle of wood, stone, and glass was draped with a huge banner bearing the RyCom logo and lettered in blue and red against a white background, YOUR PARTNER FOR A SAFER U.S.A. WE'RE ALL IN.

"Morning, Marcia." Ruth flashed a smile but kept moving. Maybe she could get to the door to the stairwell before Marcia asked the inevitable question.

"When's that boy of yours coming home?"

*Shit.* Ruth glanced over her shoulder, "Still waiting to hear. Should be any day now." It was what she'd said when Marcia first asked eighteen days ago when Ruth, reckless with joy, had told her, had told too many people, that Robbie had landed in North Carolina and was on his way home.

Marcia's eyebrows tented upward and her crows' feet arranged themselves into an expression of what Ruth took to be puzzled sympathy. The receptionist looked as though she had something else to say, but a call came through and her gaze shifted abruptly to the switchboard. Ruth escaped into the stairwell.

Sun streamed through the wall of windows that ran the height of the building and separated her from mounds of impatiens and palms grouped around a few benches. *This is what it would be like to be trapped in a terrarium*, Ruth thought, as she began to climb to the fourth floor. Ruth under glass. Like a pheasant steaming in her own juices or, in her case, frustration and anxiety. She knew, at least, that Robbie was alive and safe and would be out of danger from here on out. There was no longer any need to stand guard against her own imagination every time the men she worked with talked about "the situation" in Iraq or someone like Marcia started collecting donations for military widows and orphans. On top of that, the Transglobal deal would bring all the money she would ever need and more time, too. Lots of time if she chose. She could help Robbie start his new life. She could start a whole new life herself.

Ruth finally stopped climbing. The sun burned through the tinted glass and the air-conditioning, but it wasn't the heat that pinpricked its way up and down her nerves. It was the failure of these facts—more money, new lives—to erase the apprehension triggered every time she tried to imagine her days after Robbie finally returned.

She'd been floored by the sudden void created by his absence, especially at first. It was nearly a year before she walked into her house after work without expecting to see a pile of greasy T-shirts on the laundry room floor or to hear rap music pounding from his bedroom. When she shopped, she would put a jar of peanut butter or a gallon of milk in her cart before she caught herself. The new quiet on the fringes of her days echoed with things she wished she'd said more patiently, or simply left unsaid. She could have laughed more with him; she could have just listened.

But there was work. She'd had the most successful four years of her career, as it turned out. There was the house to build and there was Neal, her friend "with benefits" as Robbie once described it, back again in their continuing cycle of on-again, off-again companionship, his presence familiar and comfortable. After a while, missing Robbie throbbed less urgently, like a sore back that didn't hurt at all some days, ached a little on others, or flared raw and fresh when a text, a letter, or an offhand remark by a colleague reminded her where Robbie was and what he was doing and how much he was changing.

The waiting and the missing would soon be over, but Ruth didn't know what, or who, to expect when he finally came home. He was twenty-three. He'd been to war.

Wanting to fly to North Carolina was like wanting to jump into the swimming hole near her grandfather's farm: get in, get past that first gasping shock, and just keep swimming until she stopped noticing the cold. Ruth wanted enough time with Robbie to get to know him before he went on with the rest of his life.

She wanted more. She wanted him to forgive her for the mistakes she had made. But her mother had taught her that wanting anything from another person could be wanting too much. Robbie wasn't a child anymore. He could choose.

Her BlackBerry sounded from her purse. Terri's ring. Ruth clicked her nails against the Bluetooth perpetually in her ear.

"I'm almost there." The sound of her own voice steadied her.

"Good, Andrea was all set to start the meeting. I'll tell her you're on your way."

"Thanks." *And while you're at it, tell Andrea to shut up and wait her turn.* There was a fine line between taking initiative and trying to usurp your boss. Don's newest protégée didn't seem to be walking it too carefully.

Ruth wiped a few beads of sweat from her upper lip and picked a stray hair, mostly red with white near the root, from the nubbed silk of her jacket. Then she ran up the rest of the stairs.


Her staff meeting was nearly over when Gordon Olson appeared at the door to the conference room. His persistence didn't surprise Ruth, but his presence did. It wasn't like him to stand in front of a room full of people; he left that to Don and to her. Don was the idea man, at least as far as clients were concerned. Ruth executed the ideas. Gordon took care of the money and all the boring necessaries that fell into a big drum called operations. She smiled for the benefit of her staff, directors all, who had just closed their laptops and grabbed their empty coffee cups, expecting to be dismissed.

"We were just wrapping up. We've been putting the final touches on the KBR proposal."

"Good. I'll wait," Gordon said. When he stepped into the room, most of the men and women around the table got up and headed for the door, without waiting for Ruth to call the end of the meeting. Andrea, of course, lingered, but not, Ruth knew, out of any deference to her.

"How can I help you, Gordon?" The conference phone buzzed, but Ruth ignored it.

"HR's been hearing from the families of some of our contractors. Apparently, they've got complaints."

Ruth saw Andrea lift her eyes from her phone and shake her mane of chocolate hair out of her face.

"What kinds of complaints?"

"The usual, insurance claims taking too long, that sort of thing."

"Isn't that HR's problem to solve?" Ruth said.

Gordon's face cinched into a frown. "That's one way to look at it." He paused, probably expecting her to bite. Ruth decided to wait him out.

"What was a trickle of claims is suddenly a stream. Legal's gotten letters from a lawyer. Something's up."

This was ridiculous. Ruth's BlackBerry vibrated against her hip. She started to gather her own laptop and notes.

"Sorry, Gordon, isn't HR your area?"

"Isn't the contractor business yours?"

The edge in his voice sounded like a warning of some kind. Ruth glanced at Andrea. "Thanks, Andrea, you can go. Let's touch base this afternoon to go over the final proposal."

"Sure," said Andrea, but Ruth thought she saw her glance at Gordon as if checking with him first. Ruth felt her jaw tighten, but she had no more time to think about it because Gordon was already talking again.

"Do I need to remind you that we all want to make Transglobal happy? They're sending in their team to do due diligence and I don't want any surprises. That's as much your concern as it is mine, don't you think?"

"Of course, but—"

"Ruth?" Terri poked her head around the corner of the conference room door. There was only one reason she would come down personally to extract her from a meeting. "Robbie?" Without waiting for an answer, Ruth shoved her laptop into her bag.

"He's on the phone right now; you want me to patch him through?"

"No," Ruth said. She wanted privacy for this call. "I'm coming."

As she brushed past Gordon, he said, "I want you to take a look, make sure everything's as it should be, that's all."

Ruth was already thinking about what to say to her son. What not to say. She glanced at Gordon and the words were out of her mouth right on cue.

"I'll take care of it."

# CHAPTER 4

Robbie had waited until the last minute to lie to his mother. He leaned against a car in the barracks parking lot, cell phone in his hand, his pack at his feet. He took a deep breath and hit speed dial for her office.

"Ruth Nolan's office." Great, it was Terri. Maybe he could just leave a message.

"Hey, Ter. It's Robbie."

"My God, where are you? It's so good to hear your voice!"

"Thanks. Still in North Carolina."

"Hold on. I'll get your mom. She's in a meeting."

"It's okay. You don't have to bother her, I just want—"

"Are you kidding? She'll hand my head to me. Hang on."

Damn, where was Korder? They had to get to Jacksonville in time to buy his bus ticket north. A couple of grunts rolled out the door of the brick-faced unit and started throwing a football back and forth as they loped across the grass and onto the pavement. If Korder didn't show, he'd grab a ride from one of them.

Then his mother was talking in his ear.

"Robbie? Why haven't you called? It's been days. Where are you?"

"They keep us busy here. The time difference kept screwing me up." But Ruth was already moving on.

"I can't wait to see you. When's your flight?"

He took a deep breath. "Sorry, Mom. Things aren't going the way I thought. Still working my way through the reentry crap. Leave doesn't kick in for another week or so." She used to know when he was lying. He tensed, waiting for her to bust him like she did when he was a kid, but she didn't.

"I should have just flown east to meet you like I did last time," she said.

"Only would have been a couple of days. In another week—"

"I know. I know. I just need to see you."

Robbie imagined his mother standing with the phone to her ear like he'd seen her so many times. She'd be tilted forward a little, one arm across her middle as if holding herself back. Her body always seemed to be moving even when she was standing still. "Won't be long, now. Did my bag get there?" He'd sent his duffel to San Diego and stuffed what he needed into his backpack.

"Yesterday. We put it in the guest room." He heard her click her tongue impatiently.

"It won't be long now," he said. "I'll call you when I know what's up."

"You sound tired. Are you—"

The sudden softening of her tone ambushed him. If she kept on, he'd cave. "I'm fine, fine. Gotta go, though."

"We'll get you rested and take care of you; just hurry up and get here." She was speaking faster now, like she wanted to cram as much as she could into the remaining seconds. He heard the buzzing of phones, voices in the background.

"It's okay. I'm okay. We'll talk soon."

"I love you."

"Me too. Bye."

He heard her draw a breath as if to say more, but he hung up before she could speak again. Almost immediately he felt shitty about it, then angry at her for making him feel shitty. Where the fuck was Korder? He dug some cigarettes out of his pocket. He was just nervous, was all. Leaving the base was hard. Every time he did, he felt naked. No gun. No Kevlar. Nothing between him and civilians walking or driving their fat asses around with cell phones stuck to their ears. He broke into a sweat at intersections watching cars zoom through without stopping, his fingers squeezing a trigger that wasn't there. At night, he and the other grunts stayed awake together in one room until they passed out, head to foot on bunks, the floor, anywhere they could fit, anywhere they didn't have to be alone.

He just had to ignore Ruthie. She was what his old boot camp DI called a "force of nature." That was how she'd gotten herself from the mountains of New Hampshire to being a corporate big shot. Back in the desert, they kept tripping over people from companies like hers. Once, he recognized the initials of his mother's company on a lanyard worn by the woman who ran the entertainment at Camp Ramadi, a "morale technician," he'd read in the camp newsletter. Someone had brought a copy back to the outpost. Peterson had thumped the picture with his dirty finger like he was some kind of lawyer and this was his evidence.

"What the fuck is a morale technician? I'll tell you what it is: some bitch who makes more in one year planning parties and writing fucking newsletters than I'll have after four years of putting my ass on the line for my country." Peterson tossed the newsletter down in disgust.

Robbie stayed out of it. No one knew what his mother did. When someone asked, he just said she was in "business." He talked with pride about the small town she came from, how she'd raised him singlehandedly; that was something they could understand and respect. In the end no one cared what she or anyone else's parents, wives, girlfriends, or fathers did. They cared about each other. He wondered if he would care about anyone or anything like that again.

Robbie was on his third cigarette and halfway across the parking lot to the guys with the football when Korder finally showed up in his girlfriend's Chevy. He was going on leave, too. His girl, Chrissy or Misty or something that Robbie never quite caught, leaned forward from the backseat, her arms draped over Korder's neck. A tiny diamond glittered on her left ring finger. Korder told him she'd picked it out while he was in country and he'd paid it off a day or two ago. They were going to drive to her family outside Atlanta, then to his up in Pittsburgh. No one knew anyone; she and Korder met online four months ago. Korder was driving too fast; his left leg was bouncing, his finger tapping like crazy on the steering wheel while Drowning Pool blasted through the speakers. "New Hampshire?" Korder shouted over the music. "What's up there?"

"Best place in the whole world. Gonna stop in D.C. and see Rami too." Robbie thought about saying, *C'mon, Kords, grab your pack and come with me.* They'd both be all right that way. But when they pulled up to the bus station in Jacksonville, all he did was reach over, his hand open. Korder gripped it and for a moment they stayed like that, unbreakable. Then Korder let go.

"Say hey to Rami. Say hey to whoever the fuck you're bangin' in fucking New Hampshire."

There was no girl in New Hampshire, only an old farm with his great-grandmother, his uncle, and memories he'd been hoarding for months. The farm out on Lost Nation Road had been his refuge when he was a little kid. He hadn't been back since he was sixteen, yet one night, a month into his second tour, he smelled the brook he'd fished with his uncle. He'd been awake for twenty-one hours straight and was standing in a ditch up to his thighs in icy water, engine oil, and blood. For seconds, the space of time it took to sniff and wipe his nose with the back of his wrist, he picked up the clean mossy smell of the stream that ran through the maples surrounding the sugar house. Then it was gone.

He thought about that stream over the remaining months, recovering the hours he'd spent walking its edges with a rod and line, tramping down the mountain to the farmhouse with his uncle to clean the fish so his great-grandmother could cook them. During the long empty spaces between action or the nights when the pills he used for sleeping didn't work, he conjured himself at age four plunging his arm into the sack of birdseed Big Ruth kept by the back door. He tried to remember the names of the birds that would come to the feeder or pick the seed off the ground. He could almost feel the warmth of his great-grandmother's arm around him when she sat on the back step and pointed each one out. Somehow the farm had once again become his safe place, and now he needed to go there.

He'd never be able to make his mother understand. She hated the place. *Screw it*, Robbie thought as he settled into a window seat on the Greyhound. He'd earned the right to go wherever he wanted. A pimpled kid with no hair and a big belly squinted at him from across the aisle.

"Semper Fi?" The guy shrugged his lumpy shoulders and laughed a little, like he'd made a joke.

Robbie saw a glint of metal on his tongue. He wanted to reach into the kid's mouth and yank out the pin or bolt or whatever the fuck it was, make the kid understand he had no right to even think the words *Semper Fidelis*. He didn't have the right to be on the same bus with a Marine.

Robbie dug through his pack for his iPod and stuck the buds in his ears. The music lit along his nerves until he felt like they were burning right through his skin. His fingers found the prescription bottle that held the only pills he had left. He'd been ashamed at first, when he admitted to the doctor after his first tour that he couldn't sleep. "Normal," the doctor said. So was the "anxiety," as she called it. She scribbled a bunch of prescriptions and told him these things resolved on their own. If he saw the doctor now, he'd tell her she was full of shit. He pulled out a pint of bourbon and swallowed one of the pills he'd hoarded. He almost laughed. Taking drugs was supposed to keep you out of the Marines. Then they handed 'em out to keep you in. Right now he hoped he had enough to keep him in his seat for the next eleven hours until the bus got to D.C.

When it did arrive, though, he wanted to stay on it until the next bus he needed showed up. He forced himself to follow the other passengers down the steps and into the station. He asked how to get to Walter Reed, but the directions involving bus routes and subways got lost in the noise and motion surrounding him. Out on the sidewalk in front of Union Station, people bumped and pushed past him. They were too close. Everything was too close. He retreated. He bought another pint of bourbon, some cola, and a few magazines. Then he found the gate for his next bus. He'd see Rami soon, he told himself. He and Korder would go together next time they were on liberty. He pulled out his cell phone and punched in a text to Korder: *Missin' me yet?* But he deleted it without sending.

Colors and noise rushed at him. A woman draped in brown, her hair covered, jabbered into a cell phone as she wheeled her suitcase toward another woman wearing a shiny pink blouse, a gray skirt, red lipstick, and an earpiece visible beneath a shell of blond hair. She reminded him of Ruthie, the way she walked, like she knew someone was watching. A giant television screen flashed from one giant head to eight smaller ones while words raced across the screen. Over the announcements of trains arriving and departing, Robbie heard the roar of a crowd from a bar.

He couldn't monitor everything; the muscles in his neck and jaw began to ache. Right now the guys who had replaced his unit in Ramadi were going on patrol, studying every bump in the road, every car coming at them, every man, woman, and child with their phones and bundles. Right now Ramirez was lying a few miles away in Walter Reed waiting for a new leg, a new hand, and more surgery to fix the parts of his insides that had been rearranged in the blast. Robbie sank down in his chair, hating that he couldn't move, hating that he was no better than the oblivious crowds around him.

# CHAPTER 5

Nearly thirty hours after leaving Jacksonville, Robbie woke with a lurch. The brakes of the bus groaned and then let out a hiss as the driver shifted into park. Rain splattered against the metal roof and dribbled down the windows. The clapboard buildings outside seemed to ripple as though they'd been painted on a curtain.

"Gershom, New Hampshire," said the driver.

Robbie pulled himself to his feet and hauled his pack down off the rack. When he climbed down to the sidewalk, the yellow structure in front of him turned into Inman's Drug and Sundries. Still here, then; a good sign. This was where his Uncle Kevin used to buy him jaw-breakers, bubble gum, and bags of malt balls behind Ruthie's back.

He let the rain drizzle down the back of his neck and arms while the bus heaved into gear and pulled away, sending one last blast of diesel exhaust into his face. Part of him was sorry to see it go. On a bus, you didn't have to make any more decisions. The world got trimmed down to window-sized chunks that just slid past like a movie; at night the bus was a rolling cave where you could hunker down with your music and your pint and no one said anything. Sleep was possible, even if only for an hour at a time.

Here on Gershom's Main Street, there was nowhere to hunker down, and nothing slid past except a green Ford pickup that had to be from the seventies. He saw the driver peer at him from under the bill of a cap. Robbie stared back until the man looked away. His uncle might look like that; his truck probably wasn't much newer than that one either. Robbie's stomach, still sour from booze and burgers he'd snared along the way, began to hurt. Would he even recognize Kev? Would Kevin know him after all this time?

Fuck it, he was here.

Robbie pulled his phone out of his pocket and punched in the number he'd known by heart since he was old enough to count. One ring, two, five. He pulled the phone from his ear and glanced at the time. Only three thirty, his uncle should still be at the shop. He listened again. Two more rings. His hand began to shake. What if he wasn't there, what if—

Then Kevin answered with something like a grunt.

"Garage."

"Kev?" Robbie heard his voice croak; he'd gone too long without talking. He cleared his throat and tried again. "Hey, Uncle. It's me, Rob. Just got off the bus here in downtown Gershom. Think you could come by and pick me up?"

Robbie heard his uncle take a breath. Kevin used to stutter sometimes. Maybe he still did.

"Jesus H. Christ."

Robbie felt his lips twist up in a grin. "Nope, just me. I'm in front of Inman's."

"Sit tight," he heard his uncle say. "I'll be right there." The phone clicked in Robbie's ear. Kevin was never much of a talker, Robbie remembered, and he hated the phone.

Robbie stepped under the awning of the drugstore and began to smoke while the rain petered out. He smoked one cigarette, then another, trying to remind himself that even if Kevin left immediately, it would take thirty or forty minutes for him to get here from the garage and scrapyard he ran on the family property. Still, he kept looking at every truck that nosed its way down the street. The longer he waited, the more the town itself altered his memories, turning them into something he hated. Inman's, the diner, and the bowling alley looked scarred, all peeling paint and green streaks of mold under the clapboards. They were squeezed now between bigger, glassier storefronts filled with high-priced camping gear, a cell phone store, a real estate office. The chatter of skateboards on concrete drew his gaze down to the bridge where he used to hang over the edge with a fishing line. Two kids, maybe ten, maybe older, in baseball uniforms pushed their way toward him. Skateboards in Gershom. Christ.

A tan Chevy Suburban measled with splotches of Rust-Oleum pulled up halfway through Robbie's fourth cigarette. Robbie recognized the hunch of his uncle's shoulders and the hair that bushed out around the bottom of his hat. Kevin pushed open his door and started to unfold his cranelike body, but Robbie hoisted his pack and motioned him to stay in the truck; he just wanted to get to the farm.

When he climbed into the passenger seat, Kevin grasped his hand and just looked at him for a long minute. "Good to see you, Rob." He smiled and shook his head. "Can't believe how much you resemble your dad when he was your age."

Robbie saw that his uncle, like the town, looked worn. His hair used to be the color of a new basketball. Now his frizz and the beard that covered his chin looked muddy with patches of gray. His hazel eyes, the same color as Ruthie's, peered at him through a pair of black-rimmed glasses. Robbie didn't know what to say, so he just nodded and tried to smile.

They took off slow, wheels sloshing through the puddles left by the rain.

"Heard from your mom a couple of weeks ago," Kevin said. "Told us she didn't know when you'd be home."

Here it was. "She still doesn't. I'm gonna surprise her."

Silence. The truck rolled past the Methodist church and, a few hundred feet later, the cemetery shared by all the churches. Robbie found the far left corner guarded by the maple they'd planted. A few of its leaves already littered his father's grave.

"You want to stop for a minute?"

Robbie shook his head. Maybe later.

When Kevin pulled onto the North Road, past the hospital, he picked up a little speed. Very little, Robbie noticed. Hard to believe Kevin and his dad used to race cars up at the county track when they were kids.

"How's Big Ruth?" he asked as they passed a clump of new houses in a field that used to feed cows.

"Not bad for ninety-one. A little trouble gettin' around but there's nothing wrong with her mind, that's for sure. Told her I was headed out to get you. She's probably sittin' at the window right now watchin' for us."

Robbie wanted to see his great-grandmother, but he wanted even more than that to be alone. He was trying to figure out how he would manage it when Kevin cleared his throat like he was getting ready to say something he wished he didn't have to say. Robbie glanced at him from the corner of his eye. His uncle looked straight ahead.

"You sure about this surprise stuff?" he said. "Your mom sounded kinda on edge. And Big Ruth's gonna want to talk to her. Hell, she'll want her out here on the next plane."

Shit, he'd fucked this all up. Robbie curled his hands into fists. He looked out the window until he trusted himself to speak. Even when he did, though, his voice sounded harsher than he meant. "I just can't do it, Kev. I need a little time first."

He took a chance and looked at his uncle. The car slowed and Kevin pulled into the dirt driveway leading to what looked like an empty barn. He turned in his seat and Robbie saw his eyes assessing him as though he were one of his engines that sounded a little off.

"You know I'm glad to see you after all these years. But I've got to ask, what are you doing here?"

Christ, he wanted a drink. He wanted a smoke. He wanted out of the truck. He wanted Kevin to lose the worry that was gathering in his eyes and let him alone. "I don't even know myself. I just— I used to think about this place back in— I need to be here for a little while."

Kevin said nothing for a moment; he seemed to be waiting to see if Robbie was through talking. Then he nodded in that slow way of his. "I'll talk to Big Ruth, I guess."

Robbie unclenched his fists. He still wanted a smoke but he would wait. Then a new fear struck.

"What if Mom calls?"

Kevin started up the engine and began to pull back onto the road. "Guess we cross that bridge when we come to it." A pause. "She probably won't, though. She's already called this month, and as long as you're here, she's got nothing new to tell us."

Robbie let Kevin lead the way into the old farmhouse kitchen. His uncle was right; his great-grandmother was at the big picture window rapping on the glass like one of her birds pecking at the feeders that still hung all over the yard. Robbie felt too big for the kitchen, and "Big Ruth," her eyes huge behind her purple glasses, was so much smaller than he remembered. When she smiled, her skin creased and puckered like the deer hide slippers on her feet.

"Come here, son, let me have a look at you," she said, pushing her walker toward him. Robbie dropped his pack and let her hug him. He was afraid to hug her back; her shoulders felt tiny and hollow, fragile as the teacups she still kept on a special shelf next to the round oak table.

"Put Robbie's things in Ruthie's old room," Big Ruth said to

Kevin. Without a word, his uncle picked up the pack and carried it upstairs.

"When Kev comes back down, he'll make you something to eat. He's not a bad cook as long as I keep an eye on him. You must be starving."

"No, thanks. I'm not that hungry, BR." He looked out the window. He was tired of windows now, even big ones. He wanted out. "Mind if I take a walk?"

He saw her eyes widen as if she were getting ready to protest, but Kevin was back.

"Go ahead," his uncle said.

"That's right, son," his great-grandmother said quickly. "Go on and stretch your legs. We'll have something for you to eat when you get back."

It was nearly five but there was plenty of light. He followed the brook up the mountain to the fishing hole, shallow now that it was nearly August but clear. He stripped down and sat in the icy water. He splashed it on his face and shoulders and then lay shivering until his spine bounced against the rocks covered with green slime. Bits of sky flashed through the poplars and the pines towering over him. Water streamed over his cheeks, face, eyes until his teeth chattered. For the first time, calm settled over him. He felt himself sink into the sounds and wetness; for a few moments he felt like he was part of the stream itself. If it had been spring, it would be easy. The water would be higher, rush faster. One slip and his head would crack against the rocks. The brook would fill his nose, mouth, lungs and he would be part of it forever.

A memory found him. He was nine or ten. He'd caught a trout and was unhooking it from the line when a moose snorted twenty feet behind him. He remembered how he'd dropped his rod and run like hell for the sugar shack. He felt the smile forming on his lips as he thought of how he'd crashed through the brush, convinced the

moose would follow. He wished another bull would appear. He'd
stand up, naked, dripping, and face the thing. If it ambled off, that
would be a sign. If it charged, he wouldn't be afraid. He'd let the
moose make the decision.

B y eight o'clock Big Ruth had already pushed her way to bed.
She hadn't said much during dinner, but she watched Robbie
the whole time, he felt it. She kept patting his arm as if to make sure
he was really there. She hadn't mentioned calling Ruth, and Robbie
was grateful to his uncle. "Sure I can't do anything?"

Kevin put the last dish in the drainboard. "All done. Join me on
the back step."

They each drank a beer; Robbie heard rustling in the lupine
field up in back of the house, and then it stopped. A sniff followed,
a long loud sucking in of breath. Robbie startled.

Kevin chuckled. "Probably the bear that's been raiding Big
Ruth's feeders. She's caught one or two out there in the mornings.
Heard her yelling from the front step one day, and she tried to make
me shoot it." He finished the last of his beer and pulled a joint out
of his pocket.

"You still grow your own?" Robbie said as he watched his uncle
light it up and inhale.

"Yup." He passed the joint to Robbie.

"Things have changed, huh? Last time I was here, you reamed
me out for getting into your stash." He'd been about sixteen then.

"Had your mother to answer to."

Robbie held the smoke in his lungs until his eyes watered. He
exhaled slow and easy. This might help him sleep.

"Think I'll head up to the cabin after," Kevin said. "Been a while
since I spent the night at my own place. Don't like to leave her alone
much at night anymore. She sleeps good, though. Doesn't usually
get up until five or so. I'll be back by then."

"Okay." His uncle sounded like a nurse, the way he talked about Big Ruth. He felt ashamed of his mother. She shouldn't leave it all up to Kevin.

Kevin seemed to read his mind. He took the joint from Robbie. "Your mom sends money," he said. "She keeps telling me she'll pay for a nurse or a nursing home. I tell her we don't need either one, but she wants to do something. She'd come visit more if she could."

"How can you be brother and sister and be so different?" Robbie said. He hadn't intended to ask it, but there it was. Kevin stood up but didn't make a move to descend the porch steps and head out to his truck. He stared off into the shadows of the front yard as if he thought he'd find the answer to Robbie's question out there by the feeders. Then he just shrugged and looked down. Robbie wished he'd stay awhile longer. He liked his uncle's quiet talk. He felt all of a sudden like he could sit there all night, passing a joint back and forth, talking about anything or nothing, like he used to with Garcia or Korder or Rami. Kevin started down the steps. Robbie held the joint up for him to take.

"You keep it. See you in the morning."

Robbie watched him back the Suburban down the driveway. He watched until the darkness extinguished the last flicker of red from its taillights. He made the joint last as long as he could. Then he went upstairs to bed.

He woke up screaming. He rolled off the narrow bed onto the planks of the old pine floor and lay there in the dark trying to breathe, trying to remember where he was.

"Robbie? Robbie, you all right up there?" His great-grandmother's worried voice brought him back. He lifted his head. His mother's old room at the top of the house, right under the peak of the roof. He didn't remember the room being so small; he used to like the way the eaves slanted over the bed, but now it seemed like the ceiling was pushing down on him.

"Robbie?" Big Ruth was trying to yell, but her voice kept giving out.

"Sorry." He thought he shouted, but he couldn't hear his own voice over the pounding of blood in his ears. He pulled himself up and stumbled to the door. Light rimmed the door to his great-grandmother's bedroom at the bottom of the stairs. He heard a bed creak as if she were trying to get up. What if she fell?

"Sorry, BR, sorry," he yelled again, louder so she would hear. "Just a dream."

The creaking stopped. Her voice quavered up to him. "You okay there?"

He began to shiver. His skin was slick with sweat; the night air was making him cold. He wanted warmth. He wanted light. He didn't know what the hell he wanted. "No worries," he called back. "I'm good. Just a dream."

She didn't answer right away. Robbie waited, half wishing she wouldn't believe him, wishing somehow she could be the woman he remembered from years ago when he was a kid awake at night, missing his dad. She'd know. Somehow, she'd know. She'd come to his door in the old plaid bathrobe that used to be his great-grandfather's and look at him through her crazy glasses. "I'm heading to the kitchen for some cocoa. Could use some company." Now he heard only an old woman's voice, tired and uncertain.

"All right then. See you in the morning."

A few seconds later, the light clicked off in Big Ruth's room. A rage that Robbie didn't understand flared inside him. She was leaving him up here in the dark. In a few minutes she'd fall asleep. He couldn't remember the last time he'd slept more than an hour or two in a row. He couldn't remember the last time he'd been alone for this long. He didn't know how to be alone.

He wheeled around and ran his hands along the wall until he found the light switch. The eaves cast shadows over the narrow bed and the sheet he'd dragged to the floor with him. He needed a drink. He found the bourbon he'd hidden in his backpack. As the familiar burn worked its way down his throat, he remembered what they'd told him in Kuwait, where they tried to figure out who was ready to go home and who needed a little more time to "transition."

"Civilians aren't going to know what to do or say," the major told them as a chaplain passed out little notebooks, as though they were in grade school. "You can always talk to the book."

"Talk to the book," Korder had sneered. They'd taken the little journals to make it look good, then tossed them. Now Robbie started looking around his mother's old room. He yanked open the drawers in the maple dresser and Ruthie's old desk, looking for a scrap of paper, anything he could write on. He found an old composition book with his mother's name printed across the front in schoolgirl letters: *Ruth Nolan, 11th Grade.* The first ten pages were filled with lists and check marks. Robbie flipped past them to clean pages. He grabbed a pen rolling in the top drawer and began to scribble. He couldn't keep ahead of the thoughts pouring out of the hole where they'd been breeding while he was in country. The girl's eyes. A piece of Garcia's bone stuck to his jacket. Things he'd done. Things he'd failed to do. They swarmed through his brain until he had to throw the pencil down and get out. They drove him out of the little room at the top of the stairs, back out onto the front steps of the farmhouse where he listened, rigid, alert, to the whispers and scufflings of the night. He kept his eyes trained on the perimeter of the yard and smoked one cigarette after another until dawn finally broke over the mountain.

Later, when the sun warmed the morning air, he took one of Kevin's old dirt bikes up the logging trail to the sugar shack. On his sixth birthday, Kevin had brought him up here and told him all about the days when Mo, Big Ruth's husband, used to make syrup. There was no floor; the old boiling pan was rusting outside, a chunk of roof was gone. It was the right size for a kid, though. Kevin had helped him fix it up. They used to come here after fishing. His dad had come, too, until he got married again.

The bike engine vibrated beneath Robbie as he straddled it, looking over his old haven. The shingled roof sagged, but his uncle had been watching over the place. A patchwork of fresh replacement planks and old weathered wood around the sides showed some kind of ongoing care. Robbie once had begged Ruthie to let him live in New Hampshire. A mistake. What was he, eleven? She'd kept him in California most of that summer, and after that he'd only come for short visits. A bit of familiar carving over the door caught his eye. He looked closer and saw it was the sign, shaped like a fish, that Kevin made him when he was little. It was covered with tree mold, but he could still make out the letters, dingy, hand painted: *Rob's Bait & Fly Shop.*

That night, he moved his pack and his booze into the sugar shack. If he woke up screaming, no one would hear him.

# CHAPTER 6

A couple of days later, it was morning and the air coming in the window smelled like rain even though the sun was already climbing. Big Ruth sat across from Robbie at the old oak table in front of a cold piece of toast and lukewarm tea. She wore a sweater the color of a peacock's feathers, all blues, greens, purples. Her pants were red. The older she got, she'd told him, the more color she wanted in her life.

He lifted his can of Coke as if he were toasting her and said, "Nice feathers today, BR." She beamed at him as he sipped his soda.

"Vonnie called yesterday," his great-grandmother said. Her tone was cautious, hopeful. "She wants to bring the kids over." Robbie's calm began to thin at the edges. She wanted some kind of family reunion. He hadn't seen his stepmother or his half siblings in years, although both Justin and Luanne had written letters to him in Iraq. He'd wanted to write back but never could come up with the right thing to say.

"'Kay," he said to his great-grandmother, although he wasn't sure it was. He just wanted the warmth he was feeling to keep going. He wanted to please her.

She gave him another big smile, which made her bridge slip a little. She pushed it back with her hand, and Robbie looked down so she would think he hadn't noticed. He picked up his fork and scraped the last of some scrambled eggs off his plate.

"You still look hungry. Let Kevin scramble you some more eggs," she said.

"You always said I looked hungry even when I was a fat slob," Robbie told her. He reached for his can of Coke.

"You were never fat! I never understood why it was a crime to eat. I miss it now." She gestured toward the half-eaten toast on her plate. "I eat more than this and the gas just about kills me and everyone else."

Robbie caught Kevin's eye from across the kitchen. His uncle, slouched now against the sink with a mug of coffee in his hand, grinned and shook his head. Time seemed to slip for a few seconds. Any minute now Ruthie would come down the stairs and start telling him to put on sunscreen and bug spray if he was going to go fishing all day.

The desire to see his mother seized him. When he was a kid she'd show up on a morning like this in a baggy T-shirt and shorts, looking for a cup of coffee that was never strong enough for her. She never used to bother with makeup in New Hampshire, or her contacts. Her hair, a deeper red than Kevin's, swung in a ponytail back then. His uncle might tug it gently as he passed by. Only he could get away with it. Just as Big Ruth was the only person who could tell his mother to sit down and expect that she would.

Robbie used to love seeing her sit like a child across the table from him, as she read a paper or magazine or one of those files she always had with her. She looked like she was pretending to be an adult, the way he used to when he grabbed his great-grandmother's glasses and put them on to make everyone laugh. Remembering his mother this way made his chest go soft inside.

He pulled his cell phone from his pocket but stopped when he saw a text from her, all in capital letters: *WHEN R U COMING? R U OK?* He looked up to see Big Ruth's eyes wide now, and eager, like a kid's.

"You calling your mom? Tell her to get herself out here so we can all be together again." She looked so hopeful that Robbie almost said yes, but if he called Ruth now, she'd know he'd lied to her about his leave.

He shook his head at his great-grandmother. "Just a buddy," he said. The softness inside him turned to guilt. His thumbs tapped out another lie: *all ok. Cll u sn.* The guilt thickened inside him. He got up without finishing his soda and told Kevin he'd meet him behind the house, where they were going to chop some wood.

Over the next few days he chopped nearly two cords of wood. He believed at first that working his body to the point of exhaustion would help him sleep. He looked for opportunities to chop, dig, and haul just to feel the sweat stream down his skin and smell the night's booze leach out his pores. He craved the emptiness that followed when he was too spent to think. For a little while he could sit still and let whatever surrounded him fill him up. Sometimes it was Big Ruth's voice as she rocked next to him on the porch of the farmhouse, or the smell of oil and hot metal in his uncle's shop, or the gentle sucking of the brook as it bubbled unhurriedly between his ankles. In those moments he sensed something like the sanctuary he'd dreamed about in the desert.

The stillness fled with the daylight, though. Shadows fell across the mountain and sank into him. The night loomed and with it came the desire to escape even the people he'd traveled two days on a bus to find. Their attempts at conversation sounded like demands in a language he no longer spoke. As they went about their quiet evening routines, he found himself watching and realizing with every passing minute that he was the foreigner here.

The worst was when his father's second wife, Vonnie, brought the kids over to see him. Their size shocked him. In his mind, they were still toddlers, the only beings in his life who had ever looked up to him. Now his half brother, Justin, was eighteen and as tall as he was, his legs sticking out of a pair of long gym shorts, his soccer shirt flapping like a wind sock. Luanne, his sister, was a year younger but looked like an adult to him.

"Cool tattoos," Justin said the first time they came by. Robbie, who'd taken his shirt off to mow the lawn, found it and pulled it back on. Luanne showed him the brownies she had brought, and he took one even though all he wanted was a beer. Vonnie gave him a hug and immediately began to talk about the early days when his dad was still alive and all of them were little. She worked hard to get the conversation going, like she was blowing on kindling, trying to coax a flame into a fire. It was just easier to sit there and listen, or pose with Justin and Luanne for pictures that they took with their phones and loaded onto Facebook while he watched. Justin grabbed a soccer ball out of their van and began to kick it, glancing at Robbie from time to time. "Lookin' good," Robbie told him, but he didn't get up to kick it around with him. He was glad when they left.

They came back for dinner two nights later, and he steeled himself with a six-pack of Bud. They almost made it through before Justin started asking the questions he'd probably wanted to ask from the minute he heard Robbie was back in Gershom.

"You were a machine gunner, right?"

"Yup."

"You kill anybody?" Niblets of corn stuck to his lips. His eyes, Robbie noticed for the first time, were the same deep brown he saw when he looked at his own face in the mirror.

"Stop it, Justin," Vonnie said. "Eat your corn and leave your brother alone."

Robbie looked down at his plate. The smell of the meat made him sick.

"I bet you did."

"Justin—" Vonnie's voice sharpened. Robbie wasn't sure if she was trying to stop Justin from asking or him from telling. When he looked around the table, he saw his brother, his sister, Kevin, Big Ruth, and Vonnie all looking at him. He pushed his chair away from the table. "Gonna smoke," he said. "I'll help with the dishes later."

"That's okay, honey. We'll do—"

But he didn't wait to hear any more. He heard the screen door slam behind him. Outside the sun settled on the rim of low mountains to the west. A mosquito bit him on the neck, but he didn't slap it. He burned through one cigarette, then another. Then he headed for the dirt bike. Justin came to the door and yelled to him. Robbie just waved as he revved the engine. He guided the bike down the driveway and roared toward the sugar shack.

When he returned the next morning, stinking and hungover, it was nearly ten. Kevin had gone to the shop and Big Ruth was alone.

"Sorry about last night," he said. His words sounded thick in his own ears. He sank into what had become his regular chair but avoided looking straight at her.

His great-grandmother reached across the table for his arm. "No need for that." She kept her hand there until he looked at her. "I want you to go get something for me."

A job to do; he felt steadier.

"Go get your book."

No.

"Go on, go get it. It's still in the same place."

*No.* He stood up, though. Slowly he left the kitchen and climbed the stairs to the landing that separated his mother's old room from the one Kevin used, first when he was a boy and now when he looked after Big Ruth. The blanket chest was at the end of the landing, wedged back under the eaves. This was where Big Ruth kept what she called the "Nolan Family Records." He dropped to his knees in the smothering heat of the upstairs and opened the chest. He pawed through photographs, baby shoes, old report cards, a book report Ruthie had done in eighth grade marked with a huge red A+, pictures of Kevin's first car, a wedding picture of their parents whom he'd never met, crayoned drawings by all of them for his great-grandmother's "refrigerator gallery." Finally, he saw it, the old brown vinyl book Big Ruth called "The Story of Robbie."

He wished he could climb back into the skin of the child he'd been. When he was five, he couldn't wait to see what she'd added and go over the story behind each picture. Even when he'd been a teenager pissed at Ruthie, more pissed at himself, he'd gone looking for the book. It seemed to hold him between its covers, his small past and all the possibilities that still remained on those blank pages.

He opened it now. In the first picture, Ruthie held him up like a prize she had won. She was laughing into the camera, her cheek pressed to his so that his infant mouth lolled like a drunk's. He crouched on the floor ignoring the sweat streaming down his face. He looked at his mother's smile.

"Did you find it, son?" Big Ruth's voice sounded from the bottom of the stairs.

"I found it," he said.


That night the book lay open on the floor of the sugar shack next to a crowd of empty beer bottles and a pint of bourbon. Robbie lit a joint he'd rolled from Kevin's stash, inhaled, and held his breath while he looked again at the snapshot of Ruth holding him as a baby. He exhaled, deliberate and slow. Then he wedged his fingernail beneath the edges of the photograph and extracted it from the fasteners at the corners. He placed it on the table next to the snapshot of his boot camp graduation portrait.

These showed the good times, the blank-slate days. The first one was taken before he'd made any mistakes. The second one was taken when he'd started over. Brand clean, as his great-grandmother used to say. The Marines scraped the fat and laziness off him. He rose like a fucking phoenix from the ashes of his old self.

He wanted to turn back the clock and see his mother the way she'd looked on graduation day. Those big old sunglasses came off. Her whole face opened up like a door swinging wide on a sunny afternoon. He swore he could feel her surprise and relief blowing toward him from the middle of all those parents, girlfriends, and babies crowded onto the stands at the parade grounds. Later, she hugged him tight tight tight. Everything was forgiven: the drugs, the fights, the struggles. His enlistment. He wasn't her problem anymore. He was no one's problem.

His throat ached thinking about it. He reached for the bourbon and held the bottle to his lips for a few seconds before he realized it, too, was empty. "Fuckin' shit," he grumbled, and hurled the bottle across the one-room shack. He started to get up to see if there were any more beers cooling in the brook outside, but the drawings stopped him.

He squinted at the wall directly in front of him. Half of it was in shadow but he could still make out the tracings of fish he had caught over the years. Faded pencil outlined his first brookie, his first small-mouth bass, his first perch, all drawn on paper cut from brown shopping bags. Each bore a few lines of information: type of fish, size and weight, where and when caught, the fly or lure used. His uncle Kevin's blocky lettering or his father's sloppy scrawl marked the early ones. Robbie had been old enough to trace and label the last few by himself. His were better than the others. He'd sketched and shaded in the scales and fins. The fish in his drawings seemed to be moving in the shadows, as if they were underwater poised to dart behind a rock.

This was who he used to be, the kid who thought this little bit of New Hampshire was paradise. All he ever had to do was show up and his great-grandparents would break into smiles. Uncle Kevin would grab him and take him up the mountain. They'd be fishing or fiddling with engines or checking out some new kittens before his parents unpacked the car.

He never understood why his mother hated the place so much. She and his dad had grown up here. If they had just stayed in Gershom, maybe they wouldn't have gotten divorced. And if they hadn't gotten divorced, maybe his dad would still be alive and his little brother and sister would be Ruthie's children, not Vonnie's. All it took was one thing to be different to change everything that came after, like in that movie Garcia always used to talk about.

He turned to the next page in the old photo album. There he was at twelve or thirteen, a lardass with pants sawed off at the shins, Padres cap turned around on his head, eyes puffed up, all spacey. Must've just come back from smoking a fatty in the barn during a rare visit back.

He ripped that one off the page and shredded it.

Here was a good one, himself with a string of brookies, standing in the farmhouse kitchen. What was he, six, seven?

There was a photo of him and his half siblings. He recognized it as the "good-bye" picture. Vonnie had taken it the day before Ruth dragged Robbie off to California. Justin and he looked like brothers, both of them stocky with puffy cheeks and the same mop of unruly brown curls. Luanne looked like Vonnie: bird bones, big eyes, wispy blond hair.

He felt bad now for running off when Justin tried to talk to him. He should have asked him more about the soccer, about high school, about anything. He was eighteen and a senior, but he seemed like a kid. Robbie lifted the photograph and put it next to the others. He remembered how much he'd loved the idea of having a brother, but he never felt like a brother once they moved. There were too many miles between them, and the age gap loomed larger then. He'd found his real brothers in the Marines. Robbie drained the rest of the beer.

A few drops spilled onto his boot camp picture. He tried to brush them off but they left spots on the white hat, the dark blue of his jacket.

He didn't know who or what he was when he enlisted. He just knew what he wasn't. He wasn't a college kid like Ruthie wanted. He wasn't headed for any corner office like she had with a secretary and a bunch of people running around while she cracked the whip. He was no surfer, no skinny golden boy like her boss's kid. It used to scare the shit out of him when he tried to imagine what he wanted or who he was supposed to be and nothing came to him. Nothing that mattered.

The Marines didn't care, though. They were going to make him part of something bigger than whatever the hell he thought he was. No one mattered but the Marine next to him and the Corps: not his mom, not his "fat nasty civilian" friends from high school, not even Uncle Kev or Big Ruth.

It was a relief. An honor. He was a grunt and proud of it. Robbie looked again at the photographs he'd lined up on the table. He looked back at the book, open now to all the empty pages Big Ruth had saved for him. The longer he looked, the more he understood that there was nothing left to fill them with.

Tomorrow, he'd go see his mom. He was as ready as he'd ever be.

# CHAPTER 7

Ruth pressed her ear to the guest room door. Nothing. Damn door was too thick to hear anything on the other side. She didn't want to wake Robbie but she wanted to see him, just for a minute, enough time to soak up the proof that he was finally here. The night before was nothing like the homecoming she'd imagined.

Pure Robbie, though. He makes her wait and wait, and then, when he finally arrives, it's like an ambush. The phone rings after eleven as she's dropping off to sleep, and it's him. "I'm at the airport." No time for anything but pulling on a sweat suit and sneakers, finding the keys to the Jaguar, Neal telling her it wouldn't be big enough, they should use his SUV, telling her to calm down, forget makeup, Robbie wouldn't care if she had on lipstick or not.

When she first saw the lone figure standing in a pool of light outside the baggage claim area, she thought: *Not him. Couldn't be.* The man standing in front of her was too thin, too old, and something else that she couldn't get a fix on. Then Neal guided the car to a stop and she saw her son's familiar chestnut eyes peering at her from under the bill of a camouflage cap.

Just one look. Ruth reached for the doorknob and turned, but it resisted her. She rested her forehead against the door and imagined him sprawled across the bed the way she used to find him after a long night. It was still early. Robbie had to be exhausted. He probably locked the door because for the first time in four years he had one to lock.

Anyway, they had time now. Lots of time. Ruth turned and began to climb the stairs to the living room. When she ascended the final step, she was surrounded by sky. Only a wall of glass doors and windows separated her from the mist dissipating before her eyes. Slivers of sun raced across the surface of the Pacific. She snatched up a remote control and stepped toward the deck. The windows slid apart. Two steps and she was outside, looking beyond the rail at the waves breaking on the cliffs below her.

She couldn't wait to show Robbie the house. He'd never seen it finished. Ruth leaned out over the rail and looked down at the waves slapping against the cliffs. He'd sit right here, she decided. She would bring him breakfast, lunch, whatever he wanted. She'd already left a message at the office. She was taking the day off. Tomorrow too. Hell, she'd take the week. She never used all her vacation time. Her mind was suddenly crowded with plans; her heart felt unmoored. It bounced against her ribs like a trapped balloon. This was how she'd wanted to feel last night.

"Any signs of life down there?"

Ruth glanced over her shoulder, shook her head. "Not yet." She reached for the mug Neal held out to her. "Thanks." She sipped, eyed the man standing next to her wearing a towel and nothing else unless she counted the sand dusted across his shoulder blades and embedded in the silver hair around his ankles. In a few minutes, the grains would dry and drop to the tiles she'd had shipped from Italy.

Screw the sand. Didn't matter. Not today. She smiled. "How were the waves?"

"Nice steady rollers. Perfect for an old guy like me." Neal took the towel from his waist, let it fall to a chaise longue, and settled on it, head back to grab the sun burning through the last of the marine layer. He sipped from a chipped blue Chargers mug and sighed contentedly.

Ruth thought of Robbie down in the guest room. He could be up here any minute. She stepped closer, brushed her fingers through Neal's damp hair so that it stuck up in spikes like tiny stalagmites.

"We've got company. Don't you think you better wrap up?"

"He's been living with Marines. You think he'll be upset by a naked guy?"

"Come on, Neal. I mean it."

Neal put down the mug, knotted the towel around his middle, and smiled at her. "There, how's that?"

Ruth nodded, but she was thinking now about things she hadn't had to think about for the past four years. Maybe Robbie would resent Neal's presence on his first day back. Then again, maybe not. After all, he'd been in and out of their lives since Robbie was ten. Not exactly a stranger. Not exactly family either. She realized Neal was talking.

"What did you say?"

"I was just saying you look a little nervous, there."

Ruth sat down on the chaise next to him. "I am." Saying it out loud didn't help.

Neal took a sip from his mug, then looked over the rim at her. "I'm going to clear out for a couple of days, head back to my place. You guys could use some time to catch up."

Good, she wouldn't have to ask him. Ruth ran her hand through Neal's hair again. "Thank you." Then she leaned over and kissed him.

"I ought to offer to get out of here more often." Neal laughed.

Ruth grinned back, but now every nerve was tuned toward the guest room. "He looks good, don't you think?" she said. But he'd looked terrible, and smelled worse. Tobacco, booze, and of all things some kind of wood smoke, as if he'd been camping. She'd almost pulled away from him after their first awkward embrace. Then she hugged him again right away in case he'd noticed.

"Yeah. Sure." The hesitation in Neal's tone made her look at him.

He wasn't smiling now. "Things could be rough for him. At least in the beginning." Neal looked down into his mug of coffee, shook it a little. "He can't be the same kid you—"

"Of course he can't. Don't you think I know that?"

Ruth shifted away from him. She knew where Neal was going and she didn't want to listen. Not right now. There would be time enough to talk about Robbie's adjustment. Was it wrong to just wait and see? She just wanted today to be okay. To have one good day.

She thought again of Robbie's silence on the way home. She'd shown him the guest room and was ready to go make him something to eat, but he was through the door in the time it took to mumble good night. When she'd checked again before going to bed, he hadn't responded to her knock even though she'd seen a line of light beneath the door.

"He's tired. That's to be expected," she said.

Neal didn't seem to hear her. "Just a few months, a couple of years. They change your whole life," he said, looking past her shoulder in a way she'd come to recognize. He was talking about himself again. Vietnam. The things he'd seen. The end of one marriage, then another. Estrangement of his children. He'd been talking more and more lately, usually late at night after a few vodka martinis. Each telling peeled away more of the man Ruth knew, as though he were stripping in front of her. He wasn't drinking now, though. He was trying, in his way, to help but all he was doing was frightening her.

"You took orders; so did Robbie. You both did what you had to do. You have a good life now, right?"

Neal's voice grew insistent, as though he were a doctor and she were a stubborn patient. "I'm just trying to h—"

"Please, Neal, don't . . . can't we give Robbie some time to—"

"Hey."

They both stumbled to their feet and turned toward the voice behind them.

Robbie filled the gap in the sliders, shirtless above and shoeless below the fatigues that clung to his hips.

"Whoa, Neal. Towel." He croaked out a laugh while Neal caught and resecured the towel around his waist. Ruth knew she was blushing, and knowing it made her cheeks even hotter. She looked at Neal and knew she was scowling. Had he heard them talking about him?

"Geez. Kidding. Just kidding. It's your house." Robbie did not look at her or at Neal when he said it. He drove his hands into his pockets and walked past Ruth to the rail. A dog's bark, the laugh of a couple of surfers floated up from the base of the cliffs.

"Big change from the old place."

"Your mother's a big wheel, you know," Neal said. "She's got generals eating out of her hand."

*After they've taken their cut*, Ruth thought, amused by Neal's attempt to impress Robbie with her accomplishments. Neal used his ex-military network to make money as a consultant. He brought Ruth lots of business and he got a piece of the pie. She caught Robbie's eye and smiled.

"Way to go, Mom," Robbie said.

For a few seconds, no one spoke.

"You want some coffee, Rob, or is Coke still the drink of choice?" Neal cinched the towel tighter and grabbed his mug.

"Coke'd be good."

"Done."

Ruth joined Robbie at the rail, her shoulder nearly touching his. His head, still glistening with water from his shower, was razored nearly bald on each side; a small patch of black bristles did its best to cover the top. His jawline was still a surprise to her after four years, clean bones rising from what had once been a double chin. He was too thin, though. The circles under his eyes worried her.

"You look exhausted, honey."

"Just jet lag. Mind if I smoke up here?" He reached into his pocket and pulled out a pack of cigarettes.

"As long as you don't do it in the house." Ruth wanted the words back as soon as she said them. Still she was glad when he shoved the cigarettes back in his pocket.

He leaned forward on the railing. A tattoo appeared on his rib cage, just under his armpit. His name, followed by the letters *APOS*, a string of numbers, *USMC, No Religion*.

"What's this?"

"Like dog tags, only permanent."

"But why?"

"Lot of guys were getting 'em. You get . . . sometimes dog tags disappear. Seemed like a good idea at the time."

At first Ruth still didn't understand. Then she did. She grabbed his arm and pulled it to her the way she used to do when he was little and darting ahead of her near a busy street. More ink crawled up the underside of his forearm. A shield with the words *Semper Fidelis*. There were names: Hanny, Garcia, a couple of more she couldn't make out before Robbie pulled his arm back. Overhead, a flock of parrots shrieked. They swooped past in a blur of green.

"Damn, those guys are loud, huh?" Robbie watched the birds, descendants of escaped pets, now louder and more aggressive than the biggest crows. He rubbed the tattooed names, but now Ruth was looking at his hand. There was a tremor she hadn't noticed before.

She pretended to watch the parrots but wanted to pull Robbie to her and hold him until the tremor stopped. She settled for resting her palm against his shoulder, white where his T-shirt sleeve had shielded it from the sun. His shoulder stiffened under her palm. He breathed in through his teeth, the inward whistle he used to make when he was nervous. Ruth patted his shoulder and then let her hand drop. He glanced at her sideways.

"You look good, Mom. Still working out?"

She looked down at the sweat stains spread across the front of her tank top. "Every day. Did five miles on the treadmill this morning."

Her waist, still damp, itched under her spandex shorts. She'd woken at four thirty, unable to go back to sleep. She'd seen the light under his door and had to restrain herself from trying to look in on him right then and there. "I put in a little gym downstairs. There's a lap pool out back too. Feel free to use it. Not that you need to lose any weight. You're a rail." Her words petered out. He might think she was criticizing; he used to hate when she said anything at all about his weight. She started talking again before he could respond. "Start thinking about what you'd like to eat. I'm going shopping as soon as I get dressed."

"No work?" He looked at her and for the first time she felt she'd said the right thing.

"Are you kidding? I left a message last night. I'm taking time off beginning now. We're celebrating."

"Here's your Coke, Rob." Neal joined them at the railing. He'd changed into a pair of shorts and a faded blue polo shirt.

"In a glass and everything," Robbie said. "Thanks."

Ruth watched him swallow, his Adam's apple ascending and falling in one beautiful pumplike motion. Now she was thinking like him, a mechanic right from the start. At nine, fresh on the heels of a visit to his uncle's auto shop, he'd given her a lecture on hydraulics, rife with inaccuracies but packed with enthusiasm. The nine-year-old's voice sounded in her ears while she watched the twenty-three-year-old down his drink. She'd thought—hoped—he'd follow his father into engineering. Maybe now he'd do it. Robbie caught her staring at him.

"I know, I know. Coke's 'not a civilized drink for breakfast.'" His hand still shook.

"What? No. No. Just glad you're here," Ruth said. "Drink up."

Neal cleared his throat. "Look, you both'll need some time . . ."

Ruth's BlackBerry toned. All three of them looked at the phone clasped to her hip.

"This'll just be a minute. I've already told them I'm taking the day off." Ruth smiled at Robbie. "Start making that list, honey. Anything you want."

She heard Terri speaking before she'd even put the phone to her ear. "I'm sorry to have to do this when Robbie's just gotten home, but Don's calling an emergency meeting. You need to be here in an hour."

Ruth smiled at Robbie, motioned to Neal, and mouthed, *Another Coke*. She turned away from them and spoke in a low voice. "What's up?"

"There are protesters all over the front steps of the building and more keep coming. A whole busload just arrived."

So it was RyCom's turn, Ruth thought. Other defense contractors occasionally had to put up with peace groups but until now, they'd been lucky. She glanced at Robbie, who was looking back at her with an expression she couldn't read. "Isn't this something that Gordon can handle with his security guys?"

"He's the one who's telling Don you need to be here. Says he told you something was going on with insurance claims and a lawyer."

Claims. Lawyer. Ruth's stomach clenched as she remembered the morning Gordon surprised her by showing up at her meeting. Then Robbie had called, two new contracts hit her desk, and she decided it could wait a few days. That was a week and a half ago. Shit. Just yesterday, Legal had wanted to meet with her, but she'd put them off. Still, she was confused.

"What's that got to do with protesters?"

"That's who's out there," Terri said. "Ex-contractors, families. There's a lawsuit, filed yesterday. They must have told the media beforehand because there's a big story in the paper today," Terri said. "The vans from the TV stations are out there now too."

Ruth looked around her for the paper. "Neal? Where's the *Union Tribune*?"

"What?" He was in the kitchen getting the soda.

"The *U-T*? Did you bring it up?"

Robbie pushed himself away from the deck railing. "I'll get it," Robbie said. "Front steps, right? Think I heard the guy toss it there this morning."

Ruth nodded her thanks. Terri was speaking again in her ear.

"When do you think you can get here? I've got to report back to Don's office, let him know I've reached you."

"Robbie just got home. There's got to be some way I can handle this from here."

The phone line went quiet. Then Terri said, "You may want to be here in person."

"What are you saying, Ter?"

Another silence. Her assistant's voice dropped as if she were trying not to be overheard. "From what I can gather, Don is listening pretty closely to Gordon right now. He's laying it all at your feet."

The bastard. Paper rustled next to her. Robbie was back, reading the front page. Neal stood next to him, holding the can of Coke and reading over his shoulder. Ruth caught a glimpse of the headline: *RyCom Contractors Sue Firm.*

"Let me look and I'll call you back."

"What do I tell Don?"

"That he's a . . . Never mind. Tell him I'll be there in an hour," Ruth said into the phone and disconnected.

Robbie looked up at that. "You're going to work?" The catch in his voice caught her off guard. Again, Ruth saw the young Robbie in the full-size version before her.

"Just for a little while. I'll come back early. Promise. We'll have the afternoon. Tomorrow too and the day after. I'm taking the whole week off. I just need to put this fire out."

"Pretty big fire," Neal said. "I'm going to need to make some calls myself."

"Let me see." Ruth scanned the first few lines of the paper. *Families of contractors employed by RyCom Systems filed suit this morning against the local defense firm. The suit alleges the company has failed to provide insurance or pay claims on existing policies for contractors wounded or killed in the Middle East.*

"Saw some people wearing the old RyCom logo when I was back there," Robbie said. "Doin' all kinds of stuff."

"We have more than one division," Ruth said without looking up.

"Can some guy really make a hundred thousand for swinging a hammer?"

"It's not that simple," Ruth said automatically. She turned the paper over, looking for the rest of the article. "They're working under unusual conditions."

"Yeah. I know."

Ruth looked up, stricken. Robbie stared back at her like he didn't know her. Neal cocked his head as if waiting to see what she would say. "Robbie, my God, of course . . . I didn't mean . . ."

Robbie cut her off, shrugging. "It's a good deal for them. If they make it, they deserve whatever they can get. Anyway, the paper's full of shit, right?"

"Of course." Ruth's stomach churned. She needed one of those heartburn pills.

"My phone's going to be ringing today. I'll want to know what to tell my folks," Neal said, all business now. He reached into the pocket of his shorts and pulled out his phone.

Ruth shot Neal a look she hoped would silence him. "I hate this, Robbie, but I need to be there. Only for a little while, just have to set the wheels in motion, get this straightened out. You understand, right?"

Robbie looked past her. He waited so long to reply that she wondered if he'd even heard her. Finally, he shrugged again. "You gotta do what you gotta do."

*We do what we have to do. Then we can do what we want to do.* She'd said it for years to motivate or reassure herself, and to show him what it meant to be a grown-up. Now, though, it sounded like an accusation. She spoke louder than she needed to, trying to sound more confident than she felt.

"I'll be back before you know it. You need to rest anyway. Go for a swim. Take a nap. We'll have the rest of the day together." She saw Robbie glance at Neal, who was checking his messages.

"Just us. Neal has business for the next couple of days, so he's heading over to his place." Neal nodded and smiled before turning toward the kitchen.

She raised herself on her toes, kissed Robbie on the cheek, and then patted the spot she had kissed. Stubble. A beard. She patted his cheek again. Then he surprised her by grabbing her hand. The tremor she'd felt earlier ran from his hand into hers. His palm was clammy with sweat. For the first time she noticed the little white lines at the corners of his eyes. He'd been squinting in the sun so long that the fissures were left untanned. Then she saw that he was smiling at her. The smile was tentative, tired, but it was there.

"We can go out for lunch," he said. "I can meet you at work. I'll even pay."

The band of tension around Ruth's chest loosened and she smiled as she squeezed Robbie's hand. "How could I refuse an invitation like that?" She held his hand a little longer, hating to give it up. "That will be wonderful. Thank you so much, honey." She looked at his tired, smiling face and smiled back. He was home. "I love you." She squeezed his hand one more time and forced herself to let go.

Ruth stripped and stepped into the shower. She barely felt the jets of steaming water. The allegations in the article were absurd: unpaid insurance claims, lapsed life insurance policies, misleading recruitment practices. But the negative publicity could queer the Transglobal deal, which was probably why Don jumped in and called the meeting and why Gordon was blaming her.

Ruth turned off the water, grabbed her towel, and headed for the walk-in closet that opened off the bathroom. As she rubbed herself dry she tried to focus on what lay ahead. The bathroom door swung open. Neal's flip-flops slapped across the tile into the closet.

"You better get going," he said to her reflection in the mirror. "Square this thing away before it blows out of proportion."

She tossed the towel into the hamper.

"Do me a favor, buy me some time to deal with this."

"What am I supposed to do?"

"Tell your clients that when all the facts come out this will go away. Tell them not to hit the panic button." She grabbed a silk blouse from the "white section" of the closet.

"They'll want to know—I want to know—if anyone associated with our projects is suing."

Ruth caught her toe in the hem of a gray skirt and tore it loose. "Damn." She tossed the skirt aside and reached for another one, nearly the same color but shot through with black and blue threads. "I'll call you. Just give me a little time."

When she glanced in the mirror, she saw Neal's brow relax but only a little. He moved toward the section of her closet she'd cleared for a few of his clothes. Then it hit her: If they both left now, Robbie would be alone. "Neal."

"Mmm?"

"You don't have to rush off. Stay and have a little breakfast with Robbie." She shoved her toes into a pair of slingbacks and leaned over to pull the straps over her heels.

Neal looked surprised. "I guess that would work."

"He doesn't know the house, where things are, anything." And he hadn't spent more than a half hour with Neal since he was fifteen. It might help Robbie, though. She knew she'd feel better. Ruth crossed to Neal and cupped his cheek in her palm.

"You said yourself that the first day back could be difficult for him. If we both leave at once, it just seems—"

Neal pulled Ruth to him. "Sure." He gave her a quick hard hug. "I can't stay too long, though. I want to start calling folks before they call me. You've got to keep me up to date on this thing, okay?"

Ruth nodded, but she'd stopped listening. She needed to get to work.

# CHAPTER 8

R uth's BlackBerry rang again as she backed her Jaguar out of the garage. She tapped her earpiece. "I'm here."

"Stand by for Don. The meeting is underway."

Ruth kept her eyes on the road, but most of her attention was focused on the voices that pushed their way through the speakerphone into her ear. She heard Andrea, who seemed to be reading from the article in the paper. Ruth knew the men who were leaning forward, pens tapping out their impatience on the conference table, interrupting with questions no one knew the answer to yet. She knew the few who would be sitting back, creating as much distance as possible between themselves and this crisis. She was unsurprised by the baritone that plowed through the noise.

"This is all bullshit," Don Ryland said. The other voices subsided suddenly. "They're saying we didn't tell them it would be dangerous? It's a fucking war zone. Right there in the want ads, it says, 'hazardous conditions.' It's why goddamned truck drivers are making nearly two hundred grand a year."

Now came a voice with a pitch somewhere between gravel and

buzz saw. Gordon. "Perhaps the reality was more than some of them bargained for." He would be slouching in a chair at the other end of the table, eyes flicking around the room, yellowed fingers picking up and putting down his pack of cigarettes. "Ruth's on the line; let's hear from her."

"I know what I read in the paper," she said. "And I know it can't be accurate." She glanced into the rearview mirror and then pulled out to pass a minivan.

"That's reassuring," Don said. Was he being sarcastic? Ruth suddenly felt like a blind person in a room full of knives. "Tell us more."

The line went quiet then. Ruth imagined everyone's eyes on the speakerphone lying in the middle of the conference table like a beached manta ray. Acid seared the back of her throat. She steered with her left hand and grabbed her purse with her right, hoping to find some Tums.

"Every recruiting document, every insurance plan was reviewed and approved by Legal and HR—" she started.

"Still, here we are, with a lawsuit on our hands," Don interrupted. "The Transglobal people are going to be on our backs, and I want to make them feel real confident that there are no bumps. Think you can do that?"

"I'll need a team to help with the communications plan," Ruth said. "Gordon, tell the HR folks to clear their schedules. We'll need Legal too."

"They've been waiting for your call," Gordon rasped into the phone. "For a while now."

Bastard.

"I'm putting Andrea on this with you," Don said.

Great. Ruth swallowed but her throat continued to burn. "Thanks. That'll help." She hit the accelerator and blasted past the minivan.

The blare of a horn followed Ruth as she edged right again and cut toward the exit to the office complex rising on the northbound side of the 5 freeway. "I'm just pulling in now." She braked to a halt as a TV van pulled a U-turn in front of her and parked. A crowd of people clutching signs milled around the entrance to the RyCom headquarters building. A couple more vans splashed with the logos of local television channels were parked on the fringe. "My God," she said aloud.

"That's your welcoming committee," Don said. She'd forgotten the phone was still live. He must be watching the scene from the conference room window above. She disconnected the phone and slowed as she passed the entrance. A young woman stooping over a figure in a wheelchair looked up as she rolled by. Another woman, gray-haired, was climbing the steps, one hand holding a poster showing a youthful male face, the other the edge of a banner. In her rearview mirror, Ruth watched a man with a cane take the other edge of the banner and unfurl it. *Families of the Forgotten*, it read.

A woman with a notebook peeled off from the protesters and peered in Ruth's direction. A reporter. Ruth avoided eye contact and guided the car into the parking garage. A few minutes later, she'd given Danny the car to park and run to the side entrance before she could be seen.

She felt better once she walked into the lobby. No matter how fast the lights on her switchboard lit up, Marcia spoke with unhurried assurance as she routed or deflected the calls.

"Robbie got home last night," Ruth said in a low voice as she passed the reception desk. Marcia smiled and shot her a thumbs-up sign. Ruth decided the expectations waiting for her upstairs were like the black diamond ski trails she'd mastered long ago: challenging, a few sharp turns and steep drops, but nothing she couldn't handle.

She dialed Terri from the elevator and issued clipped instructions: set up a meeting with HR in half an hour, pull all files on anything to do with contractor agreements and recruiting, have it all on her desk so she could dive in the minute she broke free.

Then she went straight to the conference room, now empty except for Don Ryland. He didn't turn around. The fluorescent lighting produced a dull gleam on his shaved head. His shoulders remained square, his hands clenched together behind his back. There was a time when she'd known that back intimately, had kneaded the muscles until they relaxed in her hands. They had celebrated deals with champagne and sex in the hotels, sometimes the offices, where the deals had been made. That time had long passed but her usefulness had not; she'd seen to it. She'd been his gatekeeper, his second set of eyes, his right hand for over twenty years, longer than either of his marriages. That had to count for something.

"They want to bring me down," Don said. Ruth joined him at the window. The figures below were grouped around the banner. In front of them, a man with a briefcase was being interviewed by a woman holding a microphone.

"Who's that?"

"Their lawyer," said a woman.

The voice came from behind Ruth. Andrea. Ruth hadn't realized that she was still in the room, half seated on the edge of the table, eyes down, her thumb moving across the keypad of her BlackBerry. She glanced up. "His name is Breen."

"Candy-assed liberal prick," Don grunted. "Wants to make his name on me."

"They'll have to make a case to do that, and they can't," Ruth said. She tried to sound confident. Confidence was what he was looking for, and she'd give it to him.

Don allowed his lips to part in the smallest of grins. "Andrea has spent all morning pulling the information together on these idiots."

The implication was clear. While Ruth had been busy lolling at home, Andrea was getting the job done.

"It's all printed out and on your desk," Andrea said without looking up. "Here's the latest on Transglobal." She held the Black-

Berry out but Don crossed to her and read the screen over her shoulder, just far enough away that he wouldn't need the reading glasses he hated, Ruth thought. Old fool. He eyed her from beneath the thatch of his brows.

"Don't let us keep you," he said.

Ruth made herself smile and walk out of the room with a purposeful but unhurried stride. She wouldn't give Don Ryland the satisfaction of a reaction. He must be more rattled than she'd realized if he needed to humiliate her in front of Andrea. His rough dismissal burned as she threaded her way through the pods of cubicles to her office. She'd like to cast it as an old man's weakness for young attractive women, but Don was too practical for that to matter by itself. As his company had grown, he wanted connections. And Andrea had them: Stanford and four years of working for a member of the Armed Services Committee in Washington. The last new junior executive had been the son of a senator. Like Andrea, he'd been young, not quite thirty, assigned to work under Ruth in some vague capacity that didn't matter because the real job was to swim after Don like some kind of pilot fish. "My mentees," he called these young people hatched in nests of wealth, nurtured in private schools, and then let loose among their own kind, secure in the belief that they had earned everything they'd gotten and deserved better.

Ruth was the product of public schools in a county Don had never heard of followed by four years at the University of New Hampshire, in-state tuition being all her grandparents, and she, could afford.

Ruth picked up her pace as she neared her office, where she could see Terri and another person silhouetted in front of the frosted glass walls. She couldn't afford thoughts like this now. She had work to do. She saw Terri wave a hello in her direction and then recognized the other woman as Sylvia, the head of Human Resources, a lumpy woman so burdened with files that she reminded Ruth of a camel. Ruth took a deep breath, crossed the threshold, and dove in.

A little over an hour later, she sat back in her chair, stunned. "You're telling me that our people filed their medical claims and the insurance company still hasn't paid out? None of them?"

"These have been paid," Sylvia said, pushing a page across the desk. "Partially. The company has denied payment for the rest of the claims. It's standard operating procedure. Most will eventually be paid once reviews have been completed."

Ruth looked from the names on the single page in front of her to the eleven-inch stack of files Sylvia had dumped on her desk. The "pending" files. Some of the claims had been "pending" for eleven months. Some longer. Ruth had opened the files before she stopped, rattled by the juxtaposition of ordinary job descriptions and extraordinary injuries: interpreter, double amputee; truck driver, quadriplegic; medical technician, brain trauma. She tried not to read the names but they were right there, on the first page, their stories crammed into small boxes below: Ahmed Hazazi, born in Detroit, fluent in Arabic, IED blast. Marissa Albertson, age twenty-seven, caught when a newly built clinic she was working in collapsed after a nearby explosion; the truck driver, Clayton Massey, spinal cord severed after his caravan was ambushed.

Each name clawed at her in a way she'd never expected. By the tenth file, she'd had to stop looking. *They knew the risks*, she told herself, just as she'd told Robbie. *We told them there would be risks*. Still, she grabbed the top folder and shook it at Sylvia.

"We're paying out huge premiums. There's no reason to sit on these."

Sylvia's shoulders, straining the seams of her black blazer, rose in a shrug. "As I said, standard procedure. Out of our hands."

"Until now. Now it has landed in our goddamned laps. Why didn't you tell me about this right away?" Ruth's voice rose.

Sylvia straightened; her wattle trembled. "This information is included in every monthly report I send out. The last one went out four days ago." The older woman's eyes narrowed behind her glasses. "You haven't opened it. I track all my e-mails."

"Good for you, Sylvia." The woman was Gordon's creature, a senior executive who acted like a goddamned clerk. "But we need solutions, not record keepers."

Ruth grabbed the phone on her desk and punched the keypad. "Terri, call—Sylvia, who's the boss of the person you deal with at"— Ruth looked down at the papers on her desk—"Excel Insurance?"

Then she saw something she hadn't noticed before. The letterhead in front of her identified Excel as "a Transglobal Company." She had not paid attention to the selection of the insurer. Olson had handled it. They'd made the switch to Excel about eight months ago. That was when talks about merging with Transglobal had gotten serious. Ruth put the phone down, then stared at the files before her.

The premiums were huge, probably three times what they should have been. Neither Olson nor Don would care, she knew that. The cost would be passed on, along with a hefty upcharge, to the next client up the food chain—ultimately the Department of Defense. Giving the business to Excel was, essentially, giving a chunk of money to Transglobal. A little sugar to sweeten the pot.

Sylvia pushed another sheaf of papers toward Ruth.

"What?" Ruth's mind was racing, trying to find one small crack in the wall that had suddenly risen before her, someplace where she could get a finger hold, and pull herself up and over.

"The life insurance claims. Since you haven't seen my report, you won't have seen this. Excel isn't paying out on these life insurance claims."

"Why not?"

"The denials state that their deaths were not a result of their jobs. A couple are called accidents that happened on leave in Qatar. Two are said to be suicides. The rest were—"

"Well, suicide can't be a job-related death."

"Of course." Sylvia paused. "The families apparently see it differently."

"That's between them and the insurer," Ruth insisted. "We can't tell Excel people how to do their job."

Sylvia's lips stretched in what might have been an approving smile. "That's our view as well."

The phone buzzed. Ruth ignored it. She had to meet Gordon and Andrea in an hour. She had to understand everything before that.

"What about these?" Ruth picked up a page marked *Denied: Other.*

Sylvia cleared her throat. When she spoke, Ruth heard a note of defensiveness that hadn't been in her tone until now.

"The remaining claims have been denied because the policies never went into effect. Missing signatures, incomplete forms, things of that nature."

Disbelief mixed with a rising fury at the woman in front of her. Ruth worked to keep her tone even. "Why weren't those things taken care of before the contractors were deployed?"

"By the time Excel informed us, most of those impacted had already shipped out. We sent them reminder letters with instructions about what to do."

"And?"

Sylvia shifted in her seat; her eyes lowered for an instant before looking again at Ruth. "And nothing. We sent the notices."

Ruth tried to maintain an even tone. "How hard did we try to follow up?"

The woman's eyes, a watery blue, blinked behind her glasses. Her jaw seemed locked in place. "We provided the forms, all the information the contractors needed. The rest was their responsibility."

The image of the picketers with their signs flashed before Ruth's eyes. There was no way to make that message fly with the women carrying pictures of their dead husbands up the company's steps. She wouldn't accept it and neither would they. Ruth wanted to hurl the files at Sylvia.

"Was this in the monthly reports, too? Or was it in another of the hundreds of e-mails I get with my name in the cc box?"

The phone buzzed again. Ruth pounded the speakerphone button.

"What is it, Terri?"

"Ruth, Robbie's here."

"Robbie?" Ruth looked at her watch. He was early. No, he wasn't. It was noon. On the dot. Lunchtime, as far as he knew. She'd left the house late. She should have thought this out.

"Sylvia, let's take a break and meet back here in a half hour. I want to make sure we've covered everything. No more surprises."

When the office door swung open to reveal Robbie, Ruth did a double take. Crisp khakis. Olive button-down shirt. None of the tattoos showed. He'd done this for her. A beam of pleasure temporarily eclipsed the problems strewn across her desk.

"Hello, ma'am," he said. He looked from Ruth to Sylvia and back. Ruth motioned him inside.

"This is my son, Lance Corporal Robert O'Connell," Ruth said. "And Robbie, this is Sylvia . . ." Damn. What was the woman's last name? "From Human Resources."

Sylvia pushed herself out of the chair. Robbie shook her hand. "Nice to meet you, ma'am."

"Thank you for your service," Sylvia said. "We are praying for all of you every day."

Ruth noticed that Robbie pulled his arm back quickly; she wondered if he was trying to hide the tremor.

"Is it young Robert?" Robbie jerked his head up at the sound of Don's voice. The older man was taller, broader than Robbie. For reasons she could not understand, Ruth wanted to step between them.

"Yes, sir."

"After you, Sylvia," Don said, stepping aside to let her pass. He turned to Robbie. "Been getting the job done over there. Good for you." Ruth noticed he didn't reach to shake her son's hand, as if he weren't important enough.

"Yes, sir." Robbie's face had turned into a mask. His jaw muscle twitched in a way Ruth recognized; he was clenching his teeth the way she did when she was fighting not to say what was on her mind, or just trying to stay calm.

"I tell the folks around here to work hard because you are all depending on us." Ruth knew Don was irritated by the need to be polite; he'd come to her office for a reason.

"Is there something new?" Ruth said, to draw his attention away from Robbie.

"Only that the hyenas and their damned posters left our front door a while ago," Don said. "They got what they wanted from the media and now they're gone. But they'll be back. Came by for a briefing, to see what you've got." He glanced at Robbie and bared his teeth in what was supposed to be a smile. "Need to steal your mother for a little while. Would you like to grab something from the cafeteria?"

Robbie looked at her as though Don were speaking a language he did not understand and did not care to learn.

"Don, excuse us. I need a word with my son." Don didn't move. He was not, Ruth knew, used to being dismissed. "I'll come find you. I just need a few minutes."

"Of course." Don nodded once more at Robbie and shot Ruth a look that told her she was on thin ice. "A few minutes, then." He disappeared.

"Robbie," Ruth said as gently as she could. "About lunch."

He seemed not to hear. He looked around the office. She followed his gaze. Together, they took in the carpet, a Kilim, a present from a customer; the mahogany shelves with a grouping of antique Chinese bowls; and a gold plate on a crystal pedestal engraved with the words *Women Defense Executives Pathfinder Award*. He said nothing about the espresso machine or the photographs of Ruth flanked by a general or congressman on one side and Don on the other, but the sight of his boot camp graduation photo drew him. He walked over to Ruth's desk and picked it up.

"Guess I outrank the general over there, when it comes to pictures, anyway."

Ruth nodded. "I look at it every day and show it to everyone who comes in here." She went to his side and looked over his shoulder at the serious eyes, honed jawline, and white cap that looked almost too big for his head. "I haven't said it anywhere near enough, Robbie. I'm so proud of you." She touched his arm. His sleeve was damp and Ruth noticed sweat gathering on the back of his neck. "Are you okay, honey?" She lifted her hand as if to check his temperature. He wasn't flushed. He was pale. He stepped out of her reach and then made a show of looking in his shirt pocket.

"Here's another one for your collection." Robbie pulled out a color snapshot and handed it to Ruth. Ruth glanced at the photo, Robbie at six or seven clutching a string of tiny fish. He was standing in the kitchen of her grandparents' farmhouse. She frowned. Where had this come from?

"Good times, huh?" Robbie said.

Ruth knew he wanted her to say yes, so she nodded. For her, the small farm in northern New Hampshire was home by default, the place where her mother had dumped her nearly forty years earlier and never looked back. Robbie, though, had always loved going there.

"Where did you get it?" She took the photo and pretended to examine it. She could make out a plaid shirt in the background. It belonged to her brother, Kevin, adored by Robbie from the moment he could walk. He'd followed her brother like a puppy through the woods, barns, and garage where Kevin repaired cars for a living.

Robbie didn't answer her. When she looked up to see why, he cleared his throat a couple of times and said in a low voice, almost as if he didn't want her to hear, "Stopped there on my way here. Found it in one of Big Ruth's old photo albums."

"You went to New Hampshire?" She fought to control her voice. "Before coming here?"

"Yeah. No big deal. I was close, well, on the East Coast. I didn't figure I'd get back . . . anytime soon."

"And of course Gershom is right on the way to San Diego."

"Mom, c'mon. It's home."

"Home?" Hurt bled through her.

His voice surged past her in a frantic rush. "No. That's not what I mean. You're my . . . California's . . . I know that this is home. But Big Ruth, Uncle Kevin, the kids, they're my only family besides you."

Ruth wasn't listening. She'd waited and waited while he was sitting at her grandmother's oak table, drinking beer with her brother, playing big brother to the children of his father's second marriage. That smell in his clothes made sense now. Wood smoke and pine had seeped into his clothes while he'd been fishing, camping, or just sitting outside her brother's cabin on the mountain.

"How long? How long were you there?"

"Not that long."

She knew she should let it go. This wasn't the time or the place, but she didn't care.

"I've been waiting for months, wondering every day where you were, how you were, existing on texts, e-mails. You've been back in the country for how long? Two weeks? Three? Four? You couldn't even take the time to call me and explain what the hell you were doing and that you'd come home whenever you got around to it."

His arms seemed to twitch a little at his sides as if he didn't know what to do with them. He began to stammer. "I didn't mean to . . . I didn't come here to fight. I went because . . . it doesn't matter. I'm here, Mom. I'm here now."

Something in his voice, in the way he was standing there, caught her. She looked at him and saw the fatigue that his crisp clothes and close shave had concealed for a while. His face above the olive shirt looked drained, but his eyes shined with need.

She took a breath to steady herself. Then another one. He was right, it didn't matter, not right this minute. They could talk about it later.

"Okay." Ruth opened her arms. "Truce." She waved him closer for a hug.

Robbie took the snapshot and leaned forward to embrace her, but he startled when Ruth's phone buzzed from her desk. She looked at the phone, willing Terri to keep whoever it was at bay a little longer.

"Honey, I still need to talk to you about lunch."

"I can wait until you're free," he said. "We don't even have to eat. Let's just take a walk or something."

She heard how hard he was trying. A walk. It sounded so simple, but it was unfathomable now. She tried to speak gently. "I'm sorry, Robbie. We're in an emergency situation here. It looks like I'll be tied up the rest of the day."

"I guess I should have come here before going to the farm."

"You think I'm trying to punish you? I wouldn't do that, honey. This is punishing me as much as it is you. I have no choice."

Robbie looked past her again, the way he had that morning, pretending maybe that he didn't hear or trying to wait long enough for her to change her mind.

"Robbie, let's eat dinner together instead. We'll have more time. What do you think?"

Ruth watched the hope recede from Robbie's eyes. She struggled to hang on to her smile.

The phone buzzed again. She heard Terri's muffled voice outside the office as she tried to defend the closed door a little longer. Ruth inhaled. She had to get a grip. She had no choice. Everything would be all right. It had to be.

"The company's in trouble. It's my responsibility. I can't walk out of here just because I want to. You know how it is." She smiled her most positive smile even though it felt like weights were sewn into the corners of her mouth.

He shrugged but didn't nod or speak.

"Honey, you just got here. We have the rest of your leave and then it's only a little while before you're out altogether. We'll have lots of time. I'll even fly back east and go to the farm with you if you want. Starting tonight, I'll be all yours."

When he still didn't reply, Ruth talked faster as if that might help. "We can go out, someplace nice."

Robbie closed his eyes. His chin ducked and Ruth took it as a nod.

"Or we'll meet at home. Tell Terri what you feel like eating and I'll pick it up. Pizza, Chinese, whatever you want. If you don't know right now, call her this afternoon." Ruth paused but Robbie said nothing.

"Robbie? Honey? Are you okay?"

Robbie looked at her and nodded, but the fatigue in his eyes sapped Ruth's certainty. She gave him her cheek to kiss. His lips were soft, like a little boy's, but his arms pulled her to him in a hug so hard it made her gasp. Again Ruth picked up a whiff of whiskey or something like it. She'd have to find a way to ask him about the drinking.

Ruth placed her palms against his chest. "Robbie? Honey? See you tonight, okay?" Robbie hung on. She smiled, pressed once gently, then again, harder. He squeezed her briefly once more and then released her.

"Okay, Mom," he said in a hoarse whisper.

Relief found its way into the thicket of emotions tangling inside her. She smiled at him.

"I'll walk with you to the elevator." Ruth turned to grab the notes she'd taken while she'd been with Sylvia. They were buried under paper.

When she found them and turned back to the door, Robbie was gone.

# CHAPTER 9

It was 6:43 when Ruth pushed her chair back from the conference table awash with paper, pens, bottles of water, and empty coffee cups.

"Where are you going?" Don glared at her from the head of the table where two lawyers leaned over his chair, pointing to the lines they had highlighted on the official statement they were honing with him.

"I need to make a phone call."

"Make it fast."

Ruth was already at the door. She pulled her BlackBerry out of her pocket as it closed behind her and punched in the number to Robbie's cell.

"Please, answer," she muttered into the phone. Again the phone went straight to Robbie's voice mail greeting—a barrage of rap music followed by "Yo, leave a message." *Shit.* Ruth looked at her watch. Maybe he'd left a message with Terri.

"Ruth, Don wants to review our plan one more time." Andrea poked her head around the door.

Ruth barely looked at her. "I'll be back in a minute." She strode to her office. Good, Terri was still there. She'd been going through all the personnel files and insurance claims she'd made Sylvia give her. Terri would make sure there were no more surprises.

"Has Robbie called? I told him to let you know what he wants to eat."

Terri looked up. The halo of light from her desk lamp painted shadows under her eyes. Her lips, normally slicked red, were pale. A half-eaten tuna sandwich lay in a white wrapper near her elbow. Seeing her there made Ruth suddenly feel less alone. Terri was the only ally she had in this place right now.

"No. Do you want me to call him?"

"When I called just now I got his voice mail. Will you please try him again? Keep trying until you get him. Tell him I just need another hour or so."

"How're you holding up in there?" Terri asked.

*Like a target at a shooting range*, Ruth wanted to tell her, *full of holes but still there*. "I have to get back," was all she said.

"Okay." Terri reached for the phone. "Go. I've got this. Just hurry so you can see your son."

Ruth wheeled and threaded her way through the maze of gray cubes outside her office. Most were empty. In a few, she spied slumped shoulders or the silhouette of a head against a computer monitor screen. An analyst jumped as she passed behind him, and she saw photos of what looked like the protesters fade from his screen. Ruth looked away and kept moving.

They'd been on conference calls all afternoon. With lawyers, with their PR firm, with each other. Early on, she'd gotten Don and Gordon alone so she could propose a plan to make Excel speed up its claims process.

"We've paid three or four times the cost of the insurance. They can afford to move a little faster. We're not talking garden-variety injuries." She gave examples: amputation of both legs below the knee, burns to lower body, arterial cut from shrapnel, both legs broken, fractured pelvis. Blunt trauma resulting in death. On and on. Relentless and sickening. She didn't expect Don or Gordon to be moved by the injuries. She thought she could convince them to do something if she painted a picture of what would happen when photographs of these people and their individual stories started to circulate.

"No," was all Don said.

Gordon had explained. "The insurance division is twice the size of the business we're bringing to Transglobal. If it comes to a decision between Excel and RyCom, Transglobal will let us go and find some other company to add to their portfolio."

"But not paying the life insurance makes them look bad too," she'd said. "And we'll have to give the families something at the end of the day. Let's figure out what it will cost to make them whole and just give it to them now, take the issue off the table."

"We'll just take that out of your stock options, shall we? You're scheduled to sell a few millions' worth any day now, aren't you?" Don didn't smile. "After all, this happened on your watch."

Gordon shot a look in Ruth's direction. *I told you so*, it said. "Think about it, Ruth," he said. "Paying them anything is admitting we're to blame. Excel knows what it's doing. The worst that will happen is that they will be forced to pay a fine. They plan for that. For now, just put a story together that Don can feed to the media. Make us look good, make sure our current clients don't catch any flak, and we'll work on expediting the deal with Transglobal."

Don hadn't looked at her while Gordon laid it out. Ruth knew now it was futile to point out how Excel and Sylvia's people had let contractors go to a war zone without completing their policy applications. She understood now that Don had a backup plan. If she failed to keep him clean and the clients happy, she would be offered up as a sacrifice to Transglobal. It wouldn't make the lawsuits go away overnight but she would serve as a scapegoat, enough to demonstrate RyCom's commitment to its shareholders. Then Andrea

Baumann would step in as the new head of the contractor operation that Ruth had built from the ground up. Andrea had already let it slip that she'd met with the head of private security contracting at Transglobal. She wanted to head Ruth's division after the merger went through.

Ruth halted in front of the closed conference room door, her hand on the gleaming stainless steel door handle. Don's baritone rumbled impatiently beyond the frosted glass. Ruth closed her eyes. All she had worked for. All that sacrifice. Gone. With one sentence from Don. After twenty years, he would throw her away as she had watched him eliminate others whose usefulness had expired. The handle moved beneath her fingers. Her hand was shaking. Ruth gripped tighter. She lifted her chin. *Not without a fight.* She opened the door.


Terri was still at her desk when Ruth emerged three hours later. The sandwich was gone, the papers and files stacked neatly. She was leaning forward on her elbows, her eyes nearly closed.

"You didn't have to stay this late," Ruth said.

"I thought you might need something."

Ruth was half afraid to look Terri in the eye. Working late was one thing; she could find some way to thank her when all this was over. But Terri had always had a soft spot for Robbie; after years of working with Ruth, she'd become Robbie's agent of sorts. She was the one he called after school to "check in" and leave messages for Ruth. Terri helped research schools, ran interference with teachers and car pools, and ensured that Ruth knew when and where to pick him up. Terri would care that she'd kept Robbie waiting even if it was an emergency.

Ruth came to a stop before her assistant's desk. "Did you reach him?"

"No. I kept getting his voice mail, just like you did."

Some of the ache in Ruth's chest must have shown on her face because Terri's voice softened as if it might make her words less painful.

"I tried again a little while ago. Texted a bunch of times too. Maybe he's out of range?"

*God. Robbie, please forgive me.* "Thanks." Ruth walked straight into her office and started to stuff her laptop into her bag. Terri came in behind her.

"Here, this is easier to carry." She held out a flash drive. "I put summaries and copies of all the electronic correspondence here. I scanned several of the hard-copy reports and put them on here too."

"Thanks."

But instead of leaving, Terri pulled Ruth's office door closed behind her. She bit her lip as if considering whether to say more. Ruth glanced at her watch. Still enough time to order dinner in.

"What? Spit it out, Ter, I've got to get home."

"I'm not sure if I should say anything."

"Then don't."

"Look at the files I put on there. There are some things that Sylvia didn't show you. You should see them."

"Like what?"

"Just look."

"Damn it, Terri, I'm too tired for games." If she didn't leave now, she'd bark at Terri and have one more regret in a day full of them. "Don't worry. Things will be fine."

She had to believe her own assurances. They had come up with a public statement and had called all their clients, reassuring them that RyCom was meeting the letter of the law and they would not be pulled into negative publicity. Calls had been made to the insurers. They would handle all communications regarding life and disability claims. Don, Gordon, and she would meet with Transglobal tomorrow. Ruth hated the thought of having to tell Robbie she'd have to come to the office again. After that, though, there'd be nothing to do but sit tight and wait for the whole mess to die down. The deal would still go through, even if it took a little longer. Ruth shoved the drive into her briefcase and straightened.

Terri stood between her and her office door. "Don't forget, okay?"

"I said I would look at it and I will." Terri didn't move. She looked as though she had more to say, but Ruth was done. "Ter, we both need to get home." Terri finally nodded and opened the office door. What was wrong with her? Ruth couldn't think about it right now. She wanted to go home. She needed to see her son.

# CHAPTER 10

The garage was empty when Ruth pulled in. A couple of oil stains marked where Robbie's truck had been. Ruth fixed on them as if the splotches could tell her where Robbie had gone, when he would be back, and if he was punishing her for failing him. *I'm sorry, baby. I'm sorry.* She whispered the words like a prayer. She thought about trying his phone again, even though she'd done so twice in the past twenty minutes, once in the parking garage at work and again while she was flying south on I-5 toward her exit. It wouldn't do any good. He hadn't picked up, either because his phone was off or because it was on and he just didn't want to talk to her.

Gravity seemed to hold Ruth in her car. When she'd woken up, the day had contained such promise. Somehow, it had gone off the rails. But what could she have done differently? Ruth ran through it all again in her mind, dodging the arrows flung first by the contractor families with their banners and their lawyer, then by Don, Gordon, even Andrea Baumann with her research and her attitude. She'd tried to make it right for the people waiting for their claims to be processed, tried to press Don and Gordon for a way to make the lawsuit go away. She'd tried. Tried to make it all happen and get back to Robbie, who hadn't even told her when he was coming, hadn't given her time to prepare. Not that she blamed him, of course not, but he would see her situation, he could understand. He was an adult.

Ruth pushed the car door open, then grabbed her briefcase and purse. Robbie would be back. She'd wait up for him. They'd have a chance to talk.

Still, once she was inside the house, emptiness dropped down like a net. It closed in on her from all sides: in the shadows cast by the few security lights that came on automatically when the sun set; in the breath of the air conditioner rumbling distantly; in the travertine tiles, hard and impervious beneath her soles. A pile of envelopes lay on the floor under the brass mail slot. She strode past them around the corner into her office, where the red message light was blinking on her phone. Robbie. Ruth dropped her briefcase and her purse and hit the message button.

"It's me." Neal. Ruth turned away, stepping over the briefcase and the purse to get to the light switch. Neal's voice followed her. "Just checking in to see how things went today. Give me a call." A pause. "Hey, say hi to Rob. Enjoyed my breakfast with him this morning."

Ruth wondered if he thought Robbie was there, listening. She could see him, the way he'd been in the old days rolling his eyes as the two or three men she'd dated tried to connect. He'd never made it easy, had he? Offered a chance to go see the Lakers, he'd say he hated basketball. Would he like to try surfing? "Nah, I hate salt water." For a while, things had been different with Neal.

Robbie was just turning ten when she brought Neal home for the first time. He ferreted out Robbie's love of engines and his fascination with the desert. He showed up one Saturday with an issue of *Dirt Riders Magazine* and two tickets to what he called a "desert quad" race near Ocotillo.

"Guys only," Neal told Ruth. Ruth wasn't sure but she thought she saw relief flash over Robbie's chubby face. At any rate, he never looked back as he climbed into Neal's truck.

Ruth had thought seriously about following them. Neal would not remember Robbie's sunscreen. What would they eat for lunch? What would she do for the rest of the day? Then it hit her. She was completely, utterly free in a way she had not been since they'd lived back east and Robbie's father took him for visits twice a month. Even then, she'd been constrained by time and weather. For once, Ruth left the work she'd brought home in her briefcase and spent an entire Saturday at the beach by herself with a stack of magazines and a thermos of margaritas. She'd drifted home to find Robbie and Neal stretched out on the living room floor, arms and faces scorched. But both of them were oblivious. They'd found more races on television and barely looked up when she walked in. Neal passed Robbie his beer—"just a sip," he warned—as they compared notes on different machines and drivers. If they noticed her, they gave no indication. She backed out of the room, ordered a pizza, and, when it came, was given a race-by-race account of the day by each of them. She remembered nothing of what they said, only Robbie's eyes, unguarded and shining as he chomped his way through half the pie.

There had been other nights like that one. Ruth recalled them with mixed feelings. For a few months, she'd come home not to a sullen child but one who laughed and joked. He fell into easy banter with Neal, who seemed to know not to try too hard. She watched, first relieved, then amazed, and, finally, jealous, as her boyfriend won Robbie over. More and more often he would call her at the office and tell her not to worry about dinner, he'd pick up Chinese or pizza and meet her at the condo. A few times, she'd come home to the smell of steak on the grill and the sound of their voices mingling in the half dark as Neal explained the difference between medium rare and medium well.

Ruth found herself picking at the threads of their growing intimacy. She couldn't help it.

"He's getting too heavy," Ruth said one night after sending Robbie to bed. The memory rushed back to her as she stood alone in her office, defenseless against it.

"Relax, he's fine." Neal had responded, not looking up from a report he'd pulled out of his briefcase. He was stretched out on the couch, feet up on the arm, the sheaf of papers in his hands. They usually worked for an hour or two before going to bed. It was one of those things that Ruth liked about being with Neal; Robbie's father had always sulked when she brought work home. Still, Ruth remembered suddenly wanting to push Neal's feet off the sofa she'd splurged to buy.

"Easy for you to say, he's not your responsibility."

Neal sat up then and put the papers aside. "No, he's not, but I've been around him now for a while. He's a good kid. You're making him nervous with all that stuff about the food, and the private school. Maybe you should just—"

"Let him do whatever he wants?"

"I'm not saying that."

"What exactly are you saying?" She saw the flicker of wariness in Neal's eyes. Too late, the implications of the conversation dawned on her and, she saw, on him. His criticism only mattered if he was ready to step more deeply into the relationship. She wasn't sure she was ready even if he was. Still, she couldn't stand the indecision that was written all over his face.

"What's your stake in all of this?" she said.

"You're right. He's your kid. Sorry for interfering." Neal looked away when he said it. Ruth remembered wondering how it was possible to feel disappointed and relieved at the same moment.

Arguments flared soon after that, little ones quickly dampened by apologies. Then bigger ones. Then they were "taking a break," the first in a string of them interrupted by reunions that lasted anywhere from one night to several months and, sometimes, overlapped new relationships. They were never quite without each other, never quite all the way in. They were, Ruth once joked, each other's fallback position, the final line of defense against commitment in any form. What had brought them together this time? Getting older, probably, looking for safe harbor. No kids to worry about.

Neal had been with Robbie that morning; maybe he knew where he might be.

Ruth picked up the phone again and hit redial. It was only ten o'clock or so; Neal would still be awake.

He picked up on the third ring. Television voices talked over each other in the background and there was some kind of organ music. He was watching a baseball game.

"Didn't think I'd hear from you today," Neal said, yawning.

"Hi to you too. Did I wake you?"

"No, no."

*Liar*, thought Ruth, but it didn't make her want to smile the way it might have on another night.

"So, tell me," Neal said. "Is RyCom going to come through this mess squeaky clean?"

"I don't want to talk about work."

He laughed but sounded more alert. "Shit. It's worse than I thought."

"I didn't say that."

"Since when do you not want to talk about work?"

"What is that supposed to mean?"

For a moment Ruth heard nothing through the phone except the television. Then Neal spoke again now. "Sorry. You're off duty, we can save the rehash for later."

"Thanks." Ruth sank into the chair behind her desk. "So, tell me about your breakfast with Robbie."

"It was good to see him. Made me think of old times."

"I was thinking of those myself just a minute ago. Remember when you took him to the desert for those races and came back so sunburned you both looked like barbecue?"

Silence. "Sure. Was trying to get on his good side so I could stay on yours. Worked. For a while, anyway." Another pause. "How'd it go today?"

Ruth hesitated, but there was no point in trying to hide how badly things had gone. "We had to postpone lunch. I just got home from work a few minutes ago."

"Geez, Ruth. You stood him up?"

Ruth bowed her head. She rubbed her temple with the forefinger of her free hand. No matter how good her reasons were for not going with Robbie, the effect was the same.

"I thought we agreed to meet here tonight instead, but I ran so late," she said. "I called him. Terri called him. We haven't been able to connect." The semidarkness around her gave her office the feel of a confessional.

The television in the background suddenly went mute. When Neal spoke, his tone had shifted from tired and casual to quiet, alert. "What happened?"

Ruth straightened. "What do you mean, 'what happened?' You know what I was dealing with today." But she didn't even believe herself now. The air around her seemed polluted with doubt. What would have happened if she'd left work for an hour or two? Would the result have been much different?

"So where is he now?"

"I don't know. I told you, I've tried to call him but he doesn't answer."

Neal was quiet. Ruth remembered what he'd told her that morning. ". . . been to war . . . not the same kid." She heard that warning now like a siren.

"What did he say this morning?" She stood and began to pace. "How did he act? Should I be worried?"

"He seemed fine," Neal said, but Ruth heard an edge in his voice. "I didn't mean . . . He didn't say anything. Ruth, calm down. Look, he's probably out getting something to eat, having a few beers."

Ruth wanted to believe him but then, for the past two weeks, she thought Robbie had been in North Carolina and instead he'd been in New Hampshire. With her family. But not with her.

"Don't beat yourself up," Neal said. "Make it up to him tonight when he gets home, or tomorrow. He'll understand."

"I know." But she didn't.

"Want me to come over?"

*Yes. No.* The reason Neal was in his own condo was so she could be alone with Robbie. What if he came home in an hour or even two? She couldn't risk another misunderstanding. "No. It's late. We'll talk tomorrow."

"Ruth?"

"No, it's okay. Thanks, though. Really. I'm going to hang up. I haven't eaten since . . ." Ruth couldn't remember when she'd last eaten. "I'll call you, okay?" Ruth heard Neal say, "Sure." She was already moving the phone from her ear, already disconnecting, standing so she could get out of her office, turn on some lights, find some food. When Robbie came home he'd be hungry too.

# CHAPTER 11

An hour and a half later, Ruth wanted to throw her phone across the kitchen. Robbie's voice mail greeting echoed in her head, the pounding rap music, the disinterested "Yo." He should have answered by now. Even if it was just to tell her he was all right. She'd stopped leaving messages but hit redial every twenty minutes or so. She'd found some tamales in the freezer, pulled them all out, and hunted down a jar of salsa. He'd come home after drinking to raid the kitchen and she'd be ready for him. She'd opened a bottle of pinot noir and waited. Nothing. Not even a text.

Ruth shoved the remains of a chicken tamale around on the plate in front of her. Then she poured another glass of wine and rubbed the back of her neck. She'd stripped off her work clothes, put on some sweats and a tank top. Still, the tensions of the day clung to her. Her nerves seemed to be downloading every missed connection, every frustrating conversation, every unanswered question into the knot she could not rub away. A long soak in a deep bath might help. She picked up her phone and the glass of wine and made her way down the stairs.

She paused outside the guest room, Robbie's room. She wouldn't be snooping. She just wanted to check, make sure he had everything he needed. Maybe she'd find some clue to his whereabouts. She wanted to see his unpacked belongings strewn around the room, smile at the mess he'd undoubtedly left in the bathroom. Maybe she'd surprise him, have all his laundry washed and folded by the time he woke up.

Ruth froze in the doorway. The bed was made and Robbie's duffel was packed and zipped. Something about the crispness of the folds in the bedspread and the tidy way the duffel stretched out next to the bed unnerved her.

Slowly, Ruth crossed the carpet to the bed. She sank onto the edge, and looked around. The grays, taupes, and blacks that she had allowed the decorator to select for the guest room made it look like a hotel, not a home. What had she been thinking? There were boxes in the garage, packed with all the things she'd swept out of Robbie's room in the old house. She should have gone through them, picked out some books, a poster, something that connected him to this new house.

His duffel, he should have at least unpacked it. Ruth set her wineglass on the bedside table. She reached down and tugged on the zipper of the bag, then let go and stood up. What if he came home and found his things in the drawer; he'd be furious that she went through his stuff.

"Don't worry, I won't." The sound of her own voice startled her. If she was beginning to talk to herself, then it was time for bed.

Ruth reached for her glass. A square glimmered under the light. It was the snapshot he'd shown her in the office, his six-year-old hands raised, the string of trout dangling.

Ruth's heart leapt toward the photograph. When she picked it up, it fluttered in her hand like something winged and fragile. She was surprised to see that her hands were shaking.

A memory took shape. Her grandmother, Big Ruth, standing at

the stove heating an iron skillet to cook the fish. Kevin out on the front step where he'd shown Robbie how to slit the bellies and clean out the insides in one efficient sweep. Slime glistened on Robbie's hands, arms, even one cheek, and he was smiling wide enough to reveal the crenellated edge of his new front tooth and the pink-edged gap beside it.

Ruth traced the small face with her finger.

She'd been there too. Sitting, as always, at the round oak table in her grandmother's kitchen, paperwork spread out in front of her. Ruth searched the face smiling at her from the snapshot. Had she smiled back at the little boy covered with fish scales? Had she eaten one of the brookies he'd caught, sweet, tender, its crisp, delicate skin falling to pieces in her mouth?

Ruth pulled her legs up and curled into a ball on the bed. Her ears strained for the sound of a car in the driveway and the sounds of the refrigerator door opening, the way it always used to when Robbie came in late. She never knew when she fell asleep; in her dreams she was wide awake and waiting.

The front doorbell, not the refrigerator, woke Ruth. She sat up on one elbow. Gray light slipped around the edges of the drawn blinds. The digits on the bedside clock read 7:21. The doorbell sounded again. Ruth pushed herself into a sitting position and shoved her feet into the flip-flops she'd kicked off a few hours earlier. Robbie was home. He'd made her wait all night, but now he was back and stuck outside because she'd never thought to give him the remote for the garage opener or the security code for the door. The system went on automatically after midnight. How stupid of her to forget. She ran from the guest room to the front hall, punched the code into the receiver, and pulled open the door.

Three men looked up from their shoes into her eyes. One in khaki, a gun holstered at his waist, wore a badge on his thick chest.

The others, taller, leaner, wore the blue jackets and white hats of a Marine dress uniform. A wail began to sound deep inside Ruth, like that of a child locked in a room.

"Where's Robbie?" Her voice was loud in her own ears.

The men shifted their weight, planting their feet as if to brace themselves. The closest Marine removed his cap.

Fog hung in the air; water dripped off the spikes of the agaves that bordered the entryway. She shivered, tried to peer around the blue shoulders of the Marine, hoping to see Robbie slouched in one of the cars she now saw in the driveway. "Has there been an accident? Is he all right? Where is he?"

The blue coat answered. "Ma'am, we need to ask, are you Ruth Nolan, the mother of Lance Corporal Robert O'Connell?"

"Robbie. Yes. Yes."

"Ma'am, my name is Captain Oliver Dixon, this is Captain James, our chaplain. On behalf of the—"

"You! Tell me where he is!" Ruth said to the smaller man in khaki, a sheriff's deputy, she could see now. He couldn't be much older than Robbie. He clutched a notebook in his hand. He cleared his throat.

Ruth stilled. She smelled the man's fear, saw the dark spots in the armpits of his polyester shirt. His slightly bulging brown eyes would not meet hers.

The Marine interrupted. "Ma'am. We regret to inform—"

*No.* The man named Dixon stepped forward. She recoiled. "Get out."

"Please, Ms. Nolan, may we come in?" The chaplain's voice, kind but firm, broke through. Ruth shook her head but her legs disobeyed her. She stepped back into the hallway. They followed her. She held herself straight, arms crossed across her chest. The chaplain spoke again. "Would you like me to pull up that chair over there for you?"

Ruth shook her head. She didn't want them to touch her.

Captain Dixon spoke again. "Ma'am, I'm sorry to say that Lance Corporal O'Connell was found dead tonight in Imperial Beach. He suffered a g—"

Ruth heard herself ask the question as if she were far away. "Did you see him?"

"Ma'am?"

"Did you see him with your own eyes?"

"No, ma'am."

"Then how do you know it's him?"

She saw the captain glance at the chaplain. The chaplain stepped toward her.

"No," she told him. "You didn't see him either." She looked at all three faces, found the eyes of the young deputy.

"Ms. Nolan, we know this is very difficult," the chaplain said, but Ruth looked only at the deputy.

"You," she said. "You saw, didn't you?"

The young man stared back, frozen.

"Tell me," Ruth said. She heard her voice rising but she didn't scream. She wouldn't scream. She would listen. Then she would tell them they were wrong. "Tell me!"

Captain Dixon finally nodded at the sheriff's deputy. The younger man reached into his shirt pocket and pulled out a notepad. He stammered. Began again. His voice was young, trying to sound old. He looked at the pad, not at her.

"Imperial Beach." Ruth heard him say, then, "Motel." "Gunshots." "Responded. Time: 0233 hours."

Ruth shook her head. "Not him."

The deputy didn't look up. He took a breath and began to list what they found. "Pint of Jack Daniels, empty, dog tags hanging from the neck, also bottles of"—he stumbled over the words *fluoxetine* and *alprazolam*—"with his name on the prescription labels. An empty backpack on the bed. Khakis, a green shirt, socks, underwear, folded and placed on the pack, shoes on top. Inside one shoe was a mobile phone, battery dead. In the bathroom, a male, appearing to be in his early twenties . . ."

"It's not him," Ruth whispered.

The sheriff's deputy paused, swallowed, pushed on.

"Said male in the bathtub half submerged in water, a forty-five-caliber handgun also submerged, held in the right hand of the deceased. A towel was wrapped around his head. Red stains, red water, appeared to be blood."

Ruth began to sink to the floor. Someone's hands were under her elbows, supporting her. The deputy's voice broke like a fourteen-year-old's as he looked up from his notepad. "Ma'am . . . I'm sorry . . . It looked like he was trying to be as neat as he could."

# CHAPTER 12

January 1985

*R*uth gets to the doctor's office before they can call to cancel because of the snow. The receptionist releases a sigh of resignation as Ruth pulls off her wool hat and shakes her hair; ice particles and clumps of snow scatter on the carpet.

"My husband's coming too." Outside, the afternoon has darkened; from the twelfth floor of the medical building, Longwood Avenue looks like an artery of lights pulsing slowly through the murk. Ruth is aware of the pulsing in her own veins in a way she has never been before. From the moment the home pregnancy test strip turned blue, she has been impatient for this moment. This will make the baby real.

The door swings open and Jeff is there. At the same moment, the nurse opens the door that leads to the examining rooms. "Hurry, guys, we need to get home while we can."

Minutes later, Ruth shivers in the stirrups, the hospital gown pulled open. Jeff holds her hand while the technician moves the ultrasound wand over her belly. She hears him inhale sharply and turns to the screen. A shape, like a fiddlehead, or a fish, swims onto the screen and floats. She can see the head, the feet, the heart. Everyone, Jeff, the technician, the doctor, all disappear. The wand *skims over the greased surface of her belly and Ruth imagines she feels the baby turning inside her to look back at her through the video screen. The baby is only a few inches long; the technician is saying, do they want to know the sex? Ruth nods. Jeff squeezes her hand. A boy, the technician says. Jeff's voice rumbles nearby but she doesn't hear what he says. Her ears are filled with the liquid sound of her son's heart.*

# CHAPTER 13

If.

If she cried, it would be real.

His body did not make it real. She saw the tattoos inked onto his forearms, the pimples on his collarbone. No one made her see these things. She told the sheriff and the officers to take her to him. She said that the Marines could not be sure of who he was, fingerprints, dog tags, records be damned.

She watched while the sheet was peeled back from his body, saw the shield with those names on his arm, the "meat tag" on his ribs, his ruined face. Even as she nodded, she thought, *not Robbie*. And she was right.

Walking out of the morgue, she didn't see Neal, who had driven there to meet her, but Robbie, lounging against the fender of the SUV wearing a black T-shirt and baggy jeans. In the car, he was a child of five straining against the seat belt, craning his head so he could see her in the rearview mirror. She could summon him up, whole and unblemished at any age, just by keeping still, closing her eyes. He was inside her; to cry would be to lose him, tear by tear.

If.

If she said the things people expected of her, they would leave her alone. Neal and Terri talked of "arrangements." She agreed to nothing. At any moment, Robbie would call her on the phone, tell her he was on the next flight. He was still away, that was all.

She could not talk to her grandmother or her brother. That would make her son's death real. She'd called them both when Neal brought her home from the morgue. She dialed the number, listened to the rings. Big Ruth's voice quavered through the phone line.

"Ruthie? Baby?" Ruth saw her grandmother as though she were next to her, leaning into her walker, speaking into the yellow receiver attached to the wall phone by a long beige cord. "Kevin, it's your sister!"

She could see her brother too, leaning against the counter, drinking a cup of coffee after his lunch, getting ready to head back to the garage for the afternoon. Her shy brother who still stuttered sometimes and would avoid talking altogether if his grandmother would let him. He'd been the one who sat in patient silence when two-year-old Robbie was learning to talk, who could stop his tears just by sitting down next to him and showing him a toad he'd just caught, or how to hold a wrench. They had their own language, Kevin and Robbie, one that Ruth had never been able to follow.

As she tried to talk to her grandmother, she knew Kevin would be looking at Big Ruth, his red hair swept back from his forehead, eyebrows raised the slightest bit, as if he'd asked a question out loud and was waiting for an answer.

"Gramma," Ruth said. Then she stopped. She had not used that name in years. She called her grandmother Big Ruth or BR. Her hands began to shake. "Gramma, I'm calling about Robbie."

"Doesn't he look wonderful? Thin. Too thin. But it was so good to see him."

"Gram . . ."

Her grandmother went on, happy to relive the visit. Such a surprise. He was amazed at the changes in Gershom; did he tell Ruth about the kids? Vonnie, Jeff's widow, brought them over. Justin, the oldest, so big now, and his sister Luanne, nearly seventeen now and so pretty.

Ruth tried again to speak but her throat closed. She dropped the phone. Neal was the one who picked it up. He was the one who explained that Robbie was gone. Ruth did not have to hear her grandmother cry or her brother's silence deepen.

Neal held the phone out to her. "They want to talk to you."

Ruth shook her head.

"They want to come."

Ruth again shook her head. She turned away so he could not look at her.

A few seconds later she heard him speak again into the phone. "She needs a little time; it's been a long night. Too soon to make any decisions. We'll call back." Silence. Then, "Don't worry. I'll stay with her."

And he did stay. He was the one who called Terri, who came over with flowers and some food that Ruth could not eat. She handled communications with Don and others at work. Neal fielded the phone calls from Captain Dixon, accepted his condolences, confirmed what details he could for the reports they had to make.

She woke from a drugged sleep one afternoon and believed it was the morning after Robbie had come home. She decided to peek in on him. Anticipation filled her. She was halfway across her bedroom floor before Neal knocked on the door to tell her he was ordering out. What did she want to eat? In seconds, the true present materialized and the whole progression of events that led up to it extended before her, each interlocking, unchangeable piece.

If she'd just closed the door in the deputy sheriff's face, if she had walked out of the office with Robbie when he came for her at lunch, if she had never gone to work that day in the first place. Each "if" launched her into a waking dream, so real that she could almost believe that she had made the right decision at each of these points, that the events unfolding around her were happening to the mother of another boy.

He'd been hurting and she hadn't seen. She hadn't seen how much he needed her. Neal had tried to tell her to look more closely, but she hadn't looked closely enough.

She wanted to sleep. If she could fall asleep again, she could wake up and start over. She'd go back as far as time would let her go. Change everything.

She could bring him back.


The envelope arrived two days after Robbie was found. The plain envelope, postmarked Imperial Beach, contained one page. It confirmed that Robbie, not some other person that Ruth could find and blame, had put the gun to his head. It was his gun. He'd added it to the shotgun and the rifle that came to him when his father died, all of which Ruth had packed and locked in the cab of his truck when they moved into the new house. Then she had forgotten them.

*Mom,*

*I'm sorry for everything. It's not your fault. I love you.*

*Robbie*

The paper, a lined sheet torn out of some notebook, was still crisp. The envelope was postmarked the day after he died. He must have stopped to mail it on the way to the motel where they found him. He'd missed the last pickup of the day but it hadn't mattered. He'd made his decision.

*It's not your fault.*

The words flayed her. He'd thought to leave her absolution. He knew she would need it.

# CHAPTER 14

R uth sat up straight in bed, eyes wide, heart thudding, the doorbell reverberating in her ears. After a few seconds, she understood it had been a dream. The pills she'd taken hammered her into an hour or two of unconsciousness, but after that a dream or noise would jerk her awake and leave her stranded with hours of night remaining.

Neal's snoring ripped through the darkness. She thought of rolling him over but did not want to wake him. He'd stayed every night, often waking when she did, trying to keep his promise not to leave her alone. The promise had taken its toll. His face looked ashy instead of tan and she heard a rough edge in his voice when he made work calls from her office. She should be grateful, she knew. She lay still, trying to summon gratitude. Instead Neal's breath seemed to fill the room until she thought she would suffocate.

She rose, careful not to jostle the bed. Barefoot, she made her way across the carpet. A few minutes later, she was back in the guest room, Robbie's room, the overhead dimmers shedding more shadows than light. On the bed was the old stuffed rabbit he'd loved as a baby. She'd found it in the box from the garage that lay now on its side next to the bed, along with other boxes of Robbie's belongings she'd dragged in. Ruth scooped up the rabbit and sank onto the bed. The duffel lay at her feet, untouched since Robbie had left.

"If anyone opens it, it will be me," she'd told Neal when he asked her if she wanted him to clean it out.

"I'm sorry. I was just trying to spare you," he'd said.

"I can do it. I want to do it," she'd said. But she hadn't. Not then, not in the days that followed.

Ruth hugged the small toy, ignoring the dust and mildew that had settled into its fake fur, once white, now yellowed. She remembered how she had been proud of herself for not looking inside the duffel, for giving Robbie his precious privacy. She kicked the side of the bag; her toe bent backward as it struck something hard. She stifled a cry. Ruth dropped the rabbit and knelt on the floor to rip open the zipper. She had to know. There had to be more he could tell her.

Opening the bag released the same smell of wood smoke and pine Ruth had picked up before, combined with the sharp musky smell of his deodorant. It had always struck her as too strong, but now she inhaled until her eyes stung. She unrolled a sweat-stained T-shirt and buried her face in it, then pulled it over her head, shoved her arms through the sleeves. She pawed through the other clothes: shirts, socks, jeans, clean and dirty, all rolled and stacked. She found his green and khaki service uniform, then his fatigues. A digital camera. His Dopp kit, a couple of dog-eared copies of *Dirt Rider Magazine* she remembered sending him months ago. When she lifted out his fatigue jacket, a thick photo album dropped back into the bottom of the bag. She recognized the scuffed vinyl binder from her grandmother's house. But as she picked it up, a black-and-white composition book tumbled from between its covers onto the floor. The name on the front was hers. Dried stains obscured the last few letters of the precise script she'd practiced in high school. She picked it up and flipped it open. What had made Robbie want it?

The first few pages revealed the girl she had been: a maker of lists, a keeper of assignments, a compulsive note taker. A believer in the power of plans. The book contained lists of colleges she'd never be able to afford even if they accepted her and notes on conversations with the overweight and overburdened guidance counselor more familiar with vocational schools than college scholarships. Neat checks marked tasks completed: get applications, complete essays, meet deadlines for mailing them in.

Then her rounded *m*'s and uniformly slanted *b*'s and *l*'s gave way to Robbie's scrawl. Ruth was aware of a rushing sound in her ears, like rapids at a river bend. She crawled nearer to the bedside table and turned on the light. Words ran across the pages, unbound by dates or times, spilling into the margins. Skipped lines, sudden gaps of white space, were the only indication that time may have passed between entries.

*same fuckin dream—know they're in there, gotta get 'em out—can't find—unzip the bags but all i see are pieces—hanny's leg—pete's—try to put pieces together—too many*

Ruth stopped. She became aware of her own breathing, short, heavy, panting. Her nightshirt stuck to her chest and back. She could stop now, close the book before she read another word. *No.* Then she forced herself to open it again. Her son was in there. She had to look.

# CHAPTER 15

The guest room door opened with a click. Ruth did not look up. Robbie's half-printed, half-scrawled words slanted off the page in front of her. *so tired want to close my eyes see nothing hear nothing.*

"What's that?" Neal touched the notebook. But Ruth held on.

"Let me see." His voice was firmer this time. Ruth felt the cardboard cover slip from her fingers as he grasped it. She heard the flipping of pages slow, then stop, then the whisper of a single page as he turned it slowly.

"I should have stopped him when he enlisted," she said dully.

"That wasn't your call to make."

Ruth shook off the arm Neal was trying to put around her shoulder.

"I was his mother. I should have protected him."

"He was old enough to make his own decisions." Neal grabbed her shoulders then; the book slipped to the carpet.

She tried to twist away. "He saw someone, a counselor or psychiatrist," she said. "Why didn't they help him?"

"Look at me." Neal gripped her. "This isn't your fault. It's not the Marines' fault."

"What are you saying?"

"It's hard but you've got to remember, Robbie was not the most stable kid. He did drugs before he joined up. He had that thing that time, that bout of depression. You were driving yourself crazy trying to get his head straightened out."

Ruth wrenched herself free. "You're blaming him? He wasn't tough enough? Is that it?"

"You think I don't know what I'm talking about?" Neal said. "You think I haven't had my share of nightmares?"

"But you were tough enough to take it and Robbie wasn't?"

"Everyone's different. Every guy deals with it his own way."

"Deal with it? He's dead!" Ruth said bitterly. "Nobody helped him. Nobody." She pushed him, then threw herself at him, striking every part of his body she could reach. His bathrobe gave way and she dug her nails into his skin.

She felt Neal's fingers close around her wrists like manacles. Suddenly she was twisted around, her back pressed against his chest. His arms wrapped around her and squeezed. She kicked and twisted, but Neal hung on.

"Go ahead," she heard him say. "It's okay."

Fury made her thrash; she was choking on it. Neal was alive. He could have his nightmares, but he was still alive. Robbie was dead. Stupid, stubborn, broken boy.

She sagged. Neal's arms were holding her up now, guiding her to the bed, helping her to sit. She wanted him to go, needed him to stay. She felt his hand on the back of her head, patting, then stroking. His breath rasped in her ears. "It's okay." She heard him repeat the lie again and again as if, through repetition, he could make it true.

# CHAPTER 16

September 1987

*R* *uth clutches the bottle of champagne in one hand and juggles the keys to their Boston apartment in the other. Beyond the door, she can hear Jeff reading* Goodnight Moon *to Robbie. He's only two but he knows every page by heart. "Husssh," he says, drawing the word out with a giggle. She takes a deep breath and pushes open the door.*

*"Hi."*

*Jeff looks up at her over Robbie's curls, still damp from his bath. Then he eyes the champagne and grins. "I was going to surprise you, but I guess Mom called you already."*

*His words derail her. What is he talking about? Now Robbie is reaching for her and patting the book.*

*"Wait a minute, Champ. Mommy's thirsty." Jeff rises and sets Robbie on the floor with the book. "Give me the bottle, I'll get some glasses."*

*"Mommy wead."*

*Ruth squats down and pulls Robbie close. "Just a minute, Monkey." Then she says, a little louder so her voice will carry into the small kitchen of their apartment, "Why would your mother call me? What's up?"*

*The clinking of glasses stops.* "You don't know? What's with the wine, then?"

"I've been offered that new job, the one with Ryland." *She sings it out.* "I spent all afternoon with him and his partner and at the end of it, they wanted me. You won't believe the salary." *The giddiness she's tried to suppress emerges. She squeezes Robbie until he squeals and then she kisses him right on the nose and makes him giggle.*

"I didn't know you were going there today." *Jeff is back, glasses and wine nowhere in sight.*

"I told you. Jeff, it's a great opportunity. Getting in at the beginning of a startup," *Ruth says, talking fast now, sure that if he just hears the details, he'll go for it.*

"Hold up, I need to tell you—"

"Wait till you hear what they're paying. He said I'll start at—"

*Jeff cuts her off.* "I have a new job, too."

*So that's his surprise.* "The promotion? That's great! How much?"

"Nope. I took a job with the state of New Hampshire. We can finally move out of the city. I'll make the same as now but up there, things are a lot cheaper. You can even stay home with Robbie."

"You're joking, right?" *Her husband's hesitant smile tells her he is not.*

"That's why I wanted you to wait on the thing with Ryland—I needed to know if this was real or not," *he says.* "We're going home. The state needs an engineer to oversee construction projects up north." *This time it's Jeff who is firing words almost faster than Ruth can process them.*

*Robbie's fingers tickle her ankle, but the giddiness has evaporated. She looks at Jeff, who is staring right back at her, his smile tightening into a stubborn line.*

"No," *she says.*

"What?"

"I told you, I'm not going back. You knew it. I told you."

"I gave my notice today." *Jeff says it as if he hasn't heard her.*

"You can't do that."

"I can't?"

"You quit your job without telling me? You call your mother but not me?"

*Her voice is loud in her own ears. Jeff yells back. "Of course I called you. I called you the minute I knew, but you were gone all afternoon. What was I supposed to do?"*

*"You were supposed to wait, that's what."*

*"I've been waiting. I'm sick of waiting." His voice is hard with a bitterness she has heard more and more lately.*

*Robbie starts to cry. For once, though, it fails to stop them.*

*"You want me to pass up that much money?" Ruth says. "It's the same as you're making right now and in six months I'll get a raise. We'll have stock in the company. We could buy a house in a year."*

*"We don't need the money. We could buy a house right now in New Hampshire on my salary. That used to be the plan, remember?"*

*Ruth turns her back and walks into the cramped kitchen. His resolve scares her.*

*"Not this time, Ruth." Jeff is behind her, grabbing at her arm. She shakes him off.*

*"Stop it. Robbie's crying," she says.*

*"I'm not rolling over this time," Jeff says, quieter now. When she looks at him, she can't find a trace of hesitancy.*

*Robbie's arms are around her knees. He has followed them. She scoops him up so he's between Jeff and her.*

*"It's time," he continues. "My parents aren't getting any younger . . ."*

*"Not again. You're nearly thirty. You're still trying to please them?"*

*"I'm their only kid. Robbie's their only grandson. They want us to be closer. It's what I want, too."*

*Ruth hates that he isn't yelling anymore. "We live only four hours away! We see plenty of your parents."*

*"I'm sick of this place, sick of the phonies everywhere. I want my kid to grow up like I did. Is that so wrong?"*

*"What about my job? What about me?"*

*"It's always been about you. Every decision I've made, where to go to college, where to work, has been because of you."*

*"Don't give me that." The guilt, though, toxic and familiar, steals over her. She knows the drill now. He will recite the history of their relationship from*

teenage love to this moment, how he fought his parents when they tried to send him to prep school for the last years of high school, fought them again when they wanted him to study law like his father. He followed her to the state university and got a degree in engineering. They got married right after college even though he (and his mother, Ruth always pointed out) wanted to wait.

"Boston was always your idea," he says. He'd been stunned when she landed a job at an advertising agency before he'd decided. He ended up taking a job at a consulting firm on Route 128.

"A damn good one too," she replies. "You've made great money. You've traveled—" But she knew he'd hated everything she loved: the "starter" apartment in Somerville, riding the T to Boylston Street every morning, spending Saturday nights in a Cambridge bar or trying food at an Indian restaurant with their neighbors from Delhi. When Jeff had to spend weeks at a time in places like Charlotte or Chicago, she looked forward to flying out and meeting him for long weekends; the idea that she could fly hundreds of miles for a weekend never got old. It didn't matter where they went.

"It's my turn," he says.

"Your turn means we have to go backward?" She thought of how Gershom squeezed her down to nothing when she went back north. The mountains circled around her like an ancient stone wall. Jeff would sit for hours with older, fatter friends, lost in beery recollections of ski races and basketball games. She thought of her mother-in-law with her judgmental silences, her brother and grandparents who always seemed confused when she talked about her job.

"You used me," Jeff says now in a tone that makes Robbie bury his head in the crook of her neck. "Right from the start you used me."

Ruth listens with disbelief. He's reaching all the way back to high school. There he was, a town kid, big-fish father and bossy mother. He was popular, easygoing, got along with everyone. Even her shy brother. Even her. Most of the kids didn't know what to do with her, a farm kid who sounded like a flatlander and got good grades, from a family that went back to the early days of the county, but also an orphan whose mother was from "away." Jeff liked her red hair, her tall skinny body, even the glasses she wore for a while. "They make your eyes look bigger," he always said.

She's not that kid anymore, Ruth wants to scream now. Neither is he. He's *only reminding her of it because he knows it drives her crazy. She is caught in a confusion of exasperation, guilt, and pity. He's the one who doesn't fit in now. It's Robbie who tightens his arms around her neck, but Ruth feels it's Jeff who's dragging her down, trying to keep her, and them, from changing.*

*"When are you going to take responsibility for your life instead of blaming me?" she asks.*

*The question isn't new, but Jeff's answer is.*

*"Right now," he says.*

*He's still angry but the sadness in his eyes jolts Ruth. This isn't the change she means. She pushes past him and goes back into the living room. "It's late. We have to put Robbie to bed."*

*"NO!" Robbie struggles now, reaching for Jeff. "Daddy, too."*

*Jeff follows them into the bedroom. Robbie spreads his arms open and Jeff moves into the circle. They stand, linked by their son's small arms, one around each of their necks, so that each of them kisses a cheek. He's hanging on to each of them the way they used to hang on to each other after their fights were over. Ruth feels Jeff's hand on hers and she doesn't pull away. They can find their way out of this. They have to.*

*He starts again, though, as soon as Robbie settles down in his crib and they are standing again in the living room, Ruth's discarded coat and briefcase on the floor, Robbie's book splayed open.*

*"If we stay here, we won't make it," Jeff says. "I always told you that's where I want to live. Remember? We almost broke up over that when we got out of college."*

*"You wanted to be with me more, that's what you always said."*

*"The thing is, I don't feel like I'm with you, Ruth. Maybe it's that I don't feel like you're with me."*

*"What are you talking about?"*

*"I don't know. You're the one who's good with words. I'm just saying that you wanted a guy and I was there. I was always there. You wanted a kid—"*

*"So did you!"*

*"Yeah, I did. I still do. I want a few more, even."*

*"I never said I didn't want more children."*

"Every time I talk about it, just like every time I talk about moving back to New Hampshire, you put it off. You put everything off unless it's got to do with your job or Robbie."

The words are fighting words, but Jeff says them in a tone that sounds resigned, as though a decision has already been made. All Ruth has to do is acknowledge and accept it.

"You're just making me the bad guy so you feel better about leaving." Her words come out breathy and broken; a lump has formed in her throat.

Jeff doesn't reply right away. She sees a struggle in his eyes and suddenly she wants them to stop talking and go to bed, right now before they can say another word. She wants to wake up with the Jeff she has known since high school, the only person other than her brother and grandparents who has known her that long, and who always stayed, even when she knew he longed to be somewhere else.

"I guess that means you're not coming with me," he says.

Ruth wants to tell him he's got it wrong. Maybe she can do it. She loves him. He loves her. She wants Robbie to have his father. She wants to be the kind of woman who stays. When she tries to say it, though, it feels like an ending, not a beginning. In her ears are the words that Don Ryland said to her that afternoon when he offered her the job: "We don't want someone who knows everything, Ruth. We want someone who can figure things out and go the distance." It was as though he'd reached inside her and found both her fear and her strengths. He'd held them up where they reflected possibilities, endless and open.

She looks at Jeff's broad familiar face. She sees a pinpoint of hope in his eyes and wants to cry. "I want to be with you. But I can't go back."

"You can, you just don't love me enough."

"What about you? If you loved me or Robbie, you'd stay with us . . ."

Even though the decision's been made, they fight. They fight first in low, rasping whispers, conscious of their son sleeping one room away, and then louder and louder until Robbie is awake and crying and they are too.

# CHAPTER 17

Ruth stood at the bottom of the stairs trying to decide whether to go back to bed; it was only nine thirty in the morning, but the thought of the day ahead drained her. Maybe she would slip out the door so that Neal and Terri, deep in conversation upstairs, would never know she'd left. She'd like, for a little while at least, to be free of their worried scrutiny. It seemed to be exhausting them as much as it was her. She half turned and came face-to-face with the alcove that shadowed the guest room door. She hadn't been inside that room for three days, not since she'd read Robbie's journal. The notebook probably lay where she'd dropped it, among the clothes and other belongings scattered across the floor. She turned again, this time away from the guest room, but moved too quickly and lost her balance. The glass of water she was holding slipped from her grasp and shattered on the tiles.

"Ruth?" Neal's head appeared over the upstairs railings. "You okay?"

"Just broke a glass."

"Leave it. I'll get it later. Come on up."

"Don't be ridiculous," Ruth said. "Just toss me the paper towels." She didn't know what frustrated her more, the missed opportunity to sneak out or the mask of strained patience on Neal's face.

"Here, I'm coming." A few moments later, Terri rounded the turn on the landing and clattered down the steps bearing towel, dustpan, and broom. She crouched to sop up the water.

Ruth gave in. "Thanks, Ter."

Terri rose, a smile on her round face. She handed Ruth the sodden towel and stooped to finish sweeping the glass into the dustpan. "You head up. I'll follow."

When Ruth got to the top of the stairs, Neal was standing behind the island unit as if waiting to see how she would respond before attempting to come closer. Behind him, the television suspended from the corner was on. A cup of espresso steamed on the granite counter.

"Sorry for snapping," Ruth said. She dropped the towel into the sink and went to Neal. She touched his arm. He put it around her awkwardly and gave a quick squeeze. Terri appeared and Ruth thought she saw a smile of approval.

Then she glanced down at the newspaper on the counter, its sections spread all around. Sunday, August 17, she read. Nine days. Nine days since she'd learned Robbie was dead. When she looked up, she saw him on the television screen, a photograph of him, smiling from under his helmet, his arm flung over another set of camouflaged shoulders.

"What's this? What are they doing?" she asked, as text began to crawl along the bottom of the screen. *Local Marine, suicide . . . growing national trend.*

"Reporters have called a couple of times," Neal said. "I didn't want to bother you with it. I ignored them, but they kept at it." He frowned in disgust. "The paper, the radio, they've all got something. There's suddenly a focus on military suicides. Robbie fits in, makes the story local, I guess." He waved his hand over the papers on the counter.

On the front page of the *Union Tribune*, Ruth saw a photograph of Robbie sitting on the back of a truck with two other Marines, legs dangling, guns on their laps, grinning from under their helmets. It was one of the photographs he'd posted to his old MySpace page during his first deployment. That must have been where the television station had found the other snapshot. Ruth's stomach felt tight. "Bastards. This has nothing to do with Robbie or me."

She caught sight of another headline, this time in a section of the *Los Angeles Times*. *Marine Suicide Under Investigation*, it read. *Son of defense contractor found dead of gunshot wound.* In the gray paragraphs surrounding yet another photograph of Robbie, Ruth saw her own name: *Ruth Nolan, executive, RyCom, recently the target of a lawsuit by families of contractors the firm places in Iraq and Afghanistan.*

Ruth snatched up the pages. "What are they saying? Why are they doing this?" They had no right. They were treating Robbie like fodder, using him to fill their daily news hole.

"We need to talk," Neal said. "The thing is . . ." he started to say, but then the house phone rang. Ruth watched him pick up the receiver, glance at the display, look at Terri.

"What? Another reporter? Give me the phone."

"It's not . . ."

"Give me the goddamned phone!" Ruth grabbed the receiver from Neal. "Who is this?" she demanded.

There was a pause, and then she heard a familiar rasp.

"Hello, Ruth. Sorry we haven't spoken until now. My condolences."

Ruth fought for control of her voice. "Gordon."

"I'm sorry to be calling at a bad time but, let's face it, there isn't likely to be a good time."

"That's all right. I can talk." Confusion infiltrated Ruth's anger. A quick glance at Terri's face, then Neal's told her that they knew something she didn't.

"Don and I've been talking and it isn't necessary for you to rush back," Gordon said. "In fact, this might be a good time for a sabbatical."

"I don't need a sabbatical," she said.

What she needed was work. She wanted to lose herself in something hard, complicated, and demanding, something that would fill every hour and leave her exhausted.

"You say that now, but you may need more time than you think and we're fine. We've got everything taken care of."

"Are you saying I should stay away?" Ruth tried to steady her voice.

Another beat of silence.

"Perceptive as usual." Gordon's rasp sounded normal now, as if up until this point he'd been trying to sound like someone else.

"Forget it. I'm coming in. I'll come tomorrow," she said.

"As you can imagine, your misfortune has touched more than our hearts. RyCom's been in the papers a little too much these days for our customers' tastes. We thought it would simplify things to have Andrea take over for you, ease the bumps we've encountered with the Transglobal deal."

"No."

"You will continue to be paid your salary and get all benefits until the merger goes through. When that happens, your stock will make you a rich woman. In other words, you'll reap the benefits of all your hard work. Don wanted me to specifically reassure you on that point, in recognition of your long partnership."

Ruth slammed her hand down on the counter. She saw Terri startle and look to Neal with worry in her eyes. Ruth wheeled around so her back was to both of them. This was too much loss. Too much. They couldn't do this to her.

"I want to speak to Don," she said.

"What you need to do, Ruth, is focus on what is best for the company and remember that what is best for the company is also best for you."

"No."

"It's done. I'll tell Don that we've spoken and that we can count on your support. I've already asked Terri to provide Andrea with all the files on the contractors involved in the suit. If you have anything at home, give it to Terri. She'll be supporting Andrea now."

*No. No. No.*

"We're squared away now. Take some time off, relax, wait for the merger to go through. Then you'll be fabulously rich and can go on to the next chapter in your life."

"You prick! This was your idea, yours and Andrea's. I won't let you do this."

"I'll assume that's grief talking, Ruth. So here's a gentle reminder: The decision is made. You can go along and make it easy or you can resist and run the risk of Don losing his temper. And his generosity."

Ruth tried to think. There must be something she could do to salvage the situation.

"Good-bye."

Ruth heard a click, then a hollow buzz. She slammed the phone down on the counter and turned to Neal and Terri. "You knew. Both of you knew."

"We were going to come find you," Neal said.

"I still want to help out, Ruth," Terri said. "I told Neal that. Anything you need. All you have to do is call. Day or night." She took a step toward Ruth. But Ruth went rigid.

"You work for Andrea now."

Terri held Ruth's gaze. "I've known Robbie since he was a little boy. I want to help."

Ruth could not look at her eyes, soft now with tears and concern. Her assistant felt sorry for her. For some reason, this unnerved Ruth even more than Gordon's cold dismissal. She wanted to sweep the newspapers off the counter, wanted to throw the telephone at the television screen, which now was broadcasting a clip of dogs helping disabled children. They'd finished picking over Robbie's bones and moved on.

Neal's mouth was moving but Ruth's thoughts drowned him out. He had to have known this was happening even before today. He represented too much business for RyCom. Don and Gordon would have had to tell him what they were doing so he could tell his clients. He hadn't warned her. He hadn't fought for her.

". . . for the best," she heard him say. "You need time."

She interrupted. "If he'd been killed in Iraq, this wouldn't be happening, would it?"

"What are you talking about?"

"Your company, you, Transglobal, no one wants anything to do with a suicide." Even as she said it, she knew there was more to it. The media focus on Robbie's suicide had provided Don, Andrea, and Gordon with an easy way to move her out. Her loss was their opportunity, pure and simple. She turned on Neal. "You helped them. You sold me out."

"The contractor suit, then this . . . they just don't want anything to do with the publicity," Neal said. "You can't take it personally. You're getting the same payout you would've gotten if you stayed. We'll be able to start our own company like we—"

"Get out," Ruth said. "Leave. She swept the paper from the counter in a fury.

Neal's patience slipped; Ruth saw the flare in his eyes before he turned to face her assistant. "Ter, thanks for coming. Why don't we call you later?"

"About what?" Ruth said. "Are there more surprises you're hiding from me?"

A beat of silence followed. Neal's voice, strained but calm, broke it. "The county called. They're ready to release Robbie's body. The mortuary is going to pick him up. They'll handle the cremation but they'll want to know what to do about a service."

Her anger collapsed inside her. Words and the breath she needed to utter them went missing.

"Ruth, I meant what I said earlier," Terri said. She almost whispered the words. Tears filled the corners of her eyes. "When you're ready, I'll make all the calls. Anything you need. I'll take care of it." She paused, as if she were waiting for Ruth to say something.

Ruth nodded; it was all she seemed able to do. She watched Terri pick up her bag, step past the newspapers strewn on the floor, and make her way downstairs. Moments later, she heard the front door open, then close, then the sound of a car starting. She walked slowly across the tiles, out of the kitchen, to the bank of windows opening onto the ocean. Behind her, she heard Neal clear his throat.

"We figured you'd want your family here but we didn't know who or what else you might want."

Her family. Ruth closed her eyes to the blues and greens shimmering outside the window. She saw her grandmother's eyes, huge and sad behind her glasses, full of questions she would never ask. And Kevin, always silent, would wonder how this could have happened, how she could have let their boy die.

Neal coughed again, sounding as if he were trying to loosen the words from his throat. She opened her eyes but didn't look at him.

"A friend of mine told me about an old Navy guy with a boat," Neal said. "He'll take everyone out so you can distribute Robbie's ashes."

"Robbie hated the ocean."

"It was just an idea."

Ruth turned. She caught him looking past her out the window, checking the waves. She'd seen that gaze every morning and every night. Even though she knew he hadn't surfed in days or even spoken of it, that one long look at the water kicked the embers of her rage back into life. He wanted to be out there on the water. He wanted to pick up his life where he'd left it when Robbie died, and he could. He would. The inevitability of this, the unfairness of it, scalded her.

"Why are *you* still here?" Neal wasn't looking at the ocean any-more. Ruth saw his eyes soften, the way a parent might look at a child who made no sense.

"You really want me to leave?"

"Why didn't you . . . do what Robbie did?" she asked now. "When you came back?

She saw the condescension dissolve into surprise. His jaw tightened.

"I told you. We're all different," he finally said.

"Different how?"

"What do you want me to say, Ruth? You have a duty and you do it. You don't walk away. You do what you have to do."

Those words didn't mean what she'd always thought they meant. She didn't know what they meant.

"You're still doing it, right? You're going along with Don and with Gordon because it's what you 'have to do.'"

Neal faced her again. "That's out of my hands, you know that," he said. A shadow of something—regret, guilt, maybe both—passed over his face.

"Why did you stick around the military after you retired? You could have started another business, gotten another job that had nothing to do with uniforms or war, or any of this."

"Never would have met you, then, would I?" he asked.

He was trying to lighten things up, but Ruth didn't want light. She wanted him to tell her something that would make sense of all of this.

"No one understands unless you've been there," Neal said. "Maybe that's why I stayed in the Army all those years. I didn't have to explain myself to a bunch of idiots who couldn't understand, who hated us. You know how it is; I wasn't going any higher so I had to get out. This job . . . it's close enough. I figure you might as well stay among your own kind."

"And the money's good, right? Enough to get you through a few nightmares."

His eyes hardened. "I've done all right," he said, his voice loud now, and sharp. "We all have." He waved his hand toward the view outside the sliders and swung it in an arc that encompassed every inch of the top floor.

Ruth turned toward the room she had built. She found no safety in the sweeps of glass, the tiles of natural stone. Her thin shirt was no defense against the sun burning through the wall of glass that framed her ocean view.

"Go," she said to Neal. But she didn't look at him. She couldn't. "I want you to leave."

# CHAPTER 18

I'm only a phone call away," Neal said from the doorway of Ruth's office. She'd retreated there while he packed.

Ruth heard him, but she did not look up. Her fingers tightened on the envelope she held in her hand, a note of sympathy she'd pulled from a pile of unopened mail on her desk. She didn't recognize the name in the upper left corner. Maybe Terri would know. Then she caught herself; this was not the kind of help Terri meant. A few sentences from Gordon Olson and all the rules were changed; the last bit of certainty was shattered.

"Did you hear me?"

She ran her finger along the edge of the unopened envelope. Thick ivory paper, expensive. The note inside would be unoriginal and brief; no answers for her there, only the possibility that she would resent the writer for being able to write it and then move on. She placed the note, unopened, on the small pile of similar envelopes between stacks of bills and junk mail.

"Ruth," he said again. She felt Neal's hand on her shoulder.

"Look at me, please."

Ruth glanced up at him, saw the overnight bag slung over his shoulder, the confusion in his eyes.

She was afraid to be alone. Maybe Neal hadn't meant what he'd said. He'd been angry, that's all. He knew there was a difference between what he'd been driven to do in combat and what she did for a living.

"I don't know what you want from me," he said. "I've tried to help. I still want to help."

He would stay if she asked. Ruth was afraid to look at him. She needed to remember she'd always been alone. She'd been fooling herself to think otherwise. A moment passed. Then another. A rustling sound from the doorway told her that Neal had turned to leave.

"I'll call you tomorrow, make sure you're all right. If you need me before then, call me."

She leaned forward, hands cupped over her ears so she would not hear the echo of his steps in the hall or the bang of the door as he let himself out.

What now?

She should leave, get out, go for a walk or drive or something, anything to clear her head. How was she going to manage the next few days, weeks, months?

*Months.* Panic flickered. Ruth turned from the window looking for something that would rescue her, at least for the moment. She snatched her laptop, still in its case, leaning against the side of her desk. A few minutes later, the blue screen was filling with familiar icons. A click and she was on the RyCom server, another and she was in her e-mail, half surprised to find she still had access. She hadn't thought about what she was looking for, but the realization that she was still in the system steadied her. Maybe she could still get to Don somehow, convince him to change his mind.

As Ruth looked closer, though, she saw that many of the e-mail messages were from strangers, forwarded to her from the company's general mailbox. The subject lines chilled her. *My Sympathy. I Understand. Help for Families of Suicide Victims.* Furious at the presumption behind them, Ruth began to delete the messages wholesale, racing through them until she came to one with a single word, *Please*, in the subject line. She clicked.

*Dear Ms. Nolan,*

*I don't know if you will see this but after I saw the terrible news about your son on television, I wanted to try to reach you. I feel I have a better sense than most people of what you are going through right now and you have my deepest sympathies.*

*My husband took his own life last year after spending thirteen months first in Iraq and then in Afghanistan. He was a strategic weapons consultant. He signed on with RyCom to work with the military. Something happened to him. I didn't know him after he came home. He suffered so much. We both did, and our kids.*

*We tried to get him into a psychiatric hospital, but the insurance wouldn't pay even though it is in the policy. All he got was a few counseling sessions and some drugs. He couldn't work. After he died, I was told by the life insurance company that there would be no money coming because he committed suicide. We have four children, three boys age 10 to 14 and my youngest, a girl who is 5. We are losing our home. When I saw your story, I felt you might be the one person who could help us now. We are part of the lawsuit, but we may lose our house before it can be settled. I know this is a terrible time for you but I also know that tragedy can open the heart.*

*Please go to whoever is in charge and tell them our family and the other families of contractors you hired labored and died trying to help their country just as I am sure your son did. I don't know him or you but I have seen firsthand what going to those places did to a good man. He may have died here, but he was killed there.*

*Please help us. If you want to write back, just reply to this e-mail
or you can call me. My contact information is below. I hope to hear
from you.*

*Sincerely,
Marilyn Corning*

Ruth's finger hovered above the "delete" key but she could not
tap it. *He may have died here, but he was killed there.*

Ruth recalled the pages of Robbie's notes, scrawled with stories
of things she'd never let herself think about while he was "there."
The more Ruth reread that one line, the more it accused. There
were no parallels here, Ruth wanted to tell the Corning woman.
Robbie had been forced to do what he needed to do, but her husband, a man with four children, had chosen to go into a war zone.
*We never lied,* Ruth found herself thinking, as though the dead man
and his wife had taken up residence in her mind. There was nothing
she could do even if she wanted to. She scanned the list of remaining e-mails. There was nothing important in them. Nothing from
Gordon, Andrea, or Don. No follow-ups from that woman in Human
Resources, Sylvia. They knew she was gone. Soon enough, so would
the others.

Sunlight spilled through an opening in the blinds and swallowed
the images on the computer screen. Ruth couldn't look anymore.
She needed to get out of here. She'd go to her gym in the back of
the house. She'd crank up the music, push it hard. She'd work every
muscle until it screamed. She'd do whatever it took to get through
this afternoon. But the phone rang before Ruth reached the door.

She stood still, snared by the absurdly calm male voice leaving
a message. He was calling from the mortuary. Her son was "resting" now with them, he said. The cremation would take place that
afternoon, as instructed. They would wait to hear about the remaining arrangements. She could call any time. He listed two phone

numbers and a name she did not catch. "We'll wait to hear from you. Please accept our sympathies to you and your family at this sad time." Click.

Five hours later Ruth was still in her gym, even though she'd long since stopped moving. The floor was cluttered with water bottles, weights, and a cotton shirt so soaked with sweat she'd struggled out of it. She sat on the floor, her back against the wall, staring out at the late afternoon sky. Her shoulders ached, her knees throbbed—they'd nearly given out when she stepped off the elliptical trainer for the last time—but at least the day was almost over. Now she had to find a way to get through the night.

# CHAPTER 19

August 1995

*S*he and Robbie are in the car. They are always in the car. In an odd way it is where Ruth feels closest to him because he is all hers. Elsewhere, she loses him to day care, to school, and on alternate Friday nights, to Jeff. On Fridays it's a frantic dash to Robbie's day care to pick him up before it closes, crawling through the drive-up line at McDonald's for the Happy Meal she's promised him, and then battling the traffic north of Boston until it breaks and flings them forward. For ninety minutes, she singsongs questions to him, tries to make him laugh, or just steals glances at him in the rearview mirror as he sleeps, a French fry dangling from his fingers. Then, too soon, they arrive at the state liquor store parking lot in Concord where Jeff's truck is usually parked and waiting.

They still fight.

"He's only three!" Ruth says when she finds out Jeff took him up to the top of Cannon Mountain for skiing "lessons." Later, she is even more furious when she learns that he has introduced Robbie to his future stepmother by moving Vonnie in during one of Robbie's "off" weekends. A new baby follows quickly. Too quickly.

"He doesn't know where he stands with you," Ruth tells him in a low voice as Robbie climbs out of her car. "Try to give him a little extra attention."

"You have him in day care all day long and you're telling me to give him more attention?"

"At least he knows when he comes home that there won't be any surprises."

"For Christ's sake, stay out of it," Jeff yells in front of Robbie. "It's your constant controlling bullshit that's got him so wired he doesn't even know if it's okay to like me or not."

She's relieved then on the January weekend that a nor'easter shuts down stretches of the interstate connecting Boston with New Hampshire. Jeff tells her he'll be at the usual spot, but Ruth cancels the visit; the roads are too messy and it will take too long. The next day, he catches the tip of his ski on a patch of ice during a run down Cannon, plunges out of control, and slams headfirst into a pine tree.

In the three days before Jeff is removed from life support, the roads are cleared and Ruth brings Robbie to the hospital where his father lies hooked up to a ventilator, a host of beeping monitors, and bags of fluids. She is not allowed into the room, but his second wife, Vonnie, takes Robbie in to see him. Ruth watches through the glass while Vonnie places her hands on Robbie's shoulders and gently guides him toward the bed. She sees Robbie's hand close around his father's. Jeff's face is swollen; his eyes are ringed with black. He doesn't move. Ruth's eyes fill with tears as Robbie wheels around and hides his face in Vonnie's embrace.

After Jeff dies, they must wait for the ground to thaw so he can be buried. Robbie insists on keeping to his original visitation schedule. A child psychologist she's found for Robbie tells her this is good for him. Every other weekend, Ruth drives him all the way north where they stay at the farm and Robbie visits with his uncle Kevin, Vonnie, and the kids. Ruth does it even though it means swallowing her own confused grief and crawling back to the all-too-familiar smallness of Gershom.

You win, she thinks, as if Jeff can somehow hear her.

"Leave him here with us," her mother-in-law suggests when Ruth brings Robbie to visit them. "We'll give him Jeff's old room. We'll take care of him."

"Do you believe the nerve of the woman?" Ruth sputters that night to her brother, Kevin, after Robbie has fallen asleep. "Trying to take my own child from me?"

*"More like she was trying to be close to her grandson," Kevin says. "She's lost her child. It's understandable."*

*"She doesn't think I can handle it."*

*"You can handle anything, Ruthie. We all know that. Just let it slide."*

*She's not sure, though. Even when she isn't traveling, there isn't always enough of her left at the end of a day or a week to deal with Robbie's grief or just make him dinner, never mind remember the play date or soccer game he's been looking forward to. When she drives up the gravel road to her grandparents' farm she knows that for a while, at least, it is not all up to her to make Robbie happy.*

*She would never leave him, though. She can't. That would make her no better than her mother. When she sees him rush into the waiting arms of her grandparents or brother, longing stabs her. She wants to be the one who makes him smile like that. Maybe if they could get away from this place and its memories, she might be able to do it.*

*When Don decides to move RyCom's headquarters from Boston to La Jolla, Ruth sees her chance to make a clean break.*

*"But it's so far," her mother-in-law quavers. Even Kevin and Big Ruth go silent when she announces the move. Her grandfather, Mo, who was still alive then, asks if it's what she really wants.*

*"It's my work," she tells him. "I have to go. It'll be good for Robbie, and me, too, a new start, a new life."*

*Her grandmother's eyes tear up behind her thick glasses but she doesn't cry. She reaches for Ruth's hand the way she did when Ruth was a girl. When she speaks, it sounds like a warning. "It's all one life, honey. You can't just start a new one because you don't like the one you have."*

*Ruth snatches her hand away and turns to hide her own tears.*

*J*eff is buried in May. That June, after the school year ends, Ruth moves Robbie west. She tries to make an adventure of it. She takes her first and only two-week vacation and they drive across the country in her Honda. For the first day or so, Robbie sits hunched and still in the passenger seat. "I want to go home."

"We are going home. Our new home."

"Then let me stay at the old one."

"I would miss you too much. Wouldn't you miss me? Besides, my job is there."

"You could get another job if you wanted to."

The stops in Hershey, then Gettysburg take on the feel of a forced march. Ruth begins to regret the long drive ahead. She should have taken a plane, gotten it over with in a few hours. Sooner or later he'd have to come around. But as they see signs for Lake Erie, Ruth notices Robbie eyeing the atlas. A while later, it is spread open in his lap.

"My teacher says a big boat went down in Lake Erie."

Ruth hasn't planned to stop but she exits the highway, cruises the Ohio shoreline, and spends the night in Vermilion, where Robbie listens rapt while the docent of a small museum there tells him of one shipwreck after another. By the time they head back to the interstate, he is poring over the map.

"Six hundred miles to the Mississippi," he informs her.

For the next eight days, Robbie navigates and provides commentary. They like the arches in St. Louis, are equally disappointed in the Mississippi. "Looks like diarrhea soup," Robbie pronounces. Instead of heading south as Ruth had planned, they follow I-70 through the plains to Colorado and into the mountains. "Wow," he says as they twist and turn through the Front Range. "Dad would have loved skiing down that. Think I could get Uncle Kevin to go fishing with me out here?"

Ruth lets him talk. She has never spent so much time with him alone. The Honda has become their safe place, a capsule world. All they need is food, water, and a map. Here, he can say "Dad" and not cry. She can listen without guilt. The landscape changes as fast as they can move through it; there is no place for grief or guilt to take hold. Ruth even lets work go for a few precious days. She lets voice mail catch her calls. She and Robbie stand, speechless, at the edges of canyons, touch the sand at rest stops just to see how hot it is. She snaps his picture in front of hoodoos at Bryce Canyon, and then, on the last day, rubs sunscreen on his nose at eight in the morning as he prepares to leap into a pool in Las Vegas. He loves it all, hot as it is, dry as it is. He wants more.

"Let's keep going."

*"We're only half a day from San Diego."*

*"Death Valley is right on the way."*

*"We'll be able to see it anytime we want."*

*"I want to see it now."*

*What he wants, Ruth knows, is to keep driving. Now that arrival is imminent, their capsule is disintegrating around them. Ruth has twenty voice mails to answer, she must get in touch with the real estate agent for the condo she's bought in San Diego, she has to confirm the arrangements for the summer camp she's found for Robbie. She is eager, suddenly, to see her new office in the new building, to dive in.*

*"I'll take you next spring. I promise," she tells him.*

*When, later that day, they pass the turnoff for Death Valley, Robbie stares straight ahead. When Ruth asks him to check the map to see how much farther, he pretends he doesn't hear her.*

# CHAPTER 20

Ruth showered and changed. She thought she could eat, but all she could find in the refrigerator was leftover takeout from a ribs place that Neal liked, a chunk of Brie, and some wilted lettuce. She grabbed the cheese, found a bottle of pinot in the wine cooler and some crackers in the cabinets, and brought it all out to the deck. After the first glass of wine, she forgot about the cheese. She closed her eyes and tipped her face toward the weakening sun. The voices of people gathered on the cliffs below to watch the sunset ebbed and fell with each surge of the waves. The sounds flooded her thoughts the way the ocean flooded the rocks cairned along the water's edge. She imagined the water bubbling through the crevices of the rocks and as the waves receded, so did her ability to think about whatever it was that came next. When the phone rang, she didn't get up to answer it, and then it too receded.

A while later, the intercom for the front door sounded. And then she heard Terri's voice. Ruth tried to stand but her thighs quivered; her knees seemed too fragile to support her. She sank back into the chaise. Too much exercise, she thought, distractedly. The wine probably wasn't helping. Terri had a key. Ruth picked up a cracker and was still chewing it when the deck lights went on and Terri appeared at her side, holding a shopping bag.

"I tried to call, but you didn't answer. So I let myself in. Hope you don't mind."

Ruth was surprised to find she didn't mind. Terri's frown of concern, her confidence that she would be welcome were reassuring. She remembered the first time she'd met Terri, her blond hair piled on top of her head like a ball of curling ribbon, her eyes too made-up and too blue to be taken seriously, glasses or no glasses, résumé or no résumé. Ruth almost dismissed her before the interview even started. But then Terri took off the glasses and looked Ruth in the eye as if she could read every thought in Ruth's mind. "I'm the oldest of six kids; I raised my youngest sisters when my mom got sick. I've worked since I was fourteen and put myself through school. I'm not afraid of work, and I'm the kind of person who is going to know what you need even when you don't. You are going to need someone like me."

Ruth searched for that Terri now and saw her. Ten years older, hair shorter and looser, soft around the jaw now and thick through the hips, but still the person who knew what Ruth needed and cared enough to give it. "I'm sorry about before," she said.

Terri picked up the wine. "Have you eaten anything to go with this?"

Ruth pointed to the plate.

"Never mind. I know the answer," Terri said. She went back into the kitchen with her bag.

Ruth watched the sky turn from blue to violet as she listened to the clatter of utensils from inside the house. The marine layer had moved back in and blurred the horizon. The sun, a huge scarlet eye, slipped into the haze. Ruth stared unblinking until all that was left was a salmon glow along the horizon and the Pacific had turned the color of wet slate.

"Here," said Terri. She put down a tray of food she'd picked up from the Italian place Ruth liked near the office. A salad, some bread, a container of pasta e fagioli.

"You should be at home with your husband and your kids," Ruth told her.

"They know where I am." Terri held up the bottle and a glass for herself. "You mind?"

"Go ahead. Get yourself a fork, too. I can't finish all this. Don't know if I can eat any of it, to be honest."

"You shouldn't be alone," Terri said. "When is Neal coming back?"

"He's not."

Terri's silence bore down on her.

"Not tonight anyway," Ruth said. "I told him to go home. He needs a break." Not entirely true but true enough.

Ruth made herself pick up the bread and begin to chew. She should be ravenous after the afternoon she'd had, but eating was an effort. The bread felt like a sponge in her mouth. She poured more wine and drank. "So, how was your first day with your new boss?"

Terri sighed. "It'll take some getting used to."

"You're spoiled after working for a jewel like me."

"Well, the devil you know . . ." Terri flashed a smile over the top of her glass.

Ruth nodded appreciatively and raised her glass in salute. This was easier to take than sympathy. She was sick of sympathy.

The air had cooled; the sun was sinking faster now. Ruth ate a little of the soup. She picked at the salad. If she could just stop time for a little while, she would. The wine, Terri's arrival, and now the silence made the deck a safe place.

"Ruth."

"Yes?"

Terri hesitated. Ruth looked up from her food to see her friend sitting up straight, her wineglass on the table, the smile gone. Ruth let go of her fork and started to hold up her hand as if that would stop whatever was coming.

"Look, Ter, I'm glad you are here and I appreciate the food, but—"

Terri spoke over her. "Do you remember the flash drive I gave you that night? The last night you were at work?"

Ruth's hand fell into her lap. "You mean the last time I saw Robbie alive?"

"No! Oh, Ruth, that's not what I was going to say at all. Please . . ."

"That was the day he came to see me. I thought he could wait." Ruth's voice was loud in her own ears. Her throat burned.

"Please, listen. I didn't mean to—"

"This has been the first time in days that I have not thought of that night."

Worry furrowed Terri's broad forehead and widened her eyes. She leaned forward, full of urgency. "You were a good mother to Robbie. He was lucky to have you."

Ruth got up. Her legs felt shaky but she didn't want to sit there anymore. She walked to the rail as Terri's voice followed her.

"Ruth, I'm so sorry. I never wanted to cause you pain. Only I'm not sure when we'll have a chance to talk alone anytime soon and I wanted to . . . I gave you a flash drive with a lot of documents on it, remember?"

Ruth did not even try to recall what Terri was talking about. "No."

"A couple of days ago Andrea took all the files from me and Sylvia, all the contractor files and all the correspondence. I don't have any of it left."

"So?"

"It's all on the flash drive I gave you, along with some stuff Andrea doesn't know exists."

What flash drive? Why would it matter? Ruth turned from the railing.

"I wanted to remind you about it, in case—"

"In case what?"

"You might want to use it."

Terri was standing now, sucking on her lower lip the way she did when she was nervous.

"What are you talking about?" Ruth asked. "What's on there that I could possibly want to use?"

"E-mails. Memos. Other documents. They show that Gordon and Sylvia messed up when it came to the insurance and the claims. They knew what they were doing. They knew lots of stuff."

Ruth went still. The deepening shadows on the deck seemed to breathe now with something even darker than the pain of remembering her last moments with Robbie. "You think I should blackmail them into giving me my job back?" The idea flared into life as if Terri had struck a match. Then it fizzled. She knew Gordon. If he had screwed up, he'd also probably found a way to cover his tracks. He'd win. He had Don; she didn't. Not anymore. She started to thank Terri for having her back, but when she glanced up her friend looked at her the way someone might look if they'd opened a drawer and found a mouse.

"I never thought of blackmail," Terri said.

Through the fading light, Ruth saw Terri try a smile that failed before it got started. She wished they could go back to sitting on the deck with their glasses of wine, to be together in that small space where feeling was absent for a while. Instead, she asked a question that could only lead to more trouble. "Educate me, Ter. What exactly were you thinking?"

"I was thinking of the people," Terri said. She paused, as if she expected Ruth to understand, to lift the burden of explanation from her. Ruth waited.

"The ones out on the steps of the office the other day, the contractors who are hurt, the mothers, and the wives. They need help, and they're not going to get it from Andrea or Gordon Olson or the insurance companies."

The implications of Terri's explanation began to sink in. Terri must have seen all those e-mails those people had written to Ruth. She saw everything that came into Ruth's inbox. *Please. He may have died here, but he was killed there.* The woman's plea reached down through Ruth's grief and anger to compassion she'd forgotten she had. There was nothing she could do, she'd told herself that morning, but now here was Terri looking at her with eyes full of concern, giving her the means to fight not for herself but for someone else.

"You want me to threaten Don Ryland and Gordon Olson, tell them they better pay up or I'll go public with whatever's on that flash drive?" Ruth said, not quite believing it, hoping that Terri would somehow take all of this back.

"I'm just saying you have it. They need it. You could give it to them." Terri's brow unfurrowed. She looked at Ruth, still concerned, but also trusting, expectant.

The distance between them, just a few feet of deck, seemed to widen even though neither of them had moved an inch. Ruth saw all the ways that this could and likely would fail. Terri, she was sure, might only see that Ruth was afraid to try.

What did she expect Ruth to do? Didn't she understand that even if Ruth gave everything on that drive to the lawyers, offered herself up as some kind of whistleblower, the contractors could still lose? Lots of years and lots of lawyers later they could still lose. Ruth tried to imagine what would remain for any of the contractors, for her, after all that. She saw more loss, more loss than she could begin to think about right now. And that gave rise to a sudden and fierce resentment.

"Why not you? You take it, you be the hero."

Terri's shoulders sagged. She looked at her shoes. "My husband just got laid off. I put my résumé out but it's going to take a while. I can't lose my job right now." Her voice was subdued, embarrassed.

"And I have nothing to lose, right?" Ruth said. "Nothing more, anyway. That's what you're thinking?"

Terri flinched. She didn't look up. "I guess I didn't think. I'm sorry." She reached for the purse she'd put down when she arrived. "I'd better go."

*No, don't go,* Ruth wanted to say. Her anger turned to the panic she'd felt earlier in the day.

"Terri," Ruth said. *Stay with me. Stay just a little longer.*

"Yes?" Terri responded quickly, almost eagerly, like a woman expecting good news. Her purse dangled from her wrist, half open. In that moment Ruth thought of her grandmother, the only person in the world besides her brother and, apparently, Terri who believed that Ruth was better than she was.

*Thank you for trying.*

"Thank you for the food."

Terri looked back down at her purse. She zipped it up and slung the strap over her shoulder. "No problem." She said it in the same flat, efficient way she'd said it so often at the office. Ruth could still see her friend, but the shadows of the evening stood between them.

"I'll call you tomorrow," Terri said. "I'll call the mortuary too." She turned to go.

"You don't have to do that."

"No problem, Ruth," Terri said over her shoulder, not looking at Ruth. "I want to do it. I told you that."

She watched Terri go from the deck, through the kitchen and then disappear down the stairs. A few seconds later, she heard the front door open and bang shut. Then Ruth looked down for the bottle of wine. Empty. Didn't matter. She knew where there was more.

R uth woke up on the floor of the guest room. Pain radiated from her temples to the base of her skull and her mouth was dry. Her legs were frozen in a fetal curl. Her heart hammered against her ribs. Fragments of a dream tried to chase her into consciousness. Hands. Her mother's red nails flashing from the truck window as Ruth ran after her. Robbie's hands shaking in hers, then not moving at all.

She pushed herself up and saw through the blinds that the sky outside had already lightened. Another day was about to begin. The thought brought her to her feet; she couldn't endure another day like yesterday.

Something soft tripped her when she tried to take a step. Robbie's old stuffed rabbit. She scooped it up, then grabbed the closet door for balance. The mirror on the door startled her into stillness. Over the silk tank top and shorts she'd put on the night before, she wore Robbie's faded denim jacket, the one he'd begged for when he was twelve and would never let her give away. She cradled the toy rabbit, a crumple of plush and bare patches, its remaining ear drooping over the crook of her arm. Her eyes stared back at her, puffy and shadowed but also with an expectant look, as though waiting for the answer to a question.

She needed some aspirin. Antacids too. Coffee. Something, anything to get her going. She started down the hall to her own bathroom but stopped when she saw her laptop on her office desk, open but dormant. What would she find in her e-mail inbox if she looked? The red light on the phone blinked like a warning. The mortuary was waiting for a response. In a few hours, there would be more messages, calls from Terri, a funeral checklist to make. Terri. She might not say another word about the contractors, but Ruth knew she'd be thinking about them, and Ruth would have to think about them too.

The desire to escape rose, sudden and swift, like a pot boiling over. Everywhere Ruth looked there was something she wanted to get away from: the phone, the laptop, the house that echoed with accusation. She looked down at the denim jacket and the rabbit that somehow was still in her arms. She'd take it with her. She'd take Robbie too. They couldn't scatter his ashes until she was ready, and she wasn't ready.

A thump from the front curb startled her. The newspaper, now surely lying somewhere near the front door. A radio blared, then faded. The day was already moving forward. In a little while, Neal

would pass her house on his way back from the beach. He'd said he
would call. He might stop in. If he did, then somehow, she knew,
she might give in to his suggestions, she might let Terri make all the
arrangements. She might let go.

Ruth raced back into the guest room and began to stuff everything she could reach into Robbie's duffel. The rabbit, his clothes,
the photo album. She snatched the duffel strap. Too heavy. Didn't
matter. She dragged the whole thing to the bathroom and slammed
her palm into the light switch. His Dopp kit. She pulled it off the
shelf over the sink and unzipped the top. She grabbed the toothbrush
from the holder and jammed it in. His razor, too.

Her nose filled with Robbie's scent. She wheeled around and
ripped the towel hanging from the rack. She buried her face in it.
Everything. She would take everything.

She ran down the hall to the garage, flung open the door, and
stuffed the trunk of the Jaguar with Robbie's things. Then back in
her office, flying now, she scribbled the phone number of the mortuary. She flipped down the top of her computer. She'd better take it.
She didn't know when she'd be coming back.

# Flight

# CHAPTER 21

Casey floated in the space between sleep and the start of another day. The desert afternoon was poaching him in his own bed, but Casey didn't try to surface. He lingered in half consciousness as he did on the casino floor, not taking a step toward a table until the day's luck could find him and reveal itself.

His cell phone toned from somewhere in the back of the trailer. He squeezed his eyes tight, trying to drift a little longer, but the phone continued to harangue him. Where was it? He visualized the black clamshell and saw it folded in the pocket of yesterday's jeans, now pooled on the floor outside the toilet closet, right next to the faker and all the gear that went with it. *Shit.* Pinned by the heat to his pull-down bed, he stared at a tear in the vinyl ceiling, willing the phone to go silent. Then, to his surprise, it did.

Casey worked his mouth, trying to dredge up enough saliva for a good swallow, but all he got was the aftertaste of tequila, too many Camels, and the familiar feeling that he'd fucked up. He'd won, hadn't he? Enough to get good and drunk after and still have enough to send Emily. He'd go mail her the money right after breakfast.

Then he'd drive into Vegas, treat himself to a woman and a good book until it was time to hit the tables again.

Then he remembered the El Camino. The front tire had blown out on the way home last night. He'd driven the last three miles on the rim.

The phone shrilled again but Casey wasn't listening. He was thinking about how he could still make the day work. He propped himself up on one elbow and shook his head, jostling ideas, looking to see where they fell. Nothing. Beside him a set of red digits told him it was 1:17 p.m.

He began to push himself upright but fell back when his head began to pound. Hangover headache. Or maybe he was just hungry. He hadn't had anything but a sandwich since yesterday afternoon and those pretzel twigs they served at the blackjack tables with the drinks.

He sat up again, slower this time, and inched his right leg to the edge of the thin mattress, finding the floor with his foot. Then he swung the stump of his left leg next to it and peered at the bulb of flesh just below his knee. The skin was a little pink, nothing to be worried about. He started to pull himself up when a fist pounded against the metal door of the trailer.

"Casey MacInerney, you better be in there and you better have my rent money." The nicotine-scarred drawl lacked the sleepy quality he normally associated with its owner, his landlady, Belva Pointer.

"Go away, Belva," he yelled.

"Not today, sunshine. I already cut you enough slack. You owe me two months back rent. I'm not runnin' a charity here."

A key rattled in the lock of the door.

"Jesus Christ, Belva, get out. I'm naked."

"Ain't nothin' to get excited about, from where I'm standin'," Belva said. Her frame filled the edges of the narrow doorway like a trapped hot air balloon. Casey grabbed the sheet he'd been lying on and yanked the edges off the mattress, folding it over himself like a diaper.

"Where's my rent money, Casey Mac?" She was smiling at him, but her eyes were pellets.

"If you had called like a civilized human being, you could have saved yourself some trouble."

"Oh, but I did call you, darlin'. Called you a bunch of times last night and then again this morning. I just finished calling you. I could hear your phone ringing from outside. When you didn't answer I got kinda worried about you. Then I got worried about me and my rent money. You owe me two months. Jeezus, what's that smell? Somethin' die in here?"

Belva peered into the dusky heat of the trailer, her penciled eyebrows aiming down in disgust. Everything on Belva was aiming down—eyes melting into jowls, jowls into neck, neck into breasts straining against a leopard print tank top that could give way at any moment. The only thing that stood up on Belva was her hair and that, Casey knew, was because it was a wig. Orange coils rose like tongues above a fringe of shiny copper bangs that didn't move as she swung her head from side to side.

"You're looking particularly lovely today, Belva. You've really nailed that bovine look."

Belva's eyes stopped moving and fixed on him suspiciously. "Compliments won't pay the rent."

"My disability check's coming this week. You'll get your money."

"That's what you said last week. And the week before that." Belva looked around again. Casey had pulled the pleated blackout curtains across the skinny trailer windows, but light peeked out on either side and through a few holes in the limp fabric. "You sure somethin' ain't dead in here?" She stepped farther into the trailer and knocked into his bookshelf, a strip of paneling sagging under the weight of battered paperbacks and his few treasured hardcovers.

"Be careful, for Christ's sake," Casey said, and then he saw that Belva's eyes were moving again and he remembered his wallet, lying open and defenseless just out of reach. She spotted it before he could distract her.

"No!" Casey lunged but fell sideways on the bed.

She laughed and two seconds later she was brandishing his wallet in her fat white fist.

"Feels in here like you had a good night last night, Mr. Mac-Inerney."

"Give me that wallet, Belva!"

"What's this?" Belva flipped open the wallet and stared at a frayed snapshot of a little girl with serious eyes and no front teeth. "Cute little thing—someone you know or are you one of those pervs? Don't tell me. I don't want to know."

"Give me my goddamned wallet, Belva."

"Oh I will, darlin', I will. Just need to get somethin' of mine out first."

She was as good as her word. Casey watched helplessly as she extracted the cash and tucked most of it into the money pouch she hid beneath the rolls of fat around her waist.

"That'll do it until Thursday. Then you'll owe me for next month."

Belva paused, a twenty fluttering from her fat fingers. "Lunch money," she said. She tucked the bill into the wallet and flipped it onto his lap.

The snapshot of the child fell out of its torn plastic sleeve onto the dirty sheet beside him. It trembled in the faint, hot breath of the table fan. Casey read in the girl's eyes a question he could not answer. He drove his fist into the mattress. Then he snatched up the wallet and hurled it against the trailer door as Belva slammed it behind her.

# CHAPTER 22

Habit guided Ruth toward the freeway. She accelerated past banks of oleander, blind to the shimmer of white, pink, and crimson. Above, the sky was fading to the color of Robbie's old denim jacket. She'd pulled it back on, after swallowing two aspirins and an antacid and splashing water on her face. She wore it into the gas station where she'd bought some coffee and a stale bagel. She wore it into the mortuary office where she waited for the startled receptionist to get someone to help her. She kept it on after she'd carefully wrapped the metal box marked with Robbie's name in a towel that still smelled like him and secured it in the trunk.

The box had been heavy in her arms, the weight of a baby.

Through her tears, Ruth saw the sign for the RyCom exit. She sped by it.

She saw Robbie's smile in his boot camp portrait on her desk. She heard the catch in his voice when he asked her to lunch.

*We'll have lots of time,* she heard herself say.

Then she remembered what Neal had said. *You stood him up?*

Up ahead traffic snarled to a stop, blocking the lanes north. Ruth lurched to the right-hand lane that would take her east. A horn blasted behind her but she ignored it. She had to keep moving, it didn't matter where, she just had to get away. She turned up the radio and stepped on the gas.

W hat's the plan, Casey man?" The voice was too big and too smooth to belong to the wiry little man behind the cash register at the Cactus Gardens Mobile Home Café and General Store. Casey usually liked it when Lenny practiced for the jazz disc jockey job he'd never had and never would, but today, Lenny triggered a vibration in Casey's head that rattled his teeth.

"Jesus Christ, Len. Can't you say anything without making a rhyme out of it?"

"What's got you in such a sunny frame of mind?"

Casey pushed his Ray-Bans up on his forehead and struggled to catch his breath. Hauling himself through the 110-degree heat had kicked his headache back into gear. He leaned on the counter inside the entrance of the coffee shop that doubled as a convenience store. No noise from the other side of the cinder-block wall separating them from the showers and the Laundromat. Good. He jumped as a trumpet sliced through the static on the little black radio Lenny brought in every day because Belva was too damn cheap.

"And here comes Mr. Wynton Marsalis with—"

"Jesus, Len, turn that down, will you?" Casey said. The air conditioner prickled his skin under the black T-shirt he wore. Now he was cold, goddamn it.

"You okay?" Lenny leaned over the counter to peer up into Casey's eyes, pools of concern behind the glasses that were too big for his shriveled brown face. Casey wanted to laugh but he couldn't find it in him. He settled for a lopsided smirk and pushed himself up and away from Lenny so that he was standing, legs a little apart, shoulders back, hands loose at his sides. Ready position.

"Yeah, yeah, I'm fine. Just hungry."

Lenny busied himself with something behind the counter.

"No cash, no hash," Lenny mumbled. "Belva's orders."

"Old orders, Len. I'm all paid up with Belva."

"You are?"

"She broke in this morning and emptied my wallet. Took everything I had."

"She did that?"

"Yeah, she did. Least she can do is stake me to a little breakfast."

"Mmmm," Lenny said. His hand found its way to the back of his head, which was as bald as every other part of it. He looked once over each shoulder, then back at Casey. "Every cent, huh?"

Casey tried not to think about the twenty he'd jammed into his jeans pocket, looked Lenny in the face, and nodded.

"Yeah. Over four hundred—that should take care of me for a long time."

"Guess a couple of eggs wouldn't hurt."

"I was thinking more like a steak. You know, with some of those potatoes you make and some eggs on the side." This might be his one meal today and he knew that Lenny had already given in.

He sat down while the little man poured a mug of coffee from a stained decanter and plunked it down. Then Lenny tucked a dishrag into his belt for an apron and began to slice some onions.

"Four hundred—your luck is turnin'."

"Yeah, but now I've got nothing to get me started for tonight." Casey let the statement sit there and waited to see what Lenny did with it. But Lenny just threw the onions in the skillet he'd started on the stove and stooped to get the meat out of the little fridge under the prep counter. Casey tried again.

"You know, I could make you a little money."

"That's okay, Casey Mac. If I want to piss away my Social Security check I can do that all by myself."

"C'mon, Lenny." Casey's fingers drummed the counter. His good leg jiggled.

Lenny shook his head. "Uh-uh. You just come off a pretty bad losing streak."

"Yeah, but like you said, my luck is turning."

"Hmmh." Lenny stirred the onions and flipped the steak. "Even a blind hog finds the trough once in a while. Doesn't mean I'm bettin' on him to do it every time."

"Wrong handicap, Lenny. I'm a gimp, not blind. I'll win you some cash, c'mon." Casey hated the way the words wobbled out of him. He sounded like a whining kid.

He caught his reflection distorted in the aluminum along the back of the prep counter. Shaggy hair, yellow streaks fighting with gray ones across the top. Smudges for eyes and a nose that, in the rippling metal, lumped its way down his face like a root vegetable. He looked like crap and, on top of that, he was back to square one. The thought of his four hundred in Belva's money pouch sickened him.

Casey leaned onto the counter and ground his forehead against his palms. He needed to get more money or this would be the first month in nearly twelve years that he'd fail to send a little something over and above the child support deducted from his disability check.

"Eggs up, over, or scrambled?"

Lenny stood at the grill with an egg in one hand and a spatula in the other. "Up," Casey said, but he didn't really care. He only cared about the money, the one thing he could give her. She was seventeen now. There were a lot of ways a seventeen-year-old kid could use four hundred bucks. Maybe she'd put it away for college. He hoped so. He'd planned to buy a card and sign it this time, *Love, Dad.*

Fucking Belva.

The smell of onions and hot steak brought him back. He watched Lenny shake the frying pan back and forth over the flame. He leaned closer and his mood wrapped itself around this small success. He was about to eat and he still had a twenty in his pocket. He was hungry, that's all. He'd feel better when he had some food in him. He could get Lenny to give him a ride to the casino, and after that, forget him, forget Belva. He'd figure something out. He always did.

# CHAPTER 23

Ruth flew toward the desert in the far left lane. Other drivers, in no particular hurry now that it was past rush hour on a weekday, pulled their cars out of her path with the blare of a horn. She drew up behind a gray tractor-trailer and found herself staring at the face of a giant cartoon pig. When she pulled out to pass, she saw along the truck's side a mural of four pink pigs in running shorts under the words *Pork Run Express, Speediest Swine in the East, West, North, and South.*

*Looks like the driver needs to do some laps herself.*

Robbie, at twelve, would have said it just like that. Then he would have hooted at his own joke. She could hear him as if he were right there in the passenger seat. Ruth's foot came off the gas and for a moment she and the woman in the truck's cab looked straight at one another. The woman frowned over a pair of sunglasses too small for the cheeks beneath them, then gave Ruth the finger.

Ruth hit the gas harder. She was heading toward places she'd never been: Victorville, Barstow, Baker. Soon, she'd be passing the turnoff to Death Valley. She'd never taken him there after all. There was never the right time.

*when its your time its ur time don't have to look for it u can get blown up in your cot or just sitting on the can.* The fragment from Robbie's journal surfaced, jagged and sudden. More tried to follow. Ruth pushed the pedal down. She raced past hundreds of stolid brown houses planted in concentric circles around strip malls and industrial parks. She bored through the haze that settled over all of them in thick drifts, trapped by the San Bernardino mountains.

She raced into the openness of the desert.

L enny's ancient Ford 150 pulled up next to the giant turquoise buffalo in the parking lot of the casino.

"Here we are, Casey. Good luck, now."

"I don't need luck, Lenny. I need money." Casey knew it was a lost cause. He'd been working on Lenny all the way from the trailer park. Twenty miles and not a dime to show for it. He pushed open the passenger door and held on to it until he was standing on the pavement, steady on both feet.

"Like I said, Case. Good luck." The old man grinned. Then his eyes widened. "Watch out!"

The roar of a car engine almost drowned out Lenny's warning. Casey turned in time to see a dark blur heading for him. He tried to climb back into the truck, but he was too slow. The car clipped the rear of the truck's bed. He lost his balance and tumbled to the pavement. Brakes screeched and grit strafed his face and neck.

"You okay?" Lenny's voice boomed like a foghorn in the distance. When his face came into view, Casey saw the whites of his eyes behind his glasses.

"Think so."

Casey was sprawled on his side. The pavement scorched his

cheek; grit scraped his eyelids when he blinked. His stump bounced like a ball coming to rest; he knew the pin sticking from the end of the silicone sleeve was waving like a fucking antenna. Shit, not again.

"Where's my leg?" He twisted toward his stump, cursing the stupid pin release. He must have landed right on it. At least he was already on the ground. Lately all he had to do was bump it and the prosthesis would drop away, usually taking him with it.

"Oh, God. Are you all right?"

"If he is, it'll be no thanks to you," Lenny growled.

Casey craned his neck backward to see who Lenny was talking to. A thin woman in a black skirt, dark glasses hiding half her face. She was shaking like it was thirty below zero, even though she was wearing a denim jacket and it had to be breaking a hundred degrees.

"Jesus Christ." Lenny started for the casino.

"Where are you going? You can't leave." The woman grabbed Lenny's arm.

"Let me go, lady. I'm gettin' some help and right after that I'm callin' the cops."

That was when Casey saw the car. A Jaguar XK8, crouching like the big cat it was named for, not thirty feet away. A little dusty and bruised after hitting Lenny's truck, but it still purred money.

"Hang on, Len. Hang on. Let's not make a federal case out of this. I think I can move a little. Help me up."

The woman looked wired, everything tight and shaking at the same time. He had to calm her down, bring her in.

"Don't try to move, Case," Lenny said. "What if something's broken?"

"Maybe if the lady gives you a hand, you can get me up and we can see what's what." Casey leaned up on one elbow. "Can you get my sunglasses over there, ma'am?"

She twisted her head from right to left.

"Right there," Casey said, pointing to a spot by his knee.

She edged past him, her calves at eye level. No stockings. No tan. Slim and strong. She worked out, he bet. Probably had her own very expensive personal trainer.

"Thanks. Now if you get on one side and Lenny takes the other . . ."

Lenny's mouth pursed like he was sucking on a particularly tart lemon. But the old man did what he was told. Casey reached his free arm toward the woman. She hesitated, then walked over to his right side and crouched down.

"That's it," Casey said. He pulled himself up while they steadied him. When he was leaning against the passenger seat of Lenny's truck, he saw the woman wipe her hand on her skirt. Good, he was bleeding. That would make it easier.

"Your arm's all scraped up," Lenny said.

"I see that, Len. Looks like your truck got a little scraped up, too."

He glanced at Lenny and then the truck bed and bumper, which crumpled a little more than usual and bore a fresh scrape in what was left of the paint. Lenny followed his glance and frowned.

"And now, ma'am, my leg. If you don't mind." Casey gestured toward the limb lying on the pavement. She stared at the short metal rod with the socket on one end and a battered black sneaker on the other. "Don't worry, it doesn't bite."

She bent down and picked up the faker in both hands, nearly dropping it when she touched the metal.

"Hot already, huh? Sun works fast out here." He worked hard to keep his voice light, conversational. He needed her guilty, not afraid. He needed her to calm down.

She brought him the faker, holding it by the socket. Her hands shook.

Casey made a show of examining it, checking the socket, looking for something he could hang his demands on. Then Lenny jumped in.

"What are you going to do about this?" Lenny wheeled around and gestured toward his truck's fender. Casey wondered just which of the dents his friend had picked out to show the woman.

"I'm . . . I'm sorry."

"Sorry isn't going to fix it, is it?" The old guy sure didn't sound like any kind of smooth DJ now, did he? Old man cranky was all Casey heard.

"I'll pay for it," the woman said.

*Now we're talking,* Casey thought. He continued to run his hands over the metal bar and peer into the hollowed plastic that cupped his stump. He'd have to clean out the grit, but if he squinted hard, he could see a scratch that was not there before.

"You'll need my insurance information. It's in my purse." She turned toward the Jaguar.

"I don't want to wait around for some insurance company," Lenny said.

The woman stopped and looked at them through those huge sunglasses. She seemed to focus somewhere beyond Casey's shoulder and, unaccountably, shivered.

Casey spoke up. "I figure it'll take a couple thousand to fix, don't you, Len? They'll have to put a new one on and paint it too." He knew the old man couldn't get $2,000 for the entire truck.

Lenny tugged his ear. "That'd about do it, I guess." His eyes flicked from Casey to the woman.

"And then there's this leg, not to mention the medical care I'm going to need, x-rays and that." He made a show of examining the socket and then sat back and began to roll up his pant leg until the silicone liner and the pin were clear. He felt the woman's stare but when he looked up, she glanced away. He grabbed the end of his shirt and started to wipe out the inside of the socket.

They were almost there. Casey wished he could see her eyes. They would tell him how close he was. Beads of sweat lined her upper lip. For someone with a lot of money, she looked like shit. Why was she wearing that jacket in this heat? Maybe she was covering track marks. Or bruises. Shit, he hated bullies.

He had to get a grip. She wasn't his problem. The rent would come due again in just a few days. He had to eat. And there was Emily to consider. He positioned the socket over his stump and stood up, pushing until he heard the pin click. He took a couple of steps. "That noise wasn't there before," he said. This time he wasn't lying.

"I don't have much cash with me," she said.

"Look, it's hot out here. Why don't we all go inside, talk it over?"

She hesitated, straightened her shoulders a bit, getting a handle on herself, he thought. Not a good thing.

"I'll get my purse," she said. She turned her back on him and started walking to the car.

"Lenny'll get that for you." Casey started to motion to Lenny, but the old man was way ahead of him. He darted after the woman with more speed than Casey thought he was capable of.

She half turned back to Casey. "He doesn't need to—"

Lenny brushed past her, jerked open the door, and grabbed the keys out of the ignition. He dangled them for Casey to see. Then he shoved them into his pocket and reached back into the car. "This your purse?"

"Yes." She held out her hand for it but Lenny shouldered it, an ugly brown thing shaped like a sling.

"I'll carry it for you, lady. Let's all just head on in to where it's a little cooler and get this settled."

R uth watched the men move off. One more inch in the wrong direction and she could have killed one of them, or both. The force of the near miss sent a shudder through her.

She should follow them, she knew that. A hot gust lifted the hairs on the back of her neck. The asphalt scorched her soles through her thin sandals.

How had she gotten here? The gas pumps. That was it. She'd pulled off for gas, but something had distracted her.

Behind her came a roar, then the clatter of metal. She whipped around as screams shot through the noise. She remembered now. A roller coaster had burst out of the roof of the casino just as she'd passed. She'd thought she was hallucinating, but it was real. She'd driven through miles of nothing to a huge pink casino with a roller coaster. There'd been a giant sign near the highway with the words *Blue Bison Hotel and Casino* surrounding the head of a turquoise buffalo like a crown. If this had been here when she and Robbie drove through nearly a decade ago, she didn't remember. Since then, she'd always flown to Vegas and never looked down.

She watched the men disappear through the doors under a pink arch. She should go on alert, track down whoever was in authority and report the men. She should call her insurance company. All the "shoulds" pounded against the wall of fatigue that grew thicker with every passing minute. Soon all the decisions she'd left behind would catch up and pound her too.

Ruth knew there had been a time in her life when this would be laughable, a story to tell Neal or Terri over a drink, a story that would end with her winning, and the two men nursing their wounds, maybe in a police station. Now, though, she just wanted them to go away as fast as possible. The roller coaster roared once again. As the hideous thing snaked back into the building, Ruth began to walk toward the casino.

O ver here, Miss Nolan," Casey said, loud enough to get to her through the sirens, dings, buzzes, bells, and whistles of the gaming machines lined up like infantry across the casino floor behind them.

He shoved her license back in her wallet—no cash at all, not a single bill, incredible—and limped toward her. He picked up a sharp smell beneath the perfume or soap or whatever it was she used on her body. Nervous sweat. What was he dealing with here? Maybe he was wrong about her. Shit, maybe she'd stolen the damn car. Maybe she was as broke as he was. Maybe he should just walk away from this whole enterprise. Fuck it. Might as well play it through. "Let's go into the bar. You can buy us a drink while we settle up." She nodded. He guided her between two banks of machines to an alcove lined with big wooden booths. They found a booth and sat down. She said nothing as Casey ordered himself and Len each a beer.

"What about you? You must be thirsty standing out there the way you did. You like margaritas?"

"I don't care."

He could not read her eyes; she still had the stupid glasses on. He ordered her a margarita on the rocks. Then he took the purse from Lenny and plopped it on the table.

"Okay. Let's talk."

"You can have anything you want."

Casey felt his jaw go slack. Beside him, Lenny let out a long, low whistle.

No longer sure who was leading the negotiations, Casey settled for stating a fact. "That's fine, but you don't seem to have much cash in there. You'll have to get us some."

The woman reached for her purse and pulled out her wallet. In a minute she had all her credit cards on the table. Five of them, for Christ's sake, plus her bank cards laid out in front of her like a hand for seven-card stud. She barely looked up when the waitress brought their drinks.

"You said two thousand, right?" She'd stopped shaking, finally, and her voice was flat. Not mad. Not rushed. She just didn't give a damn. Like she had bigger things to think about than a few thousand bucks.

Lenny nodded and took a long swig of his beer. Casey noticed the waitress still standing there. They didn't need an audience for this. He handed her one of the credit cards.

"Start a tab, honey." He didn't know her. Must be new. "We'll call you when we're ready for some more drinks."

"How much do you want? I've got to get back to my car." The Nolan woman spoke to him now in the same flat voice. This time he was the one staring into the huge dark lenses. Was she hiding a black eye? Was he trying to fleece a battered woman? He tried to imagine himself getting up, walking away.

"Well?" She started to pick up the cards in front of her, one by one.

He couldn't look at her. "I'll take a couple of thousand, too."

"Fine." The woman picked up each of the cards with a crisp, precise movement, like a dealer. She slid out of the booth and stood up. "I'll start at the cash machine. Then I'll have to see someone about a cash advance or a bank transfer."

No. They did not want to call attention to this any more than they already had. Besides, he'd had enough crazy and enough guilt for one afternoon. He scrambled out of his side of the booth and pulled himself up.

"The cash'll be fine. We'll go with you. C'mon, Len." He would take whatever she got out of the cash machine and call it good. If it wasn't enough for Lenny, then fuck him. He needed to get some money in his hand, some Camels in his mouth, and then he needed to hit the blackjack tables. He needed to get away from this woman. When she crashed into Lenny's truck, he thought he'd struck a vein of good luck. But nothing, not even luck, came without a price. He ought to know that by now.

The two men took every dollar Ruth extracted from the ATM, a thousand dollars each, and seemed to vanish into the din caused by the roller coaster and the relentless dinging and buzzing of electronic gambling machines. Just before she lost sight of them altogether, the younger man stopped, turned, and opened his mouth as if to say something. Maybe he wanted more money after all. He just shook his head, as if to rid himself of a nagging thought, and raised his hand in a brief, final wave. Then he disappeared.

The gesture dove into the well of Ruth's memory and brought back with it the echo of abandonment. She closed her eyes, unshielded now by sunglasses, and leaned back against the wall next to the ATM. What time was it? She'd lost track. She was so tired. Maybe she should get gas and just drive to Vegas. Once she got a little sleep and a place where she could soak in a bath, she'd be all right. She could make a plan. When she opened her eyes, though, she saw the sign blinking over the bar not far away. She would sit a while, cool off, and then head to Vegas.

The bar seemed a mile away. People, shouting and laughing, brushed past, without seeing her: fat fathers and tired mothers, tiny Asian women with grim mouths, sticky children screaming for another ride, men in cowboy boots and dirty hats. The noise rasped at her ears; her throat stung. She wouldn't stay long, just one drink, and go.

She sat down at the same table, now cleared of the earlier order, and signaled to the waitress. "Another margarita."

"Like some company?" A bearded face leaned over hers. A blast of bourbon and fruity dipping tobacco hit her. A woman's voice laughed from behind the man.

"If she does, it won't be you, Asa. Shove off."

The waitress smiled at Ruth and set down the drink. "You want me to keep the tab open?"

Ruth nodded.

"Watch out for that guy," the woman whispered as she set down the drink. "He's horny and lonely and he's a mean son of a bitch."

"Now don't go tellin' her lies," the man said.

Ruth wanted both of them to go away. She pulled her sunglasses back down over her eyes and stared straight in front of her.

"Can I get you anything else right now?" the waitress asked. "No? Well, just wave when you're ready for a refill." As they retreated,

Ruth forgot about them. She let the drink do its work. Each sip released her a little more from herself. There was no rush to get to Las Vegas. It wasn't as if she had a plan. Just before she emptied her glass, the waitress was back with a fresh one that Ruth could not remember asking for. The man at the bar was looking at her. He raised his glass in salute.

I'm outta here, Case. You'll have to find another way home." Lenny pushed himself back from the blackjack table. A ponytailed blonde twice as big as Lenny took his place.

Casey sensed rather than saw Lenny walk away. Tommy, the dealer, was already laying out the cards. King and queen for Casey, six up for himself. Good. The woman giggled. She showed Casey her cards, a ten and a three. "Should I hit?"

*Shit.* He rolled his eyes at Tommy, who said nothing, and then he shook his head at the woman, just to get her moving.

"Case." Lenny was back, breathing bourbon in his ear.

"Jesus, I'm on a roll. If you're going, get the fuck out of here already."

The woman scrunched up her eyes, pouted. Then she slapped the table. "Hit me."

A ten, bust. Served her right. He glanced at Tommy. He busted. Yes! The dealer pushed Casey's chips toward him. Casey shook his head and slid them back. He had a good feeling.

"C'mon, Case, pay attention."

Irritated, he glanced sideways at Len. "What?"

"Don't want these," Lenny said. A set of keys with the Jaguar insignia appeared next to Casey's beer.

"What the fuck am I supposed to do with them?"

Lenny shrugged. "Not my problem. Later, Case."

Casey looked up and started to call Lenny back, but the old man moved fast. Shit. Casey glanced at his watch. They'd left the Nolan woman by the ATM four hours ago. She hadn't missed her keys yet? His conscience began to itch again. A small irritation. Tommy was already dealing. Fuck it. Ruth Nolan had waited this long; a little longer wouldn't matter.

R uth was in the parking lot. The sun had gone, though; it was dark except for the light shed at intervals by the lamps. She was not sure how she'd gotten here. She could feel her legs but had forgotten how to operate them. She heard a man's laugh from somewhere behind her.

"Time to go, Red," he said. Someone grabbed Ruth's arm and nearly yanked it out of its socket.

*Hurts*, she thought, but all that came out was a grunt of pain.

Then her arm was looped around her back, under her armpits, and she felt herself being dragged. Ruth wanted to grab the hands that held her and push them back, but her own hands didn't seem to work. Nothing seemed to work. "Let go."

"We are goin'."

"No."

"Yep." A hand gripped her left breast and clamped down. Ruth cried out.

"What you got there, Asa?" A man's voice laughing.

"Just a little something I picked up inside."

"Only way you can get 'em, right? So blind drunk they can't see your ugly face." She heard the crunch of shoes on grit. The voice disappeared. The man was pulling her, harder now. Her bladder leaked.

"Let me go. Have to . . . ladies' room."

"Jesus Christ." They were next to something big. A wheel. A truck. "There's your fuckin' ladies' room. All the privacy you need right there." Ruth's legs started to give way again. "Don't lean on me, you cunt." He shoved her against the truck and Ruth leaned against it, sinking into a squat she could not sustain. As she fell, hot liquid jetted out of her.

"Aww, Christ, you're pissin' all over yourself . . . you got it on my boots! Goddamn whore, you're ruinin' my five-hundred-dollar boots!"

The words ran together in Ruth's ears; all she heard was the man's rage. Then something sharp slammed her hip. She keeled onto her side and it slammed her again, this time in her buttocks. His boot. The pointed toe, sharp, rippled with snakeskin, was poised to strike within inches of her nose. Ruth closed her eyes, waiting for the impact. Instead she heard a woman's voice. She'd heard it before, in the bar.

"For Chrissakes, Asa! We don't have time for that. Just get her wallet. I've got to get home."

Ruth struggled to get away but she felt hands on her, yanking her back, prying open her fist. She heard the woman again.

"No cash. Shit. You can have the credit cards. I'm taking the ring."

"She owes me for these boots."

"Whatever, I'm outta here."

Ruth heard a rustle, then the hiss of a zipper. He had her by the hair again, pulled her face to his crotch. She turned her head, but he twisted her by the hair and slapped her. Ruth couldn't breathe. She began to thrash, looking for escape. He pulled her head back and began to thrust himself into her mouth. She bit. He yelled and the grip on her head loosened. Her gorge rose and she vomited. Everything went black.

# CHAPTER 24

When Tommy went off shift, Casey rose from the table, trying to hold the whoop of glee inside. He was up nearly three grand. Shit, if he totaled everything from the minute Belva wiped him out in his trailer this morning to now, he was up nearly four grand. What a day. What a fucking incredible day. His head hurt, his leg hurt—but he could send a fat envelope to Emily and still have more than enough to keep himself going for a while.

He passed the restaurant on his way to cash in his chips. The smell of roasted meat got his juices going. As soon as he cashed in, he'd come back here and have himself a king-sized prime rib, bloody, and a pile of fat greasy fries.

"You all done, Casey? The night's still young," the man behind the counter said as Casey plunked down his box of chips.

"Yep. All done." He grinned. "You're not getting any of this back."

As Casey dug for his wallet, his fingers hit the Jaguar keys. Shit, he'd forgotten all about that woman. Where the hell was she?

He limped toward the bar. Every booth was filled, but the Jaguar lady wasn't in any of them. The tables were busy but she wasn't there either. He waved to the meaty blond woman working the bar.

"Hey, Case. A nice cold one?"

"Not right now, Kit. I'm lookin' for a woman."

"Look no further, darlin'." Laughter danced in Kitty's brown eyes.

Casey grinned back. "Now why would I want to piss off that husband of yours?"

"You might not, but I wouldn't mind—it'd get him off the couch." Her eyes flicked up the bar to where a man was signaling for a drink. She nodded at him and reached for a shot glass.

"I'm looking for a particular woman. Red hair, thin. Big sunglasses. She was wearing a dungaree jacket and a black skirt."

The easy grin fell from Kitty's face. "That's your girlfriend?"

"No. Nothing like that. Got something of hers."

Kitty had lost interest. She inclined her head toward the exit and started to turn away. "Walked out of here a while ago with some trucker. If you could call what she was doing walking."

A few minutes later, Casey stood outside the casino entrance surveying the dark parking lot, counting the reasons he should just go back in, drop the keys in the lost and found, and eat his dinner. He was hungry. What Ruth Nolan did was none of his business. But the bills in his pocket bulged against his thigh, and his conscience squirmed. All the things he'd ignored earlier came back to him: her shaky hands, the carelessness in the bar, laying all her credit cards out for the world to see, the way she'd slumped against the cash machine when he and Lenny walked away with wads of her cash.

"Shit, lady, where the hell are you?" he muttered into the dusty heat that settled over the parked cars, semis, and giant blue bison. Screams of laughter split through the roof of the casino and roared behind him as the roller coaster completed its loop. A couple brushed past him and headed, hands entwined and laughing, to a car parked near the line of semis. Casey shrugged and turned to go back in.

Then a scream, the girl's, jerked him back. Half sorry he'd heard her, he limped in the direction of the couple's voices, now raised in argument, over by the line of cars closest to the semis.

"She's drunk, is all," said the man.

"We can't leave her like that. What if she's hurt?"

"Well, I'm not touchin' her."

Casey came up behind them as the woman kneeled down to get a closer look at the heap on the pavement. He knew it would be Ruth Nolan even before he saw the thin white legs and short red hair in a shaft of light cast by a nearby lamppost.

"Jesus Christ."

"You know her?" The man, a thickset guy with a goatee and a mouthful of brown teeth, twisted his face in disgust.

"Kind of . . ."

The words were out of Casey's mouth before he knew he was going to say them. The rest of his body, in fact, was half turned toward the casino, away from the stink of puke, piss, and sweat rising from the woman at their feet.

"Great. She's all yours." The man grabbed the girl's arm and pulled her, but she twisted away.

"Do you want some help? Should we go get help inside?"

Casey liked the girl for that, for giving a shit. She looked like a million other girls, bare belly slipping over the sides of her jeans, tattoos on one of the tits squeezing out of her tank top, but her eyes were soft under all the makeup. Getting help would only complicate things, though. The security folks would want explanations: how he knew her, where his money had come from all of a sudden, nothing he wanted to get into. He shook his head at the girl.

"That's okay. Thanks."

The man grabbed his girlfriend around the shoulders and pulled her away. "It's all yours, man."

"Now what, Jaguar lady?"

Her skirt was ripped and soaking, and she'd lost a shoe and her sunglasses somewhere along the line, but she still wore the denim jacket. He squatted and pushed the hair away from Ruth's face. A fresh bruise was rising on her cheekbone; blood mixed with vomit still leaked from the corner of her mouth. Gingerly, he touched her shoulder and squeezed. "C'mon, wake up."

Nothing.

How bad was she hurt? He leaned closer and felt her breath on his hand. He squeezed the shoulder again and shook it gently. "C'mon." A low moan slipped from her mouth, and her body curled into the fetal position. The faker wobbled. He pulled himself up, leaned against the lamppost. He'd have a hell of a time picking her up. Dead weight. Slippery too.

What a fucking mess. His fingers itched to drop the keys and walk away, but it would be just his luck if she woke up remembering his face instead of the asshole who actually left her here. Everyone here knew him. Besides, what if some idiot drove right over her? Ruth had nearly run him down just hours before not a hundred feet away. Because of her, his pockets were loaded with money. Casey sighed. No steak for him tonight.

He'd seen guys in worse shape. Hell, *he'd* been in worse shape. She'd be heavy, though. He unbuckled his belt, leaned down, and looped the leather strap around Ruth's belly. Then he leaned back against the lamppost for balance and pulled, lifting her up and toward him. Her hands flayed out wildly and she began to retch. He tipped forward and almost fell on top of her but jerked back just in time. He wrapped both arms around her chest to keep her from sliding down and struggled to breathe.

"C'mon, lady. Help me out here."

Somehow he held on and turned them slowly in the direction of the Jaguar, parked clear across the parking lot somewhere near the buffalo, if he remembered right. Ruth's head slumped to his shoulder and she half moaned, half mumbled something he couldn't

understand, but at least she was vertical. He cast his eye around for
her purse, not really expecting to find it. Casey heaved another sigh.

"Okay, lady. Let's take it one step at time."

An hour later, the Jaguar shuddered to a halt in front of Casey's
trailer and the rusted-out El Camino parked next to it.

"We're here," Casey said. There was no response from the passenger side of the car where Ruth slumped, unconscious.

He sighed and pushed open the door on the driver's side. A long,
crazy, goddamned day and it wasn't over yet. He paused, half in,
half out of the Jaguar. Maybe he should get Lenny to help. He
glanced in the direction of the old man's trailer and caught sight of
Belva's huge green double-wide, flanked by her beat-up brown Lin-
coln. Shit. Belva. How was he going to explain the Jag? How was
he going to explain Ruth? Belva could smell cash a hundred miles
away. He cupped his hand over the money bulging in his pocket,
thinking of the way Belva had swooped down that morning and
emptied his wallet. No way he'd let her near this.

"No . . . no . . . Robbie . . ." He saw Ruth's mouth moving, but her
eyes were still closed. He stretched to her shoulder, shaking it gently.

"You awake over there?"

Ruth erupted. She flung her body against the door with a stran-
gled cry, half sob, half scream. Her eyes were open now and her
fingers scrabbled against the door.

"Hang on, hang on." Casey pushed himself up and limped as
quickly as he could around the car to the passenger side. When he
reached for Ruth, she kicked out her legs and thrashed, now diving
for the other side of the car and kicking the faker practically out from
underneath him. He stifled the groan of pain and frustration that
rose up inside. Yelling wouldn't help. She was already scared enough.

"It's okay. It's okay. I'm not going to hurt you." The words did
not have to mean anything. She wasn't listening to the words. She
had to trust his voice. He kept speaking, low and calm, stooping to

peer into the car but not reaching for her. Her body finally loosened and she stopped thrashing.

"Let's try again, okay? I'm going to help you. Can you hold on to my arm?" Her head sank to the driver's seat. "No, don't pass out, babe. Ruth, right? Ruth, stay awake for me now, just till we get inside." He reached in and tugged gently on her arm until she was sitting upright once again in the passenger seat, her head tilted back, eyes closing again.

"Just a little more," Casey said, reaching down and pulling her legs around until her bare feet hung out the side of the car. Gripping the top of the car for balance, he guided her out. He glanced at the steps to the trailer and then back at Ruth. For a skinny woman, she was pretty heavy.

"Work with me, lady," he said. Limping, he half carried, half dragged Ruth through the sand to the trailer door.

# CHAPTER 25

Casey watched the night recede from the steps of his trailer. He pulled the nearly empty pack of cigarettes from his shirt pocket and plucked one of the two remaining joints he'd been saving. He shivered as he lit it. The cool night air was the only thing keeping him awake, that and the fact that he had nowhere to lay his head. He inhaled and held the smoke in his lungs, glancing over his shoulder through the screen door. In the dull glow of the overhead light, he could make out Ruth's form on the little fold-down bed. Her breathing was ragged and heavy but she was finally still and mostly clean. He'd done the best he could with an old washcloth, even though she'd fought him. Then she'd sobbed, not like a drunk, but like a kid in pain.

What had he been thinking? Didn't matter. She was here now. He had to look at the situation as if it were a card he'd been dealt. Like showing eleven at the blackjack table. The next move could make him richer, or leave him where he was. He'd figure it out quick enough and send her on her way.

The edge of the doorjamb dug into his back. He shifted and tried to focus. It had been a long time since he'd greeted the dawn this sober and this tired. Shit, he might as well do something useful. He glanced at the Jaguar. She'd need some clothes.

He sucked once more on the joint before pinching it out. He pulled himself up, stretched, and limped down the steps.

Even in the shadows and layered with dust, the Jaguar looked out of place next to his rusted-out, flat-tired El Camino. Casey sighed and patted the car's roof.

"We've both seen better days," he said. Then he opened the driver's door and looked around.

Something gleamed from the floor in the weak interior light. A BlackBerry. He reached down and put it in his shirt pocket. What else? A leather briefcase in the back, wedged tightly behind the driver's seat. He abandoned the briefcase and hunted around the car, looking for luggage, something fresh she might be able to wear. Nothing. He should try the trunk. Then the jingle for the morning news sounded from one of the trailers nearby. An early riser and his radio.

Casey straightened and scanned the shadows formed by the other trailers, the RVs parked in the adjacent camping area and the building that housed the café, public shower, and washing machines. The sky was already paling where it met the edge of the desert. Soon Lenny would fire up the grill and the old people who liked to walk a little when it was still cool would get up and take a turn around the campground. He didn't want to explain himself or the Jaguar to the busybodies.

"Fuck it," he said, climbing out of the car. She'd have to put up with whatever he could find.

The slam of a screen door went off like a gunshot in Ruth's ear. She jerked up and then convulsed in waves of nausea.

"I don't think you've got anything left," said a man standing somewhere nearby. "Just in case, here." His wiry forearm thrust a plastic garbage pail toward her. The smell of old coffee grounds, sour milk, and mold rose from the bottom.

She buried her face in her hands and pulled her knees to her chest. The sudden pain made her gasp. Every breath hurt.

The pail disappeared. "What you need is water. Better yet, a nice cold Coke."

Her eyes were so dry they stung; her lids seemed stuck halfway. The man slouched against a counter less than two feet away in a black T-shirt, damp hair pushed back off his face. He lifted a mug to his lips and stared back at her over the top of the stained rim. She was naked. She hugged her knees with one hand and reached behind for a sheet. There must be a sheet.

"You kicked it off. Here." The man set his mug down on the chipped surface of the counter and stooped. A bit of steel showed between the hem of his jeans and a black shoe. Images returned to her in fragments. That metal leg lying on pavement. Screams of rage. A kick that she felt all over again. She snatched the clump of material from him and backed against the wall, trembling uncontrollably.

"Easy. I'm not the enemy." He seemed to be looking for something more to say but then he shrugged, picked up his mug, and leaned back again.

"Who are you, then?" She tasted bile.

"Your guardian angel." One side of his mouth lifted in a lopsided grin that revealed a small gap between his front teeth.

Ruth sat up, pulling the sheet tight around her. Where was the door to this place? It looked like some kind of camper: old brown paneling, chipped vinyl, everything—sink, refrigerator, cheap laminate counter—in miniature and crammed into the same small space. There. The door. Right next to the microwave. She glanced at the man again and then back at the door. "You won't get far dressed in a sheet," said the man.

"Give me back my clothes."

"Lady, you don't want those clothes, believe me."

"You can't keep me here."

"You think I want to? You're free to go whenever you want to. As far as I'm concerned, the sooner the better."

Ruth stared at him, not sure of the next step. He looked equally uncertain.

"Look, first things first," he said. He put the mug down on the counter, limped over to a laundry bag just inside the door, and began rummaging around.

Ruth sagged against the wall. She blinked and found she could not fully open her left eye.

"You should probably put some ice on that shiner." He was in front of her again, holding out a dark bundle. "In fact, you should probably see a doctor. You might have a concussion or something."

Ruth watched him lay the bundle next to her, men's clothes and a faded, but clean, towel. "Who are you?" she asked again.

"You don't need to know my name. We're not going to be lifelong buds." His back was to her now; he rooted around below the counter.

Ruth glanced again toward the flimsy door. She could be out of here in two steps. She grabbed the sheet and started to push herself up, but pain shot through her ribs, arms, and legs. She fell back; her breath seemed trapped in her chest.

"Yes!" The man turned to face her holding a can of Coke. "Thought I had one of these in there. Nothing better for a hangover except maybe a beer. Even have a few ice cubes." He pulled out a child-sized plastic tray from the miniature freezer and set it on the counter.

Robbie drank Coke in the morning. He would never try coffee. *Smells like skunk, Ruthie. How can you drink that?* She clutched the sheet and tried again to stand.

"Where's my car?" She tried to breathe around the pain.

"Relax, Ruth, relax. It's just outside. A little low on gas, maybe, but it's okay. Here, try this."

How did he know her name? Ruth's hand shook but she took a

small sip of Coke. She waited for the bubbles to burst before swallowing.

"That's it." He picked up his mug.

Ruth felt soda dribbling down her chin but she didn't care. "You're the man from the parking lot," she said.

"The one you ran over, not the one who roughed you up."

"You took my money."

"You owed me, don't you think?"

Ruth eyed his legs, now hidden in his jeans. "Fixed it up pretty fast."

He glanced down at his left leg and then back up at Ruth. "Good enough to get around until I can take it to the VA for permanent repairs."

The VA. So he was a veteran. He'd been broken but he'd come home. He looked so much older than Robbie but here he was, nearly whole and still alive. Ruth forced herself to ask. "Your leg, did you lose it in Iraq?"

His eyes narrowed; a hard smile formed. "Were you about to thank me for my service? Don't bother. It wasn't this war, it was the first Gulf war. Operation Desert Storm."

Through the fog of pain came the facts that Ruth associated with that war: Robbie was six and a half; he'd lost both his front teeth the week the bombing started. Don uncorked champagne to celebrate the sale that put RyCom over the ten-million-dollar mark. She'd gotten home late and forgotten to put the tooth-fairy money under Robbie's pillow. Ruth looked down at the soda in her hands.

"Forgot about that one?" the man said. "Don't worry. You're not alone. Let's move on."

His eyes, some shade between blue and gray, flickered with a light that could be laughter or derision. The Coke was nearly full, but Ruth couldn't drink any more. She glanced at the bundle of clothes and the towel next to her. When she looked up she found her computer bag in the corner by the door.

"Where's my purse?"

"Gone."

"Why should I believe that?"

He set the mug on the counter without taking his eyes off hers. "Because I didn't take it."

"Right." She held his gaze, but it dawned on her that he wouldn't have brought her here if he'd taken everything. As the seconds ticked by she knew she wasn't fighting him as much as she was trying to beat back the thoughts of Robbie at six and a flood of new images from the evening before. The salty rim of a margarita glass, a wobbly walk across a crowded room, fingers biting into her arm like a pit bull's jaws. And then.

"Yeah, right. Because here's what happened, Ruth. You went back into the bar after we left you and drank yourself into a coma. Then some asshole followed you and took you down."

Ruth shook her head.

"I found you lying in your own puke in the parking lot."

Ruth flinched. "Stop."

"Your bag was long gone. But you can't blame me. If it weren't for me, you'd have been run over before anyone saw you out there."

"Stop, I said!" Ruth hurled the can of Coke at Casey, but he leaned to the side and it clattered to the floor.

"This place isn't much but it's mine. Show some respect." His eyes took on a flinty look, then softened into uncertainty. "Look. I don't know how to say this, but you may want to know, I don't think he . . . your underwear was still on. Didn't look like—"

"Stop. Please stop." Ruth couldn't look at him another minute.

"Sorry." He sounded relieved, and tired. "We've both had a rough night. I'm going to go get another cup of coffee and let you get yourself together. Shower's in there." He jerked his thumb toward the closet. "Works okay, not great. You can use the public shower if you prefer."

He looked at her and Ruth looked back, silent.

"You're welcome," he said. "You're a treat, lady, a real treat." A few limping steps and he was gone.

The bang of the screen door reverberated through Ruth's brain. She had to calm down. God, she smelled. The stink was alien, leaching out her pores. She pushed herself into a standing position, one hand clutching the sheet to her body and the other leaning against the wall for support.

The trailer, though shabby, had not quite surrendered to the heat, dust, and grime. She saw pockets of discipline and care. Hangers held two unwrinkled Hawaiian shirts on a short rod protruding from the wall. Cotton shirts were folded neatly on a shelf to the side, and two pairs of thick-soled black sneakers faced the wall below as though awaiting orders. A wall rack held old magazines: *The Atlantic, The Sun, Rolling Stone, Mother Jones.* She picked up an issue to look for an address label, but all she found was a sticker: *Las Vegas Public Library Copy. Not for Circulation.*

When she turned, she found herself eye level with a shelf of books above the bed. One of them was for children, *Where the Sidewalk Ends.* Robbie had loved that one. Ruth could remember his weight in her lap, his chubby fingers pointing to the pictures, the smell of his scalp, the way she would settle her chin on the top of his head so that she could sniff more deeply. He would twist in her lap and command her, "Stop tickling!"

She grabbed the clothes Casey had left her and let the sheet drop to the floor. Then she recalled the look he'd given her before he left. *You're welcome*, he'd said in the same terse tone her grandmother used when she caught Ruth neglecting her manners.

A dingy washcloth was folded on top of the little refrigerator. Ruth dropped the clothes back on the bed and held it in the trickle produced by the kitchen sink faucet. She stooped over, head pounding. On her hands and knees, she began to clean up her mess.

———————

She awake?" Lenny leaned down on the counter so his face was just across from Casey's. He was trying and failing to whisper. Casey glanced over his shoulder at the white-haired couple sharing the paper and an order of pancakes at the other end of the counter. They didn't look up.

"More or less." Casey was still pissed. Here he was, no sleep all night long, had to beg a shower from Lenny and she throws god-damn Coke all over his place. "Heat this up again, will you, Len?"

"Whatcha gonna do with her?"

"Jesus, Len, for the hundredth time already, I don't fuckin' know."

A bell sounded from the back entrance and Lenny snapped to attention. He began to move toward the older couple, wiping the counter as he went. Belva appeared in the door between the grill and the back room, wearing her Marilyn wig today, a shiny blue blouse hanging over the top of her stretch pants. Her eyes darted up to the other customers, dismissed them, and then speared Casey.

"So, you got company." She waddled from the doorway and stood in front of the counter.

"Yeah." Casey sipped from his mug and set it down again, next to a plate streaked with the remains of two eggs sunny side up, a side of bacon, and two pancakes drenched in blueberry syrup.

"You givin' away my food again, Lenny?" Belva barked.

"I can buy my own food," Casey said.

"That's good to know. How long she stayin', or is it 'he'?" A smirk planted itself on Belva's fat face.

"Not your business."

"Everything's my business at Cactus Gardens, you know that," said Belva, settling her fanny on the stool Lenny kept behind the counter. "You move another person into that trailer and your rent goes up. I'm not runnin' a charity here."

Sooner or later, everything got around to the charity she was not running, Casey thought. Usually sooner.

His head was beginning to pound and his breakfast was not sitting all that well. He stood up to pay but paused. This was no time to pull a wad of cash out of his pocket where Belva could get a good look at it. "Need a couple of things," he said, turning his back on her and walking down the single aisle of shelves sparsely furnished with packages of junk food, toiletries, and laundry supplies. He grabbed some toothpaste, a toothbrush, and a newspaper, and was working his fingers in his pocket, loosening a twenty from the roll, when Belva froze him with a shout.

"You've got mail."

"What the hell . . ." The words died in Casey's throat. Belva fanned herself with a couple of white envelopes. He stumped back, laid the toiletries and his money on the counter, and grabbed the envelopes out of her hand.

"When did those come?"

"Yesterday. One of 'em's from the VA. Might be a disability check, which would come in handy for both of us, wouldn't it?"

Casey stuffed the mail in his back pocket, grabbed his purchases, and made for the door.

"Aren't you going to thank me?"

"For what? Giving me what's mine?"

He nearly ran down the old man who was in the doorway, his hand on his wife's elbow. "Watch out, son, you'll be old too one day."

Belva's laughter followed him out the door. He was sick of the woman, sick of her bullshit and the whole crap fest she ran out here. By the time he got back to his trailer, he was sweating into his clean shirt, but he couldn't go inside yet. Ruth was in the shower. He could hear the water. He reached for his last cigarette and saw that it was crushed. Shit. No way would he go back in there now, though. He'd have to wait until Belva crawled back under her rock. He sat on the steps and pulled out the first envelope.

The VA again. The new faker was taking forever to get approved. He balled up the letter in his hand. Same old shit: His request was being processed.

Casey peered at the second envelope and felt a thump in his chest, like a blow. He stared at the familiar handwriting: *Mr. Casey MacInerney, Cactus Gardens, Jean, NV.* He did not need to check the postmark but he did anyway: Jersey City, New Jersey. The last time he'd opened an envelope like this one, a photograph of a young girl with serious eyes and missing teeth had fallen out. She'd been seven then. Ten years ago. He wiped the sweat off his hands on his jeans. Then he reached in his pocket for his penknife and slit the top of the envelope.

Inside were a couple of newspaper clippings and a short note on a square of plain white paper: *Thought you'd like to see how your daughter is turning out. She's been asking about you.* There was another line squeezed below, as though the writer had decided at the last minute to add it. *It's been too long. I'm not getting any younger and neither is she. Come home. I'll handle her mother. Moira's tough but she wants Em to know her dad.*

Casey unfolded the clippings. The first showed a photograph of a long-legged girl on a basketball floor, airborne, a look of intensity on her broad face as the ball left her hands. *Emily MacInerney*, the caption read, *a junior, scored the tie-breaking shot for St. Anne's.* The sister school to St. Francis, his old school. He could almost hear the squeak of his black Chuck Cons as he ran down the floor, playing point just like the girl in the picture.

The note was not signed, but Casey knew the compact script belonged to Katie O'Brien, Emily's grandmother, once his mother-in-law, still the woman who helped raise him. She'd written a few times before, asking if he was okay. She never said anything about the money or Emily and nothing about Moira, leaving it up to him to ask. Sweat crawled down his spine. He thought of the letters he'd written and torn up.

He scanned the other clipping. No picture this time, just an announcement of kids on the honor roll and Katie's scrawl in the margin, *Takes after her parents.* Sweat from his fingers darkened the thin newsprint and smeared the headline. Carefully, he put the articles and the note back into the envelope. He held it, square in his hands, and tried to imagine walking back into the house he'd left over a decade earlier.

He pictured himself standing at the foot of the steps leading up to the old frame house in the row of the brick ones being snapped up by wealthy young couples. Katie's lace curtains marked the window of the living room where no one ever sat. She'd be in her kitchen at the scratched Formica table where, as a boy, he and her own children, Mike and Moira, used to sit by the window eating peanut butter and jelly sandwiches, tossing crumbs out the window just to see the pigeons fight over them.

The refrigerator, the same gold color as the table and the oven across from it, would be plastered with lists on scraps of paper and children's drawings careening at odd angles after slipping from the fruit-shaped magnets she'd used to hold them. This was Katie's favorite place, the place where she held court, kept an eye on things out the window, and could keep a hand on both telephone and whatever was cooking on the stove. "Come into my office," she'd say to a child with a scraped knee, or a neighbor with an unfaithful husband. She probably said the same thing to his grandmother the day they arranged for Casey to live with the O'Briens when it became clear the cancer would kill her. Band-Aids were in the drawer next to the sink, and a bottle of Jameson was kept ready on the top shelf for adult emergencies.

The kitchen had been empty the last time Casey entered it, fresh out of the third or fourth rehab. He'd looked around him in the dim light cast by the fixture over the sink. Katie, her husband Brendan, Moira, and Emily were all asleep. Mike, the beginning and end of everything good in Casey's life, had been dead for years, but Casey had heard him that night, taunting him, telling him to go ahead and leave, he didn't belong there.

Casey left no note, nothing for the sleeping people to find when they woke up. Instead, he'd yanked Katie's bottle of Jameson off the shelf, emptied the billfold in the drawer where she kept her "mad money," and limped out with everything he needed stuffed into a blue gym bag.

The low persistent growl of the air conditioners protruding from all the double-wides called him back to the present. Sweat poured from his hairline down to his neck. The day suddenly stretched before him. The only new thing was Ruth, and he'd send her on her way as soon as he could. Then hours to go in the tin can he called home until he could get over to the casino, settle at the blackjack table, and play until another day dawned. He shifted the envelope from one hand to the other, wiped his palm on his jeans, then pulled out the clippings and the note and read them again.

*She's been asking about you*, Katie had written.

Maybe it was the heat that was making him think about things he'd not let himself think in years. Or maybe it was the lump of cash in his pocket, giving him a strange kind of courage.

Instead of a few hundred bucks, he could give Emily a couple thousand, something to put away for college or something else she needed. He could, if he wanted, bring it to her himself. He could fly to New Jersey, knock on the front door of the old town house, and track her down. Katie would help him; she all but said so in the clippings. He could hear what she sounded like, search her face for any traces of his own. He wouldn't stay; he knew he could not buy his way back into his kid's life. At the same time, he wouldn't arrive empty-handed. The cash he'd been sending these past few years proved he still thought of her and cared about her. Maybe it was enough to buy him a few hours with her. A few hours would be enough to know if they had any more to talk about. Hope, sudden and frightening, opened up in him. For a moment he did not recognize the feeling. The idea of going had already taken hold, though. If nothing else, he told himself, going away would get him out of this hellhole. That's right. Fuck the VA and fuck Belva Pointer. It was time. Maybe he'd catch one of Emily's basketball games. He shook his head. Not in summer; school would be out. He stood up. Fuck it. He didn't have to plan every step right now. All he had to do was do what he did every day in the casino. Show up. After that, anything could happen.

R uth fumbled for the faucet and turned off the tepid drip from Casey's shower. She freed herself from the mildewed curtain clinging to her shins, then grabbed the towel he'd left her. She had no strength for revulsion. She was wet, she needed to be dry. She was naked, she would put on the clothes that he'd laid out for her. There was relief in the absence of choices.

As Ruth pulled a maroon shirt over her head and stepped into absurdly long black shorts, her cell phone sounded from somewhere beyond the bathroom door. Neal. He had his own ringtone. By now, he and Terri probably knew Ruth had taken the ashes from the funeral home. Maybe he'd gone into her house and had seen the mess she'd left behind in her rush to leave.

A tapping began on the thin folding door.

"Everything okay in there?" The man was back. Her heart still pounding, Ruth ran her fingers through her wet hair and slicked it back behind her ears. She could not go back to San Diego. Not yet. It was the only thing she knew for certain.

"Yes," she said. She slid open the door.

He looked her up and down, the corner of his mouth lifting in the beginning of a grin.

"Not exactly your size, huh?"

"They're fine," said Ruth, hunched over, arms folded against her belly to keep the shorts from sliding down.

"Got some things for you—if you promise you won't throw them at me." His grin spread but his eyes looked guarded.

Ruth tried to smile. She needed him. At least for now.

"You're safe," she said. Then, "I need to sit down." She sank onto the bed as he stepped aside.

He dug a small tube of toothpaste and plastic toothbrush from his pocket and set them on the bed next to her, then pulled her phone out of his other pocket and handed it to her. "I found this in your car. It was ringing a few seconds ago. Thought about answering, but that seemed like a bad idea."

"I don't want it."

"It's been ringing a lot."

"I told you, I don't want it." She did not look at him. He set the phone on the bed next to the toiletries.

He cleared his throat. "Listen, lady. Ruth." His voice trailed off. Ruth glanced up. "You know my name," she said. "What's yours?"

"Casey, not that it matters." He dug his hands into his pants pockets and peered down at her. "So, what's your plan?"

"I don't have one."

"Maybe you should see a doctor."

"No, I just need some more sleep."

"Here's the thing. You can't stay here. Not that I'm not enjoying your company, but it just isn't a good time."

Ruth looked down at her body, adrift in the baggy clothes. She needed to think, but her mind, too, was submerged beneath layers of pain and fatigue.

"I've got no money. I can't even put gas in the car."

"I bet whoever's been trying to call you can help with all that," he said.

*No.* She would not let Neal see her like this. There was Terri. Terri had all her credit card numbers; she'd know what to do. One call would do it. She'd wait for a time when Terri wasn't likely to pick up. She'd leave a message on her voice mail. That way Ruth would not have to explain things she could not even explain to herself.

"No," she said aloud, her voice stronger now that she'd been using it. She heard a clicking and turned her head toward the sound.

It came from an ancient fan she had not noticed before, but it barely moved the hot air that surrounded her. "Jesus Christ." Casey pushed himself off the counter and wheeled around, tottering a little on the left side. "I don't need this."

He stared through the screen of the door at something outside the camper. "What's your story, anyway?" he said, a bit more gently, without turning around.

Ruth shook her head. "None of your business."

"The law chasing you?"

"No. Nothing like that."

He shrugged. "Well, I don't suppose it matters. I'm leaving, getting out of this shit hole. I'm in kind of a rush. Stay here if you want. Rent's paid through day after tomorrow."

The BlackBerry sounded again. They both looked at it. "They're giving you another chance," Casey said. "Go ahead, answer it. I'm going to pack." He went into the bathroom and closed the door. She heard the sound of rummaging, the clink of what might be the can of shaving cream she'd seen.

She scooped up the BlackBerry and stared at the display. Her grandmother's number. Neal or Terri must have called her. The phone vibrated in Ruth's palm. She squeezed the phone until the ringing stopped. Out of nowhere, another fragment of the night before came to her. She was curled like a snail on the pavement, expecting another blow, wishing for it. She'd wanted the stranger to punish her.

But deliverance, if it came at all, would not be that easy or that cheap.

She just needed a little more time. She wasn't ready to call her family. She wasn't ready to go home, either. She wheeled around and came eye to eye with the book she'd seen earlier, the one Robbie had loved. She reached up and ran her finger down the spine of the book.

"Hey! Don't touch that. What gives you the right to touch my stuff?" Casey limped toward her and grabbed the book off the shelf.

"Nothing . . . I didn't think . . ." She sank back, unnerved by his reaction. "I'm sorry."

He stuffed the book under his arm silently. His jaw was clenched tight. She could see the muscle working. His shoulders rose and fell as he took first one deep breath, then another. He was trying to calm down.

"Forget it. Just don't do it again, okay?"

Another trickle of sweat coursed down her spine. "Don't worry, I won't."

Ruth watched him until his shoulders relaxed. She would have to figure out her next move somehow. "I need some cash," she said.

He squinted at her and cocked his head slightly, as though she'd lapsed into a foreign language.

"I gave you plenty," she went on. "You don't need all of it. You're walking around just fine."

"Forget it."

"I can't leave here any other way. Look, I'll pay you back. I just need time."

"No."

She needed him to listen. "You can't leave me here."

"That's where you're wrong."

Casey pulled open a door to a narrow closet that Ruth hadn't noticed before. He yanked out a blue canvas bag and began to root through the clothes in a drawer.

"It'll only be a few days. I'll pay interest."

That stopped him. She heard him clear his throat. "Out of curiosity, where would you go if you had the money?"

Ruth looked up to see him holding a blue and lime green Hawaiian shirt. Good. He was asking questions. A negotiation was still possible. She struggled to articulate what it was she wanted. Anywhere but San Diego, was all she could think of. Anywhere she could be a stranger with no one asking questions she couldn't answer, giving her advice she didn't want. A place that didn't taunt her with what she had lost. She just wanted a little more time with Robbie.

She shrugged. "Anywhere but California."

He seemed to make a decision about the shirt. He set it back on the peg and pulled off the one he was wearing, using it to rub the sweat off his chest and arms before letting it drop to the floor. Ruth was startled by the sudden paleness of his skin and by the muscles that webbed beneath it across his shoulders and down his arms. He'd looked too skinny to have much strength. There was something both young and old in the way he hunched forward, self-conscious but defiant about his naked chest. He shrugged into the clean shirt and began to button it.

"Is the Jag yours?" he said.

She nodded.

He stepped to the screen door and stared out. "I've gotta tell you, Ruth, I'm confused. You've got money, but you can't get to it. You've got people who can help you, but you won't call them. Just how would you pay me back?"

"I'll make some calls, get my cards and ID back. In a day or two, I'll be able to walk up to another cash machine and give it to you just as I did before. I could have it wired from my bank to yours if you want."

His lopsided grin revealed the gap between his front teeth. "You have any collateral? Something in that trunk, maybe?"

The thought of this stranger touching the box or any of Robbie's things made her want to strike him. A protective, helpless rage gathered inside her.

"No," she said. "Nothing."

Casey trudged toward Lenny's trailer, his mind working over the opportunity before him. He felt sorry for Ruth in a way he could not quite put his finger on, but the woman kept bringing him luck. Here he was, ready to spend big bucks on a plane ticket and along comes a door-to-door ride and more money. As he made his way past the other trailers, he began to construct a mental checklist. He needed enough gas from Belva's pump to get to Vegas, where they could fill up more cheaply. They'd need a map and some food. Most important, he needed to stay sharp.

He paused on Lenny's doorstep and glanced back at his camper. Its shadow had shifted with the waning sun, even though the air had not yet cooled. This Ruth woman was not thinking clearly, that was for sure, and she sure as hell was hiding something. She'd just about jumped out of her skin when he joked about the things in her car's trunk. Didn't every game hold some unknowns, though? He could handle it.

"What's up, Case?" Lenny stood behind his screen door, a beer in one hand, the television blaring behind him.

"Taking off," Casey said as he pushed open the door. "Just wanted to say so long and ask you to pick up my mail. I'll call you."

"How long you gonna be gone?" Lenny settled himself back into the recliner and gestured for Casey to sit.

Casey shook his head. "No time to visit."

"What about the lady?"

"She doesn't know it yet, but she's my ride."

"You guys getting friendly?"

Casey laughed. "Let's just say we're scratching each other's back."

He was still figuring it out. He'd have to hang on to his money and the keys. She wasn't in good shape now, but once she was, he didn't want her stealing off and leaving him somewhere in the middle of fuckin' Kansas or some other purgatory he had no easy way of leaving.

"It's hot. Got a beer to spare?"

"Over there, help yourself." Lenny pointed to the nook that served as a kitchen, but Casey was already there with his hand on the refrigerator door. "Sure you don't want to sit a bit? Nice and cool here by the AC."

Casey leaned forward and pushed himself up. "No, Len. Gotta go." He remembered the El Camino. "Hey, keep Belva away from my car. All it needs is a tire. You fix it, you can drive it."

Lenny took a long pull from the can. "Where you headed?"

"East. New Jersey." There, he made it real.

"Nearly three thousand miles." Lenny settled back in the recliner, pulled the lever, and stared at Casey over the tops of his bare, gnarled toes. "A long time to be locked up in a car with a crazy woman."

He took another pull from the can and squinted like he was taking aim at something over Casey's shoulder, out beyond the open door. "Better watch out. She already tried to run you over once. She could do it again."

R uth slouched in the passenger seat of the Jaguar watching Casey and a fat, blond-wigged woman argue about gas. Their voices blew through the open window on a gust of hot dusty air.

"You're rippin' me off, Belva. I put exactly ten gallons in there. Give me my change."

"Price has gone up. Didn't have a chance to change the prices on the pumps." She didn't even bother to look at Casey. Instead, she stared at Ruth through the longest set of false eyelashes that Ruth had ever seen.

Ruth stared back through a haze of misgivings and exhaustion. When Casey stalked out earlier—to "take care of a few things," he'd said—she had curled up on the pull-down bed and given up trying to think. If he gave her enough money for gas and a hotel, that would be a start. The heat bore down on her; her throat was dry again and her stomach, empty as it was, still felt as though it were going to erupt. She was still huddled on the bed, her BlackBerry silent and waiting beside her, when Casey limped back into the camper and laid out his proposal to drive together across the country.

"My money, your car." He'd cover her expenses and, when they got where he was going, she'd come up with the cash to pay him back. For this, he would charge a fee: three thousand dollars.

"It's a win-win, Ruth."

She'd spent more money than that in one day for a new suit and a purse. If she said yes, she'd at least have more time to think things through, and she wouldn't be stuck in the trailer he called home. She nodded her assent. "I need shoes," she'd said.

A pair of men's sneakers was produced from the bottom of the closet. When she stood, the waist of the shorts slipped to midthigh. Without speaking, he'd dug through a drawer, pulled out a couple of bandanas, and made her a belt. Then he'd picked up his bag and her computer and walked out the door. Ruth watched Casey wrangle with the fat woman. This was exactly the kind of "win-win" that she helped Don create for his clients: one "winner" always made out better than the other. Casey would control the money, the car keys, and how fast they traveled. He hadn't even said where they were going. All she knew was that they were headed east.

As Casey shook his fist at the fat woman one more time and walked toward the car, another fragment of memory slipped through the wall Ruth had erected around the previous night. She was lying in the camper bed, as his hands washed her down, dabbing gently at the cut on her lip, sluicing water over her breasts, ribs, hips, and thighs and mopping it up with the care, if not the skill, of a nurse. Those same hands had lifted her up from the pavement in the casino parking lot.

The car door opened. Ruth glanced up at him and then at his fingers closing over the steering wheel. She'd made her choice. For now, she was in Casey's hands.

# CHAPTER 26

They were two hours out of Las Vegas when Casey conceded that Lenny had been right. He should have slept one more night in Cactus Gardens and gotten a fresh start in the morning. He squinted in the glare of an oncoming semi, unconsciously easing off the gas and veering away from it.

"Are you all right?" Ruth had said little since she'd agreed to get in the car, but more than once she'd reached for the dashboard as if to brace herself.

"Fine."

"You don't seem fine." Her voice was stronger now. She no longer sounded like she was scratching out each word on sandpaper. She had been sipping constantly on a bottle of water and had even nibbled some crackers he'd picked up at the gas station in Vegas.

"Okay, time for some ground rules. First, lay off the backseat driving."

"I didn't say anything about your driving."

"Next, you don't get to hold the keys until I get my money."

"Don't you think you'll get tired?"

Now she was pissing him off. Casey gripped the wheel and glared through the windshield. A sign popped up out of nowhere: Cedar City, fifteen miles ahead.

"I have to go to the bathroom," Ruth said.

Casey said nothing.

"You've got to be kidding," Ruth said. "You're not even going to stop for that?"

He glanced at her but she was looking straight ahead, her chin thrust out, foot tapping angrily. Good. Let her be mad. At least she shut up.

Twenty minutes later, Casey guided the Jaguar off the highway and into a parking lot shared by a gas station, an all-night hamburger place, and a motel. "See what a good guy I am?" he said.

Ruth shoved open the door before he switched off the ignition and slammed it behind her. Casey watched her take three steps and then stop, flat-footed in the huge sneakers. The crowd at this hour was small. He looked around and saw only a pickup at the gas pumps, and a row of semis sleeping farther back, engines idling.

When Ruth had shuffled into the restroom, Casey pushed open the driver's door, got out, and stretched. His back pinched, and his right leg cramped when he moved. He hadn't driven a car for this long a stretch since he arrived in Nevada a decade ago. The farthest he was used to going was Vegas, where he went once or twice a month for a change of scene and some female company. He had an arrangement with a married cocktail waitress who liked the stump. Casey steadied himself against the Jaguar and reached down to scratch the skin around the edge of the socket. Maybe the waitress would miss him, maybe not. She had other boyfriends.

He stared west but the road beyond the gas pumps was lost in the blackness. He'd landed in Vegas a week after kissing his sleeping daughter good-bye. Emily was five going on six then; he was twenty-five going somewhere, anywhere, where he wouldn't screw up her

life the way he'd screwed up her mother's and his own. Twelve years
of no one asking questions, no one expecting much.

When the engine of the pickup rumbled to life, he watched the
truck nose out of the rest stop and accelerate east, until the night
swallowed it. Soon enough, he'd be following it, all the way to the
place and people he'd left behind a dozen years earlier. Fear coiled
through his gut. He turned away from the road, elbows on the roof
of the Jaguar, and dug his palms into his eyes. If he'd stayed in Cactus Gardens one more night there was a chance he wouldn't have left
at all. When he told himself he was going, he'd let out the desire he'd
buried. The desire for more than a couple of hours with Emily. The
desire to explain things that could never be explained. The desire
for absolution. The odds were way against him, but it was too late to
stop now; all he had was the hope that had blindsided him when he
read Katie's note. Hope, he knew, was the last resort of desperate
and very bad card players. Nothing good ever came of it.

From the entrance to the restroom, Ruth saw Casey bowed over
the roof of the car and pulled back into the shadows. She shivered; the chill in the night air shocked her after the heat of the day,
but instinct made her wait. To surprise him when he was low might
set him off; she wouldn't want to appear weak if she were in his shoes.

*You* are *in his shoes*. It was the kind of thing Robbie would say. She
almost felt him here. *Go ahead*, she wanted to tell him. *Tease me*. She
would laugh, and think of something silly to say back, something
she'd rarely let herself do when he was growing up. She wanted to
see his pudgy thirteen-year-old face collapsed in laughter. She wanted
to hear that squawking teenage guffaw that used to sear her nerves.

"Hey, Ruth. You still in there?" Casey's voice scattered the
echoes of Robbie's laughter. He couldn't see her standing in the
shadows of the entrance.

"Cold, huh?" he asked her as she made her way back to the car.

"A little." Ruth hugged herself, rubbing her hands up and down her bare arms.

"Want some coffee or something?" His voice was gruff, as though reminding both of them that he was still in charge—but she could hear a little gentleness in it too.

Ruth nodded. "Just some tea and some more crackers. Water too, doesn't matter if it is bottled or not. I'll wait in the car."

She saw him squinting as if he had not heard her correctly. "I'm not waiting on you. If you want something, come and get it yourself."

She did want something to eat and to drink. She couldn't believe it but she did. She looked down at her clothes, the oversize shoes. When she looked up, he frowned with impatience.

"Shit, Ruth, you think anybody in a place like this is going to care what you look like?"

A flame ignited in Ruth as he trudged away from her toward the restaurant. Maybe he liked humiliating her, watching her clomp around like a clown. Maybe part of him enjoyed her tagging behind him, her lip swollen, one eye black and nearly shut. Ruth would have to look out for herself. She shuffled into the glare of fluorescent lights, toward the smell of deep fryers and grease burning on the grill. She ignored the stares of the woman behind the counter when she asked for a large tea. Then she sat at one of the orange plastic tables bolted to the floor.

Ruth saw belated understanding fill Casey's eyes when he set the tray of food down in front of her. He winced at the sight of her swollen face and then he looked around. The waitress looked back, standing with her hands on her hips as if she were waiting for him to make a move she didn't like.

"Those bruises look pretty bad in this light."

"They make you look worse," Ruth said.

"I never touched you."

"She doesn't know that. She'd call the police in a heartbeat if I stood up and screamed for help." A grim satisfaction warmed Ruth. She reached for the paper cup of hot water and the tea bag.

"You won't do that. It would screw things up for you too, wouldn't it?" His voice was steady, unworried. Good for him.

Casey pushed a bag of fries toward her. Ruth put one in her mouth. Her stomach suddenly craved more: more of the salty, greasy skins, the hot potato pulp inside. She reached for the bag.

"Look, we need to talk," she said.

Casey unwrapped a burger. Half of it disappeared into his mouth in one bite. "What about?" he said between chews.

Ruth's stomach churned. Her appetite sparked surprise, then guilt. She shouldn't feel hunger and thirst when Robbie could feel nothing. She focused on Casey. "Our agreement, for one thing. How much money do you have? Is it enough to get us wherever we're going, or are we going to be relying on you having another accident in a parking lot somewhere?"

"I've got enough."

"Good. Because I need some clothes and a pair of sunglasses."

She picked up the last two fries and nibbled while she talked. "Let's be reasonable, okay? I've already agreed to pay you back for every dime you spend. On top of that, you're getting three thousand dollars. Robbery, if you ask me."

"That's my price." He leaned back and crossed his arms across his chest.

"I've already agreed to it, haven't I?"

The French fries were gone. She glanced at the tray. Nothing but his empty wrapper, his Dr Pepper, and a couple of packets of sugar. She grabbed both of the little brown envelopes, emptied them into her tea, and looked up. "Is there any cream?"

Casey shook his head. His arms were still folded but she knew she had his attention. "What else?"

"You can't drive straight through all by yourself. You've got to either stop and sleep or let me drive."

"You're not driving."

"Fine. Then plan on spending some money for motels. Running water, no roaches. And no smoking in my car."

He shook his head. "I won't have a dime left."

"What does it matter? I told you I'd pay you back."

"Where's all that money come from, Ruth?"

"All that matters is that I have it."

"Not right now you don't. And for all I know the car isn't even yours."

Ruth put down her tea and held his gaze. "I thought you were a gambler."

She saw his eyes narrow as he tried to guess where she was going with this. "I've been known to play a little."

"So, shut up and play." She lifted the paper cup to her lips and swallowed, trying not to wince when the tea seeped into the cuts in her lips.

Over the rim of the foam cup she saw he was staring back at her. Then his mouth split into a grin that showed the small gap between his front teeth. He slapped the table in front of him and stood up. "Okay. Let's go."

The steering wheel of the Jaguar barely vibrated under Casey's fingers; the twin blasts from the radio and the air conditioner were not enough to keep him awake. His eyelids were as heavy as old Army blankets and itched like them too. He rubbed his right eye, glanced at the dashboard clock, and shook his head. No point in looking for a motel now; the night was half over. He glanced at Ruth but she was asleep in her seat, huddled like she was cold. Maybe it wasn't a good idea to keep the air on. He peered at the dashboard, trying to find the controls, but his attention was caught by a sign up ahead. An exit. No rest stop but probably another one of those ranch-only exits, a quiet place he could pull over for a while, take a leak, close his eyes.

A few minutes later, Casey turned off the ignition. The night held its breath. Quietly, he opened the door, limped a few feet into the darkness, and unzipped his fly.

"So long, Dr Pepper," he thought. He'd been having a silent conversation with himself since they'd gassed up the car and left the rest stop behind, armed with a packet of extra-strength ibuprofen for the headache she was giving him and a map he'd picked up in the gas station. They would get to a town big enough for a Walmart or Target and he'd get a real map, an atlas or something. He nodded into the shadows beyond the dirt road and zipped up his fly.

Ruth was still asleep when he opened the driver's door and set-tled back into the seat, lowering the back as far as it would go. Not bad. He turned toward her. Her breathing was heavy but regular, not the tortured gasping of the night before. The alcohol was long out of her now. She must be feeling a little better.

He leaned up on one elbow and watched her breathe. Her small breasts were lost inside that old shirt of his. She was nearly forty-seven, he remembered from her license. The hair on her temples looked dusty compared to the bottled red of the rest of it but her body was as skinny as a kid's. One of her arms angled out of its maroon sleeve. The nails at the ends of her fingers were chipped and red, like scabs. She was a mess, that was for sure. He had to hand it to her, though, she'd straightened his ass out. "Shut up and play," she'd said.

She shivered in her sleep. He glanced into the backseat for his bag. He reached behind the passenger seat, unzipped the bag, and felt inside for something warm. There, his jacket. He yanked it out and spread it over Ruth's shoulders. She rolled away from him, clutching it around her without waking. He nodded at her sleeping form, then leaned back in his own seat. In a few minutes, he began to snore.

T he snoring woke her. For a few seconds Ruth thought she was
in her bedroom in San Diego, Neal deep into the sleep that
never failed him. Reflex took over; without opening her eyes she
thrust her finger toward the sound to prod him. The motion opened
up the pain in her hip and tore back the blanket of oblivion that
had, for a few hours, numbed her.

She turned her head and blinked at the stranger sleeping in the
driver's seat. Recall swept in swiftly and without mercy. Her boy
was dead. She might have saved him. Ruth lay back in the seat, eyes
forward, staring through the film of condensation on the windshield.
Nothing moved in the murky light. She wanted sleep to take her
again. But her eyes wouldn't close. She looked from Casey's sleeping
bulk to the droplets of water on the windshield and back to her
hands, which had twined together as if they were hanging on to
each other for dear life.

*Breathe*, Ruth reminded herself. This command had never failed
her when confronted with a snarl of competing demands. A deep
breath, a list, and without fail, her next step would be clear to her.
Ruth's breath turned into a gasp. How long would her body hurt
like this?

She was so cold. She forced herself into a sitting position and
slipped her arms into the sleeves of Casey's jacket. The smell of
cigarette smoke seeped from the material, crawled up her nose. Fresh
air. Now. She scrabbled for the door handle but stopped when Casey
grunted and twisted in his seat.

He couldn't roll over entirely; his legs were in the way. She saw
the glint of metal on his lower left leg, which was jammed in the
cramped space below the steering wheel. His moneymaker. Lying
there with his jaw slack, eyes closed, he looked broken, exposed,
pretty much the way she felt. Ruth let go of the door handle. She
inhaled again. If she took it slow the breath went around her pain,

not through it. After a few minutes, she felt an easing in her chest. She picked up the crumpled map lying between the seats and squinted at it in the half light. They were heading east, that much Casey had told her. The map they had took them to Colorado. She could not make out the print or follow the red lines that branched out from the interstate, each no wider than a hair, but there was a solid blue line heading east. That was the one they needed to follow. She'd feel better once they were moving. Ruth crossed her arms and pulled the jacket tight around her, but the cold had penetrated her bones. She wanted Robbie's denim jacket, but it was gone. "Couldn't save it," was all Casey had told her.

Deep inside, a wail began to gather as it had the night Robbie died. She heard it, faint but getting stronger, coming for her. *Please,* she heard herself whisper into the dark car with its smell of leather, sweat, and French fries. *Please. Not now. Not here.* She rolled onto her side, away from Casey. Eyes wide open, afraid now to close them, she waited for dawn to break.

# CHAPTER 27

A blue and white Walmart sign flashed into view just outside Grand Junction.

"Get off, you're going to miss the exit!" Casey heard Ruth say just before she pointed a chipped nail into his line of vision.

Casey wrenched the steering wheel right and then wrenched left to avoid a Subaru. The blare of the Subaru's horn followed them as the Jaguar sailed past the Walmart exit. He heard a deep intake of breath from the passenger seat as if Ruth were getting ready to let him have it.

"Don't say anything." Casey heard himself growl the warning. "I mean it. Don't say anything. If you say one word, I swear I'll just keep driving and you can rot in those shorts."

"You won't get far. We need gas," she said.

Damn, she was right. Casey saw her fold her arms as if she were holding in whatever else she wanted to say. Good. He didn't want to hear it anyway. Whenever she broke her silence it had been to tell him where to turn or to sigh in a way that irritated him even more. Years had passed since he'd been in such close quarters with anyone, never mind a woman who could make him question his own competency simply by exhaling in a certain way.

Silence was worse. When he woke in the driver's seat earlier, he saw her shift her gaze quickly to something outside her window. He wondered if she'd been watching him sleep. Creepy. That was why he liked sleeping alone.

"There's another exit, take that and turn around," Ruth said.

"You need one of those GPS things," he said. "How come you don't have it?"

"Just take this exit and get going in the right direction."

Casey gritted his teeth and did exactly that. Maybe it would lead him not just to Walmart but to a cup of hot coffee. He'd seen the sun rise two mornings in a row now. It was killing him.

"I see it, I see it," he muttered. There was a gas station and a doughnut place right in the same parking lot as the Walmart. Things were looking up.

"You want anything?" he asked as he brought the Jag to a halt in front of one of the pumps. There was a sign in the window of the station that promised a free cup of coffee with a fill-up.

He heard the door open before he even turned off the ignition. "Coffee," Ruth said as she clopped as quickly as she could toward the restroom. Well, that could explain at least some of her tension.

But she was still testy when he found her waiting for him and the coffee he juggled on a cardboard tray along with a raft of sugar packets and creamers.

"I don't need those. I drink it black," she said, and sat back down in the passenger seat facing outside. She didn't even smile when he handed her the bag of biscuits he'd bought, steaming and hot, right out of the oven, just grabbed one and thrust the bag back at him. Maybe she'd feel better with a little caffeine.

Using the top of the car as a table, Casey dumped two creamers and three sugars into his cup and stirred. He took a sip and then bit

into his biscuit. Crumbs spilled to the pavement but he didn't care.
It had been a long fucking night. And now he was going shopping.


After several wrong turns, Ruth found her way to the aisle of
women's clothing. Casey had elected to leave her to it with the
warning not to go overboard. She was supposed to meet him at the
checkout area in twenty minutes.

She fingered a pair of tan capri pants, looked at the price tag:
eighteen dollars. Hard to go overboard here. She found a pair in
size four and put them in the basket. She selected a pair of shorts,
a couple of shirts, underwear. That was all Ruth needed, but she
kept pushing her cart down the aisles of cheap clothes, glad to be
alone for a few minutes, glad for the distractions around her.

She paused at the end of an aisle that stretched the length of the
store. Signs pointed to everything from frozen food to gardening
equipment. Standing there, she was reminded of the Globe, forty
miles from the farm where the paper mills filled the air with the
smell of rotten eggs, the place her grandparents took her and Kevin
twice a year for school clothes or other necessities not available in
Gershom or through the Sears catalog.

Her grandfather would steer the Bel Air with a resigned look on
his face while Kevin sat in the back next to her, counting the money
he'd saved up to buy some new car magazines or a fishing rod. Ruth
had nothing in her hands, but she'd memorized the pages of the
*Seventeen* magazine she shared with her friend Micheline. Maybe she
would find the one sweater or skirt that would make her feel like
those girls in those pages.


I said, can I help you?"
A Walmart employee materialized in front of Ruth. She had
no idea how long he had been standing there. He was shorter than

she was, with a high voice and a feathery gray mustache. His hands hung uneasily at his waist and his chest was puffed up under a blue store vest like one of her grandmother's grosbeaks. His gaze traveled the length of Ruth's body before settling on her face.

"I'm looking for shoes," Ruth said. She made herself look him straight in the eye and tried to speak with the same confidence she would if she were in Neiman's with her personal shopper. "A purse, too. Then deodorant, shampoo, and tampons."

A walkie-talkie cackled at his side. He looked Ruth up and down again, registering the T-shirt she wore, the shorts, the men's sneakers. Maybe she didn't meet the dress code for Walmart patrons. *Homeless woman in aisle eight*, she imagined him thinking. *Check her out.* She relaxed a little when the man finally glanced away and shrugged. "Shoes are over that way and . . . lady things are over there."

C asey was waiting for her at the checkout counter nearest the door. He said nothing as she emptied her selections onto the conveyor belt, but she saw him frown as the register displayed the totals. She noticed that his own basket held an atlas, a jar of peanut butter, a package of crackers, a twelve-pack of Coke, duct tape, roll-on antiperspirant, skin lotion, a carton of filterless cigarettes, and three kinds of headache pills. Ruth seized the carton of cigarettes, rattled it at him.

"We agreed, right? No smoking in the car."

"But what I do outside the car is my own business." Casey took the carton from her and tossed it onto the moving belt. He pointed to another box moving toward the cash register. Nicotine patches. "See? For inside." Then they both noticed the clerk watching them as she rang up the clothes. Behind her was the grosbeak, standing with his arms folded in front of him. Ruth focused on the items moving on the belt.

"Are you sick?" she asked, nodding toward the pain relievers. Advil, Tylenol, Extra-Strength Excedrin.

"Prevention," he said. "The way this trip is going, I'm going to need all the help I can get."

Any other day she would have laughed out loud at the secretive way he half turned from her, peeled out eight twenty-dollar bills, and counted the change afterward. Did he think she couldn't see where he put his money? Did he think she cared? Now she just wanted him to hurry. She needed to get out of here.

Twenty minutes later, Ruth emerged a second time from the ladies' room at the gas station to find Casey waiting for her, atlas open on the top of the car. He nodded at her as she swung into the backseat with the plastic bags holding the clothes he'd given her. She tossed his sneakers in after them.

"Feel better now?"

She looked at him through her new sunglasses, brown tortoise-shell goggles that covered her face from cheekbone to eyebrow, and nodded. Her hair was damp; she'd scrubbed, brushed, washed, and deodorized as best as she could in the restroom sink before putting on clean underwear, pants, and the sleeveless white shirt she'd bought. Lightweight canvas shoes replaced Casey's old sneakers. She still did not look like her old self, but she would not attract instant judgment. She could hide in these clothes.

Casey pulled his cell phone out of his pocket and glanced at the screen. "It's just after seven o'clock. Four hours to Denver, then another four or so to Ogallala."

"Where?"

"Nebraska. The place we'll pick up Eighty east."

"You haven't said where we're going."

He looked at her without answering for a moment. Then he shrugged. "New Jersey."

That would take at least a few days. Plenty of time to figure things out. She watched him reach down to rub what must have been his stump. Two nicotine patches clung to the inside of his forearm. His face looked washed out in the glare of the early-morning sun and a wince creased the corners of his eyes. He had to be tired. She was. Sooner or later he'd give in. She might as well rest while she could.

"Okay," she said. "Let's get going."

# CHAPTER 28

By the time they reached the outskirts of Denver, the sun was blazing and so was the skin of Casey's stump. This was the longest he'd ever gone without taking off the faker for a while. He leaned forward in his seat and rubbed around the top of the socket through his jeans. He glanced at the dashboard.

"Let's take a break," he said.

He saw Ruth glance at the atlas spread open on her knees. "I thought you wanted to make it to Ogallala by tonight."

"We'll make it all right."

"Well, you're driving. I guess we do whatever you want."

It was the most she'd said since they left Grand Junction. He'd learned a few things, though. Ruth had two speeds: on or off. When she wasn't sleeping or staring straight ahead of her, she was squirming in her seat, tapping the door handle, and checking the fucking map every time they passed a road sign.

And she hated Springsteen, quintessential driving music. She'd reached over and just hit the button in the middle of "Thunder Road" and kept poking until she found some soft jazz. No way was he going to listen to that shit and he told her so. The news was on now, nice and low, a public radio station. At least the voices took the place of the conversation that was not happening in the car. He needed something to keep him awake.

"What should we talk about, Ruth?"

"What is there to talk about?"

"We're going to be spending the next few days together. Seems as though we ought to talk about something." He waved his hand at the radio. "I'm going to be sick of these people before too long."

"That's not my problem," she said irritably.

"That's a good place to start. What exactly is your problem?"

Silence. He glanced toward the passenger seat and saw her freeze in midtap.

"I've got some theories, you want to hear them?"

"No." She turned and started to stare out the window. He resolved to make her turn and face him.

"It's a guy."

She continued to fix her eyes on whatever was so fascinating outside. "Just drive," he heard her say. "That's all you can handle right now."

"You don't like my driving?"

Ruth sniffed.

"I've got it. You don't like it that I am driving at all since this is, technically, your car."

Her head whipped around. "Technically?"

Casey shrugged and grinned. "Okay, your car." At least now he had her attention.

"So, theory number one. Your old man was messing around on you and you decided to show him a thing or two, only you got in over your head."

From the corner of his eye, he saw Ruth's nostrils flare. She shook her head and looked away again.

"Maybe you were messing with another guy, and your old man kicked you out."

Ruth flicked the back of her hand in his direction as though she were swatting the idea away. He was beginning to enjoy himself for the first time on this trip.

"What's so unreasonable about that?" he said. "I bet that was it. And your boyfriend was younger. I always liked older women. All my girlfriends are about your age."

Ruth turned to look at him again. She pulled her giant sunglasses down her nose and peered over the tops.

"How old are you?" she asked.

"Thirty-six, ten years younger than you if your license wasn't lying." He felt her stare and glanced out the corner of his eye. "What?"

"Nothing. I thought you were older."

He hadn't thought about what he looked like for years. Older. Beat up, she meant. Damaged goods. Fuck. What would Emily see when she looked at him? Suddenly he was tired, bone tired. He ran his fingers through his hair, pushing it off his forehead, trying to push the fatigue back with it. Time to change the subject.

"Okay, I've got it. Your boy toy was messing around on you. You killed him and you've got him in the trunk."

"Shut up," she growled. He saw her hands clench.

"Relax, Ruth, I was just kidding."

"I said, shut up."

"Okay, okay."

She reached past him and turned up the volume on the radio. The noise drove all curiosity about Ruth Nolan out of Casey's head. Screw her. He would get off at the next exit, whether she liked it or not. He hoped it was soon.


Ruth jammed her finger on the volume button of the radio. "Christ, it's loud enough. Just leave it alone," he said.

Ruth ignored him.

"Listen, I'm sorry. It's none of my business who you are or what you're up to. I promise I won't ask again, okay? Just stop hitting that button." He reached toward the controls, but when Ruth heard a familiar name coming from the speakers, she pushed his hand away and turned up the volume even more.

"RyCom needs to be held accountable. We will hold the company and the insurers accountable," said a man. Ruth didn't recognize the voice.

"Turn that down, for Christ's sake," Casey said.

"Wait." Ruth pushed his hand away again when the reporter began to speak. "That was James Breen, attorney for Families of the Forgotten, a group representing the families of independent contractors who have died in Iraq or Afghanistan since the war began."

"Poor bastards," Casey said.

Ruth did not take her eyes off the radio. The lawyer was speaking again.

"RyCom Systems lied to the contractors about the dangers of the jobs. They exposed contractors to unnecessary danger. Now those same contractors are coming home disabled or dead and the company is letting them and their families twist."

The newscaster's voice returned. "Although RyCom executives declined to be interviewed, COO Gordon Olson issued a statement today in response. 'We stand by our commitment to those who have served our country by helping us staff the rebuilding and security initiatives so vital to the war on terror. In the days to come, it will be clear to all that we and our insurers are fulfilling our obligations both legally and morally to each of those who have suffered injury or loss in the course of their work for us.'"

"Crap. All of it. You can tell from the way he talks," Casey said. "He's got no use for those people unless they're out there making him money."

Hatred for Gordon Olson flooded Ruth. Robbie was nothing to him but a liability—and an excuse to get rid of her.

Then she remembered Terri handing her the flash drive. It must be here in the car; she'd never taken it out of her computer bag after dropping it in there the night Robbie died. She recalled, too, the warning in Gordon's voice when he'd told her, *What is best for the company is also best for you.* The thought of what might be on the tiny drive worked its way into Ruth's conscience like a splinter.

"Assholes like him make me sick." Casey was still talking, ranting now, all signs of fatigue gone.

Ruth reached again for the radio. She needed something to drown out Casey's words, the echo of Gordon Olson's words, and all thoughts of the contractors. She couldn't help them. She could barely help herself right now.

A rap song came on; it sounded familiar. Was it the same one Robbie had on his phone? Ruth didn't remember. She'd hated it so much she hadn't paid attention to anything but the beep that followed. Now she wanted to know. Had the words meant anything to him?

"You like this shit?" Casey was asking.

Ruth's curiosity about the lyrics fell away. The music took her back to her kitchen, where she was dialing Robbie's number again and again, getting angrier and angrier when he didn't pick up. She was lying on the bed in the guest room, expecting to see him any minute. Then she was standing in her front hall with the deputy and the chaplain and the Marine captain surrounding her, telling her that Robbie was dead.

C'mon, Ruth. You've got to eat something."

Casey thrust a grilled chicken sandwich through the open passenger door, but Ruth just kept staring at her lap, where her hands were locked together. He could see her knuckles whiten every time she clenched her fingers.

She'd been like this since twenty miles back. Suddenly there was no squirming. No grabbing the map. She did not seem to notice when he turned the radio off, just sat there with her head against the window, eyes shut tight, like a kid trying not to cry.

"I'm sorry," he wanted to say. There was something about her, sitting there, one hand hanging on to the other, that got to him. He knew pain when he saw it. It was why he had bought her food she did not ask for and why he was standing here, hoping she'd take it.

"If you take the sandwich, I'll let you drive," he said, urging the sandwich on her a second time. He knew she wanted the car back. He was hot and tired, there was a pain behind his eyes he hadn't felt for years, and his stump was acting up. He was ready to take a chance on her.

When she glanced up, he thought he could see her eyebrows lift behind the lenses of her sunglasses. He waited. Slowly, she lifted her hand and took the sandwich.

"There you go. I've got a Coke for you too." Ruth swiveled until she could stretch her legs out the passenger door. She picked at the foil wrapped around the sandwich.

"Thatta girl."

She aimed her sunglasses straight at him. "You know, there's no need to treat me like a child."

For some reason, the sharpness in her voice made him feel better. Casey grabbed the bag of food off the car roof and started rooting around in it for his burger.

Good. She would drive. She wanted to grip the steering wheel and fly forward, not sit trapped in the passenger seat where grief could find her. She swallowed her impatience to get going with a sip of lukewarm Coke.

Casey leaned over and dug his fingers through his jeans, rubbing the skin below his knee. His face was paler than before and he was rubbing his leg again.

"What's wrong? You keep rubbing your leg."

"Nothing that taking it off for a while won't fix."

He took his canvas bag from the backseat and limped toward the restroom of the McDonald's. "I'll be a little while."

Ruth got out of the car and watched him limp away with a growing sense of embarrassment and shame. Here she was, glad to be given a chance to drive her own car. A man, not such a bad one maybe, but one she barely knew, was deciding everything from food to the route they would take. Sooner or later he'd want his money and she already wanted more control. She wasn't a prisoner. All she needed was her credit cards, access to her bank account.

Ruth dug her phone out of the cheap canvas purse she'd bought at Walmart. Twenty-seven unheard messages on her voice mail. Thirty unread texts. As she looked at the screen, a text from Terri popped up. *Are you okay? Where are you? Call me.* Seconds later, one from Neal appeared. *Call me if you can read this.*

*The longer you wait, the harder it will be.* Her grandmother's voice rose from the well of childhood and suddenly Ruth felt her there, saw Big Ruth peering at her through whatever crazy glasses she wore now, right down to Ruth's soul, waiting, trusting Ruth to do the right thing, even now when Ruth had failed and failed to do so many things right. Somewhere in those voice mails, she'd find messages from Big Ruth and Kevin. Terri or Neal would have called the farm looking for her.

Ruth pulled up Terri's cell phone number and dialed. She'd be at the office now, and not as likely to answer her cell. Ruth looked over her shoulder to see if Casey was coming, but there was no sign of him. "Terri, it's me, Ruth," she said after she heard the beep. "I just decided to get away for a little while. I'm very sorry for just leaving without saying anything. I'll be in touch soon. Will you let Neal know I'll call him? And if you would, let my family know I'm okay? I'll call them too. Soon." There. That covered the important things. No, wait. "Ter, I need a favor. Would you please cancel my credit cards? All of them, the bank card too. My wallet was stolen." Shit, her license was gone too. This was going to be a mess. She didn't want to think about it now. She just wanted to get moving. "I'll explain later. Can you make the calls? Cell service is iffy around here, and . . ." She was talking too much again. "Anyway, thanks. I'll call you with where to send the new ones. Soon. Thanks, Ter."

Ruth hung up and turned her phone off. She didn't want to hear it ring, as it most surely would as soon as Terri picked up the message. She needed to move now. Where was Casey?

Just then he appeared in the doorway leading to the restrooms. He seemed to be inching toward her. His shorts flapped against his pale right thigh and the combination of skin, plastic, and metal that was his left leg. The shank running from the straps to a black sneaker flashed in the midday sun with every step.

"I'm back," he said when he finally reached her.

She took the keys from his outstretched hand. "Okay," she said. "Now it's my turn to drive."

# CHAPTER 29

Fall 1976

*R*uth is sixteen, burning with humiliation that her younger brother must teach her to drive. She squeezes back tears of rage as her grandfather tosses the keys to Kevin in defeat.

"I'm too old for this," he grumbles, climbing out of the passenger seat of the old Bel Air and slamming the door behind him.

Ruth glares at her grandfather. "You kept grabbing the wheel!"

"Jesus H. Christ. If I hadn't've, you'd've killed us both!" He tosses the keys to Kevin, who's just come out of the barn. "Here, it's your job now."

"He doesn't even have a license yet!" Ruth does not care that Kevin has been driving one vehicle or another on the farm since he was nine years old.

"I won't tell if you won't. Just stick to the back roads."

Kevin slouches next to her in the car, skinny, all knobs from his knees to his Adam's apple, red hair exploding like dandelion fluff. His calm, low steady voice drones in her right ear.

"Ditch on your right." He closes his eyes when Ruth jerks the wheel toward the center of the road and then jerks again as she sees the opposite ditch approaching.

"No need to grip that wheel so hard, you've got to feel the road."

*Ruth grips tighter. It is mid-October but the air is Indian summer warm. Every time her brother speaks in that calm voice, it feels even hotter.*

*"How can I feel anything in this boat?"*

*"She's big but she's more sensitive than you think," Kevin says.*

*"Jesus, Kev. It's just a car. Stop talking about it like it's a person."*

*"Someone's got to watch out for her."*

*She's embarrassed by the old car her father loved and her grandfather kept after he died thinking it would be perfect for Kevin and her. Its rounded fenders and aqua paint make it look like a cartoon next to the Camaros and Mustangs that belong to the kids from town. The freckles of rust scream age and no money. When she gets her license, she drives the old Bel Air like she's punishing it—and punishing Kevin for his unwitting power over her in the months before her driver's test.*

*"Slow down," her brother pleads when she drives them to school, although he likes going fast enough in other cars.*

*"No." Ruth steps on the gas.*

# CHAPTER 30

They lost the tire just as Casey decided he couldn't take another minute of Ruth's driving. Her foot had nailed the pedal to the floor ever since they left Denver. She'd let the car more or less steer itself while she fiddled with the radio or checked the atlas, to see how far they had come and how long it would take them to get to Ogallala. He was about to tell her to watch the fucking road when the Jaguar lurched to the left, its front end shaking so hard Casey braced himself against the dashboard, sure they were going to flip.

A few minutes later, they came to a rattling but controlled stop on the right shoulder and the car went still. Casey pried his hands off the dashboard and tried to swallow, but his throat was as dry as the Mojave at midday.

"Are you trying to kill us?"

Ruth ignored him, but her hands still gripped the steering wheel and her chin trembled.

"What the fuck is wrong with you?"

"It's not my fault," Ruth said, angry now. She twisted to undo her seat belt.

"Not your fault? Was I driving? Whose fucking car is this, anyway?"

Ruth shoved open the door, then slammed it behind her. Casey hit the release on his own seat belt and started to stand before he realized that the faker was lying on the floor. He'd peeled off the socks and the liner, too, so the stump could get some air and he could relax.

Ruth was standing on the edge of the paved road, her sunglasses on top of her head, staring at the driver's-side wheel.

"It's down to the rim," she said. She sounded more mad than scared. He'd been scared enough, apparently, for both of them.

"Shit." Casey's head was pounding. He twisted in his seat and reached for the liner. She was staring at his stump.

"What?" he barked, looking up. "It's just flesh and bone. At least I've got a fucking spare. Where's yours?"

What had he gotten himself into?

"Come on. Just open the damn trunk." Casey heard the jangle of her keys and the bleep of the remote lock. He cursed but he couldn't go any faster. Liner, socks, socket, pin, click. Shit, he was sore. He pushed himself out of the passenger seat.

Ruth stood frozen in front of the open trunk. He limped over to her and glanced inside. A Marine's duffel. A bunch of towels. This was what she was so protective about? He shook his head and began to reach for the strap of the big canvas bag.

"Don't." Ruth grabbed the strap from his hands.

"It's heavy. I'll get it."

"I said, *don't touch it*." She hauled on the straps and staggered a few steps to the side of the road before placing it gently down.

Casey grabbed the towels and saw a metal box. He squinted at the sticker in the corner. But Ruth got to it first and clutched it to her chest. Her eyes bored into him.

"Jesus Christ, what's in there?" He started to say more, but the ferocity in Ruth's eyes stopped the words in his throat. He looked behind him at the duffel and then back at Ruth. Then he limped over to the bag and read the name printed along the side: *R. O'Connell*. What the hell?

"Whose is this?"

Ruth shook her head and hugged the box.

An eighteen-wheeler roared past them. Strands of Ruth's hair lifted in the blast of hot air, but she did not move. She scared him, the way she was so still. Casey stepped closer to her and peered into her face.

"What's in the box, Ruth?"

Her eyes flickered. She looked down and hugged the box to her chest. A gust of wind nearly carried her words away. "Robbie. His . . . ashes. My son."

*My son*. Numb, Casey watched Ruth look down at the box in her arms. Another gust whipped a short strand of red hair across her cheekbones, pale now in the green-gray light of the late afternoon. Thunder sounded in the distance and seconds later, fat wet drops thudded down.

Casey turned and grabbed the straps of the duffel. Ruth rushed to the driver's-side door and placed her burden carefully in the seat. Her son. He'd joked about boy toys and she'd been driving her dead child around. Shame licked at him. He placed the duffel into the trunk and pried loose the jack and the wrench stored there. Then he reached back in for the little temporary tire. Nothing more than a hard rubber doughnut. Ruth was already drenched. Rain streamed down her arms and her new pants hung like sodden tarps against her thighs. "Get in the car," he said gently.

She shook her head.

Casey hesitated, then nodded. They were already soaked; besides it was starting to let up. Instead of pelting, the rain was now shower-ing, soft and steady, running off the road in sheets and swirling at their ankles as they crouched. Casey stooped but couldn't get down far enough unless he sat down. The faker didn't like the rain; it kept slipping around on him. No cars went by. The trucks that had blocked their vision for miles had disappeared. She was the only help he had.

"Here, hold these until I ask for them," he said, handing her the lug nuts. Water sluiced through his fingers; the nuts slipped from his hands to hers. She caught them and then looked up, waiting. Casey could not look her in the eye. He'd taken her money, played her without wanting to think about what awful thing had happened that would make a woman like her go along with him. Most likely her son had been killed in a desert thousands of miles away while hundreds of other kids his age were drinking beer and jacking off in a college dorm somewhere. Guilt, infused with an old jealous anger, welled up inside him, cold, mean, and familiar. He lined up the doughnut and held his hands out for the lug nuts she still held. The first one slipped from his hand into the mud.

*Fuck.*

Well, they'd have to get through this, but as soon as they got to a town, he'd give her enough money to do whatever she had to do, and then find a way to get back to Vegas where he couldn't do any more harm. He felt dirty, the way he'd felt when he left New Jersey in the first place.

"Here, this will help," she said a little louder. She wrapped both hands around the long end of the wrench and when he closed the jaws around the nut, she pushed down. Her shoulder leaned into his when they repeated the move. With a few more jerks they secured the temporary spare. They were both shivering and wet. Casey took the jack from Ruth and pointed her toward the passenger door.

"Look at the atlas and see where we are while I put this in the trunk," Casey said. He dragged the bad tire to the trunk and heaved it in.

"We're about fifty miles from Ogallala," she said a few minutes later as he squeezed into the driver's seat, leaning back on the seat to squash the duffel and the other bags. They seemed to push back just as hard. Ruth was bowed over the atlas. The metal box was in her lap.

"Ruth."

"We could get there by seven o'clock, earlier if we make good time." The words chattered out of her.

"Ruth, I'm sorry." He started to reach toward her arm but froze when she looked up at him. Her cheeks were streaked with rain and mud. Her hair was plastered back like a boy's. Her eyes were empty of anger and full of tears. He closed his fingers around her arm, and then he just squeezed once, gently.

"I'm sorry."

She nodded once and looked down at the atlas. A glob of water ran from her hairline down the front of her nose and dangled off the end before plopping onto the page in front of her. On another day, Casey might have laughed. Instead, he turned the key in the ignition.

"You ready? I'm going to take it nice and slow."

Ruth stared at him a moment, eyes still watery. Then she placed the map carefully between them and clasped both hands around the box.

"Yes."

It was almost a whisper. She did not say another word for forty miles. The only sounds were the constant thump of the small hard spare and the smack of water against the Jaguar every time a car passed them on the way to Ogallala.

# CHAPTER 31

The pimpled kid behind the desk at Lilly's Wayside Motel frowned at Casey.

"We're full up."

"That's not what your sign says."

"That's what I say." Small blue eyes settled on Ruth, snagging on her bruised lip and eye before flashing back to Casey. His stub nose twitched. "You're messing up the floor."

Ruth knew she needed to do something before they ended up sleeping in the car. This was the fourth place they'd tried. She'd hardly noticed when they stopped at the first three, just sat in the car and watched Casey limp in and storm out of the little offices of the small motels that lined the highway outside Ogallala. "Some kind of rodeo's in town," he said when she asked what was going on. "The summer's their busy time. The rain. Everyone got here before us, I guess."

The words fired out of his mouth at a rapid clip, but there was no energy behind them. His face was drained of color; it was all shades of gray in the fading light, paler across his forehead, smudged charcoal under his eyes. The flesh of his good leg, stark white, shivered beneath the hem of his wet shorts. He needed help. She'd gotten out of the car with him when they pulled into the parking lot of the fourth motel.

She started to speak to the boy, trying to temper Casey's irritation. Casey grabbed Ruth's arm and held her back.

"The fucking sign outside says *vacancy*. You're either a liar or a fuckup. Which is it?"

"What's the problem, Kyle?" said a husky female voice from behind the counter.

"Nothin', Aunt Lil." The boy spoke over his shoulder and moved aside at the same time. A square-jawed woman with strong shoulders rolled her wheelchair from behind the counter to the entry area that served as a lobby. She squinted through glasses first at Casey, then at Ruth, then at the path of dirt they'd tracked over the linoleum tiles. She sighed and then smiled.

"Sorry, folks. My nephew didn't mean to be rude, he's just frustrated is all. This'll be the third time today he's had to mop this floor. It's been raining off and on all day. You two must've got caught, huh?" She was speaking to both of them but looking at Ruth. Ruth knew she was taking in the bruises just as her nephew had done.

Ruth removed herself from Casey's grasp but left her hand on his arm, ready to check him if he went off again. She smiled at the woman and spoke calmly.

"I'm sorry. We're a mess. We lost a tire and had to change it in the rain." She glanced at Casey's scowl and hoped he'd keep his mouth closed. She brushed her hand across her bruised face. "This is . . . not what it looks like. . . . You won't have any trouble."

The woman in the wheelchair was silent for a moment. Her eyes, some light color that went with her faded blond hair, squinted in appraisal. Ruth held her gaze. The woman named Lil finally nodded.

"We've got one more room open, Kyle. Give them that one."

"Thank you," Ruth said. "How much?"

"Eighty dollars a night, pay up front," the boy grumbled.

"Thank you," Ruth said.

"You're lucky it worked out," Lil said. "We've only got the one left. Things are busy this time of year what with . . ."

"Yeah, yeah, we heard all about it," Casey interrupted, but he didn't sound angry, only tired. He dug into his pocket for the cash they'd need. Ruth watched the boy's unfortunately small eyes blink behind his glasses as Casey tried to separate a hundred-dollar bill from the sodden roll in his pocket. Ruth reached over and extracted the bill. She handed it across the counter and took the key and change from the boy.

"Is there any place nearby to get some food?"

Ruth directed the question at the woman in the wheelchair, who had already started to turn back toward the desk. Lil stopped and gestured to the shelves behind her. Packets of soup, a freezer down below with some frozen dinners, a coffee urn. Beer and soda lined the shelves of a small glass cooler.

"There's a microwave right here you can use to heat it up. Of course, if you're in the mood for something fancier, there are some restaurants up at the lake or back in town, but it's kind of late. Probably have to get a move on if that's what you want." Ruth thanked the woman again and followed Casey out the door.

They unloaded the Jaguar in silence, emptying the backseat armful by armful. Casey reached for the duffel but then paused and looked at her, apparently uncertain.

She hesitated, then nodded back. "Thanks."

The last thing Ruth retrieved from the car was the metal box, which she placed in the room, on top of a low dresser with two drawers. She paused, her hands resting on the box. Beneath it was a thin strip of yellowed cloth that did not hide the chipped veneer of the dresser. Not much but it was better than the floor. She arranged her purse and the plastic Walmart bags along the wall so that there was a clear path around the single queen-sized bed.

When she turned around, Casey was standing by the window, his bag next to his ankles. He stared out through the blinds to the parking lot. His fingers tapped against the windowsill, short nervous thwacks.

"What's wrong?"

"Nothing. Just wet and tired, that's all," Casey said without turning around. "Go ahead, you take the first shower."

The words were kind enough but his tone was detached, verging on impatient. He seemed anxious for her to leave the room.

Then it hit her. He was going to leave. Hours ago she'd thought she'd welcome the chance to get away from him; now she only knew she did not want to be alone. At least not tonight.

"No, it's all right. You go first."

He faced her. "Look at you, Ruth. You're freezing."

"You're not in much better shape yourself," she said. "You won't get far like that."

He lifted his eyes, stared across the room into hers, and then his gaze slid from hers to something behind her right shoulder. "What are you talking about?"

Ruth said nothing.

Casey straightened. He dug into his pocket and pulled out the keys to the Jaguar.

"You worried I'll steal your car? Here."

She had not thought about the car or money. She had not thought at all. She'd picked up the scent of abandonment and fought back.

"Forget it," Ruth said. Avoiding his eyes, she stepped carefully around the bags on the floor and entered the bathroom. She shut the door behind her and flipped on the light switch. Weak yellow light filled the windowless room and turned the grape-colored vinyl shower curtain a muddy brown.

"Get a grip," she muttered to the face staring back at her from the chipped mirror above the sink.

Casey watched the bathroom door close behind Ruth, then sagged against the wall. He pressed his palms against his temples. His headache pushed back. He needed some pills. He needed rest. He needed to be where nothing was expected of him. That was the plan he'd made in the rain, leave Ruth the car and some money and just get out. Now he was miles from a town where he could hitch a ride or even find another place to hole up and sleep. The day was over, the room was already dark. Casey pushed himself upright and looked around for the Walmart bags. He stooped and pawed through the pile of bags and Ruth's belongings on the floor. Where were they? He rummaged through them, his ear cocked toward the bathroom, his mind on Ruth's tired face when he tried to give her the keys. Guilt fought with the pain in his head.

He seized one of the plastic bags. "Shit. Shit." He threw the bag across the room. Women's underwear, toothpaste, and other things she'd gotten for herself spilled onto the dingy carpet. She must have the bag with his stuff. He dug into his pockets and pulled out a soggy, nearly empty pack with a few cigarettes and one and a half sodden joints. He clapped his pockets. No matches.

She'd probably be in the bathroom all night. He jammed the pack back in his pocket, grabbed his bag, stalked to the door, and pulled it open. Rain sheeted down; small lakes had already formed across the parking lot. A violent longing for the scorched sand and dry air of the desert came over him. Casey stepped back inside, slammed the door shut, and flung himself onto the bed. One more night, and then he was out of here.

Ruth heard the door slam seconds after she turned off the shower. The sound echoed inside her like a rifle shot. She wrapped the towel around her shoulders and hugged herself.

Why should she care whether Casey stayed? He was a stranger, only in this for his own purposes, whatever they were.

She pulled on dry clothes, hung the towel on the rod behind the toilet, and snatched up the plastic bag full of his headache medicine and cigarettes that she'd taken by mistake. Maybe she'd start smoking. She gripped the doorknob and pushed open the door.

Casey stared back from the bed, his face a mosaic of impatience and resignation. "Finally. I need some of those pills. My head is killing me."

# CHAPTER 32

Casey watched Ruth move around the room. She turned the switch of a small lamp on the dresser and Casey braced for pain, but it was a dull light and instead of piercing his eyes, it cast a tepid glow over the dresser with the box on it. Like an altar.

For a split second he was thirteen again, sitting in the front pew of St. Francis just a few feet from his grandmother's coffin. The shoulder of Mikey's blue blazer seemed melded to his own; his friend's voice skidded from tenor to baritone to bass as Mikey sang, loud enough for both of them, the hymns that would not come out of Casey's own mouth.

"Here's some more water," Ruth said, emerging from the bathroom clutching a plastic cup.

"Thanks." Casey sat up and took the cup from her hand. It shook in his hand. She reached as if to steady it. "I've got it, I've got it," he said, but half of the water splattered the bed. He took a sip. He wished it were Jameson.

"I'll go see what there is to eat," Ruth said.

Casey dug the crushed cigarette pack out of his pocket. "Whatever." He extracted the remains of the half-smoked joint from the other night. "Matches. We need matches."

She stopped, glanced over her shoulder at him. "What's that?"

"For medicinal purposes, Ruth. And I'm not smoking out in the rain for you or anyone else."

Ruth started to shake her head. A price tag popped out of her collar and poked her in the lip. Ruth tore the tag off and frowned at Casey as though it were his fault. He almost laughed.

"There's another one," he said, pointing to the hem of her shorts. She tore that one off, too, and this time he grinned at her. She didn't exactly smile back, but the lines between her eyebrows softened, and he thought he saw her swollen lips relax.

R uth ran through the rain carrying a plastic bag over her head as a makeshift umbrella. No one was behind the desk when Ruth opened the door to the office. She crossed to the shelves of food, picked up a cardboard container of noodles, and put it back. Nothing looked good, but they needed to eat something.

"The soup's not bad if you want something hot." The woman, Lil, rolled her chair from the back room and pointed to a plastic container of tomato soup on the shelf in front of Ruth.

"Thanks," Ruth said, and reached for it. Her stomach suddenly growled.

"You just heat it up in the microwave."

Ruth picked up a second container. While she waited for them to heat up, she picked out a box of crackers, peanut butter, and two apples, then added a small box of matches with the name of the motel on the cover. "There you go," Lil said. "That'll keep you until the morning. We've got coffee, toast, and cereal from six thirty to nine. Complimentary."

"That's great, thanks," Ruth said with what she hoped was a smile. Lil returned the smile and settled back in her chair.

"Glad to help. How's the room?"

"Fine. The phone doesn't work, though."

"Costs another ten dollars and no long distance. Want me to turn it on?"

Ruth had grabbed her purse automatically but there was no money in it. Not a dime. Her stomach growled again. "No, that's okay. Can I charge the food to the room?"

Lil's smile remained but her eyes narrowed. "Sorry. Cash only. That going to be a problem?"

A blush crept up Ruth's cheeks. She straightened and grabbed her purse. "No, not at all. I'll be right back."

Casey was snoring when she got back to the room. His wet clothes were in a heap by the bed and he was stretched out in a black T-shirt and another pair of shorts. His prosthesis lay beside the bed, but he'd turned the liner inside out and stuck it pin-first into a drawer of the bedside table, apparently to dry it. Ruth avoided looking at the stump as she tiptoed to the table and picked up his wallet. The small weight in her hand triggered a realization. She could be the one who left. She could take the car, the money, all of Robbie's things, and leave him here. He'd wake up in the morning, maybe still planning to move on without her, but she would already be gone.

A moan escaped Casey as he turned on his side, away from her. He brought his knee up, covering the stump beneath. The back of his neck was still grimy from the mud and rain. He'd been too tired to take a shower. Or, maybe it was too hard to stand on one leg.

She flipped open the slim leather billfold and felt along the side for some bills. Nothing. She opened the little drawer of the bedside table and found the wad of bills wrapped in a sock. Here it was, all he had. She could take what she needed, retrieve her keys, and go on by herself to someplace where Terri could send the credit cards or wire some money. He'd be all right. Maybe even glad. She was a burden now. Just then, Casey moaned in his sleep and began to shiver. Ruth reached over and pulled the other half of the bedspread to cover him.

It was raining. They were tired. Where would she go tonight anyway? Ruth peeled several twenties from the roll of cash and put it back. The wallet slipped from her fingers to the floor and when she picked it up, she saw the face of a child, a little girl smiling back at her through a film of plastic. Ruth squinted at it in the dim light. All she could make out were dark eyes, an uneven fence of teeth framed by a wide smile, and a cloud of curly hair. She looked to be six or seven.

Ruth glanced at the sleeping Casey looking for a connection. She could not find it in the lank blond hair spreading behind him on the pillow or the hollow cheeks. She glanced at the photograph again and then, taking care to be quiet, she closed the wallet and placed it back on the bedside table.

Mikey again. The scream of a horn, the Camaro's headlights searing through the night, eighteen-year-old Mike behind the wheel, radio blaring, screaming "Fuck you!" as he hurtled into the void.

Casey woke and began to scan the room wildly. Headlights in the motel parking lot sent shards of light through the blinds. Where was he? A diesel engine roared, then fell silent. He heard the voices of two men walking across the parking lot and the rattle of a key in the lock of a nearby door. Then another sound, close to his ear. Breathing. He bolted up and reached for a light sprouting from the pine paneling above his bed.

"What is it? What's the matter?"

A woman sat up fully dressed on a little wooden chair across from the bed. Her short red hair was flat on one side where she'd leaned on her hand. Her face was puffy and bruised. He remembered now. He leaned back against the headboard and shut his eyes, trying to calm the pounding in his chest.

"Nothing. The lights woke me."

"You yelled," Ruth said, sitting up now and pushing her hair away from her face.

"Yeah, well, I'm sorry."

He yanked the spread off him and swung his legs around to the edge of the bed.

"I've got to use the bathroom," he said, pushing himself to a standing position and leaning for support against the wall.

"Do you need help?"

He looked over his shoulder at Ruth, who ducked her head, suddenly looking as embarrassed as he felt. He tried to grin. "No thanks, Ruth. I've got it under control."

He felt her staring at him as he leaned on the wall and hopped. He'd never done this with anyone watching. On top of that, the bathroom seemed a mile off. Nothing in his trailer had been more than a few feet away. Sweat formed around his temples as his right calf muscle stiffened and started to cramp. Shit. Without looking at Ruth, Casey made his way into the bathroom and closed the door behind him. He unzipped and, swearing, sat down to piss. It had been a long time since he shared a bathroom with a woman. He looked down at his arms, at the streaks of mud from the roadside.

A few minutes later he was leaning against the stained fiberglass shower stall, face lifted to the stream of hot water. He fumbled for some soap.

"You look better," Ruth told him when he emerged. She was hunched in the only chair, a small wooden one with no arms. The bed had been straightened. The dirty bedspread was piled in the corner. His stump socks, still damp, were hanging from the windowsill. Now she was cleaning up after him. Damn. Casey was in the middle of a game that he had never played. He didn't know the rules.

"There's some food if you're hungry," Ruth said. "The soup's cold. You were asleep when I got back." She sounded almost apologetic.

Casey wasn't even hungry, but all he said was, "That's okay. It'll go down the same, hot or cold."

He made his way along the wall to the bed and sat down. He picked up the container of soup and raised it to Ruth with a half-grin. "Cheers."

That can't be too comfortable," Casey said, after he'd finished his soup and devoured the crackers and all of the peanut butter. "Come over here. You're entitled to half the bed." He bit into an apple.

Ruth glanced at the other side of the bed but didn't move.

"Come on, Ruth. I'll be good, I promise. Besides, we've shared a bar of soap; that's as good as married in some places." He grinned and bit into the apple again. The food had helped. He was still tired, but he did not feel as though he were falling off a cliff.

Ruth shrugged and got up. She settled herself against the headboard and stretched her legs out in front of her.

"What time is it anyway?" he said.

"A little after midnight," she answered, reaching around to adjust the thin pillow behind her head.

The mattress shifted beneath him as she moved. Casey turned and looked at her. The bruises spread like a map across her profile. In them, he could see the route she'd taken over the past forty-eight hours. He knew now that she'd been trying to erase one pain with another. That was something he could understand. He wanted to tell her that but did not know how.

"You must be beat," was what he said.

Ruth nodded.

"Think you can get some sleep?"

She looked at him. Her lips trembled just enough for him to notice. "I'm not sure."

He understood that too. Sleep was both friend and enemy. It sucked you in, swathed you in oblivion, and then stabbed with truths you could keep at bay when your eyes were open, your mind filled with the crap you built your days around.

"Where are those matches?"

Ruth pointed to the bedside table and closed her eyes. Casey dug through the clothes he'd been wearing and pulled out the half-smoked joint from the cigarette pack. He lit up, inhaled, and nudged Ruth.

"Here."

Ruth's eyes opened. He nudged her again.

"C'mon."

She hesitated. Then she sat up and took the joint from him. She fit it into the corner of her mouth that was least swollen and inhaled. She coughed, but she took another hit. Then another. They passed it back and forth a couple of times.

Then Casey had an idea. He leaned down next to the bed and rooted around in his bag.

"A book?" Ruth asked.

"My foolproof method for getting through the night." He did not say that it had been his friend during the long desert days too. Reading saved him, at least the piece of him that wanted to be saved.

He settled back on the bed and adjusted the light. Ruth was up on one elbow, watching him. *"Moby-Dick?"*

"Yup." He began to read. She was still leaning up on one elbow, staring at him. "What?"

"I never figured you for—" She stopped.

"Life is full of surprises."

"Why that book, because of your leg?"

What? Oh, for Christ's sake. "I'm not that simple, Ruth. Made friends with Mr. Melville a long time before that happened." He saw another question gathering and decided to put a stop to it once and for all. "Want me to read you some?"

The question seemed to puzzle her. She was stoned. Casey

resisted the temptation to laugh. Ruth lay back on the bed and stared at the ceiling. "Okay," she said after a moment. "Yes."

He opened the book but the first words were out of his mouth before he'd flattened the page. "Call me Ishmael."

He read on, filling his mouth with words, lost in their rhythm and the paintings they made in his mind. When sleep started to steal over him, he glanced at Ruth. Her head was on the pillow, eyes closed. She snored. The sound was small, like the snuffle of a puppy.

He woke just before dawn. His headache was gone but the phantom pain from the missing limb throbbed. He'd thought all that was behind him. He started to turn over but stopped when he felt Ruth's hand on his. She was still asleep. He closed his eyes and made himself stay still. The warmth of her hand traveled through his fingers, deep into him where it found a memory of being held.

# CHAPTER 33

In the morning, Ruth tried to wash quietly but realized the thin walls of the motel room made the effort futile. Casey would be awake when she emerged and the day would begin whether she was ready for it or not. She turned on the water and froze, staring at the faucet. She wasn't ready.

She reached for her toothbrush, but her hand was shaking too hard to grasp it. She was glad she'd woken up before Casey. He wouldn't know she had reached for his hand like a child. The night was over. Who knew where things stood now?

With an effort, she began to brush her teeth. She glanced up into the mirror and saw that the swelling had subsided; she could open her bruised eye a bit wider. Soon enough, the bruises would fade. But she had no sense of healing inside. Instead, it seemed that the splitting open, the breaking apart was only beginning.

Casey was sitting on the edge of the bed rubbing the end of his stump when she came out of the bathroom.

"Good morning," he said, not looking at her.

"Hi."

Ruth busied herself with repacking her shopping bags, stuffing the contents into the flimsy plastic, avoiding direct eye contact with Casey.

"We'd better look into getting the tire fixed," Casey said.

*We.* Ruth glanced over her shoulder at him. He met her eyes and then reached for the prosthesis lying on the floor, then the rubbery thing with the pin on the bed next to him. At least for now, they were back to their original plan. Her relief surprised her. She allowed herself to smile a little. He shrugged and smiled back.

"I'll go get coffee and ask for directions to a car repair shop," she said.

"Bring me a—"

"A Coke, right?" Ruth said as she opened the door to the outside.

"Right."

She closed the door behind her and faced the parking lot, stirring now with early risers. The sky was still dark with clouds and leftover night, no hint of the kind of day to come. But she had a task and she was not alone. These two facts tethered her to the present. Ruth took a deep breath and flexed her hands until they steadied. She stepped forward into the dim light.

An hour later, Ruth got them to the tire place but Casey seemed more interested in arguing with the man behind the counter than in replacing the tire. From where she stood, a few feet away, leaning against the passenger side of the Jaguar, she could see him through a plate-glass window cluttered with decals and a poster for the county fair. His head jerked back in apparent disbelief, and the round man behind the counter turned the computer monitor around and pointed at the screen. Casey shook his head. The man shrugged, looked past Casey, and nodded to the next person in line. A reasonable person who was going to get what he wanted.

Ruth let a sigh escape from her. They didn't have a choice, didn't Casey see that? She straightened as Casey limped out the door toward her.

"You won't believe that fuckin' asshole," Casey said, limping toward her. "Wants nearly two hundred bucks for a new tire. Says Jaguars need special goddamn tires and that if I really wanted a smooth ride, I'd have to buy two!"

"What did you say?"

"I said we are getting one fucking tire and the hell with a smooth ride. Asshole's just trying to rip me off because he knows we're stuck."

"You have a pretty limited vocabulary for someone who reads the classics."

Casey stopped a few feet from her, with a scowl that was so much like a disgruntled two-year-old's she almost laughed.

"Oh, excuse me, Ms. Nolan. I'm sorry you find my vocabulary wanting. Let's see if we can find some better words to describe a guy who gets his jollies from overcharging the desperate. Ignorant? Small-minded? Greedy opportunist? Frankly, I think *fat, fucking asshole* is probably as good a term as any."

Ruth glanced around the parking lot. The round man was in the doorway, and the other customers were craning their necks to peer through the window. Two men working in the garage bays paused, their hands still reaching for the tires above them, watching Casey.

"I think you need to eat." She grabbed the atlas and her purse from the car and started to tug Casey across the lot, pointing to a diner across the road. She said nothing until they got settled inside a booth. She stared at him through her sunglasses.

"So, you're frugal. And well spoken when you want to be."

"You can thank the brothers at St. Francis Academy, Jersey City's finest. Made sure we knew our way around a sentence." Casey settled into the seat.

"Catholic school?"

Casey reached for the menu behind the napkin holder. "Come on, Ruth, let's order something. Prices are good here."

"Go ahead. I'm not hungry."

"You will be later. Might as well load up now."

"Were you an altar boy?"

He laughed. "Until Father Bernard fired my ass in seventh grade."

"What'll it be?" A waitress turned up, pad in hand, a perfunctory smile on her lips.

"Three eggs over easy with bacon, fries, and pancakes for me." He nodded at Ruth. "Go ahead, live it up."

"A salad."

"It's not lunchtime yet," said the waitress. She tapped her pencil on the menu where it said, *Breakfast served to 11 a.m.*

"Do you have any fruit?"

"Fruit cocktail."

"Fine, I'll have that, some wheat toast, and coffee."

"Like I say, live it up," Casey said.

Ruth ignored him while the waitress poured coffee into Ruth's mug and departed. She maneuvered the cup to her good side and sipped. Then she nearly spit the whole mouthful out. They'd given her the dregs of a pot that wasn't good to begin with.

She decided it was time she knew a little more about his plan. "Is that where we're going, Jersey City?" Casey loaded his cup with half-and-half and sugar and took a sip from his mug before nodding.

Ruth waited for him to say more but he just sat there, drinking his coffee.

"Here's your eggs and here's your fruit," the waitress said. She plunked down the plates and, without asking, topped off Ruth's mug. Ruth let it sit there.

"So, you grew up there?"

"Mmm-hmm," Casey responded, eyes on his plate, fork busy.

"I was born there," Ruth said. "New Brunswick." Why had she told him that? She barely ever thought of it herself.

"No shit?" Casey paused, a forkful of home fries hovering in the air. "You're a Jersey girl?"

Ruth wished she hadn't started down this road, but it was easier to answer than to clam up over something so inconsequential. "Not really. I grew up in New Hampshire."

Casey, mouth full, lifted his eyebrows in a question.

Ruth shrugged as if the memory meant nothing to her, but she knew her choice of words betrayed the bitterness she felt, as sharp as it had been nearly forty years earlier. "My mother dumped my brother and me there before she left us."

Casey swallowed. He put his fork down and studied his plate as if he'd shoveled something bitter into his mouth. Ruth picked up a piece of toast and began to tear off the crust.

"So," Ruth said. "What else did you learn from the brothers at St. Francis?"

"All the usuals. Reading, writing, the perils of sex. A few Shakespearean insults. Those and the sexy stuff got us through Brother Philip's literature classes," Casey said. He picked up his fork but put it down again.

"Us?"

Casey glanced up, then out the window at the parking lot. "Yeah," he said after a moment. "Mike and me."

Ruth looked out the window but saw nothing that would account for the way he was staring. "Who was he, your brother?"

"Like a brother. No relation."

"Is that why you're going back? To see him?"

"Mike's dead."

"I'm sorry," she said. This was the same stupid thing that some had said to her when they heard about Robbie. Even Terri. To her surprise, Casey said exactly what she had wanted to say.

"Why? It's not your fault." His gray eyes, now devoid of curiosity, fixed on hers. "But yeah, I'm going back to Jersey for a little visit with some folks we both used to know. That's the plan anyway. Depends on how well you navigate, right?"

Ruth picked up the atlas and spread it open next to her half-eaten toast and the cup of fruit cocktail, a collection of flaccid grapes, cherries, and citrus sections that all tasted vaguely of the metal can they'd been in until moments before. The route was uncomplicated, a single road or two all the way across the country, but she was startled by how much distance she had already put between her and San Diego. Only two days of driving and she was miles from everything and everyone she knew.

On the atlas, Ruth traced the route to her office. She stared at the spot, seeing where the RyCom building would be. There were the people she'd come to know the way some people know friends or family: Terri, Don, Gordon. Phones would be beeping, and computer keys clicking without stop while customers, lawyers, and public relations specialists filed through to the conference rooms to cement the deal with Transglobal, fend off the contractor lawsuits, keep alive new deals like the ones she'd been working on. She imagined her desk, clean now, or more likely, ceded to Andrea.

In her old world, absences were often sudden. The bigger the casualty, the less was said, at least out loud. No matter what rationale had been provided in the office memo that announced Ruth's departure, the underlying message was clear and unsettling: No one was indispensable. She'd said this often enough herself but, like most of the other senior executives she worked with, had never quite believed it. Some would be rattled by her departure; others would simply see her loss as their gain. Either way, the survivors would want new skin to form over her absence as quickly as possible and move on. Some would expect her to pop up in a competitor's company or just take the money coming to her and disappear; most would not even give it that much thought. Even Neal had expected her to grieve discreetly, bury Robbie, and then wait until the Transglobal deal went through.

The clang of metal against the counter made her look up from the map. She saw the waitress grab a tub of iceberg lettuce from the cook and start to stuff handfuls of it into small bowls. Across the table, Casey lifted a pancake from a small plate onto his egg-smeared dish.

"We wouldn't need that thing if you had GPS," he said without looking up. "How come you don't have it?"

"Didn't come with that year's model," Ruth said. "Besides, I only drive near my home. I always know where I am and how to get wherever I'm going."

"Not anymore," Casey said. He popped a forkful of pancake into his mouth.

*No*, she thought. *Not anymore.*

# CHAPTER 34

Casey spotted the state trooper in the rearview mirror before they'd gotten twenty miles from Ogallala. Reflexively, he clicked off the cruise control and allowed the Jaguar to slow a bit, but the guy stayed behind them.

"What was that for?" Ruth said, glancing at the speedometer. "You weren't speeding."

"Something about a police car on my ass makes me nervous." Now the lights flashed on the top of the cop car. The siren sounded briefly, like a shout.

"Ruth, if there is anything you need to tell me, tell me now," Casey said, pulling the car into the emergency lane and taking as long as he could to roll to a stop.

Ruth twisted around. "Maybe—"

"What?" Casey said. It was too late. The cop was already getting out of his car. Damn.

"License, registration, please," the officer said. Casey didn't bother to ask why. Chitchat would just delay the inevitable. He dug his wallet out of his pocket, grateful that he'd thought to put the cash in the sock, now safely in his bag. "Ruth, pass me the registration."

She talked past him to the cop. "Why did you stop us? We weren't speeding."

"Lens on your taillight is broken and your left directional doesn't seem to be working."

"Just give him the damn registration," Casey said.

The officer peered through the driver's window. His breath blasted past Casey's nose, a warm mess of onions and grilled beef. "Do we have a problem?"

Ruth opened the glove compartment and shuffled through the few slips of paper in there until she found a plastic sleeve holding the registration and the insurance card. Casey passed them to the cop. The trooper glanced from Casey's license to the registration and back.

"Whose car is this?"

"Mine." Ruth's voice was chilly.

"What's your name, ma'am?"

"Ruth Nolan."

Casey saw that Ruth was trying not to look straight at the trooper. With a rush of gratitude, he realized that she was trying to hide her bruised eye and swollen lip, which the guy would automatically assume had something to do with him.

"May I see your license, please?"

Shit.

"I don't have it with me, officer. That's why my friend is driving." She was cool. Very cool. Casey glanced at the trooper, who had now pushed his own sunglasses up on his head, a balding head, freckled and burned. He was not a young guy. *That's good*, Casey thought. He hated young cops. Full of shit and testosterone. On the other hand, this one seemed to be stuck, wondering what to do next. Then he shrugged and walked back to his car. Casey kept watching the trooper in the rearview mirror, but he spoke to Ruth quickly from the side of his mouth.

"Tell me now."

"Tell you what?"

"Whatever it was that you were going to say before the cop got out of his car before."

Ruth hesitated. Casey saw the trooper pick up his radio and start to speak into it. "He's stopped writing the ticket. What the fuck, Ruth? What's going on?"

"It's possible that my friend got them to look for me. Or maybe my secretary. Or both."

"Why would they do that?"

"They are probably worried about my state of mind. I left without much warning. I left a voice mail back in Denver telling them I was okay, but maybe they didn't believe me."

"And now they're going to think I kidnapped you or something." A pain lit up in Casey's temple. He was clenching his jaw.

"Relax. I'll just tell them you're extorting money from me."

Casey couldn't believe it. She was smiling at him. She was acting suddenly like this was a joke—or worse, like she didn't give a fuck what unfolded, just like she'd acted in the casino, laying all her credit cards out for the world to see. He rubbed his head between his hands. Suddenly the cop was back at his window.

"Miss Nolan, do you have anything that would identify you?"

"Is that really necessary?"

"Afraid it is, ma'am."

Casey looked at Ruth. She seemed to think for a moment.

"Move the seat up, I need to get my briefcase," she said to Casey. Casey felt the eyes of the trooper on him as Ruth reached behind the driver's seat. What was taking her so long?

"Here, will this do it?"

She held one of those plastic company ID cards with a photo on it and a lanyard, like the security guys at the casino wore. Her company's name sounded familiar to him but he couldn't figure out why. RyCom Systems. Casey passed it to the trooper. "Would you mind taking off your sunglasses, please?"

"Why?"

"Then I would be absolutely sure the woman in this picture is you."

"First, tell me who sent you and why, if we haven't broken any laws, I should put up with any of this," Ruth said. The throbbing in Casey's temple intensified.

"We have a missing-person report. Don't see a lot of Jaguars. License plate matches up with the report."

"Well, you found me. Your job is done."

"You want to tell me how those bruises on your face got there?"

From the corner of his eye, Casey saw that the trooper was looking at him, not Ruth. He forced himself to stay still.

"No, I don't," Ruth said.

She wasn't even looking at the guy. She was going to piss him off.

"It's okay, Ruth," Casey said. He tried to make his voice sound gentle, the way he imagined a concerned friend or brother would sound. "Tell him about the accident."

In response, Ruth whipped her glasses off and stared directly at the officer. Casey winced at her eye, still puffy, ocher and purple and black. He hoped like hell she would take his cue and make up something about an accident.

"I was nearly raped by a trucker. As it was, all he got was my wallet. This man helped me. Now we are traveling together."

Casey felt his jaw go slack. He heard the cop let out a long breath.

"Did you file a report?"

"No. I had other things on my mind."

"What kinds of things were those, ma'am?"

Casey glanced at her and shook his head. He wanted her to stop; she didn't owe this guy a thing. Ruth either didn't notice or decided to ignore him.

"My son." Her voice sounded flat, hard.

"Ma'am?"

"I didn't want to bury him just to make a lot of other people feel better. That's why I left. They expected me to shut up and take his ashes out on a boat and throw them in the ocean. My son hated the ocean."

Casey watched the trooper's face. He seemed to be searching for the right words. But before he said anything, Ruth started in again, her voice growing colder as she went on.

"Would you like proof of that, officer? Would you like to see the box that holds his ashes?" Ruth twisted again in her seat and brought forward the metal box. "Here it is. Would you like to see his duffel with his Marine uniform and the sand he hauled all the way back here from Iraq? Would you like, officer, to tell me the right way to handle the death of my kid? A few bruises don't come near it."

The trooper winced. He put his glasses back on. For a moment no one said anything. Then the trooper cleared his throat.

"Look. I'm sorry."

Ruth's shoulders slumped in a way that made Casey want to hit the cop. When she spoke, her voice was low.

"It's not your fault," she said. Casey heard those words and remembered how he'd felt just a little while ago when he'd said them. He wished there were a way he could show her that he understood, but he didn't move. No one moved. The silence stretched until, finally, Ruth broke it.

"Tell me who filed the missing-person report. I'll call them right now, in front of you. If they agree that it is me, then you can let us go on our way, right?"

The trooper looked hard at Casey as if he were trying to make up his mind.

"Never mind," Ruth said. She grabbed the phone from its spot on the console between the two front seats. She'd been charging it;

Casey had forgotten it was even there. A few seconds later, Ruth said, "Terri? It's me."

Casey was at the mercy of Ruth and whoever was on the other end of the line. He looked straight ahead but felt the officer's stare on him while Ruth went on.

"I'm fine. Really." She was trying to sound cool, businesslike, but from the corner of his eye, he saw Ruth look down at her lap where her left hand had clenched into a fist. Whatever Terri was saying, Ruth didn't like it.

"I know. I'm sorry I worried you. I told you in the voice mail, I just needed to get away for a little bit, to think things through. Nebraska. I know, I said . . . Terri, stop talking. Please. Just for a minute. You need to tell the officer here . . . what's your name, sir?" Ruth leaned past Casey to look at the man still standing outside the driver's-side window. *Sir,* that was a nice touch, Casey thought.

"Jennings. Sergeant Jennings."

"Terri, tell Sergeant Jennings that I'm who I say I am." A pause. "I don't have my license, it was in my wallet and . . . Just do it, please? We can talk about all this later." Ruth reached past Casey and handed the phone to Jennings. "I would appreciate it," she said in a low voice to the trooper, "if you would not dramatize the situation."

Ruth put her sunglasses back on, covering her shiner.

"Jennings here, Nebraska State Police. Who am I speaking to?" He paused. "Would you please confirm that the woman you just spoke to is Ruth Nolan?" A pause, then. "Red hair, thin. Has an ID from your company. She informs me that her son has died recently. Yes. Thank you. Please hold on." Jennings leaned down and talked through the window.

"What is your son's name, ma'am?"

"Robbie. Robert Nolan O'Connell." Ruth turned her head toward the passenger window.

Jennings straightened. "That's all I need. Thank you." He

handed the phone back to Ruth. He handed back the registration. "You are free to go, ma'am. You should get medical attention for those injuries." Casey tensed as the trooper eyed him one more time. No doubt there was more he'd like to know about Ruth's story, but Casey figured that in the absence of charges or witnesses, there was not much the guy could do. Casey watched him walk back to his car.

Beside him, Ruth sighed and lifted the phone to her ear. "Injuries? Nothing serious. Can I call you later, Ter? Yes, of course. Tell Neal I'm fine. Tell him he can call off the dogs. Yes. Yes, I promise to call him. Yes, my family too." Ruth sounded tired now and, to Casey's ear, abashed.

"He's a . . . friend. I'll explain later." She paused. Casey saw from the way her jaw pulsed that she was hating every minute of this. "Thank you for handling the credit cards and all that. What? I don't know yet. Can you hold on to the new ones? I'll let you know where to mail them."

A longer pause. Casey thought he heard a woman's voice, faint and rapid on the other end of the phone. Ruth broke in, gentler now but firm. "I've got to go now. I promise I'll . . . Yes. Ter?" She paused and glanced at him before lowering her voice. "I'm . . . I'm sorry for putting you through this. I never meant to . . . anyway. Thank you." Casey saw her nod to whatever the woman on the other end said. "'Bye, Ter." Then Ruth clicked a button on the phone and brought it down from her ear.

Casey stared at her. The back of his shirt was soaked with sweat. "If that guy could have, he would have hauled me in."

"But he couldn't, so here you are."

"Is Neal your boyfriend?"

"No. Sometimes. A friend . . ."

"And Terri? Who is she? What's RyCom?"

"I already told you Terri's my assistant. Was." Ruth paused a moment. "She's a friend, too."

RyCom. The name was familiar but he couldn't think of a single reason why. He started to ask what the company did, but he noticed Ruth looking down at the box in her lap, smoothing the edge of the label with her son's name on it.

"You okay, Ruth?"

She glanced up but he couldn't see her eyes through the dark lenses. "I'm fine." She turned and gently placed the box in the backseat, securing it by packing a couple of plastic bags around it. "I want to drive."

"Are you out of your mind? Now they know you have no license. Forget it. We don't need to run that risk."

"No one's going to stop us again. It's done now. Let me drive. I need to do something."

Casey's head ached. It felt like a crab had seized a nerve in his neck. The desire to escape returned. Accommodating the needs of another person was something he'd forgotten how to do, if in fact he'd ever really learned it. He didn't have the first idea about what to do for Ruth and it made him feel deficient, the way he'd felt in the days after coming back from the Gulf, minus half a leg and the will to be anybody's good boy. He shook his head.

"Please."

Damn it. She wasn't alone in the world; people were looking for her. Let them deal with her mess. Next stop, he'd figure out what to do. Maybe he could call her boyfriend to come get her. He'd have to get the name; the number was probably on her phone. If that didn't work, there was always the secretary. The thought calmed him. Some of his resistance gave way.

"Why do I have the feeling that you won't let me alone until I say yes?"

"Because it's true."

The thought of riding with an irritated, restless Ruth dissolved the rest of Casey's resistance. "All right." He shoved open his door so they could switch seats. "If we're stopped again, that's it. You're on your own."

# CHAPTER 35

Ruth glanced at Casey, his head lolling against the window, apparently oblivious to the sunlight streaking through the windows or the sweat gathering on his skin beneath the rims of his sunglasses. He'd dropped into sleep within minutes of giving her the wheel, as if he were trying to get away from the mess he'd gotten himself into the only way he could.

She hit the accelerator but the landscape seemed to push back. Sky empty of clouds or variation of any kind stretched endlessly over a road that seemed to reproduce itself every twenty miles. The same median of yellowed grass coursed through the middle; on either side stretched fields of the same color, some cordoned off into patches by small lines of trees. Green highway signs were the only way she could gauge their progress, if it could be called progress. A hundred miles to Omaha. She'd never been to Omaha, had no desire to go, yet here she was racing toward the city as if by driving fast enough, she could escape the fumes of self-disgust triggered by her short conversation with Terri.

Terri hadn't said anything about the flash drive or the contractors on the phone. Maybe she'd given up on Ruth, which should have been a relief but somehow wasn't. Instead, Terri had just asked her to call Neal and her family. She'd sighed in a way that suggested she wasn't even sure that Ruth could be counted upon to do this.

Ruth looked again at Casey, half wishing he'd wake up and distract her but he snored on, leaving her with the echo of Terri's sigh and her own shame when she pictured her family. She imagined her grandmother's gentle eyes, surrounded by wrinkles of age and worry. Kevin would hide his concern as well as he could, but he would be checking the answering machine at his shop to see if she'd returned any of his calls.

*Mom, c'mon. It's home.*

There was a sensation in her chest like a balloon inflating, pushing against her heart, her ribs. Her fingers cramped. She flexed them and glanced at Casey again to see if he was surfacing, but his jaw remained slack and his eyes closed.

Damn him. Damn them all. If she talked to them, they would tell her to come home, to bring Robbie's ashes so they could say good-bye. *Not yet. Please, not yet.*

Ruth started to pull out to pass the pickup in front of her, but a horn blasted as an RV appeared suddenly behind her. She jerked the wheel to get back into her lane.

"What are you doing?" Casey's voice was the sharp, startled bark of the newly awakened.

"Driving." The sound of her own voice steadied her.

"Keep your eyes on the road. Where are we, anyway?" Casey rubbed his eyes underneath his sunglasses so they tipped cockeyed across his face.

"We're somewhere past the middle of Nebraska heading for the middle of nowhere," she told him. Yes, this was better. Talk like this kept her in the present. They had miles to go before she had to make any calls, any decisions. The tightness in her chest began to ease.

"What the fuck is that on the radio?"

Ruth had not realized it was even on.

"Jesus, let me do it." He leaned forward and started pushing the tuner. "Don't know why I bother, you hate anything good anyway."

"That's not true."

"Okay, what's your favorite song? I don't mean that crap you made me listen to before. What music did you make out to when you were a kid?"

"The Allman Brothers. 'Melissa.'" Ruth said it without hesitation, and when he laughed, she felt her cheeks warm.

"Look at that, you're turning red," Casey said. He fiddled more with the tuner. "So, Ruth, what did you do for fun when you were a kid?"

She thought about changing the subject but couldn't think of anything new to say. "There wasn't much to do. It was winter nine months out of the year."

"What do you remember about Jersey? Ever go to the shore?"

"Yes."

"Yeah? Where did you go?"

"I forget the name of the beach. But I remember the waves seemed huge."

Once, in the days before her mother left, a wave had knocked Ruth down, but before she could panic, her father swept her up and lifted her to his chest. Her mother wrapped a towel around her and Ruth was enclosed by her parents and filled with a bliss she could recall even now, forty years later. Lost in the memory, she inhaled deeply, half expecting the tang of salt, sweat, and baby oil. Instead she smelled spent coffee cups and sweat. Without looking, she sensed Casey eyeing her from the passenger seat.

"They probably weren't that big; I was pretty small," she said. "Hey, is there any water left?"

Casey reached down between his legs into a plastic sack and pulled out a full bottle.

"When did you leave Jersey?"

Ruth couldn't tell if he was really interested or just filling time. She wasn't sure it mattered. "We moved when I was nine and my brother was seven. My father got sick. Cancer. We went to live with my grandparents. My father died. Then my mother left." Ruth tilted the bottle of water to her lips and swallowed.

A minute passed. Ruth turned to Casey and saw him staring straight ahead, as if seeing another landscape entirely. "Where'd she go?"

"Back to New Jersey at first, then New York. She was supposed to get a job, then find a place for us all to live." She wanted to stop talking, but before she could think of a way to derail his questions, he asked the very one she'd asked her mother when she finally tracked her down.

"Why didn't she come back?" Casey mumbled, as if he weren't sure he wanted to know. He was staring down at the backs of his hands as if he'd found something he didn't like in the tanned skin and ridged knuckles.

"She got married again. Then again. It was never the right time." That was all he needed to know. Ruth took another slug from the water bottle.

The truth was harsher. "The longer I was gone, the easier it was to stay away," Stella had finally told her when Ruth found her twenty-six years later in Boynton Beach, Florida. Her mother had stared at her over the top of a gin and tonic and said those exact words. She'd started out defensively, leaning back into the corner of her shabby brocade sofa in the darkened condo: she cared so much about Ruth and Kevin; she would sacrifice rather than uproot them; her second and third husbands had not wanted more children. Then came the truth: just easier.

"I did you a favor," Stella had said, her voice as cold as the cubes in her gin. "Look how you turned out."

Now Ruth shook her head. "Let's talk about something else."

Casey reached into the backseat and wrestled a can of Coke out of a bag. "We have a lot in common, don't we?"

"What?"

Still holding the can, he wiggled two fingers. "Both of us were born in New Jersey and both of us were raised by old people." He ripped the tab off the top, sending a froth of brown down the front of his Hawaiian print shirt, the same one he'd worn the day they left.

Ruth glanced sideways at Casey while he mopped up the mess, swearing under his breath. Sure. Twins under the skin. Ruth shook her head. He was obviously intelligent, but he apparently wanted to obscure that most of the time. Right now, he was hiding behind a lot of questions he kept throwing at her like darts. She didn't want to talk about herself anymore.

"Who's the little girl in the picture?" Ruth asked, looking back at the road. The shifting in the passenger seat ceased.

"What picture?"

The sudden wariness in his tone startled Ruth. "The one in your wallet," she said, carefully.

"What were you doing with my wallet?"

"I needed money to pay for that peanut butter you ate last night."

He went quiet and stared out the passenger window. Ruth thought he was through talking, but he cleared his throat. "That girl, she's Mike's daughter, the guy I told you about. I'm going to see her, give her something that belongs to her."

Ruth glanced sideways again. "Must be something pretty important if you have to deliver it in person."

Casey grunted.

"She looks pretty young. Does she know you're coming? Or maybe her mother?"

Casey shook his head.

"Well, kids like surprises, they say." That was a lie. She'd always hated surprises, especially when she was young.

"It's an old picture."

Ruth was about to say something about surprises being worse when you're older, but Casey cut her off. "You've driven over two hundred miles. My turn."

"I'm fine." She didn't want to stop.

"I don't care. Pull over, up there." He pointed to a turnoff about two hundred feet ahead. "It's my turn."

She could not get him to start talking again after he started driving. The withdrawal was sudden and complete; it stung. Ruth found a news channel on the radio and turned it up loud to goad him. But he didn't seem to notice. She might as well have been alone.

The sun lowered in the sky behind them, but Casey was too busy counting the miles to Omaha to notice. Only ten more to go. They'd agreed to stop then, anywhere they could find. He was almost sorry he'd made Ruth let him drive. His back was stiff, his stump throbbed, and the pain in his head winched tighter. The sides of the Jaguar seemed to be closing in on him, but he knew some of that was his fault.

*My daughter.* The words were right on the tip of his tongue when Ruth asked about the photograph. He had no right to say them, was the way he looked at it. He'd left all his rights behind him, buried in the bits and pieces of plans he'd dared to make before he'd fucked it all up. She'd been close to five when he left. She was seventeen going on eighteen now, old enough to hate him the way Ruth obviously hated the mother who'd walked out on her. If he'd told her the truth, she would have wanted to know why he left, why he never went back, and none of his answers were good enough.

Her name, Emily, filled his mouth. He wanted to say it out loud, but when he opened his lips what came out was a lie. An easy lie to say but a hard one to swallow. He'd made her Mike's. Even dead, Mike ended up with the best of him.

Damn Ruth, hitting every nerve with her questions, like a kid running a stick along a fence just to hear the noise. His life was none of her business. He knew why he'd lied about Mike being Emily's father. He didn't want Ruth to know he was no better than the mother who'd walked out on her. He was a fucking liar and a coward. One more reason to get the hell out of this arrangement. He needed to pass Ruth to someone else.

"Pull over, there's a restroom up ahead. I can't wait for the next town," Ruth said.

Casey said nothing as he guided the car into the rest stop and parked.

"Be right back." The door slammed shut behind her.

He saw her phone on the console between the two seats. He turned it on and, keeping watch on the ladies' room entrance, found the list of her most recent calls. There was Terri, her assistant. Several earlier calls were from Robbie. Casey hesitated. Poor kid. Then, amid these and others with no names, he saw *Neal* over and over again. Bingo. Casey pulled his own phone out of his pocket and punched in the phone number attached to *Neal.* Just as he finished, he looked up to see Ruth emerging from the bathroom.

"My turn," he told her, pushing the car door open.

"Why didn't you get out when I did?" She sounded irritated.

"Relax, Ruth, it's not as if we're on any kind of schedule."

As he limped over to the low brick building, he saw her stretch her legs, then lean first to one side and then to the other like a tree bending in a strong breeze. Once he was inside, he called Neal's number. As the ringtone filled his ear, he looked over his shoulder and then chided himself; Ruth wouldn't hear him in here.

"Neal Treadwell." The voice on the other end of the phone set Casey's teeth on edge. The guy sounded like a pilot or a high-level cop, all business, prepared to go either way—polite to someone higher up, curt to someone wasting his time. Casey started to speak and then the phone beeped. *Fucking voice mail*, Casey thought. *Arro-*

*gant son of a bitch doesn't even bother with any kind of message, just says his name like it's supposed to mean something all by itself.*

"You don't know me but I think you know Ruth Nolan," Casey began. Damn, he hadn't thought through what he was going to say. "Listen, I've tried to help her, but she's got more going on than I can deal with."

A plan, Casey thought desperately. He needed a plan.

"We're headed toward Chicago and should be there late tomorrow or the next day. Call me back and leave a message telling me where you want to meet her and I'll make sure she's there."

He stopped and tried to think about what else to say. "This is no joke. If you know her, you know she's been through a lot. I've done my best, but it's time for someone else to take over."

He stopped again and then began to worry that the voice mail would cut him off before he finished. "That's it. Call this number and leave a message about Chicago and where to meet you. I'll make sure she gets there."

He rang off and shoved the phone back in his pocket. Why did he feel so shitty all of a sudden? He should feel relieved. Three quick bursts on a horn sounded from the parking lot. Had to be Ruth. "Hold your horses," he muttered as he stepped over to the urinal.

When they were under way again, he couldn't resurrect the tentative connection born in the previous day's rainstorm. For over an hour he rode elbow to elbow with her in the litter from road meals, the car echoing with aborted conversations, radio stations changed at will, the impatient snap of each atlas page as she flipped through it. He tried not to think about what he would do once they got to Chicago and he could get away from her. He had options. He could still go to New Jersey. But the more they drove, the decision to see Emily seemed as crazy as whatever Ruth might be doing. The idea that he could walk into his daughter's life after being gone for so many years was the kind of thing soap operas were made of. He felt like a fool. His leg began to hurt below the stump. This was the second time in two days that he felt pain in the leg that wasn't there, as though he'd woken it just by leaving Nevada. The headaches were back too. He rubbed around the edge of the faker but nothing helped. He needed some aspirin. He needed a cigarette. The nicotine patches weren't enough.

"There, up ahead." Ruth pointed. She gestured to a road sign rising from the side of the highway: something called the Motel 50 wedged in among a line of other motels and chain restaurants outside Omaha. Right next to it was a steakhouse. Casey sat up, taking in the neon pink letters and the outline of a T-bone. Fuck the cost. They were going to have a decent meal. He could give her that as a going-away present. And he could use a drink.

R uth waited until Casey took his turn in the shower before dinner. When she heard water slap the tiles in the motel bathroom, she grabbed her purse and dug out her phone. It was nine o'clock on the East Coast; she could call Kevin's shop and leave a message. She'd tell him she was okay, that she'd be in touch soon. She could do that much.

She rapped on the bathroom door. "I'm going outside to make a call."

"What?" Casey yelled over the shower.

"Never mind."

"What?" he yelled again. But Ruth had already closed the motel room door behind her.

The smell of diesel mixed with French fry grease hung in the humid air, so dense she could imagine wringing it out. She headed for the car to get away from the stench, and from the drone of the highway that bordered the parking lot. Once in the driver's seat of the Jaguar, she took a breath. Then another. The smell in there was only slightly better. *Just call.* Ruth shoved her hair, still wet from the shower, behind her ears and then scrolled her contacts for the shop number. She pressed send. One ring, two, then three. There was a click. Ruth opened her mouth when she heard her brother's low halting voice.

"Hello."

She waited for the rest of the message but it didn't come. Instead she heard a breath, then another "Hello?"

"Kevin?" She heard the shake in her own voice, as if she were getting ready to cry, or run. "I didn't expect you to be there."

Anyone else would have shot back with *Why did you call, then?* but Kevin only said, "I'm glad I am." Then he paused. "How are you? Are you all right?"

Ruth fingered the glasses she'd put on even though it was dark. She was glad he couldn't see her. "I'm okay. I was calling to tell you not to worry."

"A little late for that," he said. Kevin's voice was gravelly with fatigue. Ruth braced herself for reproach, but all she heard was a sigh so deep it was as if he'd waited until this moment to take a full breath.

For a few seconds she was a nine-year-old again, gripping Kevin's hand as they watched their father's casket descend into the grave. He'd slipped his hand into hers as their mother waved good-bye for what turned out to be the last time. Then, when Jeff died, Kevin found her hand again. He gave one hand to her, one to Robbie. Kevin never knew what to say, but he somehow knew to reach for her hand and let her believe she was doing the holding. Now, listening to him sigh, she finally understood that he'd never stopped holding her hand. She'd been the one to let go. She closed her eyes against the tears gathering, burning.

"Are you coming home?" Not *where are you*, or *what are you doing*, all the questions she knew Neal would ask when she finally called him. Kevin had never thought of California as her real home. Neither had Robbie, apparently. In the end, he'd gone to the farm first, not to her.

*Ruthie, come on. It's home.*

Except that going there hadn't saved Robbie. Ruth pulled off her sunglasses and pinched the inside corners of her eyes with her free hand. Why hadn't they saved him? Kevin had had days with him, days. She'd had only a few hours.

"Why didn't you call me when he showed up in Gershom?" Ruth asked. The words tore out of her even though Kevin didn't deserve them. She knew there was no one in the world who could answer all the *why*s that boiled inside her, Kevin least of all.

Ruth heard a few ragged breaths, then the mewling of a cat in the background. Her brother was alone in the night with his pain; she was only hurting him more. She shouldn't have called.

"Never mind, Kev, it's—"

"I should've," her brother said, his voice so low she could barely hear him. "Gram was all over him to call you, have you come east, but he asked us not to. He wanted to surprise you." A long pause followed, and then Ruth heard her brother gulp back a sob. Ruth's grief rose to meet his and she understood then why she had not called her family. She could not hold on to her grief in the face of theirs. She would have to yield.

"I can't . . . I can't do this now." She looked up toward the motel room door. Casey would be out soon. She didn't want him to see her like this.

She tried to think of something that would move Kevin and her to safer ground. "Why are you working so late?"

"Well . . ." He hesitated, cleared his throat. "Been spending more time with Gram during the day. Have to catch up here. Not sleeping much anyway, so might as well."

Ruth went rigid in her seat. "Is she sick?

Kevin hesitated as if reluctant to explain. "Not in the way you'd think, I guess. She's eating herself up with worry, doesn't like being alone. She wants me there in case you call. You know her. She wants to come get you and bring you back here where she can take care of you."

"The days are gone when Big Ruth can make things better," Ruth said.

"Maybe you should give her a chance. She keeps saying she knows what it's like to . . . to lose a child."

Ruth struggled against the urge to shout. "But Dad lived to be a man! He didn't *choose* to die. He had cancer. There wasn't anything she could have done to save him." Ruth's throat went dry, but her eyes began to fill again. Then she saw the door of the motel room open. Casey was wearing one of his Hawaiian shirts, his damp hair slicked back. He peered out into the haze of night, fluorescence, and fumes.

Ruth slipped her glasses back on and tried to swallow. "I've got to go, Kev. I'll call again. I just need a little more time. Tell Big Ruth I love her and that I'm all right. Promise me, okay?"

"Ruth, wait . . ."

"Kevin, please, I promise I'll call. I just can't talk anymore right now." But she couldn't hang up on him. She needed him to let her go.

Her brother seemed to be struggling for the right words. "Robbie was . . . It's not your fault. We know that it isn't your fault."

*You need to believe that. You need me to believe it. But I don't.* The image of Kevin as a boy returned. She could almost feel his hand slipping into hers. She wondered if she could ever again face the love he was trying to give her or the love that was making her grandmother stand guard at the telephone.

"I love you, Kev," she managed to say. "I'll call you soon. I promise." Ruth disconnected the phone and looked up to see if Casey was still looking for her. He was leaning in the doorway, half in shadow, half in the motel room light. She couldn't make out his features but she could tell by the direction of his gaze that he'd spotted her. He was hungry, she knew that, but she couldn't eat a thing now. She should tell him to go over to that steak place by himself, but then she'd be alone in the motel room with the echo of Kevin's voice in her ears.

She took a breath. Then another. She pushed open the car door, stood up, and called to Casey.

"I'm coming."

C asey never asked Ruth who she'd been talking to on the phone. It was none of his business. The steak the waitress plunked down in front of him was definitely his business, though. He glanced across the oak table at her, sitting beneath a mural of cattle thundering across the plain, cowboys with kerchiefs over their noses, and horses galloping under them. The smell of sizzling meat rose from his plate. Just what he needed.

"Want a bite?" he asked Ruth.

"Another drink." She pushed her empty glass toward the edge of the table and looked around for the waitress.

"Try some of this, it's better than that damn chicken salad or whatever it was that you ordered." He sliced off a chunk of his T-bone and put it on her plate, next to the sandwich she'd barely touched.

Ruth shook her head and caught the waitress as she was passing. "Another vodka martini, please."

"Jameson's for me," said Casey, smiling up at the woman. Then he switched back to Ruth. "At least eat some potatoes."

"Afraid you'll have to rescue me again?" She was looking toward him, but he couldn't see her eyes through the damn sunglasses she insisted on wearing even in here.

"Neither one of us wants that." Casey popped the chunk of meat into his mouth and chewed. The waitress delivered both drinks and Ruth began to sip hers.

"Tell me what happened to your leg," she said.

He'd been wondering when she'd get around to asking that. He reached for his water glass and guzzled enough to move the meat down his throat. When he put the glass down, Ruth was still waiting. He leaned back in the booth.

"Not much of a story. I left it behind in Kuwait in ninety-one."

Ruth stopped midsip. She put down her glass. "Were you in the Marines?"

"Army. One of the hundreds of thousands of bodies parked in the desert to protect all that oil under the sand."

"But I thought there weren't any—many—casualties."

"You mean not on our side."

Ruth looked down at her martini. Casey decided to keep talking.

"Yeah, one of the big success stories of all time, unless you happen to be one of the few who was in the wrong place at the wrong time. The kicker is most of our casualties were friendly fire." Casey stuck out his left leg and knocked on the plastic socket, the sound muffled by his jeans. "This happened when we came across some unexploded ordnance dropped by our guys."

Casey paused and tipped his drink up to his lips. He liked the way the whiskey stung a little and numbed his mouth before settling in with slow, spreading warmth.

"What happened?"

"I'm riding shotgun in a vehicle and we run over the thing. Truck's destroyed, everyone catches shrapnel. One minute I've got a leg. The next, it's just a slab of meat bleeding out in the desert."

Casey picked up his fork and knife again. He glanced across the table. Ruth's lips were frozen in a grimace that could have been sympathy or disgust.

"Sorry," he said, popping another bite into his mouth.

"No, you're not," she said.

She was right. He wasn't. He'd been thinking about it a long time and now it wanted out. "Look, Ruth, it's a fucking waste. No matter how you look at war, that one, this one, and probably the next, it's all a fucking machine set up to make a few people rich, or guard their property, or both. What's a leg when their billions are at stake? What's a life?"

The words were out of Casey's mouth before he could stop them. He dropped his fork and looked straight at Ruth. She didn't look away but he saw her fingers tremble against the glass in front of her.

"I shouldn't have said that. I didn't mean that Robbie . . ."

"Was a waste?"

Casey couldn't speak.

"Why did you join the Army?" Her hands were still shaking, but she lifted the glass and nearly drained it. He wished she would take off the sunglasses so he could look her in the eye.

"Wasn't my choice. It was either that or jail."

Ruth's eyebrows rose above the rim of the sunglasses. "And you a good Catholic boy?" Her voice sounded strained, but determined to push the conversation forward or just away from Robbie. Casey pushed his plate away and pulled his drink closer. He wasn't hungry anymore.

"I wasn't a model student," he said, trying for a smile. He was lying again. He had been a good student. He'd just been a better friend, until one night when he failed to be any kind of friend at all.

Ruth did not say anything; she just set down her glass and stared at the table.

"Look, you want anything else?"

Ruth tapped the rim of her empty glass.

"Okay. Another one for the road and then we head back." She nodded. Casey signaled the waitress and, stood up. "'Scuse me. Nature calls."

R uth did not look at Casey when he got up to head to the bathroom. She sensed his pause at the edge of the table to be sure of his footing. She heard his first few imbalanced steps across the wooden floor before they were swallowed by the noise of clinking forks, beery laughs, and cheerful waitresses. A waste, he'd said. His leg, Robbie, both wasted.

A cash register dinged through the noise around her. *Cha-ching.* "They want me. Guess I'm good enough for once," Robbie had said the day he told her he'd enlisted. "Besides, there's a war on—but you know all that, right? Cha-ching." He'd rubbed his thumb and forefinger together, accusing her the way Casey had without knowing it. Ruth grabbed her water glass. It was empty. Her eyes fell on Casey's plate and the greasy scraps of steak he'd left. *A piece of meat in the desert.* She shook her head to clear it but then remembered something Robbie had written in his journal about the desert, about blood and oil, how he should have been driving, not someone else, how it should have been him. *i can still smell it i will always smell it.*

"You okay, miss?" The waitress stooped as she placed two more drinks on the table. Her casual tone, her dark eyes curious beneath the cowboy hat all the servers wore, snared Ruth before the tears surfaced. Ruth nodded and reached for her martini with both hands.

"Then here's the check. You want me to wrap that steak up for you?"

"No," Ruth said. "Thank you." Then she closed her eyes and drank.

# CHAPTER 36

Casey lay rigid, aware of every breath from the other side of the bed. He knew Ruth was awake. She had not moved in twenty minutes but she wanted to, he could tell; the stillness of her body was too exaggerated, each inhalation too hushed, too controlled. She was trying not to wake him and her obvious effort made him want to yell at her to just roll over already.

The booze at dinner should have knocked them both out after all that driving. They'd fallen into the double bed, the border between them drawn without discussion. Ruth curved away from him on her side. He stretched out on his back, hands folded on his chest. For a little while they must have passed out. Now each was wide awake and pretending not to be.

Ruth's stomach growled through the darkness. Her breath caught and the bed shifted under them as she curled into a fetal position. He turned in her direction. "I told you to eat more."

"Go to hell." Her voice was hoarse and ragged but she said the words without real rancor. He laughed out loud.

"Guess I had that coming."

The mattress squeaked as she craned her neck, looking over her shoulder at him. "Why aren't you asleep?"

*Because my head hurts, because every time I close my eyes, I see a guy I haven't seen since I sent him off to die and he isn't happy with me. Because I'm scared shitless and I don't know why.*

"Just can't," was all he said.

Ruth sighed. She leaned up on one elbow and fumbled on the bedside table for a bottle of water. She gulped down the water until the sides of the bottle buckled. Then she burped.

A laugh exploded out of Casey. Too loud, out of proportion to the event that triggered it, but it was a relief to let it go. He gave it all he had.

"You're still drunk, aren't you, Ruth?"

She didn't answer, just seized her pillows, jammed them against the flimsy headboard, and settled back against them, her head tipped back and eyes aimed at the ceiling as if looking for a place to put her irritation. He could make out her profile and follow it down the outline of her body under the thin sheet. She was wearing the same top she'd worn all day and a pair of shorts, but her skin smelled like the minty soap in the motel. That had been the high point of their day so far, taking turns in the motel's shower and shedding the road. He wanted another shower to wash away the remnants of that last awful conversation where he got on his high horse and called her son's life a waste.

"Go ahead and read if you want," she said. The way she said it, kind of tough but also eager, made him feel good and bad at the same time. He wanted to make up for what he'd said but his head was throbbing, and so was his leg.

"Not right now. Maybe later."

She sniffed and wiped her nose with the back of her hand, pale in the half light. She looked like a kid, an exhausted, sad kid. He reached for the bedside lamp.

"I changed my mind. Go ahead and get the book. It's over there, in my bag."

The bed shifted under him when she rose.

"I'll take some water too, if there's any left," he said. He reached for the white plastic bottle of pills next to the bed.

"Didn't you just take some of those?"

She was right. More pills now probably wouldn't do anything but screw up his stomach. He leaned back against the headboard and opened the book. Beside him, the bed shifted again and Ruth leaned back, too, her legs stretched in front of her. He began to read aloud. The letters swam on the page. He pushed on for three or four pages and then paused for a drink of water. Ruth was still sitting up but her eyes were closed as she listened.

"I used to read to Robbie. When he was a baby." Her voice was low.

"I'm sorry about what I said back at the restaurant."

Ruth opened her eyes but did not look at him, just nodded and stared at her hands, entwined in her lap.

He picked up the book, then let it fall flat on his lap again. He was a little too drunk and way too tired. His head hurt like it used to after he was blown up. The headaches used to come all the time. Now they were back.

"Tell you what," he said. "Why don't you take the next few pages?" He handed her the book without waiting for her answer.

Ruth didn't move. Then, "Why not?"

She was self-conscious at first, but as she went on, the pinch in her voice relaxed. Casey knew she'd climbed into the story, could see the room Ishmael and Queequeg shared at the Spoutwater Inn while they waited for the boat to Nantucket.

Casey stopped listening. He knew how it went. He thought instead about another woman lying next to him in bed, reading. Lifetimes ago, when his future stretched in front of him like the Manhattan skyline, millions of possibilities living in those buildings, roaming those streets, lighting up the night.

Carla's voice was husky and sweet. Not like Ruth's, which

emerged from her mouth in flat, abrupt volleys, the voice of a person who wanted to sound strong. Carla was already strong. She would make love to him and then read to him. He was seventeen and she was twenty-eight. She taught literature in a private school on the Upper East Side but lived not far from him in Jersey City, in a one-room apartment with a Murphy bed.

She'd found him in the Strand, browsing the stacks and piles of books on a rare afternoon when Mike was gone off somewhere and he had nothing but time. Then he fucked up, Carla cut him loose, and Mikey died. Out of it all came Emily.

"Are you getting tired?"

He opened his eyes and saw Ruth peering at him, appraising him, like a nurse.

"Yes. No. You're doing good, Ruth." Still, he was glad when she marked the page and put the book on the floor next to the bed. She slid down a little then, her head still propped up on the pillow, and let out a sigh. Her hands were looser, her body not so tense.

"What did you read to Robbie when he was a kid?"

Ruth looked at her hands. "He liked animals. I must have read *The Jungle Book* a thousand times."

"Mowgli."

She looked up. "Another one of your favorites?"

"My grandmother told me I used to cry when we got to the part where the big black cat brings Mowgli to the village and tells him he has to go live with his own kind."

A smile started in the corner of Ruth's mouth but flickered out before it was finished. "Robbie did too, until he got older. I think he thought if we kept reading it again and again, someday the ending would change."

Casey had tried that. He'd gone over and over everything. Each time, he saw how one word, one decision, one accident of timing could have changed everything. A fleet of trucks droned by on the highway; the bed shook slightly as the noise swelled and then abated.

"What ending do you want, Ruth? If you could rewrite your life's story?"

Instantly, the current between them shifted. Casey felt Ruth retreat even though she did not move.

"I shouldn't have asked that. Sorry."

Ruth nodded without looking at him and gulped down some water.

"They're getting a little better, the bruises."

Ruth put her fingers to her lip and then walked them slowly to her eye, as though rediscovering the purpled skin. "Yes."

The need for physical contact, raw and selfish, flooded through him.

"Do that to me."

"What?" Her hand froze, suspended next to her face.

Casey took it and pulled it toward him, pressing his forehead into her palm. Her skin was cool from the bottle of water. He closed his eyes.

"Just touch me. It feels better when you touch me." The words welled up. The loneliness he felt had been part of him for so long he did not know where it ended and he began. It hurt worse than the pain in his head. When he turned toward Ruth, she was only inches from him. She shook off his hand and then placed her palm back on his forehead, as if checking for a fever. Then, hesitantly, as if she were afraid she would do something wrong, she began to stroke the skin along his hairline and then, with more confidence, along the ridges beneath his eyebrows and then, finally, traced circles in the hollows of his temples. He sank back into the pillow, as Ruth leaned over him, working her fingers across his skin. Words of gratitude started to form but fell away before he could utter them. What came out was a sound, half moan, half sigh.

"Shhh," Ruth whispered. It was the last sound he heard before sleep overtook him.

S ometime later, one hour or maybe three, Ruth woke up. She'd fallen asleep curved toward Casey's body, her arm across his chest. The light from the wall above the bed shone down on her. She glanced at Casey's face, his closed eyes, the furrows of his forehead smoothed out. Carefully, so as not to wake him, she leaned up on her elbow and reached to click off the light. In seconds Casey's hand was reaching for her. His hand ran up her back under her shirt. He buried his face in her neck.

"Don't go."

Ruth lay completely still for a few seconds. Then she tightened her arm around him, gathering him into her chest, pressing her leg between his so his stump could rest on her thigh.

"I won't."

R uth had lost all sense of time in the slipping in and out of sleep. She was aware of Casey's back spooned against her belly and breasts. Her arm still covered him; it rose and fell with each breath he took. Without realizing it, she began to breathe with him. She pulled herself closer, felt his heart beat beneath her palm, pressed her cheek against his thin cotton shirt until it too rose and fell with each breath. He stirred and turned toward her. Ruth began to pull away, until he closed his hand over hers possessively. She remained still when he lifted her fingers to his mouth. Slowly he explored her hand with his lips, brushed them against each of her fingers and then took one, then another into his mouth and began to suck gently.

Ruth did not look at his face. He did not look at hers. His hands traveled over her breasts, lifting her shirt so he could reach them with his mouth. Then he moved his mouth down her belly; Ruth pushed down her shorts so that he could keep going. The bruise on her hip flared again when he pressed his hand to it and pulled her closer so that his tongue and lips could find her. She clutched his hair, dug her fingers into his scalp, and then gave herself up to his mouth and his tongue.

Afterward, when she was quiet, Casey leaned up on his elbow; he was still hard. His breath came shallow and fast.

Ruth pushed him back and then straddled him. "Your turn," she said.


The sun lasered through a break between the curtains and burned against Ruth's eyelids. She rolled over and peered through slitted eyes at the dented pillow and tangled sheets, and listened to the drumming of water against tile in the bathroom. Casey was in the shower. She pushed herself up and then sank against the headboard, pinned there by hangover and shame. She closed her eyes so she wouldn't see the green box on the bureau across the room or the duffel on the floor below it. Robbie couldn't see her, she told herself. He didn't know that she'd left him for a while. Still, the guilt washed over her like it had been sitting on the edge of the bed waiting for her to wake up. She wanted to be the one hiding in the bathroom, washing the sex off her body.

A phone rang, and Ruth jumped. His cell, on the table next to his side of the bed. She had forgotten he even had a phone. The sound kept coming, and each ring drilled down behind her eyes. She couldn't stand another minute of it. She reached for the ancient mobile on the bedside table and flipped it open. *Neal.*

"Oh. You're awake." Casey froze in the bathroom doorway, his expression as uncertain as his tone. He gripped his toothbrush in one hand and a black shirt in another. His hair, wet and slicked back, dripped onto his shoulders. "Ruth. Let me explain."

"You didn't do much explaining last night."

The phone went silent in her hand. She'd held Casey, touched him, let him touch her, and all that time he'd been waiting for a call from Neal. Everybody was trying to make decisions for her, even a man who hadn't made many good decisions for himself as far as she could see.

"I never planned that," he said. "I'm sorry."

Ruth couldn't look at him. She saw Robbie's duffel and couldn't look at that either. Neither one of them had planned what happened the night before. "It doesn't matter. It's done."

# CHAPTER 37

They were halfway to Des Moines before Casey heard another word out of Ruth. He was beginning to think the
silence would last all the way to Chicago when she broke it with a
question.

"Who's the money for?"

He pretended to be checking the rearview mirror as he drove,
and tried to think of ways to change the subject. He'd been thinking
about the money. They would be in Chicago soon enough and then,
whether she called her boyfriend or not, they could settle up and
part ways. It would be for the best.

"Who's the money for?" she repeated.

Casey drummed his finger on the steering wheel, glanced again
in the rearview mirror. He didn't want to talk about Emily, not now.
Then she surprised him and changed the subject herself.

"Tell me about your friend Mike."

"Why does that interest you?"

"It doesn't, but I'm tired of sitting here hating you."

"We could talk some more about what you are going to do."

"I'm also tired of your advice. And the radio. And I'm sick and tired of cornfields and tractor-trailers. It's your turn."

He didn't have to answer, but what did it matter? Soon they were never going to see each other again. Casey felt guilty for reasons he couldn't understand. Maybe he owed her something to make up for last night. Certainly he owed her something for calling Neal, an act she obviously viewed as a betrayal. Still, he waited; talking about Mike was not an easy place to start. He passed a van full of kids and a couple of trucks before settling back into the right-hand lane.

"What do you want to know?" he finally said.

"You said he was like family but not family. Obviously he was important to you."

Casey nodded. "He was. We met on a playground when we were four or five. I ended up living with his family when my grandmother died. We were both thirteen then."

He remembered how they all stood in the kitchen of his grandmother's apartment on the day of her funeral. Mikey hunched in the doorway, shifting his shoulders under the jacket he'd borrowed from his older brother for the service. "You'll live with us, of course," Mike's mother, Katie, said. "Your grandmother arranged it before she went. Besides, haven't I always called you my eighth kid?"

Katie had always liked Casey and so had her husband, Brendan, a captain in the Jersey City fire department. Adults generally did. He'd grown up with two old people who did not believe in talking down to children or spoiling them. His grandmother had taught him to read at four; she wanted him to go into school ahead of the other kids. "I won't have people look at him like he's less than they are because he's an orphan," she'd said to her husband one night when she thought Casey was asleep. "I know those teachers, those nuns. They're hard enough on the boys as it is."

Ruth's voice again broke into his thoughts.

"What about your parents?" she asked.

"They died when I was a baby. My dad in Vietnam and my mom a year later in an accident. That's why my dad's folks raised me."

He didn't wait for Ruth to ask the next question. "Granddad passed when I was six or so and then it was just me and Mary Fran, my grandmother, until I was thirteen. Then she died, too. Cancer, like your dad."

Mikey, the youngest of six boys, had been Casey's best friend since he was four years old. He told Ruth how they met—head-on, literally—two blocks from their houses in a little playground with a metal jungle gym, a triangle of grass, and a sandbox. The kicking, wrestling, slugging, spitting, bleeding was all over a small red metal fire truck each claimed he found first. It was Casey's granddad, Timothy MacInerney, who pulled them apart.

"Okay, okay, that's enough, now."

He remembered his granddad's voice and his strong, big-knuckled hands. Timothy was a fireman, like Mike's father. That was why each boy thought the truck ought to be his. But Timothy had taken the toy, walked over to a woman comforting a crying toddler, and handed it over. The little boy stopped sobbing the minute he had the truck in his fist. Both Casey and Mikey mourned the loss of the truck and instantly began to conspire about ways to get it back, or, better yet, find an even better one.

"We were never apart after that," Casey told Ruth, his eyes fixed on the road ahead but inwardly scanning years of memories. "Holidays, it didn't matter, we saw each other every day." The O'Brien household was a Ferris wheel of activity and Casey couldn't wait to get there. He'd walk in the door and find himself hoisted up in the commotion of shouts, laughter, arguments, reconciliations, near violence, and ready affection.

He shuffled through the images of himself and Mikey, stopping when he came to the ones that were easy to talk about. Finding Moira's first bra and then hanging it from the kitchen window that looked out over the avenue. Hiding the priest's reading glasses just before mass, eyes wide with innocence as they sat alongside the altar, their hands in their laps, their knees bouncing under their cassocks. Stealing gum or candy on a dare from the bodega in the neighborhood that served a growing number of families from Puerto Rico and South America. Later, pushing the car they bought together, a Camaro from the late seventies, to a speed of a hundred miles an hour down the Garden State Parkway, getting to the shore at midnight on a Friday and then sleeping in that same car before hitting the beach on Saturday and staking out their claim.

Casey felt Ruth's eyes on him. Her head was cocked a little, the dark glasses pushed up onto her hair, like a headband. "What?" he said.

"Nothing. It sounds like a Disney movie, is all. A couple of scamps in altar boy outfits."

"What, you think I'm making it up?"

"Are you?" She smiled a little. "No, tell me the rest. What did you do that was so bad you had to choose between jail and the Army?"

Casey knew he didn't have to answer her. But her question kicked open a door inside him.

"You know how the movie goes. Disney stuff turns into crazy shit or stupid shit. We did our share of both, wound up in juvie court a bunch of times. Then Mike got into coke and decided to sell pot to pay for it, got in over his head. Got busted in his senior year. After that, his dad told us we were on our own. We were nearly eighteen. Judge gave us a choice. And the Army looked better than jail."

"Us? I thought you said it was Mike's business."

It had been. Even as a kid, Casey knew where the line between wild and stupid lay. You had to pick your spots, let some stuff go. But Mike never knew when to stop, and he expected Casey to be right by his side. They all did, even the parents. "I know he'll never go too far if you're with him," old Brendan O'Brien said when Casey first moved in. And four years later, when Mike's father came down to the police station to bail them out, he had nothing but weary resignation to offer Mike, but he cut Casey to the core with a look of sad puzzlement and one sentence. "I counted on you."

Casey did not bother to explain to Ruth that Mike had stored his inventory in the car they shared. He'd also made sure that some was in Casey's locker at school. Casey hadn't understood it all then, at least not in a way he could articulate. All he knew was that underneath the old Mike-Casey bond ran a sewer of feelings that had begun leaking fumes soon after Casey moved in with the O'Briens. Suddenly it was a crime to get the excellent grades that came so easily to him and so hard to Mike. He cringed inside every time Katie or Brendan O'Brien laughingly told Mike to stick with Casey so he'd "keep out of trouble." Years later, in one of his unsuccessful stints in rehab, someone had pointed out what should have been obvious: Once he'd moved into the O'Brien house, Mike was not supposed to be at the bottom of the O'Brien brothers' pecking order anymore.

"Are you still there?" he heard Ruth say. He didn't realized that he'd fallen silent.

"I told you, he was like my brother."

Ruth shook her head. The look on her face reminded him of Carla's when he saw her for the last time. "Fuck it, why am I telling you all this anyway?" Casey said.

"Sorry. Really. What happened to Mike? Why didn't you go to college after you got out of the service? How did you wind up in Nevada?"

She prodded him with more questions, but Casey was through talking. He turned up the radio and tried not to think about the answers raised by Ruth's idle curiosity. He fought the resentment she'd awakened but there it was, as hot and mean as it had been all those years ago when he'd also loved Mike and the whole O'Brien family. He loved Mike, who had known him better than anyone else. He also hated him. Hated him for the way he fucked up and expected everyone else to figure out how to fix it. For the way he used his looks and his smile to get what he wanted from his parents, or from girls they knew. For the way he derided Casey for getting decent grades and talking about college. For his secure claim on all the things that had been taken from Casey: home, parents, acceptance. Mike just assumed that whatever he had, Casey wanted and that whatever Mike shared would be enough. The way he saw it, Casey owed him.

They stopped for gas at a rest area before they reached Des Moines, and then Ruth took the wheel. Pieces of Casey's story were missing; she heard the spaces between the things he chose to tell. She didn't care. As long as she could keep him talking, she didn't have to think about the night before, or what lay ahead when they reached Chicago. From the corner of her eye, she saw him lower the back of the passenger seat. He settled back and closed his eyes. "Wake me when it's my turn again."

Then he was asleep, or pretending to be. The anxiety she'd been struggling to keep at bay since the morning sensed an opening. Ruth grabbed a bottle of water from the holder, tilted it to her mouth, and sucked it dry. She tossed the empty to the floor by Casey's feet. He didn't stir.

Ahead of Ruth unspooled more pavement, more tired grass, more stands of corn but no answers. A sign for Des Moines loomed and then the city itself appeared. Only five or six hours until they reached Chicago. That was where he probably would take his leave. Get his money and try to hand her over to Neal if she had to guess.

Casey had asked her that morning why she was running, and she couldn't answer. She had no answers for anyone: not Kevin, not Neal, not Terri or the woman who had e-mailed her for help.

Ruth's heart was beating too fast. The steering wheel grew slippery under her palms. She hit the scan button on the radio, looking for something innocuous. No words, just sound. The traffic thickened and slowed; it seemed to wrap itself around the Jaguar like a trap. A thought reached out like a rope and she grabbed it. It was her damn car; she could drive it where she wanted. She took the next exit, and in seconds she was heading south, through some suburbs. They didn't need to go to Chicago. They could handle their exchange anywhere. Casey could still get to New Jersey. An hour passed. Then another. Her left hip stiffened and a nerve running up her right leg into her back felt like a hot wire from sitting in the same position for so long. But she didn't want to wake Casey by stopping. He'd be surprised when he woke.

*I don't feel good, Mommy.*

Ruth whipped her head around to look in the backseat as the car swerved. She knew Robbie wasn't really sitting there in the backseat, his comic book tossed aside, but she saw his face, plump and flushed with fever. She heard the scratchy voice he'd had at eight when he was coming down with strep throat. She'd left work early that day to take him to the doctor, then drove him home where her babysitter was waiting. She was supposed to meet Don at the airport for a flight out that night. She hated leaving Robbie, but she and Don had been through this before. "Children are sick all the time," he said. "They get better. Business opportunities come and then they disappear just as fast. I'm investing in you for a reason. Are you willing to invest in yourself?" A meaningful pause. "Your choice, of course."

The horn of a passing RV jerked Ruth's attention back to the road but once it passed, she glanced again in the mirror. She saw only the metal box and the duffel that wedged it tightly in place. Inside the duffel were the photo album and the diary. The photos of him as a boy and the words he'd scrawled before he died squeezed in with the clothes that still smelled like him, except for the shirt he'd worn in her office, all dressed up. She'd pushed Robbie away and told him she'd see him later. Ruth struggled to breathe, but this time the panic won.

"You okay over there?" Casey finally woke up and tilted his head toward her. He glanced out the window, then at his watch. "Shit, Ruth, it's nearly four. Where the hell are we?"

He yanked off his sunglasses and grabbed the map. "What the fuck? How did you get off Eighty? Why didn't you wake me up?"

A wave of nausea broadsided Ruth. She aimed for the shoulder running along the road.

The Jaguar skidded on the gravel and came to stop on an angle. Ruth pushed open her door. She stumbled around to the back of the car and leaned against the fender trying to pull fresh air into her lungs, waiting for the heaving to subside.

Casey came up beside her but he did not touch her. When Ruth finally stood up, she felt like she'd been punched in the stomach; she couldn't seem to catch her breath.

"You look like shit," Casey said.

Ruth shook her head. "It's nothing. The lunch. Something must have been off."

"I had the same stuff. Hours ago. I feel fine."

"I can't get back in the car," she told him. She stumbled forward and then sank halfway down the embankment, in the tangle of grass and low shrubs.

"What are we supposed to do? We can't stay here."

Ruth pulled her knees to her chest and began to rock. She knew now that no matter how fast or far she drove, the end was right there in the backseat waiting for her. It always would be. She would never forget how she had let him down the last night of his life. Hanging on to Robbie's ashes wasn't going to help her. What she wanted was to have him back. What she wanted was another chance. What she wanted was forgiveness.

"I'm sorry, so sorry." But the words were too far away for Robbie to hear.

"Go," she said now to Casey. "Take the car. Go."

But worry had clouded his eyes. "C'mon, tell me what's wrong. Was it—" A flush of embarrassment colored his cheeks and he cleared his throat. "Was it last night? Because if it was, it won't happen again. I don't expect anything like that."

Casey grabbed Ruth's elbow and tried to lift her up. "C'mon, Ruth. Snap out of it. I'm not leaving you by the side of the goddamn road."

Ruth felt his hand on her shoulder, trying to pull her up. When she struggled to her feet, she felt him lose his balance. He crashed down the rest of the embankment into a ditch she hadn't seen.

*Oh my God.* His plastic and metal limb lay twisted, half in, half out of his pant leg. Blood flowed from a cut on his arm. Ruth stumbled to him and knelt by his side.

"Oh God, Casey, I'm sorry. I'm sorry. What should I do?"

He didn't look at her, or wouldn't. His anger was palpable but there was something else too: shame. Or maybe it was her own. Ruth was almost grateful when he gestured toward the prosthesis and said, "Give me a hand with this fucking thing, will you?"

Ruth tugged on the black sneaker. It came off in her hands, revealing a foam foot on the end of the limb, once clearly flesh-colored, now the color of an old sponge. A strip of duct tape ran along the side.

"You folks okay down there?"

R uth swung her head toward the voice above them. She saw a pair of blue-jeaned legs, an orange shirt, the bill of a black canvas cap with an orange logo she did not recognize. A silver pickup, sitting high above its tires, was parked behind the Jaguar, the door open, dust still settling around it. The owner didn't wait for a response.

"Hang on. I'll give you a hand."

Ruth felt Casey's weight shift from her shoulders. Heard Casey's mumbled "Thanks, man."

"Easy now." The stranger's voice was young but not a boy's. The knuckles of his hands paled as he gripped the area under Casey's armpit. Ruth hesitated, then let the stranger take Casey from her. All three of them stood, staring at each other.

"I saw the car, thought there might be a problem." He peered at Ruth's face. Her hand flew to her cheek. Where were her sunglasses? Then she saw the plastic frames twisted on the ground, one earpiece gone. Well, there was nothing to do about them now.

"He needs to see a doctor," she said.

"No, I don't," Casey barked. "I don't need a doctor." His face was pale. Sweat shone above his upper lip.

Ruth watched the man's face swing from the bruises on her face to the blood on Casey's shirt. He cleared his throat.

"It probably wouldn't hurt, though, would it? We're not far, as it happens. The medical center for the whole area's just ten miles up the road. You can follow me there. My wife's a nurse there, she'll take good care of you. Name's Alvie, by the way. Alvie Munroe." Without waiting for a reply, he began to guide Casey up the incline to the road. Ruth followed him.

What's the situation with your prosthesis?" The nurse, Mary something, bent over his stump, swabbing it down. Casey's arm was still numb where she'd put in the stitches, and his shoulder throbbed from the tetanus shot she'd insisted on giving him. She'd helped him strip off the silicone liner when he told her his stump was a little sore. He was embarrassed about the rips in the socks that covered it, then humiliated when she sniffed and tried not to make a face when she smelled the liner itself.

"It's getting old," he said, struggling to keep the embarrassment out of his voice. "I'm due for a new one but you know how the VA works."

"Yeah, I know. I used to work at the VA in Iowa City. They do a damn good job. You haven't, though, have you? When's the last time you gave this thing a good wash?" She pointed to the liner.

"If you'd been me the last few days you wouldn't ask that."

The woman glanced up. "Hmppfh."

Casey pretended not to notice. "Looks like I need a repair job. Know any place that fixes these things?"

"Iowa City'd be your best bet, or Peoria. But it's Saturday. I don't think you'll have much luck until Monday." She blotted the skin of his stump dry and frowned at the knob of flesh that always formed after he'd been wearing the faker all day. "What's the story with your lady friend?"

"She's not my friend."

"That why she's got that shiner?" The woman's tone was even, but Casey felt her probe his stump a little harder than she needed to.

Casey winced. "No, I don't hit women. She got herself in trouble and I, if you really want to know, was the one who bailed her out."

Mary eyed him for a moment and then let go of his limb.

"Sorry." Casey dropped his gaze. "It's been a long day."

Mary looked at him, head cocked, a skeptical look in her eye.

"She's a basket case," he said, although he knew it probably wouldn't change the nurse's opinion of him. "Lost her kid in Iraq. Has his ashes in the back of the car. I didn't know that when we hooked up, but now . . ." Casey looked toward the door that separated the exam area from the waiting room. He spoke more quietly. "Now I don't think she knows what to do. I sure as hell don't." He felt like a fool. He should have just gotten out of all this while he could. All he'd wanted was a ride to fucking New Jersey.

"You want me to check her out?"

"Probably a good idea, but it's not my call."

Mary pushed the stool back and stared at him. "You bail her out, then you say it's not your call."

"Listen, lady, I know you mean well. There's more going on there than I can handle. Just fix me up and I'll get out of here." He wanted out now. All the way out. Wanted to find his way back to the desert and forget this whole mess.

Mary considered his words as she turned and tossed the soiled towels and swabs in a covered waste bin. After a moment, she spoke again.

"Alvie's trying to get over to Iraq."

"Trying to? What's wrong with him?"

Mary glanced up.

"Found himself a job driving trucks. Can make more in six months than he has in the past two years. Wants to pay down the mortgage, put something by for the kids."

"You want him to go?"

Mary looked at him. "It's a long time between construction jobs now. We could use the money, but I see guys, women too, coming home. . . . I don't know that the enemy takes the time to figure out who's a soldier and who isn't."

She was talking low like she was telling him a secret she wasn't sure she believed. "They tell him he'll be working in a construction zone. Not where there's fighting."

Casey pointed to his stump. "This happened to me when the fighting was supposed to be over. Our side did it, no enemies involved."

Her brown eyes behind the glasses bored into him; her mouth straightlined. She stood. "I'll give you some antibiotics to prevent infection, although the wound on your arm looks clean. The stitches will need to come out in a week. As for that"—she pointed to the stump—"your skin will look a lot better if you give it some air and clean that liner. You may need to put it on to keep your stump from swelling too much while you're waiting to get the prosthesis seen to."

Yeah. He didn't need a lecture. "Got any crutches I can use?"

"You don't have any?"

Casey reddened. "Left them behind. Didn't think I'd need 'em."

Mary gave him a look. "I may have a set that'll get you around. If you need better ones, they have some at Walmart."

# CHAPTER 38

Ruth saw Casey jiggle his leg impatiently as he stared out the passenger window. The town was nothing but a few blocks of clapboard and brick buildings, awnings yanked down tight against the afternoon sun. Equal portions of violet lobelia, crimson geraniums, and white dianthus were served up in half-barrel casks and planters along the sidewalks of the main street. Twin silos loomed over an auto parts store where the street ended.

"We can't keep going without gas," Ruth had told him when she turned off the highway. She squinted. Her fingers ached from gripping the steering wheel. A fatigue she'd never known before had frozen her into position. She wasn't even sure she'd be able to get out and pump the fuel into the car.

The pump was one of the old kind; she'd have to go in and pay first. She paused, trying to gather herself for another encounter with a stranger. The air around her was hot, unforgiving; her throat stung.

Behind her, she heard the passenger door open, then Casey. "What's the problem?"

"Nothing. I'll be back in a minute."

The clerk behind the counter looked up from a newspaper and rose from her stool. Ruth averted her eyes and kept her chin down, as if that would hide her bruises.

"What can I do for you?" the woman asked. Her full cheeks pushed up the half glasses she wore so that her eyes were magnified.

"I'd like to fill the tank." Ruth fumbled for her wallet and then remembered she had no wallet and Casey had all the cash. "Sorry."

"That's all right." The clerk hit a button somewhere behind the counter and leaned forward. "All set to pump." She peered at Ruth over the tops of the glasses, a summer Santa Claus. She did not smile but Ruth glimpsed something like sympathy in her eyes.

When Ruth fled back to the car, Casey was still sitting with the door open.

"I need money," Ruth said. She reached for the nozzle.

He cleared his throat. "Look, Ruth, we made a wrong turn but we're not that far from civilization. Let's fill up, figure out the route to Iowa City or Davenport. Neither one is more than a few hours' drive."

Ruth turned away, closed her eyes, squeezed the nozzle. The pump gurgled, then hummed as gas poured through the hose into the tank. She couldn't face another two hours of driving. Or another two hours of Casey's frustration. "I need some cash," Ruth said again. She held out her hand. But Casey kept talking.

"I'll get the leg fixed and take a plane. You can get going wherever it is you're going. It's better this way. I'll give you some money. You can pay me back. Like you said, I'm a gambler, I'll take a chance on you."

Ruth said nothing.

Finally, Casey dug into his pocket and pulled out a couple of wrinkled bills and handed them to her. His bandaged arm banged the door. She saw him wince.

The woman was waiting for her when she returned with the money. "Got everything you need?"

Ruth looked around, saw a cooler. "I'll take a Coke and a bottle of water." She looked around some more. "You don't have any sunglasses, do you?"

"Not for sale, but there's a pair in the back in the lost and found. Wait a minute."

While she waited, Ruth picked up a couple of chocolate bars and placed them on the counter. A counter easel loaded with brochures caught her attention. Red letters splashed across one card, over an ink outline of a tree bending over a river. *River Bend Motel, RV Park and Campground*. She plucked one of the cards just as the woman returned.

"Not a bad place if you're just looking for a night's rest," she said. She handed a pair of black-rimmed sunglasses to Ruth. "These should work. Nothing fancy but they'll do the job." She began to ring up the gas, water, and chocolate. She nodded toward a copy of the *Des Moines Register* on the counter. "You want a paper? That's the last one and I'm done with it. Take it."

Why not? Ruth gathered the paper up with the small bag and change. "Thanks."

Outside, Casey was still sitting, facing out the passenger door, his good leg on the ground, his shoe tapping out his impatience on the pavement. Ruth handed him the bag and then dropped the paper onto the console between the seats. "You can do whatever you want tomorrow, but it's getting late. I'm tired."

"It's my money," Casey said. "Maybe I don't want to spend it here."

"I don't want to drive any more tonight, and you can't right now."

She stared him down until he slumped back in the passenger seat. "Whatever."

Ruth dug into her purse for her BlackBerry as she took the driver's seat. No calls. Just a text, from Terri. *Cards will be ready tomorrow. Call me so I know where to send them.* Ruth read the message twice, then deleted it. She called the number on the brochure. She would call

Terri, but first they needed a place to stay. A woman answered the phone.

"Campground."

Ruth watched Casey's eyes, still clouded with frustration and leftover anger. But he did not protest as she made reservations for the night and got directions. He pulled the crutches into the car, then picked up the newspaper and began to flip the pages. "Keep an eye out for the sign to South River Road," she told Casey as she pulled out of the gas station and headed down the street. He ignored her and picked up the paper.

"Look at this," Casey said. "That guy again. The bastard that hired those contractors is fucking them over. It's a sweet deal, isn't it? At least when I got my leg blown off, the government had to pay for the new one. No one wants to pay these guys anything. Use 'em up and spit 'em out."

Ruth glanced over to the open page and saw the face of Don Ryland. The photographer had caught him walking from his office to his car past a group of women with placards. A security guard flanked him, arms spread wide as if to keep the women from swarming forward. *Defense Contractor Under Fire*, the headline read. She looked away.

"Watch for the sign. I don't want to miss our turn."

"That guy, Alvie, who showed us the way to the hospital? He got himself a job over there driving a truck. His wife, Mary the nurse, she doesn't like it. She's not going to feel any better when she reads this."

That was right, the nurse was Alvie's wife, kind Alvie and his nice nurse wife who had pressed into Ruth's hand a card bearing the name of a domestic abuse hotline. She wanted Casey to stop reading the paper. "Watch for the turn we need to take, will you?"

Casey glanced up and then back at the little map on the back of the business card. "Try the next left." He went back to the paper. "Jesus. Look at that asshole. Walking right by that woman like he has nothin' to do with it. Picture of her dead husband right there on her sign. Look at that guy in the wheelchair."

Ruth missed the turn. Her jaw pulsed. She waited while a blue Pontiac pulled out of a driveway and then turned back. Beside her, Casey continued to read the article, shaking the pages and swearing as he read. When they pulled into the campground fifteen minutes later, her fingers were cramped from gripping the wheel, her neck knotted as though Casey had been shaking her, not the paper.

The cabin room was a wallpapered cave enclosing two beds, a bath, a closet, and a corner with a small refrigerator and a hot plate. Casey leaned into the sill of a window for balance and tugged on the sash until sweat formed on his temples. Nothing. He tried again until a riffle of air seeped through the inch he'd managed to open between sash and sill. A mosquito floated through a tear in the screen and landed on the back of his hand. A scout for the invasion sure to follow once the sun went down. Christ.

"I'm out of here," he said.

Ruth heaved the duffel and a couple of smaller bags onto the floor. "Where are you going?"

"Not as far as I'd like to."

Ruth's mouth opened, but he didn't want to hear anything from her right now. Casey pushed past her to the screen door and let it slam behind him. He swung on the crutches down a narrow dirt path to the water. The air was thick with humidity. Sweat lined his upper lip and slicked the surface of his palms so that the crutches slid beneath them with each step. He stopped well short of the riverbank, gasping, looking for a place to sit. The only bench, attached to a picnic table, was twenty or thirty feet away. Two squat adults, four children, and an ancient Labrador retriever were already trudging toward it.

Fucking crutches. Fucking leg. Fucking goddamn Ruth.

He lowered himself to the ground by inches, careful not to let the crutches get away from him. He'd been stupid to let the faker go so long without maintenance, to let himself run out of clean stump socks. Stupid to hook up with Ruth, to leave Las Vegas. He swatted at a pinch on his left forearm below the bandage. He rubbed at the bloody smear left by the mosquito.

A child squealed. Casey looked up in time to see a small girl hoisted into the air by her father, hip deep in the river. A pause, her mouth snapped shut, and she was launched, a missile in a pink and green bathing suit with a bright orange foam bubble on her back. She burst through the surface of the water, hair flattened and dark, skin shining, mouth wide and laughing. He watched her paddle back to her father, begging for more, saw the stocky man's teeth flash in the sun, radiating confidence. Casey looked away. Who had taken Emily to the shore in the summer? Who had taught her to ride the waves? Moira? Probably some guy Moira had found along the way to replace him. Casey thought of the letter and the clippings Katie O'Brien had sent, the ones that had launched him on this latest stupidity. Emily was seventeen, a big strong girl. She'd learned to propel herself into the air and make jump shots, to get on the honor roll, and she'd done it without him. She didn't need him or want him. Too many years had passed. He didn't deserve her.

Another splash. The father called, "Last time," as he waded over to his daughter and pointed to the shore. She began to paddle furiously while he stayed behind her in the water. A lumpy guy, losing his hair, the kind of guy who would hit the five-dollar blackjack tables and walk away the minute he lost. Casey tried to summon the derision he felt for men like this. Lightweights, losers, he'd called them as he raked in his own chips. Now, for the first time, he saw that men like this walked away because they had someplace to go.

Behind him, a screen door squeaked, then slapped shut. He glanced over his shoulder. The Jaguar squatted silently next to the motel room door. He thought he saw Ruth moving behind the screen. All settled into a fucking dump of a motel room with hours ahead of them and no way for him to escape. Casey turned back to the river. A few hours earlier Ruth had wanted out, told him to take the car. He tried to picture himself behind the wheel of the Jaguar. In a couple of days or less he'd be parked in front of the house he'd left all those years ago. Emily might be sitting on the steps, just like he used to sit with her mother and her uncle. Casey closed his eyes, trying to arrange the girl from the clipping into the picture forming in his mind. He tried to see himself getting out of Ruth's expensive sports car like it was his, walking up the steps, and sitting beside his daughter. But he couldn't do it. The girl on the stairs would look right through him. He wouldn't be able to get out of the car.

A mosquito whined in Casey's ear. He slapped at it. His eyes opened to the river, empty now, unmoving. The father and the daughter were with the rest of their family grouped around the picnic table, eating food that came out of a big blue cooler. The Lab sat under the table, in the shade, alert for falling scraps.

Casey knew he'd missed his chance.

And he was in the middle of the fucking heartland with a woman more lost than he was.

The bags seemed heavier than they had that morning, or maybe it was just that the day had sapped Ruth's strength. She struggled first with the duffel and then with Casey's bag. The straps slipped in her hands and her shoulders ached. When she laid Robbie's ashes on top of a small dresser, she paused to catch her breath.

Pineapples, palms, and parrots splashed the walls, defying the dull brown and tan of the early American braided rug and knotty pine of the ceiling. Her mother had had a bathrobe like that wallpaper, Ruth remembered. A cacophony of oranges, purples, reds, and greens. Cheap shiny material. She would wear it to breakfast in the morning at the farm. Next to the olive work pants and plaid wool shirt worn by Ruth's grandfather, Stella looked like a caged lorikeet. She hadn't stayed in the cage.

Ruth blinked away the memory as she stood in front of a narrow mirror on the outside of the bathroom door. Her reflection displayed evidence of her own attempt to flee: Casey's dried blood on her Walmart shirt, now filthy with grass and dirt, the bruises stippled across her brow and cheek. She recognized loathing in the eyes of the woman staring back at her. The force of it sent her back out of the cabin to the car, driven suddenly to erase the dregs of the day, to blot out the coffee smell, the memory of Casey's face twisted in pain and the panic that had driven her into the field in the first place. She stuffed old coffee cups and fast-food wrappers into an empty plastic bag and brushed off the seats with a napkin before stuffing that in the bag as well. She yanked her briefcase out of the backseat for the first time since leaving San Diego.

What else? The prosthesis lay across the passenger seat. She grabbed the metal shaft, hoisted the briefcase over her shoulder, and rose with her arms full of trash, looking about for a can. A black plastic drum stood a few feet from the path Casey had taken to the river.

She spotted him sitting in the grass about a hundred feet away, his back to her, shoulders hunched forward, shaggy hair limp in the heat. There was something doglike in his resigned slump, and in the way his head snapped up at the sound of a child's laughter. Ruth saw a little girl vault out of her father's arms into the river. A mother called to a toddler nearby and a little boy chasing a soccer ball nearly careened into him, but Casey never took his eyes off the water. Ruth watched him as he watched the little girl paddling toward her father. Maybe he was thinking about the girl he'd told her about, Mike's daughter, the one he was going to see. Then Casey's head bowed, he wiped his hand across his eyes, and she understood. Not Mike's daughter. His. He had a daughter and he was going to see her.

*Good*, Ruth thought, trying not to think about Robbie. *Good for you.*

She wanted to go to him and say it out loud, but he'd not told her himself and now he'd made it clear he needed to be alone. The stretch of grass that separated them was only a matter of feet, but she had no idea how to cross the distance that yawed between them now.

Inside the cabin, she dropped Casey's prosthesis on his bed and the computer bag on the kitchen table. She'd open it, get out a pad and paper and make a list, figure out her next steps. No. First she'd go to the campground store, get some food and something to drink. No. She'd call Neal. No.

Her hands covered her face as she sank to the chair at the table. Then her foot slid over something, producing a crinkling sound. The newspaper. She reached down and picked up the pages, now crumpled with a ragged hole in the margins, like a bite.

Ruth stared at the photograph of Don Ryland. He wore the same dismissive half smile he did whenever he felt his time was being wasted. One of the women in the background held up an enlarged photograph: a male face, young, open, with numbers in bold beneath: 1978–2006.

Don's statement affirmed the company's commitment to its employees, to the service of the country, and its faith in Excel Insurance Group, "the largest and most experienced insurer in the defense industry." These were the same words hammered out in the conference room two weeks ago while Robbie was . . . where? On his way to that motel? Or had he given Ruth a chance, and waited at the house for a little while? She gripped the pages of the newspaper. Don hadn't cared about that. He'd had his assistant send flowers to the house when he heard about Robbie. No note. No phone call. All those years, and all he gave her was a vase of lilies.

Ruth looked up at the metal box on the dresser. Robbie had deserved more than lilies. He'd deserved more from her. The green metal edges blurred; she blinked back the tears that stung her eyes and thickened in her throat. The box contained what was left of the best things she'd ever done and the reminder of all she'd failed to do. She'd blamed Don, Gordon, even the contractors for pulling her away from Robbie when he needed her. Ruth closed her eyes against the truth, but it found her anyway. Here in the stuffy stillness of the cabin, she faced her decision to ignore Gordon when he alerted her to the problems with the insurance claims. She tried to remember the days afterward when she postponed her meetings with the company lawyers. The days had been so full of urgency, but now she couldn't recall a single thing that seemed more important than returning the lawyer's call. If she'd just done one thing differently, maybe all of it would—

She was gripping the newspaper so hard the pages were giving way. Ruth smoothed it out and flipped to the back page for the rest of the article. She read what Casey had missed during his tirade in the car. The lawyer for the families, the man Terri had told her about, Breen, was challenging RyCom to prove that its executives met the requirements of the law. He wanted records, files, full disclosure. "It's not enough to say you are committed. Prove it," he was quoted as saying.

Ruth put down the paper and stared at her computer on the table in front of her. The cabin's stillness felt now like the silence that follows a question. The manager in the campground office had said something about a Wi-Fi signal. Ruth lifted the top of the computer and hit the power button. She pulled the briefcase closer to her while the computer booted up. God, it was slow. She clicked on the link to the company's VPN as soon as it became visible on the screen and typed in her password. But she was already locked out.

No surprise, they'd cut her off. But the e-mails she'd downloaded before she left were still on her hard drive. She pulled them up now and scrolled again through the messages until she found the one from Marilyn Corning. *Please.*

Ruth read the message twice. She looked at the box of ashes and Robbie's duffel. *Please Help.* Where was Casey? Ruth got up and opened the screen door. There he was, still hunched on the grass by the river, his back to her, no sign that he was getting ready to come back. The evening light lingered as though too lazy to move toward night.

She returned to the table and clicked on the Internet icon before unzipping the front pocket of the briefcase to find the flash drive. Which file was the one Terri had told her to open? Ruth scanned the lists of reports and files that appeared on the screen. There. *Personnel—For Ruth.*

A half hour later, Ruth leaned back in the hard wooden chair. The folder was still open on the screen in front of her with e-mails and documents that Olson's flunky, Sylvia, from HR, had not brought to her attention.

She'd learned from them that RyCom was delaying the reporting of injuries sustained by contractors to the Department of Labor by as much as six months, a year in some cases, instead of the fourteen-day window required by law. This made it even harder for the contractors to prove they were injured on the job. The next set of documents, in a subfolder Terri had called *Life Insurance Notice,* contained the original letters sent to contractors who needed to make corrections on their life insurance paperwork in order for the policies to go into effect. Excel had notified the contractors and copied Sylvia in HR. In all cases, the letters were sent after deployment, and half of them were dated after the contractors had died.

The most damning documents were e-mails, part of a two-month-old trail of correspondence between Sylvia and Gordon Olson regarding several hundred contract construction workers and truck drivers who were thought to be at the end of their assignments. Their insurance policies, written under the company they'd used before switching to Excel, were set to expire. And Gordon Olson had told Sylvia not to renew the insurance.

Ruth knew that the assignment had been extended for another six months; most of the workers were still in Iraq or Afghanistan.

Her own e-mail had notified Don and Olson of the extension. Olson had forwarded it to Sylvia with a cover note: *No rush. Talk to Excel about how to handle.* There was nothing else. Ruth was familiar with the projects. They had all been extended. None of the contractors had yet come home and all were working without the required insurance.

Ruth stood. She strode to the screen door, looked through the gray mesh without registering what lay beyond it. She paced back to the table. The screen shimmered quietly, waiting for her to do something. There were more files in the group that Terri had saved for her, but she didn't want to read them. She'd already seen enough. She thought again of Alvie, of his strong hands and calm voice. She thought of his wife, the nurse, who had gently cleaned Ruth's lip and probed her ribs for damage.

Ruth knew what these people had been told by the recruiters because she'd helped to develop the message. *We are all in it together. Your country needs your skills and strength. Yes, the conditions are hazardous, but you have the best military in the world at your side. And you can make more in eighteen months than you made in the last five years.* "We have your back," was what the interviewers would tell the contractors when they asked about health or disability or life insurance. The insurance was required by law. *Do it for your country. Do it for your family. Do it.*

These messages were like knots in a rope the contractors were using to climb out of their lives. The men and women she'd built her business on were just like her. She'd known what would motivate them because the same hunger for more had driven her out of Gershom, New Hampshire. More money, more security, more choices. Just more. Robbie, too, had been seduced. By images of young men clambering up the cliffs and standing at the top, stronger, shinier, made new.

Ruth wheeled away from the table and grabbed her purse. She needed air. A drink. She needed more than anything to get out of the suddenly crowded cabin.

# CHAPTER 39

Shadows from the few willows draped over the river gradually lengthened and then merged as the sun dipped behind them. Gnats crowded into Casey's ears and nose, and mosquitoes bit, but Casey did not rise until the sun slid fully and completely down. When he clomped through the door, he found Ruth sitting at the cabin's table, a pen in her hand, staring straight ahead at a dark laptop screen. Her BlackBerry and a blank pad of paper rested before her with a half-filled glass of what looked like orange juice. A pint of vodka was open on the counter. She'd apparently paid a visit to the campground store.

She glanced at him, pointed to the dwarf refrigerator. "There's some Coke in there. A sandwich, too."

Casey recognized the peace offering for what it was. "Not that hungry right now, but thanks." He opened the small white door and grabbed the can of soda. He drank half and then poured some vodka into the can. She looked away.

He lowered himself into the chair across from her and set the crutches on the floor where he could reach them. He held the bottle over her juice glass. "Want some more?"

Ruth started to shake her head but stopped. She pushed her glass toward him.

"What are you working on?"

Ruth looked down at the blank page before her. "A plan, I guess." She put down the pen. "Not much of one, so far."

She picked up her glass, drank.

He avoided her eyes. "So, we'll stick with mine. Tomorrow, you drop me off in a city of some size and I'll take it from there."

Ruth put her glass down. "What about your leg? Will you be able to get it fixed over the weekend?"

"I've used crutches before. I'll do it again."

"What about New Jersey?"

Casey shrugged. He took a long pull from the can. None of her business where he went. "I changed my mind."

Ruth stood and turned toward the door. She stopped at the screen and crossed her arms against her chest. Moths batted against the screen, trying to get into the lighted room.

"So, you chickened out."

"Ruth . . . don't, okay? Please."

Casey leaned down for his crutches. He didn't have to go but he wanted to be behind the bathroom door, away from Ruth's eyes. His hand was on the doorknob when she spoke again.

"She's not Mike's daughter. She's yours."

He turned too quickly on the crutches and almost fell. "You don't know what you're talking about."

"It's the only thing that makes sense." Ruth's arms were still crossed. She took a few steps toward him but stopped. "If she were Mike's—if Mike is even real—you'd have mailed her whatever it is you're carrying across the country. You wanted to see her and now you're bailing out."

Casey didn't answer her. He stepped into the bathroom and shut the door behind him. The nurse had told him not to get his arm wet. Fuck it. He began to strip down. He'd fill his ears with the sound of water, wash Ruth's words out of them. In the morning, he'd get out of here, find his way back to Vegas.

But it didn't work. When he stepped under the stream of water, trying to balance, trying to keep his arm dry, the memory he'd been trying to avoid since he'd left Nevada found him and crushed him. He sank until he was sitting on the fiberglass floor of the shower stall, lukewarm water raining down on him.

# CHAPTER 40

July 1989

*H*e's yelling at Mike on the sidewalk in front of the O'Briens' row house. The Army gets them on Monday morning and Mike is drinking his way through their last weekend of freedom. Casey hates the sight of him. Mike is the reason they have to go away. Mike is the reason Carla has cut Casey loose. He's a fool, she says. His loyalty to Mike is weakness, not love. "Come back when you're all grown up."

"C'mon, Case, get in the car. We can be at Long Beach by midnight. We'll drink all night and watch the sun rise. Who knows when we'll be back?" Mike slaps the hood of the Camaro and digs into one pocket of his leather jacket, then the other for his keys. But Casey has them. He used the car to try to talk with Carla but she wouldn't listen. He watches Mike stagger drunkenly. The streetlamp forms a pool of light around him, like a stage; each black curl on his head is backlit.

Moira is there. She's shouting at Mike to hand over the keys and come inside. "Go tomorrow. You're drunk, Mike."

Mike ignores his sister. "You fucker, Mac, you've got the goddamn keys. Give 'em to me." He snaps his fingers clumsily and holds out his hand.

The snap of Mike's fingers ignites the anger that has been building in Casey. Still, he controls himself.

"Uh-uh, Mikey. Moira's right." He turns away and starts down the street. He'll get drunk but not with Mike. Footsteps sound behind him.

"I'll go with you," Moira says as she catches up to him. Greens and blues shimmer on her eyelids. Her lashes are heavy with mascara. Her hair, curly like Mike's, rises a couple of inches on the top of her head before arcing down to her shoulders like raven wings.

Casey shakes his head; he wants to be alone.

"Just one beer," she says. "I'll buy. To see you off."

Then Mike is on him, wrestling for the keys. "He's coming with me, right, Case?" Mike pulls Casey to the ground.

Casey rolls away and stands up. "Fuck you, I'm not going." He starts to walk away again but Mike is on his feet and running at him, screaming.

"You owe me, MacInerney," he said. "You owe my whole family. Without us what would you be? Shit. That's what."

Casey hits him once, hard, and blood gushes from Mike's nose. Then he pulls out the keys, hurls them.

"Take 'em. Go already. I'm sick of saving your ass."

Mike wipes his hands across his face and looks from the blood smeared on his wrist to Casey and then back again. His eyes water; Casey can see them glittering. Mike screams out another "fuck you," runs to the Camaro, and jumps in. The rear lights flash on and the engine roars as he hits the gas and pulls away from the curb.

Part of Casey wants to run after the car, hurl himself through the window, and get the keys. The other part of him wants to scream, Die then, you motherfucker. Get the fuck out of my life.

"C'mon," Moira says. "Let's get out of here for a little while. You need to calm down." She tugs on his sleeve again and then reaches for his hand. "He'll be okay."

One beer leads to another and then another. Moira keeps touching him, holding his hand, rubbing his back, moving closer.

"What are you doing?" he finally asks, as she fits herself under his arm and leans into him.

"Mike's not the only one who can be blind," she tells him. They leave the *bar, his arm around her shoulders, her face turned up to his. They walk up the familiar stairs of her parents' house, going quiet as they pass Brendan and Katie's room, all the way up to the third-floor room he shares with Mike. There, she undresses him and then herself. For the first time in his life, he sees the girl he's grown up with naked. He's ashamed of the way his body responds. He sits on the bed, his hands on her hips, and buries his head between her breasts, smaller than Carla's and paler. She lifts his head and he sees her eyes dark and shining.*

*"I've wanted to be your girlfriend since I was twelve years old," she says. "I love how smart you are and I hate the way you get into trouble to protect Mike. I love him, too, but he's wrong when he says you owe us."*

*Casey pulls Moira's hips into him. She kisses the top of his head and then pushes him back onto the sheets and crawls over him. "I love you," she says to him as she kisses her way up his chest to his mouth. "I've loved you for a long time." She pauses and Casey senses she is waiting for him to say something. He starts to pull away. She pulls him back, covers his mouth with hers.*

*"It's okay." She breathes the words into him. "Just let me say it."*

*The next morning, before Katie and Brendan are up, they steal out of the house and take the train into the city. They spend the next twelve hours walking, talking, feeling the early-summer sun on their backs. Casey is trying to forget Carla, Mike, and the Army, and Moira is trying to make him love her. He feels better when they board the train back to Jersey City. He begins to look at the Army as a way to go to school, a pause, not a roadblock. He tells Moira this and she smiles like a person whose gift has been accepted.*

*When they get home, Katie's face is wet with tears and Brendan can barely speak. Mike is dead. He's rolled the Camaro across the median and two lanes of the Garden State Parkway. While Casey and Moira had been wandering through the city, a rescue team had been prying what was left of Mike's body from the twisted metal.*

# CHAPTER 41

Ruth paced back and forth from the table to the beds, stopping every so often to listen for Casey. He was hiding, the coward. He'd left his daughter the same way Stella had left her. Ruth walked over to the dresser where the box with Robbie's ashes lay. She cupped her hands on either side of the box.

"I didn't leave you. I never left you," she said, and then, realizing she'd spoken out loud, shot a glance at the bathroom door, but the water continued to run. She pressed her palms against the metal sides of the box until the edges made grooves in her skin. That last day, she'd told Robbie she'd see him later, just as she had done countless times when he was a child, each time believing that it was a sacrifice she had to make.

The rush of water in the bathroom ceased. Ruth waited for Casey to emerge. *Please. Come out. I won't ask you any more questions.* But the door did not open.

---

Casey steadied himself on the crutches in front of the bathroom door. He leaned his forehead against the damp wood and waited for the echoes of Mike's voice, and his own, to fade. Maybe Ruth had left enough vodka for him. Maybe he could get her to take one of those painkillers from Walmart and go to sleep without talking. He straightened, turned the knob, and swung through the crutches into the room.

"All done," he said. "Sorry I took so long."

Ruth was almost lost in shadow over by the screen door. Her skin looked gray in the light cast by the string of lights running through the trees of the campground.

"Going somewhere?" he asked.

Ruth turned. She leaned against the doorjamb, her hands behind her back, defenseless.

"Every time my mother called, I'd ask her when she was coming back to get me and my brother. Every time, she gave me another reason why she couldn't come."

"You don't have to tell me all this again." Casey looked at the kitchen area where she'd left the overhead light on. The pint bottle of vodka glinted back at him.

But Ruth didn't stop. "I hated the place I lived because she hated it. I counted the days until I could leave my grandparents' farm." She looked down at the floor. "I hated myself because if I were someone different, maybe she wouldn't have left me in the first place."

Casey flinched. "Maybe she knew she couldn't give you what you needed." He wanted it to be true. "I was afraid I was going to hurt my kid. I hurt everyone who cared about me."

He had to sit down. He made his way to the bed, lowered himself to the edge, and put his crutches on the floor. He leaned over, with his elbows on his knees, his face in his palms.

"Why did you want to see her all of a sudden?"

"I never forgot her. I always meant to go back when I was clean. Even when I wanted to forget, I couldn't." He looked up at Ruth. She looked back at him, eyes narrowed, brows lifted in a skeptical frown. "I sent her money. Not just what the government takes out of my disability check for child support—more, so she could save it for college, whatever she needs to have the life I didn't. Every time I went to the table, I'd be thinking about how much I could send." That commitment got him out of bed, pulled him through the empty days. When he wrote Emily's name on the envelope at the post office every month, it was the closest he came to touching his daughter.

Ruth's frown deepened. "None of that explains why you wanted to go now."

Casey inched to the end of the bed and pulled up his bag. He rummaged around in the front flap and pulled out the envelope Katie had sent with the newspaper clippings. He handed them to Ruth. She leaned over and switched on the small lamp between the beds so she could read them under the light. After a moment he handed her the letter, too.

"I got this in the mail the day after you came along with your fancy car. The note is from her grandmother, Mike's mom."

"Mike? What does he have to do with all this?"

So Casey told her. He told her about the fight. He told her how every tear running Katie O'Brien's cheek cut like a razor, how she and Mike's father made it worse by worrying about him. He told her how he and Moira gripped hands when they heard the news, but couldn't look at each other. He described the funeral, the way the casket seemed to grow heavier and heavier as he and the O'Brien boys walked it up the center of St. Francis Church. He was grateful when the extra week the Army had given him ended. He fled to basic training and for the next nine weeks pounded his body as if he could pound the guilt and grief out of himself.

Ruth broke in. "What happened to Mike's sister?"

"She didn't give up on me. She wrote, she called. She came down to Kentucky to see me graduate from basic training. She visited a couple more times and we talked every week."

"Did you love her?"

"No. Yeah. Like I loved all of the O'Briens, but not like . . ."

"Not like who?"

"I was gonna say, not like you're supposed to. I felt like she was still grieving and she needed me. I thought she'd figure it out and just stop. I wanted her to. I was beginning to think about how things would go after I got out; I'd have money for school. I could still do something." Teach. He'd wanted to teach literature; he'd have been able to read all the books he wanted.

"But you wanted her to make the decision."

He closed his eyes. It wasn't that simple. Moira brought love with her, and a sense of home, but she also unleashed a confusion of pain, anger, and loss that was all tied up in Mike. When she was gone, Mike disappeared behind the drills, the tasks, the blackjack in the barracks, the nights of liberty with a lot of guys Casey was coming to know like the fingers on each hand.

He heard Ruth sigh. A moment later he heard the springs give on the bed opposite him. He saw her sitting on its edge, facing him, the papers still in her hands. "She gets pregnant, right?"

Casey nodded. "It happened right after Easter. I'd gotten some time and gone to New Jersey. She came down a month and a half later and told me. She said her parents knew, they were happy. 'A new life is what this family needs.' Moira wanted me to know that that's exactly what Katie said." Casey remembered how Moira's lip quivered a little when he didn't respond. He remembered how she brushed her hair out of her eyes, eyes the same greenish brown as Mike's, and told him, "You don't have to marry me."

A life for a life, that was how it was supposed to go. But Mike got three. The baby's. His. Hers. "What about your nursing degree?" he'd asked her.

"I'll take time off and then finish," she'd said so fast that he knew she'd figured everything out. He saw it all: the wedding, the baby. Christmases, birthdays, Thanksgivings. Mike would be right there with him, in stories around the table, in photographs that lined the O'Briens' hallway, and in the eyes of his own child.

"I love you, Case," she said. "I always will."

There, with Ruth watching him, waiting for the rest of his story, Casey saw his younger self slumped on the motel bed, next to Moira, a beer in his hand. She was the only woman who'd ever said she loved him except for his grandmother. She meant it, he saw now. She meant it and still he couldn't say it back. Instead he'd drained the bottle of beer, set it on the floor, and grabbed her hand, and looked at it, looked at every freckle on the back of her hand instead of her eyes. "Okay."

"I got stationed in Georgia but in between, I had some liberty. I went to New Jersey and we got married," he said. "She wanted to move closer but before any of that happened, Iraq invaded Kuwait and in August I was on my way to Saudi. I was still there in January when Emily was born."

Ruth made a sound, as if she were starting to say something, but Casey didn't wait. He told her how his vision cleared when he was stuck in miles of sand waiting for a war to start. He saw what a miserable fuck he'd been to Moira and how he wanted another chance. He kept the photograph she'd sent of Emily in his helmet. He looked at it until he memorized the tiny, sleeping face at the end of a pink tube of blanket. After years of living with a borrowed family, he had one of his own.

"I met her for the first time at Walter Reed. They shipped me there after the amputation in Germany."

He stopped and looked at Ruth, saw her look toward the duffel. When she faced him again, her eyes were wet. "I'll shut up," he said.

"No, you've gone this far, tell me the rest. Tell me why you left. What could an infant do to you to make you leave?"

Casey shook his head. "Nothing. She did nothing. Moira did nothing. It was me. I couldn't give them what they wanted, what I wanted." He reached for a crutch thinking he had to move, get away from the shame raining down on him, but the crutch slipped from his hand. Neither one of them moved to pick it up. "Tell me," she said.

"I was useless. Everything hurt all the time, my leg, my head. I couldn't get away from the pain. We had to live with her parents because we couldn't afford a place. Moira went back to school. I stayed with her mother and the baby. Her dad was still working then at the fire department. All I had was my damn disability. It was only supposed to be for a year or so."

He pretended he believed Moira when she told him it was going to get better, that he had to be patient, but his head worked unevenly, like a clock that had been dropped down the stairs. A door would slam and he would drop whatever was in his hands. He was afraid to pick up Emily. He tried to get better, he told Ruth. He stumbled through the next few years, trying to work, doing stretches in rehab to unhook himself from the painkillers, weed, and booze. He failed at all of it.

"I left three times, the last time for good," he said. "I was out of chances with Moira. After the second time I left, she told me not to come back."

Ruth leaned forward, eyes dry now, her nose flared. "What about Emily?"

"Moira told me if I wasn't going to hang in there for the long haul, I'd better walk away. That I would hurt Em with the on-again, off-again crap."

"So you did. You just stayed away."

He nodded. Behind him moths batted against the screens; the soundtrack of a *Star Wars* movie burst through the open windows from an RV, then faded. Casey waited. There was nothing he could say to make any of it better. Maybe Ruth would. If not better, then clearer.

Ruth walked over to the lamp between the two beds and sat down. She held the clippings and the letter. Casey braced himself for a verdict. Instead, she asked a question.

"What would you tell Emily if you saw her?"

Casey leaned forward on his knees again, face down. "I don't know. I don't know. I just wanted to see her. Just once."

"What do you mean, 'wanted to'?"

"I don't know if I can do it."

Ruth looked down at the papers in her hand. "When, then?"

"What?"

"If you don't do it now, when will you go?"

Casey shook his head. He shrugged.

Ruth sighed. She rose and dropped the article and the letter onto Casey's lap and then entered the bathroom. He didn't look up. His eyes remained on the photograph of his daughter going up for a jump shot, pushing through the air, reaching with both arms. A perfect release.

# CHAPTER 42

When Ruth came out of the bathroom, she sank onto the bed across from Casey. He was sitting with his back against the headboard. On the table between them was the flattened tube of cortisone cream he'd gotten from the nurse at the hospital. The end of his stump stuck out from under the rolled-up hem of his shorts, a raw lump smeared with traces of white cream. His eyes were closed. The letter and the clipping had disappeared.

She eased down farther on the bed. As the minutes ticked by, her arms and legs grew heavy but her eyes remained wide open. A mosquito's whine filled her ear. She slapped at it and rolled over, facing the wall. The faint outline of a pineapple emerged from the shadows, then another, and another until she realized she was counting them on the wallpaper, trying to quiet her mind, which switched from Casey's story to her own and back. He blamed himself for his friend's death, abandoned his daughter, had apparently spent the past decade or so trying to lose himself. Yet here he was, with her, because he'd let himself think he could find a way back.

Casey's voice rasped from the other bed.

"Ruth, you still awake?"

She ignored him.

"What would you have done if your mother came back after all those years?"

As a teenager, Ruth used to imagine what it would be like to turn her back on a penitent Stella. In these fantasies she was the powerful one who could inflict pain or mercy. Even in fantasy, however, Ruth's need would betray her. When she imagined her mother's face crumpling in defeat, Ruth's resolve always softened.

"I don't know," she said. "I don't know what would have happened. She never tried."

"Do you wish she had?"

Ruth thought of the day she'd hunted Stella down in the cheap Florida apartment. "You're better off," Stella had told her. And Ruth had tried to believe her, but she didn't, not then and not now.

"Yes," she said.


Casey dropped a crutch coming out of the bathroom. Shit. He looked up but Ruth did not move. She must have finally gone to sleep. He leaned against the wall for support, stooped and felt for the fallen crutch. His armpits and his shoulders hurt. He wasn't used to the damn things. He adjusted them under his arms and then stumped his way to the kitchen, stooped over to get another Coke out of the refrigerator so he could swallow another ibuprofen. He didn't know why he bothered; the pain in his head seemed to be there all the time now, as it had after his accident.

Thunder cracked the silence; Casey nearly dropped his can of soda. The wail of a child sounded from the RV parked by the picnic tables. He glanced at Ruth, who stirred but did not wake.

Shit. Another fucking rainstorm. He used to wish for rain in Nevada, but the novelty was gone. A cloud seemed to have followed him out of there and wouldn't quit.

He made his way to the Formica table again but nearly lost his balance. He grabbed the edge and then sank into the chair in front of Ruth's laptop. He set down his Coke. This was nothing like the computers in the public library he sometimes used. He poked the touchpad on the front and watched the screen flicker to life. Ruth had been busy; a bunch of windows tiled across the screen. E-mail, articles, the results of an Internet search, and something that looked like letters and memos. He guided the cursor over to the e-mail and peered at the screen. The open message was addressed to *ruth.nolan@rycom.com*. That name again, RyCom. The subject line read, *Please Help*.

He read the e-mail and his insides went cold.

RyCom. He knew now why it sounded familiar. So Ruth was some muckety-muck in the same company that was screwing those contractors. He looked around for the newspaper she had brought with her from the gas station. There it was, its rolled-up edges poking out of the small wastebasket under the counter.

A whimper came from the bed. She was having another dream. He got up and retrieved the newspaper, opened it to the photograph of the asshole walking by the woman with the sign. There was a guy in a wheelchair behind her too. Disgust surged through Casey. Then he caught sight of the metal box on top of the dresser. The woman in the e-mail had mentioned Ruth's tragedy. Had Ruth tried to help her? He remembered now how Ruth had gone quiet when he'd ranted about the story in the newspaper.

Not his business. None of this was his business.

Then he thought of how he'd felt when he told her about Mike and Emily, half hoping she could help him, as if she had some kind of moral authority.

The skies thundered again. This time lightning lit up the inside of the cabin.

There would always be people like Ruth. People who had everything. Took what they wanted and tossed the rest away. Mike. The Army. A few years of his life, a leg, a daughter, a future. If he hadn't had something Ruth needed, she wouldn't have looked twice at him. This was the woman he'd trusted with his story.

The paper in his hand rustled as he gripped it. These contractors thought they were scoring a sweet deal, but where were they now? People like Ruth were the ones who made out. Then he remembered something she had said after the trooper stopped them. She was no longer with her company. Maybe she had been thrown out, too.

Either way, he needed to know. He propelled himself out of the chair and over to the bed across from Ruth's.

"Wake up!" he hissed.

She moaned and clutched the pillow to her chest. Strands of hair webbed against her cheek and forehead. In the shadows, it looked as though she were trying to hide behind what little hair she had.

"Look at this!" He reached across the small divide and gripped Ruth's shoulder, rolled her toward him.

She turned onto her back. He switched on the lamp between the beds. Her eyelids fluttered open, struggled, and then squeezed shut against the sudden glare.

He shook the paper at her. "You work for them, don't you?"

"What? What are you . . ."

"You work for the son of a bitch who is hanging those contractors out to dry, don't you?"

Ruth seemed to shrink from him. "Don't. You don't understand," she whispered.

"Try me. And don't tell me they knew what they were getting into. No one knows what they are getting into. Robbie didn't know, did he?"

Ruth went still. Slowly, she raised her face to his but her eyes were not focused on him. She was staring straight through him.

"It's my fault," she said so quietly he wasn't sure he heard her correctly.

"Yeah, it is. You guys were making money off these people."

"No. Robbie. It was my fault. He died because of me."

"What are you talking about?"

"Robbie. He was alive when he came home. Then he died. He killed himself. It was my fault."

Casey's anger rushed out of him. He was silent in the half light. Ruth sank to the floor and clutched her knees to her chest. He wanted to look away but he didn't.

"What happened?" *Don't tell me. Don't make me go there with you.*

She began to rock back and forth. "He was home on leave. He had just gotten back from Iraq. A few more weeks and he was done, going to get out for good." Ruth pressed her head against her knees. "He checked into a motel and put a gun to his head.

"I might have been able to stop him," she said.

Her voice was muffled but he could hear every word.

"He came to me that day. He wanted to go to lunch. But I couldn't. I thought there would be time. I want more time. I need more time."

There was nothing brittle about Ruth now. The pain came pouring through undammed. Casey pushed himself to her bed. He eased down and pulled her to him. He thought about telling her it was not her fault, that there was nothing she could have done, but she would think he was lying to her. And she would be right.

"I know," he said.

He wrapped his arms around her and curled around her like a shell. His back stiffened and his stump throbbed, but he did not move. He held on until the night was over and a gray dawn filtered through the blinds above them.

# CHAPTER 43

That morning Casey limped his way to the office and paid for another night. He brought back coffee and a couple of rolls, but Ruth didn't touch them. She lay on her bed, curved toward the wall, not asleep but not what he would call awake either. Helplessness rained down on him. The book he'd been trying to read lay facedown on his lap and he shifted in his chair.

When Ruth finally turned over it was nearly one o'clock. Casey stood, half thinking he should go to her. But she looked fragile. He was afraid to touch her.

"You okay? You hungry? Coffee's cold now, but the rolls are okay. I can go get you something else."

But she didn't respond. Casey glanced at his watch. "You should eat. I'll go out, find something better."

"You were wrong," she said at last. "He wasn't lucky to have me."

"He didn't think that."

"How would you know?"

Casey did not know. He couldn't know. He just wanted to keep her from slipping back to wherever she'd been. Questions that had earlier run through Casey's mind surfaced. He wasn't sure he could handle a confession. But he opened his mouth and there it was.

"Did he, Robbie, leave a note or anything . . . anything that would explain?"

Instead of answering him, Ruth pushed herself up from the bed, went to the duffel, and unzipped it. He saw the usual crap as she peeled it open: blue jeans, shirts rolled up and wedged in, a pair of running shoes, barely used. Ruth picked up one of the white T-shirts, shook it out. The front was printed with a face of Osama bin Laden in the center of red rings meant to look like a target. She reached in again. A camouflage hat, an iPod, a faded camouflage jacket splotched with bleach.

Ruth had stopped rummaging. She held a notebook in her hands.

"He wrote in this," she said to Casey. "The things he did, had to do . . . I didn't know. I just didn't know. He came home, and I was so glad to see him, but then there was this emergency at work. He wanted to see me and I told him to wait. He had all this inside him and I told him I would see him later. As if we had all the time in the world."

He didn't want to open it, but Ruth seemed to expect him to. As he read, Ruth picked up the stained jacket and pulled it to her chest. She wrapped both arms around it and bowed her head.

*. . . u call em haji, enemy, bad guy, target got 13 kills first guy stayed alive even after his whole face was gone—Sarge says corpsman can't help just finish him—he watches me—guy's body jumps like a fish on the ground— hear a click and Hanny's takin the guy's picture on his fuckin phone—*

*feel like a freak. kicked the soccer ball with Justy in the front yard and suddenly i see the kid, all the kids, chasing the humvee looking for fuck all peterson pisses in a water bottle and tosses it—we r laughin—saw myself laugh and laugh like it was the funniest thing i ever saw to see the kid stop in the middle of the street all covered in piss—made sense then—you could at least understand why you hated the little fuckers sometimes—you never*

*knew who they really were or if it was their brothers or fathers or uncles
trying to kill you*

*its like a movie that won't stop—think about one thing and the rest of
it all starts up. gun makes no difference—wrong vehicle wrong time is all
it takes—one night, Garcia is pissing and moaning about his skanky
girlfriend cheating on him and the next his guts and brains are smeared on
ur uniform u try to put him back together but u can't—u wonder why it
wasn't u—you wonder when its gonna be ur turn—*

*get scared enuff long enuff and the real u comes out*

The sound of the rain receded. If Ruth moved, Casey didn't hear
her. As he continued to read, he felt like a witness to an accident he
couldn't prevent.

*we're all standing aiming guns i yell at the driver to go back—we r yelling
in english—he can't understand—keeps coming he screams shit we cant
understand—Hanny drags him out of the car i pull Hanny off the guy—I
yell go home go home but there's an old lady in there, a woman and baby
plus the girl—and i see girls bleeding shes bleeding out into the car—we
try to stop it—we call the corpsman—but she's dying and there's nothing
we can do—the mother's crying and screaming at us and all we understand
is that she hates us—the girl lying across the other woman's lap. eyes open.
the eyes are always open*

*chaplain says we don't get to choose who dies bullshit—kords and me,
after the others died, we fired on 2 guys diggin—they were carrying
shovels—they had cell phones—they were burying an IED we decided—
we got commendations for that—you aim a gun and fire and that makes
you the decider right? u can wrap it in a reason but fact is we were angry
and someone had to pay but im lookin back now and i can't feel that any
more—i don't understand why they died and i got to live when i was no
different from them—no better than any of em—good guys or bad guys—*

*don't fit anymore—don't deserve to be here. don't deserve the corps. im
deciding now.*

*wanna see ruthie first. gonna tell her I love her—always loved her even when I fucked up—even when she fucked up don't blame her—look what she had to work with.*

*need to see my mom. one more time. just want to see her, sit down with her and be with her a little. no other people. no fancy stuff. just sit with her just breathe the same air for a little.*

*like Hanny said when it's your time, it's your time—ok then, it's my time. one more night—wanna sleep here in my bed with my rods and my flies. then I'll be ready. almost.*

Casey read the last line through a blur of tears. *need to see my mom one more time then I'll be ready.*

"I'm sorry, Ruth," Casey said without looking up. All he got in reply was the thrum of rain on the cabin roof. He stood to seek her out in the gloom of the cabin, not sure what to say or what to do, hoping the right words would come to him. But Ruth was gone.

# CHAPTER 44

She couldn't have taken the car. The keys were still on the table next to her computer.

He swore, yanked first the right crutch, then the left, and tumbled toward the door. He stood in the opening and called, but the rain drowned out his words. He squinted into the gloom. It was only midafternoon but the gray light and the rain made it seem later. Then he thought he saw her at the river's edge.

"Ruth!" He started down the path. His eyes were getting used to the murk, but he lost sight of the figure. He slipped and fell in the mud but used the crutches to push himself up. His fingers were slippery with rain and mud; time was slipping through them too. He could feel it. Calling Ruth's name, he advanced down the path, moving as fast as he could without falling.

He saw her now. A blurred form standing in the shallows of the river's edge.

"Ruth!"

She took a step and disappeared. Casey dropped to the ground and dragged himself and the crutches through the mud to the river's edge. Her head rose again to the surface. She was swimming but her movements were awkward and slow, like she was trying to stop her arms and legs from doing what they instinctively wanted to do. He couldn't be sure she was trying to kill herself; if she was, she was going about it all wrong. But an accident could make the decision for her.

"Ruth! Look at me!"

Her head turned. He thought he could see her eyes but he wasn't sure.

"Come back, Ruth."

He was not sure how much she could hear through the rain, with the river nearly in her ears. He kept talking into the wetness.

"That's right. Come back. It's not your fault. Don't you see? Not your fault. Don't let the fuckers take you both. Robbie doesn't want this."

He was in the water himself now. Practically crawling. He held out one of the crutches toward Ruth. "Come on, Ruth. Take it. I need you to take it. I need you to come back here. You can't do this. Please don't do this."

He saw her face bobbing pale and blurred in the water. A wave slapped the side of her head and for a moment he couldn't see her. Rage filled him.

"Ruth! Ruth, goddamn it. If you want to die, do it on someone else's watch. Don't do this to me."

He held his breath. When she bobbed to the surface again, he felt a tug on the end of the crutch.

A few minutes later she was beside him, on all fours in the water. He latched onto her arm and did not let go even after they crawled out of the river into the mud on the bank. He held on while she rose to her feet and then helped him up. His breath spilled out of his lungs as he heaved in air. Ruth started to explain.

"I didn't mean to . . . I wasn't going to . . . Robbie loved fishing. He loved the river on the farm. I thought if I came here I'd feel him.

I almost thought I could. Then there was a hole or something . . .
the current was stronger than I realized . . . I just wanted to feel
him, close to me."

"C'mon, Ruth," Casey said. "Let's go home."

One step at a time, they made their way back to the cabin.


Ruth heard the rain stop. One final burst and then nothing but
the drip from the eaves. Casey was pressed next to her now.
Skin to skin, his arm tight around her. The pillowcase under their
heads was damp from their hair. Casey had made her take a shower
with him. She'd let him guide her into the stall, then took the soap
from him as he leaned for support against the fiberglass. They stayed
together under the water until it began to lose its heat. He'd toweled
her off as best he could before half leading, half pushing her to her
bed and falling in next to her.

"You awake?" Casey's breath filled her ear when he spoke.

"Yes."

"Are you hurting?"

Every thought hurt; every breath seemed a betrayal. She was
alive and Robbie was dead. From those two facts flowed a river of
pain she would never be able to crawl out of. But Casey meant her
ribs, her eyes. The things he could see.

"I'm okay. I'd be better if you weren't squeezing me."

He relaxed his grip. She rolled onto her back, felt his breath on
her cheek. "You had some peanut butter, didn't you?"

"Had to. I needed strength in case you made another run for it."
He leaned up on one elbow. "You want some?"

"Robbie ate peanut butter for breakfast. And Coke. Like you."

Casey ran his hand down her right arm, twined his fingers in
hers. "You should eat something."

"Not hungry."

"A bite. I'll sleep better if you do."

"Okay. But I'll get it." She could see that his arm was red and tender around the clean bandage he'd put over his stitches. He needed help too. "Just tell me where it is," Ruth said.

"On the table."

Ruth moved as quickly as she could over the damp floor and grabbed the jar of peanut butter and a plastic knife lying next to it on the table. A flash of silver caught her eye; it was the drive with Terri's files protruding from the side of the computer. The screen was dark but it was only in sleep mode; she'd left it on.

"I read your e-mail," Casey admitted.

"It doesn't matter now."

She looked at Casey's face, peering at her from the rumpled bed. It would be like this for a long time, she knew. She would think of Robbie and someone or something would pull her back into the present. She would feel as she did now: resentful, grateful, lost.

"I need to take Robbie home," she said. She'd known all along, she just hadn't been able to face it.

"Back to California?"

"No. To New Hampshire. I need to take him there. It's what he would have wanted."

"What about San Diego?" Casey asked her. "What about your company?"

"What about them? The company let me go." She wanted to go back to the silence they'd created earlier. She wanted to lie in this bed with his arms around her. She'd made her decision and now all there was to do was wait until the weather cleared. "That woman who e-mailed you," Casey said. "Can you help her like she thinks you can?"

*I don't know.* She was no crusader. For years she had told herself she was doing what she had to do. She'd told Robbie that her work was hard, important, and that she was doing it for him. Someday, she'd always said, they could do what they wanted to do. She didn't know what that was anymore, if she ever did. She removed the thumb drive from her laptop and picked it up.

"Terri, my secretary, gave this to me. The night before I left San Diego, she told me that it had information on it that could help the people suing the company. She was right. It might help them. But it might not. At least not as much as she thought."

"I don't follow."

A sigh escaped her, born of nerves, or fatigue, or both. "I could call Marilyn Corning and tell her to connect me with the attorney for the contractor families. This has information on it that he would like to have." Then she told him about the files, the insurance lapses, the lies.

"How can that not make any difference?" Casey asked. "If the lawyer has that, won't he have everything he needs to pin them to the wall?" His face, a map of righteous anger and confusion, would have once made her smile knowingly. Now all she saw was the slimmest of possibilities.

"If he's good and has a little luck, he might be able to use it to make trouble, force the resolution a little quicker. If he's really good, he could get his clients some money because the timing is right. My company, my former company, doesn't want anything to screw up a big deal they're trying to make. When it goes through, everyone gets a lot of money. On the other hand, Don, the man in the newspaper, doesn't like to be pushed around. He's fighting it."

"Isn't this shit against the law?"

Casey's brow furrowed just as Terri's had that night when she'd first asked Ruth to help the contractors. When Ruth said *can't*, they heard *won't*. She tried to explain.

"It's against regulations. There's a difference. All they have to do is pay a fine and they can walk away, start all over again. Most of the time, the government doesn't have the resources to police them unless something like this forces the issue. Contractors like RyCom just build the fines into the cost of doing business."

"But you're an insider," Casey said. "If this information comes from you, it'll raise the stakes, won't it? If those people see you out there explaining how the system works, it'll do more than help those families get their money, it'll make these assholes sweat. It might even make the government do its job."

Ruth shook her head. *No.* Passing the files to the lawyer was one thing; becoming a poster girl for whistleblowers was another. Even if she tried to give up the files anonymously, it would be easy for Gordon or Don to trace the files back to her, maybe even to Terri. The only way to protect her former secretary would be to step forward and attract all the attention herself. She saw Casey's eyes narrow. "What'll it cost you?"

Ruth sank into the chair without looking at him. She knew the answer to part of his question. Don would do everything he could to punish her. The millions coming to her from the deal would not materialize. She'd have to get a lawyer to defend herself against Don, maybe even to defend herself against the contractors—because, after all, she'd headed the division responsible for hiring them. She would be a pariah; no one in the industry would work with her again. The balloon payment on the house would come due. Even if she sold it, there would be nothing left.

Those were the things she could predict with confidence. What about the rest? She looked up then and searched Casey's face as if she'd see the answer there. *How do you start over when you are nearly fifty,* she wanted to ask him. She saw Casey's face shutter the way Terri's had.

"Sorry. Never mind," he said. He got up and reached for his crutches. "I'm no one to judge you or anyone else."

Ruth looked at the laptop. With one touch she could fill the blank screen with Marilyn's e-mail. One phone call could put it all in motion. Ruth averted her eyes. Her hands were in her lap now, fingers twined together as though she were playing the child's game her grandmother used to play with her and the one she'd then played with Robbie. Church, steeple, look inside . . .

"Do what you have to do, Ruth. I gotta take a leak."

*What you have to do.* She closed her eyes and watched Robbie move toward her on the deck that last morning, the newspaper in his hand. She saw the tattoos, the acne, the flicker of surprise when he scanned the headlines. *The paper's full of shit, right?*

*Of course*, she'd said. *Of course.*

Ruth straightened and faced her laptop. She touched the keys. Marilyn Corning's e-mail appeared on the screen. Ruth read it through one more time. She looked over at the box of ashes resting on the bureau, waiting. She reached for the phone.

# CHAPTER 45

Casey woke to find Ruth sifting through their bags, looking for something clean to put on. She wore an olive T-shirt that was too big for her. She must have taken it out of Robbie's duffel.

"Everything's either wet or filthy," she said.

She'd cracked the blinds, and shadows from the louvers ran across her chest like railroad tracks. Her good eye looked bruised now, too, purple with fatigue. Another bad night, but he supposed it would be a while before she had a decent one.

"So, the sun decided to show itself," Casey said.

Ruth shrugged. "We need to do some laundry."

"You did the right thing, you know," he said. He did not say that he would've bet against her ever making a call like that. He did not say that he'd felt something almost like jealousy, just a flash, when he'd emerged from the bathroom and realized she'd actually gone ahead and done it.

"It's done, anyway. I can't undo it," Ruth said. She shook a pillow out of its case and began to stuff dirty clothes in it. "She's going to have Breen, the lawyer, call me. Throw me that shirt."

He did and then sat back and let her figure out the day. Clean
their clothes, clean themselves, rest. Listing the tasks, moving around
the room seemed to steady her. Then she surprised him.

"Come with me."

"What? Where?"

"New Hampshire. Come with me."

"New Hampshire?" She could have said Cameroon. The idea
of New Hampshire was just as unexpected, just as foreign.

"You could let your arm heal properly, get some rest. You could
even get a new prosthesis," Ruth said. "Then you can go where you
want to go without worrying about it." She went back to folding clothes,
but in her too-casual tone he heard how much was riding on his answer.
She must be as afraid to face her family as he was to face the O'Briens.

"Thanks, Ruth, I mean it. Thanks. But I'm not sure it's a good idea."
If he decided to cut and run back to Las Vegas, it would be a lot harder
to do from New Hampshire. And if he wanted to go through with seeing
Emily, he didn't see how going there would make that any easier, either.

"Don't tell me now. Think about it."

That seemed to be all that Ruth had to say for a while. She didn't
argue when he ordered her eggs in the little snack bar near the
campground Laundromat. She ate all of her breakfast, which Casey
took as a good sign.

"Hey," he said, finally.

Ruth looked at him. Her eyes widened slightly as though she had
just noticed he was there.

"Just thought I'd see if you could still hear me," he said. He hesitated,
then plunged on. "You want to think out loud, it's okay with me."

"That lawyer is going to call me. And I've got some phone calls
I need to make and I don't want to."

"Your boyfriend?"

"Neal, yes. Terri too. My family."

"What's holding you back?"

"I'm not sure."

"Will it get any easier if you wait?" He was full of wisdom when it came to someone else.

Ruth tried to smile but gave up on it. She shook her head and reached for her purse.


She called Neal from the Laundromat. She was half hoping the phone would go right to voice mail, but he answered on the first ring.

"Ruth?"

She closed her eyes and leaned forward, elbows on her knees for support. She wished now she could see him, hold him and just not have to say anything, but he was repeating her name again as if afraid she was going to hang up.

"I've caught you at a bad time," she said. "You've got people there." It was Sunday, where would he be? A meeting maybe, or golf.

"I'll be right back," she heard him say. "Got to take this." When he spoke again, the background voices had disappeared and so had the controlled calm she'd heard when he answered.

"Where the hell are you?"

"I'm sorry I haven't called. I don't know where to begin."

"Who's the guy?"

"He's . . . a friend." There was no word that would describe who Casey was to her. She couldn't understand it herself. How could she explain it to Neal?

"Are you still with him?"

"Yes, but it's okay, he's not . . . there isn't time to explain. He's not the reason I'm here."

"Tell me the reason, then."

"I'm sorry. That's all I can say."

"There's a lot more you can say. I try my best to be whatever it is you need and you kick me out of your house. Then you disappear. No explanation. No phone calls. The only word I get is from a stranger who could have kidnapped you for all I know."

His words peppered into her ear like bullets from a silencer. She'd never heard Neal sound so angry, at least not at her. Beneath that, though, Ruth heard concern and hurt. She pictured his long, lean face, the blue eyes behind the reading glasses he always forgot he had on.

"Listen to me, please," she said. "I know you were trying to help me. And you did, so much. I realize I didn't make it easy. I'm so sorry, Neal. I shouldn't have treated you that way."

The phone went silent. Ruth heard the Laundromat door open. When she looked up, Casey backed out with a wave of apology. Neal's voice drew her back.

"I just want you home. It's been a tough time for all of us."

Home. Like that, she saw it, felt it, wanted it. She wanted the sand he tracked in from the beach, the cracked Chargers mug he refused to let her toss away, the copy of *People* magazine that he'd buy for her when he stopped for milk or gum on the way home. No other man had known her as well or for as long. And Neal had known Robbie. In the silence that expanded between them, Ruth understood that none of these things were strong enough to sustain her; if they had been, she would have stayed.

Ruth took a breath, and then the words spilled out of her. "I'm going to help those families who are suing RyCom."

The silence stretched between them until Ruth wondered if he'd even heard her. "What are you talking about?" he said at last.

She imagined telling Neal to forget what she'd said. She wasn't herself. She would return to San Diego after she buried Robbie, and then they could try to figure out where they stood. That was the reasonable thing. But as more seconds ticked by, the words would not come. She didn't want to say them anymore. She didn't know what she wanted, but she knew that much. She stood up and walked away from the dryer.

"Neal, I'm going to give their lawyer some information that might help." She needed to make everything clear to him. She needed to be clear for herself.

"What are you talking about? What information?"

Over the phone, she could hear the sound of a door opening. A man called Neal's name.

"A couple of minutes," he said to whoever it was.

"I'd better go," Ruth said.

"Where are you headed?"

"To New Hampshire, for now," she said. "I'll let you know when I get there." They could talk again. He needed time. So did she.

"Ruth, you've been through a lot. Tell me where you are. I'll get there as soon as I can. We can go to your grandmother's together." All business now, ready to step in the way he had when Robbie died.

"You don't need to do that." She saw Casey leaning against the fence outside the Laundromat and she lifted her hand to get his attention, but Neal's next words stopped her cold.

"You blame me, don't you?"

"What?"

"You blame me for Robbie."

"What are you saying?" Ruth found another chair and sat down. She could handle anything but the thought that somehow Neal knew something and hadn't warned her.

"I don't know." His voice dropped so low Ruth could barely hear him. "I keep thinking about that morning. I told you not to expect Robbie to be the same . . . I keep wondering if there's something I could have said after you left for work. Instead, we talked bullshit and I made him pancakes."

Ruth slumped forward; the edge of the plastic seat dug into the back of her thighs. "I don't blame you," she said. "I never blamed you." That was the truth, even though she couldn't help imagining Neal and Robbie eating pancakes, talking, drifting into conversation that might have made Neal cancel his meetings or call her to come home or any of a million events that might have changed that day, moments missed that she would want back for the rest of her life.

"Come home, then, Ruth. Or let me come get you."

"No," Ruth said. She drew a breath and sat up. "I've already told one of the contractors' wives that I would help."

"Why? You'll only bring a shit storm down on your head, and for what? The cards are stacked against those people and you know it. No one in the industry will touch you ever again."

Ruth didn't have an answer for him that he would understand. She waited for him to speak, but she knew he was running through the consequences he'd face, just as she had not twenty-four hours before. His consulting business would take a hit. It might dry up altogether if things got nasty. Guilt by association.

"I'm too young to retire and I'm too old to start over," he said at last.

"I understand."

If she'd been standing in front of him at that moment, Ruth might have touched his cheek and pulled him close so he would know that she did not blame him. She'd never given Neal any reason to go to the wall for her.

"Don't do this, Ruth." His voice sounded rigid with disbelief, warning.

She closed her eyes and imagined the feel of her palm on his cheek, a last kiss.

"Take care, Neal."

As she ended the call, her heart tumbled in her chest like the clothes in the nearby dryers. There was a woman shoving coins in, one after the other. When had she come in? Where was Casey? Ruth caught sight of him slouched against a rail outside and relaxed a little. He waved. She lifted her hand in return. There was no turning back now. She had to call Terri. She would let her know without spelling it out that she was doing what her friend had asked. Terri could send the credit cards to New Hampshire. After that no more talking, at least until Terri was safely in another job. Ruth would be on her own.

---

From the doorway of the Laundromat, Casey couldn't tell how Ruth was faring. He shifted on his crutches and resumed pacing. Sooner or later she'd finish her calls and then he'd have to make his decision. Going back to Nevada would be easy enough. If Belva had already rented out the trailer, he'd bunk with Lenny until he got settled somewhere else. All Ruth would have to do is drop him off in Indianapolis.

Casey stopped and leaned against the hood of the Jaguar. Bits and pieces of the last twenty-four hours came back to him as he watched her stand, walk to the far wall, head bowed, hand pressing the phone to her ear. She looked the same but she was not the same. She'd taken that first step and now she could not go back. He envied her.

She was turning now, looking for him. He waved and picked up the crutches. Maybe he should go with her.

That night they ate dinner outside, at one of the picnic tables. The RV family had emerged. Children burst out of the vehicle and ran through the mud toward the river and back. The adults followed like newly liberated prisoners—cautious, blinking a little against the sun that had wavered all day but now lit the sky to the west. Everyone slapped at insects on their skin but no one complained.

Ruth watched the family from behind her sunglasses. She jumped when she felt a mass of fur, muscle, and bone worm its way between her thighs. The Lab had sniffed out a piece of grease-soaked bread she'd dropped and was looking for more.

"Looks like you've made a friend." Casey chuckled. He reached for another drumstick.

Ruth tore a piece of chicken from the thigh she'd been toying with and tossed it toward the RV. She watched the dog run away and then head toward the other table, where the wife was unpacking a cooler. Their son began to toss a softball in the air and swing a bat. Ruth couldn't take her eyes off him. She pushed the rest of her food toward Casey.

"You eat it. I'm done."

He pushed it back.

"Two more bites."

"I'm all right now. You don't have to nurse me anymore."

She saw Casey glance at the boy and then back at her. He put down his drumstick and leaned across the table, crushing the empty paper bag that had carried their food. He groped for her hand.

Ruth watched the woman wet a napkin with a bottle of water and dab at her daughter's cheeks. Then she felt Robbie sitting next to her as he had once, years before, as a toddler on a sunny Saturday in a park somewhere. His curls stuck to his scalp, moist in the heat, and his eyes were aimed at the ice cream cone melting in his hands. He lifted it to his mouth. Chocolate ice cream trickled down his arms; a gap-toothed grin lit up his sticky face. Ruth heard her own laugh, watched herself pretend to sneak up on him with a wet cloth. He'd thrown his arms around her, burying his face in her neck. For once she hadn't pulled back from the mess. She hugged him and the smell of milk, chocolate, and baby skin overwhelmed her. Her eyes filled as the memory slipped away.

"Ruth? You okay?"

"I never saw it."

"Never saw what?"

"What you said, what Neal said before I left. I was part of it. I was part of what killed Robbie. Nothing will change that."

"I didn't mean it. You don't know what he was thinking. You can't know."

"When they sent him over there, I told him I was proud of him," she said to Casey. She leaned forward, her words urgent: a confession. "I told everyone that. It's what you are supposed to say. I didn't say it enough before then. Nowhere near enough."

Casey leaned across the table, grabbed her arms. "It's okay. It's okay."

Ruth shook her head. "Then he was deployed. He sounded so happy. I went to work the next day and I heard that word, *deployed*. Everywhere. I said it myself. Told my clients how we could assemble and deploy all the personnel they needed, like we were selling them jeeps or spare parts."

"Ruth . . ."

After Robbie's deployment, she'd felt it, hadn't she? That stab of unease running through the celebration of every new contract. Then the days had passed; the work went on; quotas were defined, filled. No bad news came from Robbie, just poorly spelled e-mails or texts, a battered pink card a few weeks after her birthday, and intermittent requests that Terri helped fulfill: a new cell phone, CDs, socks, magazines. The construction on the house accelerated, distracted her with an urgency that now seemed ludicrous.

Ruth stared at Casey until his face and the campground came back into focus. "It was so hard between us sometimes," she said, her voice hoarse and low. "He seemed to spend all his time trying to get away from me. When he enlisted, I got mad. I wanted to try to fix it, get him out of it. But he told me not to." She stopped, took a breath. "And then, when he did go, things got easier. They got easier and . . . I liked that."

Once the words were out, she wanted them back.

Casey gripped her hands and just looked at her. She could see his eyes like shadows behind his Ray-Bans. He couldn't seem to think of what to say. But she didn't need him to say anything. Listening was enough. Hearing the worst she had to say and continuing to hold her hands in his, that was enough.

Later, Ruth sat on the edge of her bed, watching Casey roll his pant leg up over his stump. The knob of flesh and bone emerged pink, smooth, uneven, like the fist of an infant.

"It's red. Does it hurt?" she asked.

"Nah. It's a lot better. Pass me that tube of gunk."

"Let me," she said. She twisted off the cap and squeezed the tube until a coil of white cream appeared in her palm. She was careful not to press too hard. "We'll have to get more bandages for your arm, too. You weren't supposed to get it wet. It might be infected."

"You're not as bad as you think you are, Ruth."

She looked up to see Casey studying her, his eyes half hidden in the shadow cast by the small bedside lamp. As absolution it fell short, but Ruth was grateful.

"Neither are you." She replaced the cap on the tube and tightened it.

They made love that night. Later, in the dark, Ruth lay next to Casey, her head against his shoulder, her hand resting on his chest.

"Did you think about New Hampshire?" She thought she felt his heart jump below her palm.

When he spoke, though, Casey's voice was distant, as though he hadn't heard her question. "Sometimes, I feel like there's someone inside me who got locked up when Mikey died."

"Who is it?"

"The guy I was supposed to be. I blamed Mike. Then I blamed Moira, Emily's mom. I blamed everyone but me. The other night, when you said that stuff about my daughter, you made me look at myself."

"Was that a good thing?"

He rolled toward her. "That stuff we were talking about before, outside at the table. I don't think you ever get away clean. If you've fucked up, you've fucked up. It's with you for the rest of your life."

Ruth didn't want to hear this. She tried to sit up.

"No, Ruth, wait. Look at me." He pulled her back until they faced each other on the pillow. His face was all shapes and shadows, but she could see his eyes and they bored into her. "The thing I got wrong is that that's not the end of the story. The bad stuff's with you but it doesn't have to kill you. Look at you. You're brave. You're giving up a lot to try to make amends."

*Try.* The night no longer seemed safe or sheltering, just another place where uncertainty could find her. As for brave, that was the last thing Ruth felt. She lowered her head until it was once again on Casey's chest. His body went still against her.

"I want to see Emily, but I don't know if I can face her. It's been a long time. She was just a little kid when I left."

"She's alive. You have the choice." Ruth didn't intend for the words to sting, but she heard the strain of bitterness beneath them. She placed her hand over his heart. "I'm sorry."

He sighed. "It's okay. You're right. I've pictured walking up those steps at the old house a million times. I've pictured her face. I just can't see . . ."

"What happens after that . . ." Ruth whispered. "I thought gamblers were used to that."

"The truth? I'm a shitty gambler. I'm just a guy with too much time on his hands. For nearly a dozen years, I've been killing time and all I really know is that I can't get it back."

She reached for his hand and pulled it close. "You can't get it back, but maybe you'll get a shot at a whole new life."

"That stuff's a lie. It's all one life."

Ruth's heart seemed to pause when she heard the familiar words. "My grandmother used to say that to me."

"Wise woman."

Ruth leaned up on her elbow and looked down at his face. "Come to New Hampshire, meet her. Let your arm heal. You can think about how you want to approach Emily so you get it right."

"What about Neal?"

Ruth shook her head. "He won't be coming."

"Yeah. Okay, maybe I will." Casey rolled onto his side; Ruth curved herself around his back. He stopped talking but he wasn't sleeping. Neither was she.

# CHAPTER 46

Ruth lay still in Casey's arms, but he knew she was awake. Her breathing was uneven; the muscles in her upper arms tensed against his. He glanced at the clock. Just after four. Jesus, what was that smell? A skunk must have let loose. Casey released Ruth and leaned up on one elbow. Just a hint of light coming through the window. Fuck. Too early to get up; too late to go back to sleep.

And he had to take a leak.

"Maybe we should get going," he said. "We can drive for an hour and find breakfast along the way." They'd already decided to head to Peoria. Ruth had tracked down a couple of prosthetists on the Internet, and an urgent care place where she insisted they go to have his arm checked. If he was lucky, they could clean out the lock on the faker, maybe replace the pin and he could keep going for a little while more. Ruth pushed herself up next to him and nodded. "Let's get out of here."

She leaned into Casey's shoulder; he leaned into hers. They looked around the darkened room, at the silhouettes of the Formica table, the chair holding the stack of folded laundry waiting to be packed. Casey felt Ruth's fingers lace through his and squeeze. He gripped her hand, squeezed back, hung on until the knot in his gut eased.

"Okay, then. Pass me the crutches."

He read to Ruth while she drove. Not Melville. The Silverstein book, the one he'd bought and read to Emily when she was a baby. He'd read it to her sober, drunk, tired, high—any time she asked him to—until the day he left. He'd taken it from the table by her bed while she'd been sleeping. For months he swore he could still smell her on the pages: her baby shampoo, the cocoa she liked to drink before bed, and the straw-colored kitten Moira had given her for her third birthday. When he could no longer summon Emily's scent, he would trace the lines she'd scribbled on the pages when she was two or three.

After four hours of driving, Ruth had shut off the radio. She didn't want to talk, but her tension was palpable. She kept flicking her eyes to the rearview, drumming her fingers on the steering wheel. The shadows beneath her eyes, visible when she shoved her sunglasses up to peer more closely at the dash, had deepened along with the ocher stains of the healing shiner. He knew she was tired. They both were. Too much drama. No real sleep.

They'd spent a day and a night in Peoria, where he'd gotten lucky. A prosthetist fixed the lock and gave him a bill he could send to the VA. The urgent care place had cleaned his arm and given him a dose of antibiotics. Now they were already well into Ohio, where they would spend another night. The day after that would bring them deep into Pennsylvania. He would have to make a decision.

Lacking the attention span for reading *Moby-Dick*, he'd pulled this book from the bag in the backseat. He read to Ruth about being swallowed by a boa constrictor. She laughed, surprising them both. He kept going. "Messy Room," the one about the bear in the Frigidaire.

An ache formed at the base of his neck but he ignored it. He pretended he was reading for his little girl. Maybe he was trying to summon her presence; maybe he was just trying to hold on to the image of her face lighting up when he read to her.

"You're good at this," Ruth said. "Emily must have loved listening to you."

From the corner of his eye, he caught her glancing at him through the sunglasses she'd gotten after the accident. He'd made her smile.

Casey focused back on the book, flipped a few pages to find another poem. "She did," he said. "I did, too. It was about the only thing I knew how to do."

"You mean you were one of those guys who ran from dirty diapers?"

"Should have said it was the only thing her mother trusted me to do. I was . . . not in great shape."

He'd found his favorite poem, about that space only children know between the end of the sidewalk and the rest of the hard concrete world. But he couldn't get started.

"She'll hate me," he said to Ruth.

"She has to know you to hate you."

He turned toward Ruth, his hand flattening the page in front of him. He had not expected tough love at this point.

"That's comforting."

Without taking her gaze off the road ahead, she reached across and rested her hand on his. "She won't hate you."

He didn't believe her, but the exchange, the feel of her hand on his, settled him. He thought again about just keeping on: driving with Ruth, living with her in the contained world of the Jaguar, cheap motel rooms, and the intimacy they'd somehow stumbled into. Traveling like this reminded him of being back in Nevada, where, before the start of every day, before going into the casino, probabilities were at least temporarily eclipsed by possibility. And for the first time in years he was not alone.

Casey's eyes dropped to the book in his lap. "Want me to keep reading?"

Ruth didn't answer him. "Emily's mother, though," she said. "What about her?"

The cord in Casey's neck tightened. The note he'd received from Katie had been cryptic; the article and photos were all of Emily. He'd not allowed himself to think too much about Moira, how she had been living since he left. She had to know where he was if Katie had tracked him down. If she cared to, she could have found him through the VA.

"She probably despises me, if she thinks about me at all. She's found some guy by now, I'm sure, forgotten I existed."

Ruth shook her head. "As long as Emily is around, she's not going to be able to forget altogether, is she?"

Casey shifted in his seat, rubbed the back of his neck. He looked back at the book but the words swam before him. There was so much he had not thought through. He didn't feel like reading anymore.

"It'll be okay," Ruth said.

"Sure."

"Anyway, you have time to figure it out. You can stay in New Hampshire as long as you need to."

"How's that going to work, anyway?"

"What do you mean?"

"I mean, how's it going to work, bringing a stranger home at a time like this?"

A mile ripped by with no response from Ruth. He looked at her. She was sucking on her lower lip.

"It'll be fine," she finally said. "My folks are kind people. Not like me." She flashed what she probably thought was a smile at him. Her mouth wobbled like a kid fighting off tears.

Casey looked away, and gripped the book in his lap until a cramp flared in his little finger. He watched the silver jaguar on the nose of the car, dusty, scratched, but leaping relentlessly forward.

# CHAPTER 47

They reached Columbus without talking again about Jersey City or New Hampshire. By the time they checked into a motel and found something to eat, they were too tired to talk much about anything. Ruth rested with her cheek on Casey's chest while he read. If she could just pause time, she thought. Not forever, just for a little longer.

Later, she woke in the dark to the sound of her cell phone. In the bluish light of the display she saw an unfamiliar Los Angeles exchange and knew she would not sleep again tonight.

"What is it?" Casey asked, half asleep.

"I think it's the lawyer for the contractors," Ruth said. "Marilyn Corning said she would give him this number."

She thought of letting the call go, waiting until she got to New Hampshire. That was the smart thing to do, the kind of thing she would have done in the past. Get her ducks lined up, a lawyer on board, see if there was some way to protect herself from any repercussions.

But the longer she waited, the harder it might be. Ruth shook her head and took the call.

"Ms. Nolan?"

"Yes."

"James Breen. Marilyn Corning gave me your number."

"She said she would."

"I'm sorry. Did I wake you? It's only nine o'clock."

He didn't sound sorry. "Maybe in California," Ruth said. "It's midnight for me."

"Shall I call back?"

"No. I'm up now." Ruth pushed aside the covers and stood. She couldn't talk to this man lying down. The bedside light clicked and she saw Casey glance toward the bathroom. Ruth passed him the crutches and waited for Breen to speak. Never talk first, was what Don had taught her, as if that were relevant now. Ruth began to pace. No matter who talked first, this conversation would make her decision real.

"I understand you have information that may be helpful to my clients," Breen said in a neutral tone. Ruth tried and failed to remember what he looked like from the day on the steps of RyCom. She'd never seen his face from the conference room window, only a mop of gray curls and a wrinkled suit surrounded by reporters.

"I don't know how helpful it will be. I told Marilyn not to expect too much," Ruth said.

"Marilyn has learned the hard way not to expect anything at all," he said. "I'm curious, why are you offering to help us?"

"Is that important?"

"It might be. I'm not in the vengeance business."

Ruth was taken aback. "If you were, you'd be a fool and so would I."

He surprised her with a rueful chuckle. "There are all kinds of fools, Ms. Nolan. If you help us, you might be called one of them."

"I said I would help, and I will." But he'd unnerved her. She bit her lip and resumed her pacing. The room seemed smaller with every step she took.

"Do you have legal representation?" Breen said.

"Yes. No. Why?"

"I recommend that you have an attorney advise you before we speak—before you take any further action, really."

As the bathroom door opened and Casey swung back into the room, he caught her eye and then jerked his thumb up in a gesture of encouragement. He nearly lost his balance, but Ruth couldn't smile. She turned away. "Can't I just send you the material? You can do what you want with it."

"Of course. But I may see something that would make me want to depose you along with anyone else involved in the decisions—or the nondecisions—that led to the lapsing of life insurance policies or health insurance that my clients need. There is the possibility that you will become a target for individual lawsuits."

This was it. If Ruth proceeded, there would be no way to control everything that unfolded. She was momentarily overcome by an instinct to hang up, buy time. She looked up to find Casey but instead saw the metal box, which she'd carefully placed on the desk.

Time could not be bought, only used or wasted. "I understand," she said.

"So does that mean you would like to have your attorney advise you before you share the material with me?"

Ruth hesitated. This was her chance to try to protect whatever assets she could before moving forward. She would still be helping Marilyn Corning and the other families, but she would be making them wait.

She'd made Robbie wait.

"Ms. Nolan?"

"I'll have my attorney get in touch with you, but it won't change my decision," Ruth said. "I'll e-mail you the materials tonight, if you want. Or tomorrow, I can send a hard drive by overnight mail."

"I'll give you a site where you can upload the files securely," he said without hesitation, as if afraid she might change her mind. "I promise to contact you or your attorney before we proceed."

Ruth found a pen on the motel room desk and scribbled the information Breen gave her. When he finished, he paused, and when he spoke again, the neutrality was completely gone. He sounded kind, grateful but also a bit sorrowful.

"None of this is going to be easy, Ms. Nolan. You and I both know that my clients may not get everything they deserve, but you are giving them their first break in a long time. They may not be able to fully appreciate what you are doing, but I do. Thank you."

When the call ended, Ruth placed her phone on the desk next to Robbie's ashes. She noticed that her hand did not tremble even though every nerve vibrated with alarm.

"Good for you, Ruth," Casey said. "You did it."

He couldn't have heard everything Breen had told her on the phone, only that she had agreed to help. But it didn't matter. There was nothing to do now but keep moving. She pulled her laptop from its case, turned it on, and inserted the flash drive. She followed the instructions Breen had given her and watched a long blank bar appear across her screen. In seconds it began to turn solid blue as the files uploaded. Twenty-five percent complete, forty percent. So fast. She looked at Casey. He smiled and lifted his hand in a thumbs-up sign. Sixty percent. One click and she could stop this. Seventy percent. Ruth closed her eyes and thought of all the lives captured in those files. She thought of Marilyn Corning's tears when she heard why Ruth was calling. She thought of Terri standing on her deck that last night, her eyes full of concern but also trust. She thought of how Robbie's hand felt so small in her own when he was a toddler, how tightly he'd hugged her that last day. When she opened her eyes, it was done. The bar was solid blue.

# CHAPTER 48

They reached Harrisburg after dark on the next night. Ruth suggested that they stop in Hershey the next day. "It's close," she told Casey. "We can drive by and smell the chocolate." She had been there years before with Robbie, she explained. Casey thought she might be looking for ways to slow down now that they were nearing the end of the trip.

"Maybe," he said, but he wasn't sure he could do this for her. When he'd watched Ruth sit down in front of her computer the night before and upload the files, he'd felt a shift inside, like a gear freed after years of being frozen. It was his turn now.

He guided the Jaguar into the parking lot of another motel amid the usual fleet of vanilla sedans used by salesmen. Across the lot, next to a combination gas station and a couple of restaurants, a handful of semis were parked in diagonal formation.

"There's a pizza place over there," he said. "You hungry?"

"A little."

"I'll go over and get a couple of slices and some drinks. You get us a room." He peeled some bills from the shrinking roll of cash in his pocket. Then he reached for the faker.

"Let me do it," Ruth said. "It's too far for you to walk."

"It's no big deal," he said. He felt her watching him as he slipped the prosthesis over the liner with the new pin and then stood up. His stump had shrunk more than he realized, but he didn't want to stop and add another sock right now. He took a cautious step, then another. "Go on, get us a room and I'll meet you back here in a few."

Each step strengthened his resolve. He knew in his bones that he needed to try now with Emily. Even a few weeks more was too long to wait to see what the future held.

He was closer to home than he'd been in years. The smells of onions, peppers, and sausage and the way the guy behind the counter said "You got it" after he ordered were both familiar and foreign. Grits, gravy, and burritos were not staples here. Adrenaline filtered into his bloodstream. He eyed the trucker in front of him, watched him pick up a pizza box and head to the soda machines to fill his extra-large cup.

"Where you headed?" he found himself asking.

The driver reached for a straw and a plastic cover for the soda. "Hoboken, then north. But not till tomorrow morning. Been driving twelve hours straight. Need to take a break." He rolled his eyes. "At least that's what the law says."

"Any room for a passenger?"

"Where you headed?"

"Jersey City."

"My boss won't like it."

"He doesn't need to know."

"I'll have to charge you something."

"No problem," Casey said. "Let's talk."

He'd made the right decision, he told himself as he picked up the pizza and Cokes. He stepped back out of the restaurant and paused. One more night and he'd be standing in front of the

Jersey City house trying to screw up the courage to walk up the steps and knock. All the smells and sounds that were so familiar just minutes ago seemed the opposite now. Emily wouldn't know him from any one of these men walking from building to car or climbing into one of the semis. He wished now they'd picked up some beer or something, anything to take the edge off his nerves. He began to make his way back toward the car. How was he going to tell Ruth?

He found her leaning against the fender, her chin practically on her chest.

"Hey. Wake up."

She lifted her head, gave him a tired smile. "You're back."

The smile opened him up inside, made him feel strong and weak, both. "Ruth," he began.


She knew he was leaving before he told her. The resolve in his voice was unmistakable. Still, she argued.

"Let me take you. Some trucker isn't going to let you off at the door."

"He'll get me close enough," Casey said. He sat across from her at the small table in the motel, the pizza untouched and cold between them.

"But why?"

"This is for me to do, just like seeing your family is for you to do." He leaned forward and reached for Ruth's hand. "At least you know they want you."

She pulled back her hand like a child, a frightened, angry child. *They love me*, Ruth thought to herself. *But they don't know me.* Casey had worried about being a stranger in her family's home, but she was the stranger. Since Robbie's death, everything she'd built, everything she knew about herself had been shorn away like shingles in a hurricane. Casey had seen her at her lowest. He hadn't lied to her. He had tried to help her find a path. He'd been her friend. And she needed her friend when she gave up Robbie and was left with her family's grief, and her own. She wanted to delay a little longer whatever was coming next.

"Ruth. Look at me. It's important that you understand, okay? I care about that a lot."

She looked up. His eyes were clear and steady but his lips tightened. Bracing for her disappointment, maybe. She felt her shoulders slump.

"I understand," she said. She pushed herself up from the table.

"Ruth," Casey said. "It's not easy. Not for either one of us. I know that."

Ruth couldn't speak. "You got me this far," he said. "Closer than I've been in a long time. I just need to do the rest on my own."

Ruth nodded, then turned away so he would not see her cry.

One more time, Ruth fell asleep in Casey's arms in a hotel room, listening to him read, his voice mingling with the whoosh of highway traffic. Again, she woke in the dark but this time she was alone in the bed. She heard Casey talking to someone right by the door.

"Fifteen minutes," she heard another man say. She sat up and pulled the sheet tight around her. Casey paused on the threshold when he saw she was awake. Then he crossed to her and sat on the bed. She felt him stroke her cheek and cup the back of her head gently. He kissed her on the corner of her mouth. Ruth took his hand and pulled him close, and she felt him wanting to give in, to hold her and to be held, but something wasn't letting him. When he pulled back and switched on the bedside light, Ruth saw his bag by the door, packed and ready. He looked away from her now, down at his hands as though he'd never seen them before. He had fresh nicotine patches on his arm. He'd put on the dark blue and lime Hawaiian print shirt, his best one.

"What time is it?" she said.

"Nearly five."

"Why didn't you wake me earlier?"

"I wanted to let you sleep," he said. "But I couldn't leave without saying good-bye. You'd never speak to me again, right?"

Ruth sat up. "Let me take you."

"I can't."

Outside, the truck's horn blasted.

Casey grabbed Ruth and hugged her hard. He started to rise, but she pulled him back. "You'll call, right? No matter what happens?"

He nodded into her neck. "Yeah. I'll call. Call me, too. Tell me how you are."

Ruth wrapped her arms around him and pressed her face against his chest. Then, just as quickly, she released him, her eyes closed. She heard his shoes fall unevenly on the carpet, the scuff of his bag as he lifted it from the floor, the creak of the door as he opened it. Diesel fumes and morning air swept over her. She grabbed the sheet around her and scrambled from the bed.

"Casey, wait."

He turned in the doorway. "Yeah?"

Ruth crossed to him and squeezed his hand one last time. "She won't hate you."

She saw the gap between his front teeth as he smiled. "Thanks, Ruth." Then he turned and called out to someone she couldn't see. "I'm coming."

# Lost Nation Road

# CHAPTER 49

Casey's absence was already waiting for Ruth there in the hotel room, in the shadows cast by the small bedside lamp. There was no going back to sleep; she only wanted to get out of here now. Then she saw his copy of *Moby-Dick* on the desk across from the rumpled bed.

Ruth rushed to pick it up—maybe she could still catch him. A sheaf of bills fluttered from between the pages, like a bookmark. Four hundred-dollar bills and a torn scrap of paper bag from last night's pizza. *Gas money*, read the scrawl. *Don't worry about the rest—I know you're good for it. I'll call you. Better yet, I'll collect in person. I've never seen New Hampshire.*

The last line settled on Ruth's nerves like a calming hand. She read the note again and then looked at the cash. He wouldn't have much left for Emily. The trip hadn't gone at all the way he'd planned, had it? Or maybe he'd realized that it was never about the money.

*Good for you, Casey.*

Ruth put down the note and the money and looked up. A seam of light glimmered between the drapes. She walked to the window and pulled open the curtains to see what kind of day it was going to be. She surveyed the parked cars in the dawn and the headlights streaming on the interstate beyond the pavement. It didn't matter if it rained or was clear, or if traffic might slow her down.

Understanding took hold like a friend who'd been waiting for her for a long time. She couldn't know what was coming after she buried Robbie, or when Neal realized that she would not change her mind, or when Don learned she'd turned on him and the company to which she'd given most of her adult life. Like Casey, she knew where she needed to go and, for now, that was enough.

Ruth put the last bag back into the Jaguar and reached in her purse for the keys. She was among the last guests to leave the motel, even though it was barely six thirty. The sky was light now but the sun was obscured by the same humid gray haze that had followed them east. A straggler in a red tie and shirtsleeves sat in his car with his door open, a computer in his lap, steam rising from a foam cup in his hand. He glanced up and Ruth suddenly wanted to hear another voice besides the one in her own head. She nodded at him.

"Good morning."

She saw him take in her wrinkled shorts and shirt, the highway grime layered over the Jaguar's black paint. He narrowed his eyes. Well, whatever he was thinking wouldn't come close to the truth about her. More than that, she knew he didn't want to know the truth. It was so much easier not to look. *I understand*, she wanted to tell him. *But it isn't that easy.* Instead she waved. The man shook his head and took a long pull from the cup before looking back at his laptop.

Ruth climbed into the Jaguar and looked at the empty seat beside her. Then she got out, pulled back the driver's seat, and extracted the box holding Robbie's ashes from the jumble of bags and clothes she'd used to cushion it. She set it carefully in the passenger seat, reentered the car, and put her palm over the box. Then she started the car and headed for the interstate.

It was dusk when Ruth turned onto Lost Nation Road. The crunch of sand and gravel told her she was close to the house. Years ago, this would be the moment that Robbie woke up in the car. He would stretch high in the backseat so he could see out the window. Ruth slowed, turned left up a smaller road, and began to climb past fields and through more trees. She was back in time, a five-year-old Robbie bouncing now with excitement, calling out each landmark like a train conductor. *There's the stone wall, Mommy. See it? Almost there!*

*There's the cemetery, Mommy. I see Grampa Mo's stone.* He would wave at the small granite marker, next to her father's in the plot of land where all the families out here buried their dead, a hilly pasture bordered by the river, woods and this winding road.

Ahead lay one more dirt road leading to her grandmother's place. Robbie's five-year-old voice once again filled her ears, triumphant. *That's it. Big Ruth's Bumpy Road.* His brown eyes would be fixed straight ahead, already picking at his seat belt, ready to climb out the minute the car rolled into the driveway.

Ruth guided the dusty Jaguar up the hill. As she rounded the final curve, a rabbit launched itself from the middle of the road and Ruth hit the brakes. She watched the animal disappear into the grass-filled ditch behind a wooden post and dented black mailbox that read *Nolan*. The image of young Robbie vanished with it, but Ruth still felt him. She would always feel him here.

"This is it," Ruth said. The sound of her voice startled her after all the hours of silence.

She turned left into the small driveway. A low white house stood on a rise just to the left of her, a screened porch clinging to the front, but it was the side door leading from the kitchen that Ruth kept her eye on. Nothing. No movement. Fear lit through her. She should have come sooner. She should have called. Where was her grandmother?

Ruth struggled with the seat belt and then with the door. Her muscles, stiff from nearly eleven hours of driving by herself, didn't seem to work. She scrambled to her feet.

A truck rumbled up behind her. She turned in time to see Kevin pull into the driveway. He peered through the windshield, his glasses glinting under the bill of his hat. Then he was out of the truck faster than she'd ever seen him move in his life.

"Ruth!"

In a few long steps he was at her side. He wrapped both arms around her and even though it woke every bruise on her ribs, Ruth held on. A rapping began inside the house. When Kevin released her and stood back, she saw her grandmother pushing open the side door from behind her walker.

"You better go in or she'll drag herself down those steps," Kevin said. He started to lead her toward the house.

"Wait." Ruth turned to the car and reached across the driver's seat to the passenger side. She brought out the metal box. He looked at her. His eyes grew wet behind his glasses.

"Give it to me," he said. "I'll carry him."

Ruth nodded. She closed her eyes and let Kevin lift the weight from her arms.

"Ruthie!" Her grandmother's voice rang out like a cracked bell.

Ruth opened her eyes and saw Big Ruth balancing in the doorway, white wisps of hair clinging to her scalp, a bright green sweater hanging from her shoulders.

"Come here, girl. Come to me."

Then Ruth was on the steps, leaning in. Her grandmother's fingers traveled over Ruth's face, as if making sure of her. Big Ruth stroked her cheeks, brushed her hair back from her temples, lifted the sunglasses from her face. Ruth didn't move. She saw the faded blue of her grandmother's eyes shimmer with tears when she touched Ruth's bruises. Her own tears rose up. They spilled into her grandmother's waiting hands.